I Know it's YOU

Susan Lewis is the internationally bestselling author of forty-nine novels across the genres of family drama, thriller, suspense, crime and romance.

I Know It's You is book number FIFTY!

Her earlier titles include Richard and Judy picks *One Minute Later* and *I Have Something to Tell You* as well as the heart-stopping series, *No Child of Mine, Don't Let Me Go* and *You Said Forever*. There are too many books to mention here, but you can find them all at www.susanlewis.com

Susan is also the author of *Just One More Day* and *One Day at a Time*, the moving memoirs of her childhood in Bristol during the 1960s. Following periods of living in Los Angeles and the South of France, she currently lives in Gloucestershire with her husband, James, and their beloved, naughty, little dog, Mimi.

Also by Susan Lewis

Fiction

A Class Apart
Dance While You Can
Stolen Beginnings
Darkest Longings
Obsession
Vengeance
Summer Madness
Last Resort
Wildfire
Cruel Venus
Strange Allure
The Mill House
A French Affair
Missing
Out of the Shadows
Lost Innocence
The Choice
Forgotten
Stolen
No Turning Back
Losing You
The Truth About You
Never Say Goodbye
Too Close to Home
No Place to Hide
The Secret Keeper
One Minute Later
I Have Something to Tell You

Books that run in sequence

Chasing Dreams
Taking Chances

No Child of Mine
Don't Let Me Go
You Said Forever

Featuring Detective Andee Lawrence

Behind Closed Doors
The Girl Who Came Back
The Moment She Left
Hiding in Plain Sight
Believe in Me
Home Truths
My Lies, Your Lies
Forgive Me
The Lost Hours
Who's Lying Now?
No One Saw It Coming

Featuring Laurie Forbes and Elliott Russell

Silent Truths
Wicked Beauty
Intimate Strangers
The Hornbeam Tree

Memoirs

Just One More Day
One Day at a Time

SUSAN LEWIS

I Know it's YOU

HarperCollins*Publishers*

HarperCollins*Publishers* Ltd
1 London Bridge Street,
London SE1 9GF

www.harpercollins.co.uk

HarperCollins*Publishers*
Macken House, 39/40 Mayor Street Upper
Dublin 1, D01 C9W8

First published by HarperCollins*Publishers* 2023
1

A catalogue record for this book is available from the British Library

ISBN: 978-0-00-847191-0 (HB)
ISBN: 978-0-00-847192-7 (TPB)

Typeset in Sabon LT Std by Palimpsest Book Production Ltd,
Falkirk, Stirlingshire

Printed and bound in the UK using 100% renewable electricity
by CPI Group (UK) Ltd

This book is produced from independently certified FSC™ paper
to ensure responsible forest management.

For more information visit: www.harpercollins.co.uk/green

For my wonderful husband, James

*This is the only 50th anniversary we'll share,
which makes it extra special.
Thank you, my darling, for all your patience and support and for all the fabulous times we have when my head isn't elsewhere.
I couldn't do it without you.*

Prologue

She doesn't hear the footsteps approaching, but she wouldn't, she has ear buds in, is submerged in the heady beats of the Black Eyed Peas, 'I Gotta Feeling'. She is so focussed on singing along, chair dancing and the work at hand that even a fire alarm might not have disturbed her.

She is alone in a meeting room, a glassed-in space tucked away from the main office and close to the lifts. The walls are cluttered with shelves containing books of all genres and sizes, and brightly coloured posters, most of them promoting an upcoming TV series. There's a large blank screen at one end of the room and a coffee station at the other.

She hasn't made herself a drink yet, but she might when she's finished. Or more likely, she'll head home as it's close to seven thirty and everyone else has already left for the day.

No one popped in to say goodnight on their way past; this didn't surprise her, but it upset her. It's awful being ostracised.

She only has herself to blame, she knows that, but it doesn't make it any easier. She shouldn't have given in to him, should have steered well clear, but he'd been so very hard to resist. He'd made her feel breathless every time she saw him, caused wild and greedy flutterings in every part of her; his eyes when they met hers seemed to set her on fire.

He said she did the same to him.

He couldn't resist her either.

She'd stopped it now, told him they couldn't continue, but it's too late to repair the damage she's caused.

He'd taken their break-up hard and his wife had gone to pieces.

His wonderful, beautiful, talented wife who, some were saying, had already met someone else. So maybe she hadn't been that broken-hearted after all.

Her task this evening is to pack up the props that were used for a promo shoot yesterday. It's for a book soon to hit the screens in a major new horror series. The props had been returned from location earlier, all bundled up in a sheet like dozens of little corpses. Apparently they'd been on loan from a doll's hospital. Who even knew there was such a thing? Do people really take their broken dolls to have limbs repaired and faces remodelled? It seems so . . . weird.

For two hours yesterday, the dolls had been positioned around a deserted, cobwebby house in the countryside, perched ghoulishly on shelves and chairs, laid out on the floor and twisted into odd shapes to suggest violence and thwarted escape. Some had been placed face down, or up, in a bath and one – blonde-haired, ruby-lipped and nude – was hung by its neck from a dusty chandelier. All those miniature bodies; the grisly suggestion, the turbulence of grotesque innuendo. It had been as spooky as hell. She'd been very glad when the camera stopped and it was time to get out of there.

This evening she's carefully wrapping each of the dolls

in tissue before laying them gently into a large padded box. Even in this brightly lit and benign setting, they somehow seem disturbingly real. It's as though they're in their own doll-world, looking back at her through hard, unblinking eyes, grimacing and grinning, pouting, coy, startled, menacing. A few even have teeth. They're thin and brittle, fat and rubbery. Some are made of porcelain or china, others are moulded from plastic, even from wood. She senses them watching and listening, breathing silently and knowing everything.

She doesn't hear the door open behind her, has no idea anyone is there until they're standing right beside her. She starts to look up, to say, 'Aren't they creepy?' or, 'I thought you'd already gone home,' but – before any words can form on her lips – something hard and solid slams into her head. The thud is more of a crunch, the sound of exertion is exhaled in soft, ragged grunts.

Moments later the door closes as quietly as it had opened. The dolls stare lifelessly from their wide eyes, faces splattered in blood and brain, the only witnesses to a scene as appalling as their silence.

On the floor '. . . *I gotta feeling* . . .' plays tinnily, over and over, from a fallen ear bud.

CHAPTER ONE

'I think it might work for you,' Noel Hadigan is saying, seeming both certain and curious as he assesses the landing of his proposition. His eyes are mischievous, and then less so, as he gives a quick wave to someone he knows – bad choice of restaurant, he can never come to the Ivy in Covent Garden without being recognized and he'd much rather be focusing on the woman seated opposite him.

Marina Forster treats him to one of her famously wry smiles as he turns back to her. She's always happy to spend time with this man, especially when he's up to something, and he clearly is, so it's easy to allow her turquoise blue eyes to show interest in spite of having heard him start a pitch this way many times before. She's a tall, strikingly lovely woman in her mid-forties, with thick dark hair usually wound into a single French plait, delicately pale skin, lusciously defined features and an air of confidence that's easily matched by her natural warmth. Her reputation for being a great boss and insightful publisher is, according to most, entirely deserved for, over the past eleven years – since returning from the hiatus of becoming a mother – she's steadily built up the dedicated fiction division of Hawksley Maine, an international publishing house. It is now an award-winning, widely respected and highly profitable arm of the business. She'd even named the imprint Janus, after the god of beginnings, transitions and endings.

'Can't wait to hear what it is,' she teases, and pops a forkful of deliciously baked salmon into her mouth before raising a glass of sparkling water. He knows, as do most literary agents in town, that she, as an executive publishing director, rarely takes on a new work. She has a superbly talented and mostly independent team for that – however, there are exceptions. Usually they come in the shape of celebrities or politicians whose egos – and agents – insist on being handled by the person at the top, even if the actual editing is carried out by a senior member of the team.

'It's coming from an unknown,' he tells her, 'unless the name is a pseudonym, and I guess that's likely. All I have right now are initials and a surname.'

'Don't tell me, J.K. Rowling.'

He laughs. 'Hardly unknown, but certainly Rowling set a trend and it isn't such a bad one if you don't want your identity to influence early judgement.'

'So, are you thinking someone famous could be behind it?'

He shrugs. 'Too soon to say, but the author is definitely going for gender-neutral right now and the first chapter is . . .' He searches for the right word and is clearly disappointed in himself when all he can muster is, 'interesting.'

She smiles. It is unlikely they'd be discussing it if it weren't.

He meets her eyes and smiles too. He actually looks more like a surfer than a leading literary agent – curly russet hair, ripped and tanned; unsurprising since he hails from Sydney where, in his earlier years, he was a regular champion of the waves. He'd moved into publishing during his late twenties and had left his homeland for London just over eight years ago. Since setting up his agency in Chelsea, he's acquired an impressive client list and plenty of friends – Marina and her husband, Maxim, being two of the closest.

'OK,' she says, helping herself to one of his French fries, 'if I'm going to bite, and no promises that I will, let's start with genre.'

He's about to reply when they're interrupted for the fourth time since their arrival.

To Marina's dismay it's Rosie Shell, the deputy managing director of a rival publishing house. Back in the early days of Janus, Rosie had been a senior editor with more chips on her shoulder than hairs on her head so, when Marina returned from her maternity leave, she had wasted little time in moving her on. The woman was – and is – a renowned gossip, unpleasantly competitive and not always honest. She'd also been a part of Hawksley Maine's old regime, so she'd been around during the height of the scandal that had almost forced the company's new owners to lay off everyone in the division and close it down completely. Fortunately it hadn't come to that, but it had been a terrible time that, all these years later, Marina tries not to dwell on. It serves no one, least of all her, to get caught up in the past when the future has so much to offer. She was appointed exec publishing director at the beginning of 2012, and since then she's done everything in her power to purge what went before. This has been helped enormously by the company moving from its old premises to a brand-new office block in South Kensington. There are no reminders there to stumble over at any given moment, and these days there are very few staff who were around back then.

In spite of Rosie's sunny smiles and gushing warmth,

Marina knows very well that this woman still, to this day, will tell anyone who'll listen that Marina Forster is only in position because she's married to Hawksley Maine's CEO. Rosie detests Marina with a passion, and probably prays – even plots – daily for her downfall.

Hard, fast and fabulously humiliating would do it for Rosie.

'So, what are you two cooking up here?' Rosie's tone is at once playful and arch and sets Marina's teeth on edge.

Noel says, 'Well, Rosie, it's possible I've just discovered the new Stephen King, and I'm trying to persuade Marina here to give me a second opinion.'

Rosie's smile tightens around the edges as she glances at Marina. 'Not quite your thing, is it, horror? There again, maybe it is.'

Marina stares at her icily. She knows what Rosie is referring to, but there's no way she's going to bite.

Belatedly realizing Noel isn't serious about his new discovery, Rosie says, waspishly, 'How's your *wife*, these days, Noel? Do you ever hear from her?' Noel had briefly been married a couple of years ago to a historical fiction editor at Penguin who'd run off to the States with one of his top crime-thriller writers.

He says, quite affably, 'Sherry's good, thanks. I'll be sure to tell her you asked after her.'

As Rosie moves on, in a rush suddenly to get to her table before one of her *celebrity* authors arrives (Rosie loves nothing more than to be seen with a famous face), Marina says, 'You never fail to impress me with how nice you are to her.'

He shrugs. 'It wouldn't do me, or my clients, any good if I spoke my mind, but she's not entirely stupid – on the spectrum, yes, but not all the way there – so she knows I have nothing but contempt for her. Lucky she has some good people around her, or Ashwells could be in serious trouble with her at the helm. Now, back to my *actual* discovery and why I'm here with you and not one of your crack team.'

Marina waits for her glass to be refilled and treats him to her best expectant expression.

With a self-mocking grimace, he says, 'Actually, I've only got a prologue and opening chapter so far, and I get that a good opening is no guarantee the book will go anywhere, but why not take a look? I can email it over by the end of the day.'

Because it's him and she likes him so much, she says, 'You still haven't told me the genre?'

'Well, it's hard to be specific about that from what I've seen so far, but it's not literary. Modern day, stylistically easy, and as I said, an interesting start.'

'Tell me about the author.'

'The name is E.L. Stalwood.'

She shrugs; it means nothing to her and presumably not to him either. 'Have you actually met or spoken to him/her/it/them?' she asks.

'Not yet. The opening arrived by email a few weeks ago. It was sent out to a reader who contacted Jaz, my assistant, yesterday morning with feedback on everything he'd recently been sent. This was amongst it and Jaz forwarded it on to me.'

'So you were impressed by it, got in touch with the author . . .?'

'Jaz did, by email, to ask if there was more. Apparently there is, but Stalwood isn't prepared to send it unless you, personally, are on board with it.'

Marina treats him to her best impression of amused exasperation. This sort of thing happened a lot. Many wannabes did their research ahead of time in the hope of exercising some authority over their precious new work and who handled it. They invariably chose someone at the top, and Marina's definitely there. 'And you think it's good enough for me to give it some time?' she says, sitting back as she finishes her meal.

'Let's just say we haven't done a book together for a while, so why not see how this one runs? I can always redirect or reject if you end up deciding it's not for you.'

CHAPTER TWO

By the time Marina arrives home that evening she's all but forgotten the lunch with Noel. Her day has been crazy busy, and a good part of this afternoon has been taken up by phone calls and Teams meetings with the Toronto and New York offices. Later she'd caught up with producers and clients on the West Coast regarding various TV and movie adaptations of books Janus has published. At the crack of dawn tomorrow she'll be dealing with her colleagues in Australia and New Zealand, so this evening she needs to focus on what's likely to be expected from her when she gets to the office first thing.

It is just after seven thirty when she finally lets herself into her and Maxim's Holland Park home – a grand double-fronted, Georgian townhouse, red brick, with tall sash windows and a smart black front door. Maxim bought it thirteen years ago as a wedding gift for them both. (Though he is certainly well paid as the CEO of Hawksley Maine, he also has a large personal fortune that he inherited from his grandfather at the age of thirty. His father, Paul Forster of Forster Inc, Hawksley Maine's parent company, regularly appears on the Forbes billionaires list, but he's another story.)

'I'm just walking through the door,' she's telling Maxim on the phone as she shuts it behind her. 'Are you here?'

'Downstairs in the kitchen,' he replies, 'but I have to go out. Last-minute dinner arrangement with a couple of out-of-towners. Can you come?'

Stifling a groan, she says, 'Where and what time?'

'The Shard – they're from Kentucky, want to see the hotspots – and we need to leave about . . . now?'

Dropping her heavy bags on the hall floor, she sighs as she says, 'Darling, I'm sorry, I've got so much to do this evening.'

'It's OK, I get it's short notice. It'll be dreary anyway.'

Suspecting it will, and loving him for not minding, she rings off, pops her coat in the cloakroom and descends the short flight of stairs to the kitchen to find him. He's standing with his back to her, hands either side of a newspaper he's spread out on the centre island, and is so focussed on whatever he's reading he apparently doesn't realize she's there until she asks if he has time for a drink before he leaves.

Without glancing up he gives a brief shake of his head and stretches out a hand for her to take.

She brushes her fingers against his and goes to fix herself a large gin and tonic. 'Is anyone else at home?' she asks, going to the fridge for a lemon.

'I haven't heard anyone since I came in,' he replies, 'but I was just a few minutes ahead of you.' He finally turns from the paper and folds his arms across his chest as he tilts his head curiously, regarding her. 'Are you OK?' he asks.

Surprised, she says, 'Don't I look it?'

He breaks into a smile and, for a startling moment, she wonders when she stopped noticing how incredibly attractive he is. She hasn't, of course; it is just when you see someone every day . . . He is tall, broad-shouldered and fair-haired, with intense dark eyes, strong features and an easy way with him that is as disarming as it can sometimes be deceptive. Although American born and educated, he'd moved to the UK fourteen years ago when Forster Inc had taken over Hawksley Maine and he'd been appointed to run it. At the time he'd had no way of knowing what an unholy hell he was walking into and, in spite of being a senior editor back then, Marina had had no idea herself how bad it was going to get. If it weren't for him, she dreaded to think where the publishing house might be now, or indeed she herself.

'You're always beautiful to me,' he tells her, pulling her to him, 'but you look tired, stressed maybe? Bad day at the office?'

Inhaling the wonderfully familiar scent of him, while enjoying the sensation of how well they fit, she says, 'Not really, it just seems never-ending at times.' She smiles up into his eyes, loving the way they can still snatch these moments, even if they have other things on their minds. 'And how was your day?'

'Frustrating on some levels, productive on others.' As overall head of European operations, he is based at the company's executive offices on Pall Mall. This means they rarely run in to each other during the day, or even travel to and from work together. They like it that way; being around one another at the office isn't without its complications, and she doesn't much enjoy the way they're scrutinized by some on the occasions they're at the same meeting or official function. The fascination with them seems to have a longevity all of its own, and the rumours of how they'd got together in the first place have never completely gone away. They both suspect that newcomers to the company are regularly filled in by the old guard that remain, though nothing is ever said in their hearing.

'I dream,' she says, 'that one of these days we'll get to spend an evening, just the two of us – no work, no children, no phones, no interruptions at all . . .'

'We need a holiday,' he states, and reaches for his mobile as it buzzes on the table. 'That's my driver, five minutes away. Sure you can't come?'

'Even if I could, I'd never make myself presentable in time. No, you go, enjoy the Kansans – is that what they're called?'

'They are – or Jayhawkers, and they're a pretty dull pair. If they weren't, I might have invited them here. Anyway, I shouldn't be too late, but if you're tired, don't wait up.'

After a tender though brief kiss on the mouth, he grabs his keys and phone and leaves through the back door, taking a call as it comes in. 'Hi, Ed,' she hears him say chirpily, 'what's new?'

She stands for a moment, watching him head through the garden to exit by a gate next to the garage. Ed is his twenty-one-year-old godson, currently living with them while studying anthropology and law at LSE – and causing considerable hormonal havoc for his godfather's thirteen-year-old twins, Sophie and Olivia. It's a blessing the girls were at boarding school from Monday to Friday, or the chaos in the house, if they were around all the time, would enjoy few limits.

After popping upstairs to change into something more comfortable, Marina returns to the hall, scoops up her heavy bag and carries it down to the kitchen. Ordinarily she closets herself in her study when working at home, but this evening she decides to spread everything out on the breakfast table in front of the floor-to-ceiling French windows. From here she can easily reach the fridge, the coffee machine and the drinks cabinet. It's also possible to gaze at the garden for a while, always a welcome distraction when she's tired or overthinking a problem.

Since she already has a G&T on the go, she pulls open the fridge in the hope of finding some leftover frittata, and almost melts with love for Maxim and Ed when she sees that neither has finished it off and left her with an empty plate to stick in the dishwasher.

After helping herself to a generous slice, she quickly whips up a French dressing for the lettuce and single tomato she finds lurking in a lower drawer, and carries it to the table. As she sits down her phone rings and, seeing it's the marketing director she's been trying all day to get hold of, she quickly clicks on.

Twenty minutes later she's partway through another call and upstairs in the hall, having popped up to find out who's ringing the bell. No one's there, so she closes the door and continues to listen to one of her New York colleagues droning on about a changed publication schedule – he's already put it in an email, so did they really have to have this conversation? Too polite to protest she pauses a moment in front of the mirror to check just how tired she might be looking. She is a little pale yes, but that's normal at the end of the day, as are the loose strands escaping her French plait.

When the call finally ends, she leans in closer to the mirror. Maybe the lines around her eyes have deepened, or the lids are drooping more than she'd realized. Certainly the frown line is increasing in length and depth. Her mouth has always been full and wide and still is, but are the corners starting to tilt downwards? The girls would tell her if she asked, there's no doubt about that; they're becoming more outspoken and critical by the week. Anyway, Maxim had said tired, not old, and forty-four isn't too bad, is it?

Maxim is going to be fifty next year.

Fifty!

Even so with his looks, wealth, charm and standing in the world, he's always going to be an absolute magnet for just about every female who fancies her chances. And he isn't averse to a little flirtation here and there, it has to be said. Nor is she, although she knows it would never go any further in her case, and he always swears it wouldn't in his. She believes him, insofar as she's able, for she knows how much she and the children mean to him – and he's never given her any reason to doubt him. It just creeps up on her from time to time, stealing in like a shadow, planting thoughts in her head and suspicion in her heart. Mostly she's able to push it away, as if it is no more than the resonance of a long-forgotten chapter, or the drift of an old movie scene. Lived experience can be hard, traumatic even, and at times unsuppressible, but Maxim would never hurt and humiliate her the way her first husband did. It simply isn't in him to behave that way.

Thank God.

Shaking herself out of the unwanted introspection, she returns to the kitchen and finally starts her snack-supper while scrolling through emails on her laptop. Eventually she comes to the one Noel sent about his new discovery – if that's what E.L. Stalwood actually turns out to be.

Since she's more or less finished for the day, and as it's apparently only a prologue and opening chapter, she decides to relocate herself upstairs to the sitting room and relax on the sofa as she reads.

She gets as far as the hall when the doorbell rings again.

Putting her laptop and G&T on the console table, she goes to find out who it is.

Once again there's no sign of anyone.

It's unusual to get children playing knock-down ginger in this area, but it's hard to imagine who – or what – else it might be. She's about to go back inside when she spots something on the pavement at the end of their short path.

Going to pick it up she turns it over in her hand and feels an unsteady beat in her heart. A broken doll. No, not broken, its limbs are intact, but skewed in odd directions, its small head twisted around so the face is at the back.

A child must have dropped it on their way into the park – there's an entrance less than fifty yards away – so she pops it on the wall and returns to the house.

Time to get started on E.L. Stalwood's first – and maybe last – attempt at writing a book.

CHAPTER THREE

That Girl by E.L. Stalwood

Prologue

Getting into Christy Grant's flat was easy.

There was a key.

It was well hidden, of course, no one would think to look in the spot she'd chosen, but few secrets were as safe as their holders liked to believe. The task now was to get in and out before Christy came back and there probably wasn't much time.

The purpose was not to steal anything, or to cause damage. There was no desire at all – at this stage – to harm her. That would come later. The intention tonight was simply to leave a little something where she won't immediately find it.

Not difficult.

A bedroom drawer will do.

Mission accomplished, time to leave, and minutes later the apartment was as silent as the furniture within.

By the time Christy has realized what's been left for her, it will already be too late. All hell will break loose – for Christy anyway. For the intruder there will only be anonymity.

Poor Christy. Maybe not what she deserved, but life is like that sometimes: simply not fair.

CHAPTER ONE

This tale is a tragic one, awash with vanity and betrayal, fraught with ambition and duplicity – I wish I could tell you that it ends well.

It doesn't.

There are three main players – Katie Beech, Christy Grant and Amy Summers. You might wonder as you read on about my own part in the story. It will become clear, I assure you, although perhaps not straight away.

Katie first.

She was in her late twenties, with curly fair hair, a cutely freckled complexion and a beautifully wide smile. She was the presenter of an afternoon TV show, three times a week, and was a favourite with the viewing public. She and Christy Grant, the programme's series producer, were known to be the closest of friends. They always had each other's backs and they rarely disagreed on anything, at least not openly.

When Christy employed her eighteen-year-old niece, Amy Summers, to act as a PA to Katie, Katie took to the girl straight away. She saw her almost as a gift, a prize even, for it soon became clear that Amy was lively, intelligent, enthusiastic, and always ready to go the extra mile.

It wasn't long before Katie began encouraging Amy to come up with stories for the programme: unusual weddings; holiday nightmares; hilarious online dating. In effect, she appointed herself the girl's devoted mentor, and no one was surprised when she suggested that quirkily pretty little Amy should present some of the inserts herself.

Amy on camera turned out to be a dream! With her big blue eyes, pouty smile and playfully irreverent humour she was a natural, and very soon, under Katie's guidance, she was building up her own fan base of mostly younger viewers. She was overjoyed by this amazing turn in her luck, and Katie was sublimely happy for her. Actually, everyone was happy for Amy, at least to her face. Christy, her aunt (a couple of times removed) knew that behind the girl's back many of her colleagues were starting to find her irritating. Uppity, even. They were resentful of all the breaks she kept getting, and the way she seemed to hold so much sway with those in senior positions.

Katie never engaged with the discontent. The grudges would work themselves through in time, and everyone would start to see all the qualities in Amy that she did. In fact, Amy was already bringing a lot more to the programme than other people Katie could mention, but of course she didn't name them. Katie wasn't like that. She was mostly kind and generous and often first to recognize talent in others. (This was what Katie wanted everyone to think of her, and most did because it was largely true; however, I'm afraid there was a dark streak in her soul, as you will discover.)

She had a great need to be admired, even adored. Her extravagant beach wedding in Mallorca was its own proof of that. It was covered by *Hello!* magazine, so the rest of the world could swoon and cluck over how blessed and beautiful she was. Her husband, Robert – Rob – Nicholls, was the main anchor for the go-to sports programme broadcast by the same TV station. He commentated on all the big matches, appeared on many sporting quiz shows and was, for some people, a bit of a heartthrob. In fact, he had a lot going for him in the looks and charm department, and no one would ever try to claim that he and Katie didn't make an extremely handsome couple.

It pleased Christy a lot to know that everything was perfect in Katie's world. She wanted Katie to be happy, everything on the show ran much more smoothly if she was, but it wasn't just about the programme. Katie really mattered to Christy. She was, in many ways, the sister Christy had never had, and Christy knew it was the same for Katie. Even though Katie was married now, they still had their special girlie evenings, usually at Christy's flat, drinking wine and sharing confidences that were both heartfelt and hilarious. There was only one truth Christy determined never to share with Katie, and that was her low opinion of Rob. On the surface she had a friendly enough relationship with him – after all, he did have some good points and he wasn't bad company, but she could see beyond – or beneath – the public façade to the shallow and self-serving man she knew him to be. He drank too much, was far too full of himself, and he flirted outrageously. Indeed, there was a reasonable chance he wasn't entirely faithful. Christy had no evidence to support that, it was just an instinct she had, and her instincts where men were concerned were rarely flawed.

'You know, I think men are intimidated by you,' Katie often observed during their frank discussions of Christy's love-life. 'It's not just the fact that you're so successful and often their intellectual superior, it's being unspeakably beautiful that might put them off. I mean, look at you! You're even lovelier than Claudia Romani, who, I might add, was voted one of the world's sexiest women not so long ago. No bloke in his right mind is going to *not* be drawn to you when your Spanish blood makes you so exotic and takes your sensuality to smoking levels. The trouble is, you're so much cleverer than most of them, and in the end they feel so diminished, inadequate, that they just can't cope.'

Christy was of course touched – and embarrassed – by the compliments and the loyalty, but there was still no getting away from the fact that her relationships always seemed to start off so well and yet none ever lasted.

'What is wrong with me?' she wailed to Katie. 'Why does nothing in my personal life ever work out?'

'It's going to take someone really special to win you,' Katie insisted, splashing more Sauvignon into their glasses. 'He'll see past everything else and appreciate you in a way no one else is smart enough to, apart from me, of course. More importantly, you'll appreciate him – and you'll *love* him every bit as much as he loves you.'

Christy had to smile. Wouldn't that be wonderful? Wasn't Katie the very best of friends to offer her such a dream, and to try to make her feel so much better about herself?

Christy was still waiting for this paragon of male excellence to find his way into her world and, at thirty-seven, she was having to try very hard not to lose hope that he ever would.

It was one Thursday lunchtime that Christy went over to the news and sports building of the TV studios to take a lift to the dressing-room floor. (The day and time isn't actually important, it's simply when she chooses to go in search of Rob Nicholls, who should have just come off-air following a midday bulletin.) She was keen to discuss an idea she'd had for Katie's birthday surprise and, as he'd asked her to come up with something, she was hopeful he'd go for it.

The dressing-room corridor was empty and most doors were closed as she made her way to Rob's at the far end. She was only a step away, her hand already raised to knock, when she came to a sudden stop.

She waited, motionless, hardly breathing. She knew she should walk away now, and it was all she wanted to do, but she was rooted, caught in the grip of what she could hear coming from beyond his partly open door.

The sounds were as unmistakable as they were descriptive; so intimate and filled with the absorption of pleasure that it was clear no thought had been paid to the chance of discovery. She knew the woman in there wasn't Katie, because she'd just left Katie in Studio Three discussing the set.

Christy's eyes closed as a quiet rage rose in her.

He hasn't even bothered to close the door. Were they in such a rush to get to one another that he didn't notice, or is it a part of the thrill?

She looked at his name writ large in the panel below the number 5 and then, to her horror, she realized who the female voice belonged to.

It was Amy!

Katie's cherished little protégée; Christy's eighteen-year-old niece; Rob's . . .

How the hell could this be happening?

Of all the females she could so easily imagine him cheating with, Amy had never crossed her mind.

What a fool she was! What a low-life he was.

'Are you sure Katie doesn't know?' Amy's husky voice carried to Christy from inside the cocoon of betrayal.

'I'm sure,' Rob replied, sounding breathless, distracted.

'But are you going to tell her?'

'No, not yet. It's too soon. Can you . . .? Is this . . .?'

Amy giggled as she murmured something Christy couldn't make out, followed by, 'How about I take them off? It'll be easier.'

Christy couldn't bear to hear any more, or to be caught eavesdropping like some sort of sexual deviant, so she quickly retraced her steps back to the lifts.

An hour later she was in the production gallery for her own programme, standing behind the director and his crew as they orchestrated rehearsals for the upcoming recording. As series producer she was always around at this stage, ready to iron out any last-minute issues, or to make sure no one inadvertently wandered into the realms of inaccuracy or libel.

Today's programme was a hard watch after what she'd just – almost – crashed into. Katie's beautiful face filled the screens in front of her; she was luminous and engaging, professional and completely unaware of her beloved husband's unspeakable duplicity. Worse, was watching her banter with Amy as the girl settled into the chair beside Katie, her lovely eyes sparkling with laughter and happiness. She showed not a single sign of her outrageous treachery.

Christy felt sick to her soul.

At the end of the rehearsal, as the credits started to roll and make-up artists swooped in to apply finishing touches before the recording, Rob suddenly appeared in the studio.

Christy watched in silent, rigid disgust as he went to perch on the desk next to Katie, and gazed down at her playfully, adoringly, as he reminded her he was commentating on a game at Chelsea later so he wouldn't be home until late. He didn't so much as glance in Amy's direction, but as he kissed Katie with the mouth that only an hour ago had been kissing Amy, and touched her with the hands that had caressed and fondled the girl, Christy wanted to kill him.

How could he? The bastard!

Who the hell did he think he was?

How could he not know that Christy, at least, saw straight through him?

Maybe he did, and just didn't care.

Later, knowing what she must do, Christy messaged Rob to ask if they could meet in his dressing room the following day. He would assume it was to discuss Katie's birthday, but Christy could hardly think about that any more. She was practically consumed by what she'd discovered. She knew it wasn't her place to tell Katie, it was Rob's, but she was afraid that being of low moral fibre he simply wouldn't.

'You're crazy,' he sneered when she confronted him with what she'd overheard. 'You're making stuff up to try and cause trouble between me and Katie. It's the kind of thing you do. It's called jealousy, and we all know you've got a whole lot of that going on where Katie's concerned.'

Though his words stung, Christy forced herself to remain calm as she said, 'How serious is this . . . *thing* with Amy?'

'For God's sake!' he shouted. 'I just told you, you're making it up. What happened in here yesterday was nothing more than me having a bit of a joke with the girl, who, if you must know, has been coming on to me practically since she started. Maybe it runs in the family, like aunt, like niece, because you're a bit keen on putting it out there, aren't you?'

Christy slapped his face, hard.

He looked for a moment as if he might slap her back, but with one hand on his flaming cheek and the other clenched in a fist, he said, 'You need to get your facts straight before you start accusing me of something I didn't do. I know it might suit you to break up my marriage, but get this into your head, it isn't going to happen. Now, if you don't mind, this is my dressing room. I'd like you to leave.'

Two days later, Christy still didn't know what the heck to do for the best. The last thing she wanted was to tell Katie, but if she didn't, it would make her feel complicit in the sordid affair and she certainly wasn't that. Of course, she could talk to Amy, even fire her, but Katie would want to know why, and how would Christy be able to answer that?

What the hell was the right thing to do in a situation like this?

Speak out, dear reader. Have you ever been in such a position? If so, did spilling your conscience over the innocent party turn out to be the wisest and kindest thing you ever did? Or did it backfire horribly and kill a friendship you valued more highly than any other in your world?

For Christy . . . Well, you will discover in the coming chapters what Christy's decision meant for her, for Katie, and for poor, used little Amy.

CHAPTER FOUR

'So what did you think?' Noel asks, propping his feet on the coffee table as Marina fixes them both an end-of-day gin and tonic. They're in her spacious, booklined office, with its floor-to-ceiling glass frontage, overlooking the large open-plan area where a dozen or more of her fiction team are still at work. Georgia, the most senior editor, whose desk is closest to Marina's office, is chatting animatedly with someone on the phone – she's often the last to leave.

Marina wishes she liked Georgia more, but for some reason she can't summon up any real warmth for her, in spite of being endlessly impressed by her editorial skills. She's often wondered if it's because Georgia reminds her of someone – she does, although the two women could hardly be more different in looks, or age, or personality. The unsettling and bizarre truth of it is that Marina sometimes feels that Georgia is watching her with eyes that see too much.

What a strange quality to have.

Even to think of it makes Marina want to shudder.

Out of nowhere her mind flashes on the doll she found outside the house last week, all twisted and starey-eyed. There had been no sign of it when she'd left the next morning, suggesting it had been reclaimed by its owner, or carried off by a passing child, maybe a garbage collection.

She hadn't thought of it again until now, and it was soon gone from her mind.

'Please tell me you've read it,' Noel prompts.

Marina smiles teasingly. Though a week has gone by since he sent the opening chapter of Stalwood's book, and much has happened at Janus in that time – they're constantly busy – Marina knows exactly what he's referring to. 'I have,' she confirms, bringing the drinks over and moving a pile of hardbacks aside to sink into the sofa facing the armchair he'd slumped into. She knew he'd been in the building for most of the afternoon, attending meetings and presentations with one of his authors, so it hadn't surprised her when he'd put his head round her door a few minutes ago to find out if she was free.

'Oh hell, I'd better take this,' he grumbles, checking his mobile as it rang. 'I'll be right back.'

As he steps out into the main office Marina feels, as she often does during unexpectedly quiet moments, the friendly presence of the hundreds of books surrounding her. She's published so many over the years that she lost count long ago, everything from crime thrillers, to historical romances, literary masterpieces, suspense, comedy, family drama; so many genres, so much talent in the millions of pages. She feels a special connection to them all, and in so many different ways, but especially to their authors and the way these special people bring an extraordinary mix of characters into her life, like a new set of friends, or adversaries – imaginary lovers, even. Their names often stay with her long after she's finished reading, as does the essence of their stories and the dramatic, tragic or hilarious experiences they've shared in a literary, and sometimes even in a physical sense.

The names of E.L. Stalwood's characters have been

floating in and out of her mind this past week – Katie, Christy, Amy. She can't quite picture them yet, but they're coming into focus, and the fact that they've stayed with her at all is a credit to the author.

Or maybe it's all to do with resonance; pressing the right notes at the right time, or stimulating old memories so long suppressed that it's hard to find a way back to the light.

'Sorry about that,' Noel says, returning to the room. 'So, you were about to tell me what you think.'

Taking a sip of her drink, she says, 'Well, to begin, I'm not sure about the narrator's voice. I find it a little . . . *arch*? And addressing the reader directly is . . .' she pulls a face, 'unusual.' While unwilling to engage with this book, she's finding herself, oddly, doing so.

Nodding his agreement, he says, 'Anything else?'

She tilts her head to one side. 'It needs fleshing out,' she says, stating the obvious, 'more backstory, certainly more character depth. As it stands, it's reading more like a precis—'

'Which surely can't be a bad thing at this stage?' he interrupts. 'In other words, the sooner it cuts to the chase, the sooner we can assess the story's merits, and I think it shows signs of having some, don't you?'

She considers this for a moment. 'Well, there's a clear attempt, as it stands, to engage with women who have either been betrayed, or are afraid of it, or are indeed fascinated by it.' She wasn't going to admit how that particular element had resonated with her, making her think of how she'd felt when her first husband had cheated on her. It had even got her wondering how she'd feel if Maxim were ever to have an affair with someone she'd taken under her wing.

Georgia, for instance.

She knows they're drawn to one another; she'd noticed it most recently at a launch party when she'd spotted them talking animatedly together at the side of the room.

But Maxim is always sociable, and nothing less than gifted when it comes to inclusivity and putting people at their ease.

'But you want to know what "Christy" does about the affair?' Noel urges. 'And how "Katie", with the "dark streak in her soul" reacts when she finds out her husband's a sleazy bastard. And she's going to find out, isn't she? It's got to happen.'

'There won't be much of a story if it doesn't,' Marina says wryly. Then, 'I must admit I'm intrigued by the prologue and the "little something" that's planted in Christy's flat.'

'And who planted it?'

'Exactly. I guess we won't find that out for a while. Anyway, ending the first chapter on Christy's dilemma is good, direct address to the reader notwithstanding . . . Have you had any further chapters yet?'

'No. Stalwood has requested some feedback before releasing more.'

Marina frowns at the sense of being played. New authors don't have this sort of power, no matter how much they might like to think they do.

When is the right time for a set-down?

She looks up as Georgia, still on the phone, gives a shout of laughter. 'OK,' she says to Noel, 'you can tell Stalwood that I've read better opening chapters . . .'

'You have? Name one.'

She does, several, and he laughs.

'OK, I concede,' he says, 'but you can't deny you want to read more.'

Yes, maybe she did, but what she said was, 'I think you should give it to Alexa or Toby. You know they're both great editors and they've a lot of experience with first-time authors.'

'I'm not going to deny their skills. I've worked with them both and have a lot of respect for them. Trouble is, this author wants you.'

'Because he or she has read my name in some trade magazine, or online posting. And you know better than to let someone – especially an unknown – call the shots.'

He nods slowly, sips his drink and rests it on the arm of the chair. 'How about I get Stalwood to submit another chapter or two? Will you at least take a look before passing it on?'

She can't refuse him; he's too good a friend and she actually enjoys working with him when they get the chance. 'It could be that these first pages are all there is,' she points out.

'True. Leave it with me and I'll get back to you when – if – I have more.'

After he'd gone, Marina returns to her computer, intending to prepare for a budget meeting the next morning, but for the moment her mind remains caught up in the last few minutes. It isn't so much the book – or chapter – that's lingering as the anonymity of the author.

It isn't normal for a new writer not to engage fully with an agent who'd shown interest in their work.

So who was E.L. Stalwood?

A lesser royal? A leading politician who needs to hide behind a pseudonym in order to protect the innocent from a fictionalized account of real events? The latter is the most likely answer, and if it does turn out to be the case, Marina and Janus will need to tread carefully or they could become swept up in a very public and ugly libel suit.

There's another reason E.L. Stalwood could be withholding their real identity, which ties in with the insistence that the book should come to Marina. However, it seems a little far-fetched and makes her uncomfortable to think it, so for the time being she simply dismisses it.

'Hey,' Georgia says, popping her head round the door, 'just to say I'm off now. Maxim rang while Noel was here to say he and Ed are heading out to the cinema. They'll call when the film's over to find out if you want to join them for pizza.'

Marina inwardly groans. She detests pizza, but loves Maxim and Ed, so she probably will meet up with them. 'I'll send a text,' she says. 'And can you come in about eight in the morning? I'd like to go over a few things prior to the foreign sales review.'

'No problem. Don't stay too late.'

Marina smiles, and for a moment she's tempted to ask Georgia what she'd been laughing about on the phone just now. Had she been talking to Maxim at the time? If so, why didn't she just put him through when he'd rung?

Sighing irritably to herself, she opens up a set of spreadsheets and tries to fix her attention in a more sensible and productive direction. It works for a while; in fact almost an hour passes before she realizes that she's stopped taking anything in.

Giving up on it, she sits back in her chair and closes her eyes. This is the trouble with books, fiction in particular, the stories – the authors – often have an uncanny and even powerful way of arousing a reader's lived realities. Different though they might be to those on the page, tapping into a person's emotional, even physical experiences, and connecting them with a character or a narrative, is a vital part of the alchemy that goes into making a book work. For a reader it can be like watching two plays at once – one created by a writer, the other by memory. They aren't the same, but the resonance can be as haunting, as disturbing, as if the past had somehow caught up with the present.

Stalwood's first draft chapter is, albeit in a small way, doing that to her.

Checking the time, she turns off her computer and texts Maxim to say she'll pass on the pizza and see him at home.

There's somewhere else she ought to go before returning to Holland Park, somebody else she'd like to talk to.

CHAPTER FIVE

'Well, this is a welcome surprise.'

Marina smiles as her ex-husband, Patrick Cain, pulls wide the front door of his ground-floor Bayswater apartment to make room for her to come in. 'If you'd given me some warning, I'd have dressed for the occasion.'

She almost laughs at the absurdity – as if he needed to get a suit out for her. Besides, he's looking pretty smart in his expensive jeans, designer polo shirt and leather loafers. There's no doubt his style and rugged good looks have staged an impressive return over more recent years. In fact, it's hard to think of him as the crushed and shameful drunkard he became during the break-up of their marriage.

'So, to what do I owe the pleasure?' he asks, ushering her into a sitting room that somehow manages to seem both sterile and cosy. Anthea's influence, of course – the new, or latest, live-in girlfriend. So, like the woman herself, who's a yoga instructor/nutritionist/colonic-irrigationist. (Marina isn't sure about the last, but she generally adds it in her mind simply because the woman irritates her.) 'Can I get you a drink?' he offers.

'No, I'm fine thanks,' she replies. 'I can't stay. Is Anthea here?'

'She's taking a class at the local fitness club. Was it her you wanted to see?'

'No, you.'

He eyes her cautiously. 'What have I done?'

She laughs. 'Nothing that I know of.'

Seeming relieved he says, 'So, is everything OK? Actually, you look a bit . . . Gorgeous of course, but . . .'

She puts up a hand to stop him. 'I'll come to the point. Has anyone been in touch with you recently from . . .' She searches for a euphemism that he'll have no trouble understanding. 'From the time of trial,' she says.

His eyebrows arch in surprise as he waves her to a sofa. 'The answer is no, but does this mean you have heard from someone?'

She shakes her head. 'No. It's just . . .' Wishing she had a clearer idea of why she's here and what she's expecting from him, she sits on the arm of the chair and says, 'It was a horrible time, wasn't it? One I'd never want to go through again.'

Clearly puzzled, he says, 'What's going on, Marina? I thought . . . I mean, yes, it was hellish, for you most of all, but I thought that – between them – Maxim and the therapist had helped you put it all behind you.'

'They did,' she replies calmly, 'but it's been playing on my mind a bit lately. I'm not sure why . . . Well, actually, there's this book, a new submission . . .'

With a knowing smile he sits back in his seat and folds his arms. 'OK, I think I'm getting the picture,' he says. 'Is it about a – let me guess – a husband-stealer?'

She nods, smiles and feels foolish. He knew as well as anyone how a book could affect her and there was never any telling why one did more than another. As she often says in the talks she gives, 'Fiction can do strange things to a person. It messes with reality and memory and sometimes puts old nightmares back at centre stage.'

It's happened to her more than once. She wonders how often he's reminded of the past – and what might trigger it? Probably not a book, but a young girl walking down the street? Appearing on TV? Knocking on his door with an election leaflet?

He says, 'So what's got to you about this one?'

She gives it some thought, and decides that – rather than try to explain it – she should change the subject. 'Let's talk about you,' she says. 'How are you getting along with Anthea's daughter these days?' *How old was the girl? Probably under twenty. Did she or Anthea know about his past?*

There's an exasperated irony in his eyes as he pulls a face. 'All I'll say is I'm glad she doesn't live with us. And I strongly believe she shares the feeling.'

'Does Anthea mind about that?'

He sighs and shakes his head. 'I'll be honest with you, Anthea and I were a mistake. We both know it, but we've yet to do anything about it.'

Unable to stop herself thinking of the mistakes he'd made in the past, not least of all the one that had ruined their marriage and set in motion a series of events that had devastated many more lives than theirs, she says, 'Will you mind being on your own again? Or, no, don't tell me, you've already met someone else?'

There's no offence in his tone as he says, 'I haven't met anyone else, and no, I won't mind being on my own for a while. With the amount of travelling I do, it'll be good not to have anyone complaining about it.' For the past six years, thanks to an introduction from Maxim, he's been the sales director for a well-known, middle-market hotel chain. It's the longest job he's held down since he was forced to leave his marketing position at Hawksley Maine.

'So you're still away most of the time?' she comments. 'I guess I was lucky to find you at home.'

He raises an eyebrow and takes his turn to change the subject. 'How are the twins?' he asks.

She softens inside at the mention of her teenage girls. 'They're good, thanks,' she smiles.

'And Maxim? Have you talked to him about this new book?'

She shakes her head. 'There's no reason to.'

'Yet you're here, talking to me.'

'Yes, and I'm not entirely sure why. Except, as you know, the kind of memories we share never really go away. Don't things trigger it for you at times too?'

His eyes aren't unkind as he says, 'I probably find it easier to compartmentalize than you do. It comes with being a bloke.'

Suddenly deciding it's time to go, she gets to her feet. 'There's always been a lot in your life that comes with being a bloke,' she comments dryly.

'I won't ask what that means, I doubt I want to know.'

As they reach the door he says, 'Tell me, do you and Maxim ever discuss what happened?'

She purses her lips. 'Not really. Not any more. There doesn't seem a lot of point.'

'So you don't know if anyone's been in touch with him?'

'I'm not saying anyone's been in touch with me,' she points out. She leans in to plant a kiss on his cheek. 'It's good to see you looking so well.'

'You too,' he says, and tilts her face up to look into her eyes. 'Let it go,' he advises gently. 'It's a long time in the past, and that's where it needs to stay.'

She doesn't argue, only turns to walk away.

As she reaches her car, she looks up to find him still watching her. She smiles and waves.

'Who wrote it?' he calls out.

'Wrote what?'

'The book that's getting to you.'

She shrugs dismissively and gets into the car. An author hiding behind a pen name, she reminds herself, is simply someone trying to get themselves noticed, to cause a stir by creating intrigue around their identity that might set them apart from the crowd.

It's after nine by the time she arrives home and, since there's no sign of Maxim and Ed, she slots some bread into the toaster and checks her phone for messages.

We don't have to go for pizza, Maxim had texted. *What would you prefer?*

After not hearing back from her, he'd messaged again. *OK, you must be caught up with something. Ed and I will continue as planned and see you around 9.30.*

There are at least half a dozen posts on the family WhatsApp group, all from the girls, some of which Maxim has replied to, others Ed has bravely taken on before apparently shutting down to go into the cinema.

Deciding there is nothing for her to get into this evening, she types in, *Goodnight, Love you* and switches to her emails.

One of the many is from Noel. *Your wish is my command. See attachment.*

CHAPTER SIX

That Girl by E.L. Stalwood

'I'm truly sorry,' Christy said gently. Her heart was aching with the pain she was causing; she almost wished it could be her own rather than see Katie suffer like this. 'I wish to God I hadn't told you, but I felt – hoped – it might be easier coming from me.'

Her words fell into silence as Katie stared past her own reflection in the dressing-room mirror to Christy's just behind it, not really seeming to see her, for the moment not seeming to react at all.

Christy watched her quietly. She could only imagine what was going through her mind, how devastated she must be feeling, how shocked and betrayed. Naturally Christy had avoided the most lurid details of what had been going on in Rob's dressing room. She'd said, simply, that she'd heard Rob and Amy together and that there had been mention of telling Katie about their affair but they'd decided, at the time, that they wouldn't.

Exactly when that might have changed, or if it even would, Christy still had no idea, but she was aware now that just about everyone on the programme had known about the affair for some time.

'Can I get you something?' she offered, more for the need to say something than because she thought anything would make a difference.

Katie shook her head. She was so beautiful in her heartbreak, so dignified in her gradual acceptance of the fact that it was actually happening. 'No, I'm fine,' she replied hoarsely, even though she obviously wasn't. She couldn't be.

'Would you like to talk about it some more?' Christy suggested. How helpless she felt, and guilty for having brought this to Katie's world.

'Not now, thanks.' Katie's voice was a dull, empty whisper. She cleared her throat and pushed her hair back from her face. 'I know you need to get to a meeting,' she said. 'You don't want to be late.'

Christy grimaced. 'If it weren't so important you know I'd call and cancel.'

'No, you can't do that, not when so much is at stake, and I'll be fine. I promise.' Katie attempted a smile.

Reluctant to leave her like this, Christy said, 'What are you going to do?'

Katie swallowed and gave a shrug. 'I'm not sure yet. I guess I need some time for it to sink in.'

Christy got to her feet, wishing she didn't have to. 'I'll call as soon as the meeting's over,' she promised. 'Maybe you should wait here and I'll take you home?'

Katie nodded, although it wasn't clear that she'd actually heard the words.

Christy turned to the door.

'Do you think,' Katie asked, 'that the company's new owners are going to pull our programme?'

Hearing her own fear in Katie's voice, Christy felt her insides tighten. 'No one's mentioned that yet,' she replied. 'As far as I can tell, a lot will depend on the direction they want the company as a whole to take. Unfortunately, our programme's ratings have been dropping off a bit lately, but we still have a pretty strong following and, thanks to you, Amy is proving quite a hit.' She winced even as she said it. She really hadn't needed to add that.

Katie said, 'She's only appeared on camera a handful of times.'

And you know that each one of them has received a very positive response. Christy didn't say this, wouldn't actually have dreamt of it. 'Don't worry,' she smiled, 'I'll be fighting hard to keep our show on the road.'

Katie nodded dully and, because she really couldn't be any later than she already was, Christy left.

Katie drove herself home. She didn't want to see Christy again today, couldn't face discussing what she'd been told, wanted only to convince herself that Christy was wrong. It happened; people misunderstood situations all the time and jumped to wrong conclusions.

There was no sign of Rob when she got in and he hadn't yet responded to any of the messages she'd left on his voicemail. That didn't have to mean anything. He could be in a meeting, or interviewing someone, or simply out of range somewhere. Of course she hadn't mentioned anything about Amy, had only said she was looking forward to a night in, and was there anything in particular he'd like to eat?

She hadn't yet decided whether she wanted to talk about Amy tonight. Over a week had passed since Christy had 'stumbled' upon them. It could be over already – if it ever began.

Sighing, she dropped her coat on a chair and went through to the kitchen. No matter what she tried to tell herself, she knew deep down that she couldn't just ignore it. Something needed to be said, and it seemed she would have to be the one to say it, given that he hadn't mentioned anything at all so far.

It was just after seven when she heard him coming in through the front door. She was in the bathroom adjoining their bedroom and, as a powerful surge of anxiety overcame her, she gripped the edge of the basin to steady herself.

She was clearly more nervous, more afraid than she'd realized until now. Did that mean that in her heart she'd already accepted it was true?

Amy and Rob? *Amy, so young and talented and loyal . . .*

It was beyond disturbing how she could more easily believe it of Rob than she could of her cherished protégée.

Weren't women, girls, meant to look out for one another?

Of course, they rarely did, but it was different with her and Christy. They really did put one another first.

When he failed to call out to let her know he was back, she left the bathroom to go in search of him. He was in the sitting room, standing at a window, gazing out at the moonlit street. He didn't seem to hear her come in; or if he did, he didn't acknowledge her.

'There you are,' she said, turning on a lamp to bring more light into the room. 'Is everything OK?'

He nodded and went to pour them both a drink.

After passing one to her, he tapped his glass to hers, but made no toast. His face was taut, pale, and he wasn't meeting her eyes.

She could feel her heart thudding too hard and too fast; she just knew he was about to confirm what Christy had told her and she had no idea how to stop him.

In the end she broke the silence with the very words she didn't want to hear. 'You're sleeping with Amy.'

His failure to answer was answer enough, and she felt her world silently, irrevocably imploding. She stared at him, dizzy, unanchored, as if she was losing all sense of reality.

'Aren't you going to deny it?' she heard herself ask.

He pushed a trembling hand through his hair and turned to face her.

Suddenly there was only craziness in her head. Panic and anger. She wanted to scream and rage, to tear him apart for his stupidity and the pain he was inflicting. What the hell was wrong with him? How could he get himself involved with a child when he was already married – to her?

'Is it serious?' she asked in a voice that didn't sound like hers.

He swallowed and said, 'I – I guess . . . Yes, it is.'

He seemed both certain and uncertain and her temper exploded. 'For God's sake, you're old enough to be her father . . .'

'Please . . .'

'You must surely realize you're in the grip of some deluded middle-aged fantasy? You can't really think you're the answer to that little tart's dream? That she's going to give you everything you've ever wanted . . .'

'Don't talk about her like that—'

'Don't you dare defend her to me—'

'Katie, stop!'

'She's a tart,' she screeched. 'She's a fucking whore and you, you pathetic moron, are so damned stupid that you think you're something special. Well, you're not. From what I hear she's getting laid by half the camera crew and . . .' The breath suddenly left her, and not even the sting to her face was as great as the shock that he'd actually hit her.

She stared at him so stunned that she could find no words.

He stared back, clearly equally as shaken. His eyes were wretched, grief-stricken, as he said, 'I wish to God I could take that back.'

She looked away. She felt numb now, deadened by the horror of where they were. She wanted to walk away and pretend none of it had happened, that this was no more than a nightmare.

Why didn't he say something, for God's sake?

In the end he turned and left the room.

She went after him, into the bedroom. 'What are you doing?' she demanded as he took out a suitcase. 'No! Rob! Please, stop this. You have to pull yourself together and remember how much we mean to one another. Our marriage is strong, you can't break it up for a . . . a crush that's bound to pass. Darling, this thing doesn't even stand a chance, can't you see that? No!' she shouted as he started to walk past her. 'Please.' She clutched his arm so tightly, her nails might break his skin. She didn't care. Anything that might hold him to her.

'Katie, don't make me say things that are only going to hurt you more,' and prising himself free he went into the bathroom.

She followed. 'I don't know you,' she choked. 'You're not the man I married. Don't I matter to you at all?'

'Of course you do.'

'But she matters more?'

Again his failure to answer was answer enough.

He walked around her, back to the bedroom and she watched him, feeling so helpless and afraid that she hardly knew what to do. 'Don't go,' she whispered. 'Please, Rob . . .'

'Don't beg,' he said.

Her fists clenched and her eyes blazed. 'I will, because I'll do anything to make you stay. I'm your wife, I love you. I can forgive you for this . . .'

'Amy's pregnant,' he said softly and, picking up his case and keys, he let himself quietly out of the flat.

CHAPTER SEVEN

Marina always loves spending time at their home in the Cotswolds. It's a characterful eighteenth-century rectory with roughly hewn whitewashed walls, a black tiled roof and an abundance of climbing flowers currently creating an early summer display. The local church is nearby, amidst a cluster of stone cottages, and sprawling, undulating countryside is all around filled with paddocks and streams, tangled woods, quaint villages and mile upon mile of beautiful walks. She and Maxim find it so much easier to relax here than in London, and the girls – always lively – generally seem less querulous and competitive than they often do at other times. Of course, having Maxim's American godson Ed around this weekend is helping a lot although, as Maxim commented quietly last night, 'I don't know who's more embarrassed by the way they're coming on to him – me or him.'

Although Marina had laughed, she is just as concerned about how much more worldly the twins are attempting to make themselves appear these days. Livvy, as always, is stealing the lead with the wearing of a tiny bikini top and skimpy shorts, while Sophie, the quieter and usually slightly more modest of the two, is trying to keep up with a selection of minidresses that are just a little too tight in all the wrong – or right – places. Certainly they're maturing way faster than either Marina or Maxim feel ready for. One of their friends' mothers had commented recently that puberty seemed like a tsunami preparing to break, and Marina couldn't have put it any better.

Maxim will undoubtedly end up dealing with it much better than she would; he's always pretty chilled and is completely adored by his girls. Also, he's done a much better job of moving on from the demons in their past than she has. He shows no signs at all of being afflicted by the horrendous memories that still, at times, make her nervous and irrationally fearful of what might be coming next. To her dismay, the latest chapter of Stalwood's book in which 'Rob' walks out on 'Katie' has brought back some unpleasant memories of the time Patrick left her, and she isn't finding them easy to shake.

'I think he's locking his door at night,' Maxim comments, wincing as he and Marina watch from the kitchen terrace as a whooping Olivia leaps onto Ed's back and wraps her skinny legs around him. Going with the spirit of it, Ed runs her down to the apple trees at the far end of the lawn, spins her round and unceremoniously dumps her in a pile of mown grass.

Sophie screams with glee as she takes off to smother her sister in the pungent heap.

'They're going to come to blows over him,' Maxim warns.

'Any time now,' Marina agrees.

'Lake?' he suggests.

'Great idea.'

'I'll find out if anyone else wants to go.'

As he goes off to the summer room, where friends who've come for the weekend are relaxing with coffees, hangovers and the Sunday papers (it had been an extremely indulgent and raucous dinner last night), Marina descends the stone steps of the old terrace and starts across the lawn.

'Hey, Mum,' Livvy calls out as Marina approaches. She is brushing the grass off herself and making a self-caressing performance of it.

'Dad's going to take you water-skiing,' Marina announces and laughs as they cheer.

'Can I drive the boat?' Sophie demands. 'He let me last time. I know how to do it,' she tells Ed. 'Livvy hasn't got the hang of it yet.'

'I think Ed should drive,' Livvy declares, her angry eyes turning coquettish as she casts a little glance at her 'cousin'.

He really is an exceptionally handsome young man, Marina reflects; tall, fair-haired like his father, Joel, Maxim's oldest friend, with the same strong jaw and a runner's physique that even she can't help admiring.

'Is anyone else coming?' Ed asks, picking grass from his T-shirt and cut-off jeans.

'Maxim's gone to find out,' she replies.

'Great. I'll go get the boat ready.'

As he strides off up the lawn ahead of them, Marina has to smile at the way the twins fall silent watching his progress.

After a moment they link her arms and start towards the house.

Sophie says, 'Mum, you know when you first met Dad?'

'Mmm,' Marina responds, having a fair idea of where this might be going.

'Well, like, did you *know*? I mean, right away, that he was the one?'

Allowing her mind to touch briefly on that turbulent time, Marina says, 'I guess not right away, no.'

'What?' Livvy cries in protest. 'I asked him last night and he said he fell for you at first sight.'

Marina has to smile, certain it hadn't been as rapid as that, while knowing he'd tell the girls what they wanted to hear. She should have done the same.

'Remember, she was still married to that doozy Patrick when they first met,' Livvy points out. 'Although it was all like more or less over, wasn't it?'

'Yes, but why are you calling him that?' Marina protests. 'Apart from anything else, you barely even know him.'

'No, but you have to admit he was a loser until Dad got him that job in hotels.'

'Dad was also the one who fired him from the publishing house,' Sophie added.

'Yeah, but that was ages before he found him another job,' Livvy ran on, 'and he deserved to get fired after the way he cheated on Mum and screwed up—'

'Hang on, where are you getting all this from?' Marina interrupts, as shocked by their knowledge as she is unsettled by hearing them express it.

'We're not deaf,' Livvy retorts, 'we hear you lot talking when you've had too many.'

'Yeah, it all comes out then,' Sophie teases. 'So admit it, you were actually married to a doozy.'

'That's not how I'd describe him,' Marina objects, annoyed by their cruelty when they have no real idea of what they are talking about. However, she doesn't want to make a big deal of it so she says, 'If you're going water-skiing, you need to get changed, but I'd rather you didn't wear bikinis. You know they'll come off in the water, which is probably what you're hoping for—'

'No way!' Livvy protests. 'I am not the exhibitionist around here. She is.'

'That is so not true,' Sophie cries hotly. 'You're the one who went skinny-dipping at Jolyon Wheatcroft's last weekend.'

Marina turns to Livvy. 'Is that true?'

'So not!' Livvy growls, shooting a warning scowl at her sister. 'She's making it up to get me into trouble so I won't be able to go to the lake. It's her way of trying to get Ed to herself.'

Before it can go any further, Marina says, 'Listen to me, you two. Ed is twenty-one and you are only thirteen, so you have to stop with all this flirting. If you don't, you'll end up having Dad on your case – and think how embarrassing that would be.' *For all of you,* she doesn't add.

'Who says we're flirting?' Livvy pouts. 'We're just being friendly.'

'Whatever you want to call it, one-piece swimsuits for the skiing, with shorts and sunblock, or you won't be going.'

As they skip off to their rooms, Marina finds herself smiling in spite of the stern words, and feels such a rush of love for them that she wants to pull them back into her arms just to squeeze them. Being a mother means everything to her; it can make her quite emotional simply to think of how fortunate she is to have them. There's nothing she wouldn't do for them, no world in which she could imagine existing without them. Her life might have taken a very different turn back before they were born; if it had, there was no way she'd be standing where she is now. For certain she wouldn't be a publisher, or a wife, or a mother; she'd be someone else entirely, someone she never wants to engage with, even in a tortured form of what-if . . .

Returning to the kitchen to start packing a picnic, she finds Noel loading beers and soft drinks into a cool bag. He often joins them at weekends, usually as a single even if he is dating someone.

'Shall I put some wine in?' he asks, selecting a bottle of white from the fridge and looking it over. 'God, we got through some last night, didn't we?'

Marina groans as her head acknowledges the truth with a dull thud. 'Don't remind me,' she scolds. 'You're a bad influence.'

He laughs. 'Like anyone needs any encouragement. So yes to the Sauvignon? Or are you giving up alcohol for the day?'

'For life, actually, and I won't be skiing . . .'

'Oh, come on, you're made of stronger stuff than—'

'It's not that. I need to prepare a meal for this evening and with everyone out of the house, I can maybe even manage a siesta.'

He puts the wine in anyway, closes the fridge door and says, 'So what did you think of Stalwood's latest chapter? Myself, I reckon "Katie" is gearing up to do something truly terrible, don't you?'

Marina thinks it highly possible, and says, 'We know from the prologue that Christy has seriously upset someone, so I'm interested to know what *she* might do going forward and how it ties in.'

He grins. 'Reckon I'm getting you hooked,' he teases, and heads off to the front of the house where, half an hour later, a small convoy of vehicles starts down the drive, with Maxim at the wheel of the old Volvo they keep in the garage mainly for towing the speedboat. Noel and Ed are with him, and the girls, she sees, have jumped in with

Caroline and Ted Wren, lawyer friends who often come for the weekend with their eight-year-old son and five-year-old daughter.

After deciding on what to cook later, Marina makes herself a coffee and takes her laptop out to the terrace. She isn't intending to work, just to check over the girls' critiques of *The Secrets Act* before they hand them in tomorrow. And perhaps she can make a start on some of the reading that has piled up ahead of several meetings this week.

She's midway through Livvy's ponderous appraisal of a book she doesn't seem to care much for, when she hears the chime of a mobile somewhere nearby. Recognizing it as Maxim's text tone, she looks around and spots it on one of the loungers, half-tucked inside a newspaper. Obviously he's forgotten to take it, which isn't a big deal, she can always get hold of him on someone else's phone if need be, although she probably ought to let him know where it is in case he thinks he's lost it.

She's about to unlock it to call Sophie when she sees the text on the screen and pauses.

Where are you? Waiting for your call. G

She feels her insides starting to swim. It's crazy how fast her thoughts go to Georgia, but they're there now and she can't seem to move them on.

Why would Georgia want to know where he is? When did he promise to call? Why are they even in touch?

Quickly she enters the passcode and follows through to the text thread.

It takes her a moment to realize the messages are from Graham Robbins, a wine merchant based in Stow who supplies them with an excellent champagne at a very good price.

He's apparently expecting Maxim to be in touch to arrange collection of his latest order.

She presses the phone to her chest as relief makes her faintly light-headed.

It isn't that she doesn't trust Maxim, it's that blasted book again and the incipient similarities to her own life that are creeping in. They're obviously coincidental, and barely even that, actually – and she only has to remember that the world is full of betrayed women who'd find their own equivalences in this story, to feel slightly foolish for letting it get to her. After all, few know better than she does that it's the power and purpose of fiction, to engage a reader in emotions and events that might not be their own but could so easily be.

Hearing her phone ringing inside she goes to answer and, seeing it's Livvy, she clicks on.

'Mum! Dad's lost his phone. Can you see if he left it there?'

'He did,' Marina tells her. 'Can you let him know that Graham Robbins is waiting to hear from him? Are you at the lake yet?'

'Just getting the boat on the water. Hang on, Dad's asking if you need us to pick anything up for dinner on our way back.'

'I'll text if I do. Have a good time all of you and focus, OK? Showing off for Ed could end you up—'

'Dad! That's mine!'

'Honey,' Maxim says, apparently having snatched the phone. 'Why don't you come? Believe it or not, there aren't many people here and you know you love to ski.'

It's true, she does, but she says, 'I need to read the girls' essays before they go back to school tomorrow . . .'

'We can take one each later. Come on, it'll be more fun with you here, and we can all muck in to prepare a meal later.'

With a smile she says, 'OK, I'll get in the car. Will I find you easily enough?'

After giving her the exact location, he says, 'And can you bring my phone?'

'Ah, so that's why you want me to come?'

He either doesn't hear or they lose the connection so, ringing off at her end, she begins to lock up the house, annoyed with herself for having suspected him of being underhand. It isn't what he deserves. He is no Patrick.

And certainly no *Rob Nicholls*.

What the heck is the matter with her? She has to get this book out of her head. Neither she nor Maxim, nor Patrick, have ever worked in TV, and as for the girl who wrecked her and Patrick's marriage, she might have been eighteen, and yes, she'd been Marina's PA, but she wasn't the niece of anyone Marina knew.

She really has to stop this now or it will start driving her crazy.

CHAPTER EIGHT

That Girl by E.L. Stalwood

Christy already knew quite a bit about Johan Johannsen, the man who was destined to be her new boss when the takeover went through. As the owner of an Amsterdam-based media empire, with TV and radio stations all over the continent, he wasn't hard to find online. She'd spent some considerable time reading about him, most entries being focussed on how he and his father started the company and built it up to what it was today. She'd also learned that he was forty-three, Norwegian by birth, had a passion for sailing, skiing and fine arts – and was two years divorced from a Swedish supermodel.

Christy felt a quiet frisson of pleasure as he stood to welcome her to the restaurant table he'd had his assistant book for them this evening. He was even more attractive in person than in his official photos – and no one could say he didn't look good in them. Tall, muscular, short fair hair, strong jaw and haunting, mesmerizing blue eyes. Actually, this wasn't the first, or even the second time they'd met. He'd attended a few of the meetings set up by his senior executives to discuss the future of her programme, and during the last one she'd found him listening with apparent interest to her ideas for streamlining and modernizing the show.

Then, yesterday morning, an invitation to join him for dinner had turned up in her emails.

From virtually that moment on, she'd been in a state of nervous anticipation; one minute determined not to read anything but professional interest into his gesture, the next allowing herself to wonder if he found her as attractive as she found him.

She wanted desperately to discuss the situation with Katie, to laugh and plan and be as outrageous as they always had in the past where a possible new romance was concerned. However, talking about herself and the very improbable scenario of anything meaningful – or personal – happening between her and Johan Johannsen, would be unforgivably insensitive given the awful place Katie was in right now.

Since Rob had walked out with the shattering news that Amy was pregnant, there had been a curious and, in some ways unnerving, change in Katie. Although she was clearly devastated – how could she not be? – she didn't seem to be reacting in the way Christy would have expected. Not hysterical, exactly, but furious, vengeful, emotions of great passion and depth. Instead she seemed to have turned in on herself, as though dealing privately, secretly even, with the torrent of reaction that must, on so many levels, be tearing her apart. Every time Christy tried to approach her about it, she said she didn't want to discuss anything, and no, she had no need to take time off, thank you. She hadn't even asked Christy to fire Amy, which was the very least Christy had expected.

So Katie didn't know that Christy was meeting Johan Johannsen tonight, which was saddening, and in a way frustrating, because Christy just knew she'd be dying to tell Katie all about it later.

And in another world, Katie would want to hear it.

'Thanks for coming,' Johan said, taking her hand as she reached the table. As she smiled politely into his eyes, she was aware of the suppressed power of his grip, the strong bones of his fingers, the resonance of his low, faintly accented voice.

'It's my pleasure,' she replied and, as he stepped behind her chair to hold it while she sat down, she thanked him for inviting her.

Once he was seated too, he kept his eyes on hers, seeming to search and assess her thoughts as he raised an arm to call for a waiter. 'Will you drink wine?' he asked. 'Or perhaps we could start with champagne?'

Her heart skipped a beat. Did they have something to celebrate? 'Champagne is always welcome,' she said wryly.

He smiled and gave the waiter the order.

As they waited for the drinks, he asked if she'd had far to come this evening; did she take a taxi; had she been to this rooftop restaurant before? The answers were no, yes and no. She asked him the same and his answers were no, his apartment was just around the corner so he'd walked, and yes he'd been here on several occasions.

Glad he wasn't able to read her mind, although she wasn't entirely clear about what she was thinking, or if she was even breathing quite steadily, she watched his hands as he took out a phone to check a message.

'Sorry,' he said when he finished reading, 'it's not always easy to be off-duty, and I'm afraid I need to return this call.'

'Please, go ahead,' she encouraged. This wasn't a date, after all.

To her surprise he didn't leave the table, simply made the connection and began speaking in a language she had no knowledge of at all. She almost smiled to herself as she decided it made him seem even more interesting and, as she looked around the room, she noticed that several fellow diners were glancing their way.

Did they make an attractive couple? She imagined they must, though she'd never compare herself to a Swedish supermodel. In fact, she wasn't inclined to think about his ex-wife at all, or to wonder if he'd made the comparison at any point. This evening was simply a business meeting, a way of getting to know one another in order to create an easier, more productive relationship in the office.

Unless he'd invited her here to soften the blow of axing her programme?

She'd fight for it, of course, but she'd be careful to do so in a calm and dignified manner, something that usually came easily to her, although not always when confronted with a man she was so drawn to.

He laughed at whatever was being said to him on the phone, and she felt an unwelcome stab of apprehension piercing her resolve to remain friendly, but aloof. It was shaming, pathetic, how easily she could feel intimidated by someone she found attractive. She knew it was rooted in her father dying so young and the fear of losing someone she loved so much again, but that didn't make it any easier to control. Fortunately, over the years, she'd learned to keep it hidden behind a careful façade of self-confidence, at least in the early days of a relationship. It was only later that she seemed to go into self-destruct.

It couldn't keep happening. Surely Katie was right: one day she'd meet someone she could trust enough to stay – to love her enough to want to stay.

As he ended his call, two flutes of champagne arrived and he raised his to make a toast. 'To the future of your programme,' he declared. 'You have some good ideas and I like the fact you're ready to make some fairly radical changes.'

Surprised, and pleased, she touched her glass to his. 'To the programme,' she echoed. And, after taking a sip, 'Can I ask what in particular has caught your attention?'

His eyebrows rose comically, seeming to suggest it might be her; however, his answer was entirely professional as he began to go through the suggestions she'd put forward during their last meeting. A shorter transmission time; a celebrity-focussed interview slot; a variety of guest co-presenters; a review roundup for movies, TV, books, music, anything in the arts.

'I'd like you to shoot a pilot, showcasing how you'd bring it all together,' he continued, taking the menu he was being passed. 'We'll give you a budget for it – perhaps you could come up with some figures – and while you're doing it, I'd like you to consider the overall look of the show.'

Regarding him curiously she said, 'In what sense?'

With no hesitation he said, 'I believe it needs someone younger to give it new energy, bring in fresh ideas. Your use of Amy Summers is working well. She's a little anarchic, but not offensively so; she's quick-thinking, engages well with banter and she's good to look at. That always helps, although I'm probably not supposed to say that.'

He wasn't, but that wasn't what had caused Christy's heart to start racing. Had he just suggested removing Katie from the programme? Worse, that he wanted to replace her with Amy?

Christy couldn't allow that to happen. It would be the worst imaginable blow for Katie to lose her job on top of everything else. 'Have you – do you have an objection to Katie Beech as a presenter?' she asked carefully.

He seemed surprised. 'Not at all, she's very professional and clearly experienced. I wouldn't want to lose her, but I see her more as an occasional presenter, someone to bring gravitas to a situation should it be required. Mostly, though, I see your show as a more light-hearted look at current events, something audiences will feel comfortable with – and, as you know, big viewing figures bring in the big advertisers.'

Christy couldn't stop herself. 'Because it's all about money?' she murmured.

He looked amused and rueful. 'I'm sorry it has to be a consideration,' he said, 'but without it, you wouldn't have a programme at all.'

Unable to argue with that, and admiring him for being so frank, she took another sip of champagne and turned to her menu.

'I hope I haven't offended you,' he said curiously.

She looked up and found herself melting at the concern in his eyes. 'Of course not,' she assured him. 'I'm enjoying our chat. I just . . . Well, I should come clean about this: first, Amy is my niece; second, and actually more importantly really, Katie Beech is my best friend and the programme means a great deal to her. I think she'll take it quite hard to find herself demoted to "occasional presenter", especially if Amy is going to take over her role.'

He nodded his understanding and picked up his glass. He had the deepest, shrewdest blue eyes; was it any wonder she couldn't stop looking at them? 'I read the papers,' he said, his voice low and pensive, 'so I'm aware of Katie's marriage break-up and Amy being the cause of it. So I realize what I'm suggesting is going to be extremely hard for her, but I thought she might prefer it to leaving the programme altogether. Am I wrong about that?'

Slightly thrown by this . . . was it sensitivity?, she said, 'I'm not sure. I mean, ultimately it will have to be Katie's decision. I just don't want her to think that I'm behind the proposed change.'

'Of course not. I'll be happy to speak to her myself if you think it would help.'

She was in no doubt about that. 'No, I should do it. I don't know if it'll be any easier coming from me, but she won't feel able to speak freely to you.'

'OK, I'll be advised by you. Now, shall we choose what we're going to eat?'

His summary dismissal of Katie didn't feel great; however, Christy was certain he meant nothing by it, he was simply a man who liked to deal with the issues at hand and move on. She had to admit there was something intrinsically appealing about this.

By the time the second course arrived he'd taken two more phone calls, while still successfully steering their conversation through various additional proposals that might work for the programme. He was clearly as focussed as he was direct in his approach, and yet, all the time, in spite of never once talking about anything personal, she was sure she sensed an undercurrent of chemistry building between them. He must be aware of it too. She wondered if he'd act on it in some way, or if he had a strict rule of never mixing business with pleasure.

She had her answer – at least she thought she did – when, at the end of the meal, he looked across the table and let his gaze rest on hers. His eyes were so intense that the pressure felt almost physical. 'I've a hunch we're going to get along well,' he said. 'I'm certainly looking forward to finding out.'

CHAPTER NINE

Janus's main office is alive with celebration. Champagne corks are popping, glasses fizzing as the editorial team ecstatically cheer the great news, while staff from other departments are beginning to pour in.

The poaching of Thomas Jackson, an international best-selling thriller writer with six TV series to his name and four feature films, is a major coup for Janus. Led by Marina, the team has been trying to tempt him across from Ashwells for at least five years; and finally, only a few minutes ago, his agent had rung to let them know he's theirs. This means that from the middle of next year, his consistent high-quality, multimillion-selling output is going to make a hugely positive impact on their bottom line, and no one can feel anything but thrilled about that.

Unless you're Rosie Shell, of course.

Rosie will have heard by now that she's lost one of her star authors, and is very probably swearing all sorts of vengeance on her arch nemesis, Marina Forster. There would be no point telling her it wasn't personal, for she'd be unable to see it any other way (Marina has to admit she wouldn't be able to, either, if the roles were reversed). However, these things happen, Rosie knows that as well as anyone in the business – all is fair in publishing and poaching. Just keep watching your back.

For the moment, Marina is standing aside from the impromptu party, allowing Georgia centre stage for a while – as senior editor she played a significant role in developing the presentation and offer that no author in their right mind could refuse. It had mostly happened yesterday, over a very boozy lunch at the Delaunay, which both Marina and Maxim had attended (to land someone like Jackson, it was always a good idea to have the CEO on board). As it turned out, Maxim had been an even bigger asset than imagined, for the two men had bonded over a mutual passion for rugby and fine wines, and by the time the bill was paid, it was clear to everyone that the deal was all but done.

Just after the call an hour ago to confirm that the multimillion-dollar, global-rights offer had been accepted, Maxim dropped her an email to say he'd already invited Jackson and his new husband to the Cotswolds for a long weekend, subject to everyone's availability. Tomorrow Georgia and Carina, the publicist, will prepare an announcement for the trade press, but this evening is all about the celebration.

From her desk, Marina smiles at the way they are laughing and high-fiving – editors and assistants, art directors, sales and marketing managers, foreign rights negotiators, publicists, strategists and copyists. A cheer suddenly erupts as Maxim arrives with a handful of board members in tow – everyone wants to toast Janus's success. Marina stays where she is in her office, watching as Maxim hugs Georgia with so much affection it makes the girl blush.

It isn't so much that which holds Marina rooted to her chair, as the most recent chapter of *That Girl*.

She simply can't get Christy's dinner with 'Johan Johannsen' out of her mind. Although the story is still being presented as an overblown synopsis, it contains a resonance, a similarity even, to the time when she, Marina, had been a senior editor here at Hawksley Maine. It was before Janus's inception and during the time she was married to Patrick. Her closest friend then had been Shana Morales, the publishing director; in other words, her immediate boss.

She wonders if the roles of senior editor and publishing director are equivalent to those of a TV presenter and producer?

It seems likely.

'Christy' was nothing like Shana, certainly not in character, but as this was supposed to be a work of fiction, the details didn't have to be right. In fact, nothing was bound to reflect reality. However, the proposed takeover of the TV Station by a Dutch-based media company was disturbingly analogous to Maxim's father's US organization taking control of Hawksley Maine. And Marina hadn't forgotten Shana's hopes and expectations where their new boss, Maxim Forster, was concerned. She never would.

Could it be Shana writing?

It makes her feel sick to think of Shana coming back into their lives at all, never mind in this way.

It could, of course, be Rosie Shell. Rosie knew all about what happened back then and this . . . *book*! was the kind of thing Rosie would do – although Marina has to wonder why it has taken her this long? Did it matter? The point is, Rosie would do just about anything to injure or humiliate Marina, and if the past got raked up again, it could be utterly devastating in ways Marina doesn't even want to imagine.

There is no 'Rosie' character in the book, at least so far, but Marina can't decide what, if anything, that might mean.

She closes her eyes. *What the hell is going on in her head?* Maxim isn't 'Johan'; 'Katie' isn't her; and 'Christy' isn't real. None of it is!

And as for Georgia being an older version of the editorial assistant, Amelia Spence, who Patrick broke up their marriage for . . . There's no way this could be happening again with Maxim and Georgia. It's crazy even to think it.

'Hey, what are you doing in here?' Maxim declares, pushing open the door and coming to pull her from her chair. 'You don't want to miss the best bit, do you?'

Breaking into a smile, she allows herself to be led into the main office, where everyone is waiting, glasses refilled, for Maxim to propose a toast.

With an arm around her shoulders, he raises his drink and says, 'Congratulations to you all for the clearly irresistible presentation you put together. I know a great deal of time and talent went into creating it, from mocking up jackets, to outlining proposals and publicity opportunities, to showcasing just what an outstanding team we have here at Janus and why anyone would be mad not to join us.'

Everyone cheers and bangs the tables, and Marina can see how thrilled they all are to have their efforts recognized by the boss.

'To all of you,' he cries, holding his glass high.

'To us,' they chorus and, with a clinking of glasses, they down a collective four bottles of champagne in one go.

'Of course, we must not forget the man himself, Thomas Jackson,' Maxim continues, 'who, incidentally, would have joined us for this party if he hadn't already returned to his home in Yorkshire by the time the offer had been accepted. He wants me to pass on how excited he is to start working with you all, and how moving it has been for him, after all these years, to have another publisher so keen to take him to even greater heights. I know you can do it, and I know that having him on our list won't only be of great benefit to the company and many of our other authors, it will also be a great boost to you as a team. You've done exceptionally well, in every department, but I'm sure you'll all agree that a special mention has to go to Georgia, without whom it wouldn't have happened.'

Marina's eyes go to her senior editor as she beams with delight and everyone cries,

'To Georgia.'

'Go babe!'

'Love you.'

'Are you getting a cut?'

Marina's heart catches on a sudden image of Amelia Spence coming out of the past and seeming to impress itself fleetingly on Georgia.

Feeling Maxim's arm tighten around her, she leans in to him and continues to watch Georgia. She is radiant, beautiful, exceptionally smart, and without doubt the most ambitious member of the fiction team. Next stop for her will be Marina's position, provided Marina vacates it, of course; but Marina is in no hurry to move on, and she can't imagine Maxim ever allowing her to be forced out. So what will Georgia do next? Go to a rival publisher?

Or has she found another far more subtle and ultimately devastating way to achieve her goals?

She hadn't been around fourteen years ago, but she could be working with Rosie Shell.

'You didn't seem yourself earlier,' Maxim comments as they travel home in a taxi later. 'Are you OK?'

'It's been quite a day,' she smiles with a sigh, 'and I'm fine. Thrilled for Georgia, for everyone . . .'

'And no one could have done it without you. I should have said that in my toast.'

'No, you were right not to. I wanted it to be about them – it would have felt wrong for me to take the credit, especially when it's dished out by my husband.'

He laughs. 'Nevertheless, it was you who gave everyone the space, and encouragement to be their best selves.'

Touched by the praise, she turns to look at him and can see in his eyes that he truly means what he says. How can she not love him for that alone – as well as for so much else?

As he takes a call, she turns to gaze out at the passing streets, the very same streets that were a backdrop to her world all those years ago. Time might have moved on, she might feel like a different person now, but she can't help wondering what the gossip is about her these days. Nothing ever gets back to her, but she knows very well that people like Rosie Shell don't mind telling anyone who'll listen that – if it weren't for Maxim Forster – Marina Cain, as she'd been back then, wouldn't be where she is today.

'In fact,' Rosie would no doubt say, 'if there were any justice in the world, Marina Cain would be in prison.'

After a torturous night with memories shifting and tangling, running up and down the years and trapping her into all sorts of bizarre and frightening scenarios, Marina waits for Maxim to leave the next morning before sitting down in her study to email Noel. Maybe, if he'd been in London during the time it had all happened, the story of *That Girl* might be ringing bells for him too, but he hadn't.

Nevertheless, with the way gossip never rests in this business, someone has surely told him about it. In fact, it would almost certainly have made it to Australia at the time – to every part of the globe where there was a publishing industry – so he had to know something.

She gets no further than opening a new message box when an email arrives from him.

There's more. I'll be really interested to get your take on what comes next. Be prepared for a lot of hot sex.

CHAPTER TEN

That Girl by E.L. Stalwood

Katie stiffened as someone tapped on the door of her dressing room. Everything put her on edge these days: a laugh, a cough, a car backfiring as if a gun had gone off.

She closed her eyes, not wanting to pursue that thought.

She wondered if Rob had come to beg her forgiveness; or maybe Amy wanted to tell her that there was no affair. Christy made it up, because that was the kind of thing Christy did to manipulate and control people.

Katie knew that wasn't true about Christy, but she wished it were, because then none of this would be real.

There was another knock and Christy put her head round. 'Can I come in?' she asked.

Without waiting for an answer, she closed the door behind her and sank into one of the leatherette sofas. 'It's been a crazy day,' she sighed, stretching out her long legs and crossing one over the other. 'Great show, by the way, you were on good form.'

How beautiful and relaxed she looked, Katie remarked to herself. Well, she would, wouldn't she? Her life wasn't falling apart.

'My phone's been ringing off the hook,' Christy continued, checking her mobile and pushing a call through to messages.

Knowing that Johannsen's takeover of the company had been

made official, Katie said nothing, simply continued to stare at herself in the mirror. She was ashen, strained, almost ghoulish, with shadows of tiredness around her eyes and bloodshot rims.

Please let Amy's pregnancy be a lie.

As far as she knew, Amy hadn't told anyone about it, and she continued to bounce around the office as if nothing unusual was happening – as if Katie Beech's husband hadn't just moved in with her. Earlier Katie had watched her working on her computer, appearing absorbed by whatever was on the screen. The hatred, violence, she'd felt was dizzying, and building to a pitch that scared her.

She wondered if the girl had read any reports of Rob's drunken rampage last night, when he'd apparently got himself thrown out of a pub and threatened to beat up a policeman. How was Amy feeling about that? Why hadn't he been at home with her?

'I have some news,' Christy announced, turning off her phone.

Coming back to the moment, Katie put her hairbrush down and half-turned in her chair. A sixth sense was telling her to leave, to get as far away from everyone as she could, but all she was able to do was listen as Christy told her that Johan Johannsen was keen to have a younger person fronting the show. And after seeing Amy in the role, he'd decided she was a good fit.

Katie could feel the pounding of her heart echoing in her head, as though trying to drown out Christy's words. Her husband, her job, was there anything else Amy was planning to take from her? And where the hell was Christy's loyalty?

As though reading her mind, Christy said, gently, 'I'm afraid that if I don't go along with his plans, he'll axe the show—'

'Did you tell him Amy's pregnant?' Katie cut in.

Christy fell silent and Katie wondered if she was more concerned about how this might affect her plans for the show than she was about her best friend, or her niece. 'Are you sure about it?' Christy countered.

'She's told Rob she is, and he seems to believe her.'

Christy inhaled deeply and got up to go and pour them both a drink.

'Does Johan Johannsen know about Amy and Rob?' Katie asked.

Christy handed over a glass. 'Yes, he does. As you know, it's all over social media . . .'

'So he's aware of what it will do to me, to lose my programme to *her*?'

'It's not personal, Katie, you must know that. Besides, no one's suggesting you leave the programme. There will be a role for you . . .'

Katie put down her drink, got to her feet and walked out of the door. She didn't know where she was going, or what she might do, she just couldn't continue the conversation. She wasn't even sure if she could ever speak to Christy again.

Later that day, Christy was in conference with one of the studio directors when Johan called. 'Am I interrupting?' he asked drolly.

'It's allowed,' she responded in a similar tone. 'What can I do for you?' Her eyes bored into the director, willing him to go away, but he was fixed on his phone.

'I was wondering,' Johan said, 'if you've spoken to Katie?'

'Actually, I have,' she replied.

'How did she take it?'

Swivelling in her chair to put her back to the director, she said, 'She left the building when I told her and I haven't been able to find her since.'

'Mm, that's not good. Did you explain that we're not asking her to leave altogether?'

'I tried, but she wasn't ready to listen. I need to give her some time.'

'OK. How are you doing with the draft budget?'

'It's almost there. I'm not sure you're going to like it. No one does when it comes to parting with money.'

He laughed. 'I'll brace myself, but prepare for cuts.'

'Of course. Have you been able to read through the other proposals I sent over?'

'Not yet, but I'll get to them by the end of the week.'

Her heart was thudding so hard she barely heard herself say, 'When you're ready, maybe we could discuss them over dinner? At my place?'

He paused, and she so desperately wanted to take the words back that she already started to as he said,

'Does that mean what I think it does?'

A spasm of fiery heat shook her voice as she said, 'If you want it to.'

Another pause, her breath stopped; then she heard his smile and almost saw his eyes half-closing as he murmured, 'Send me your address.'

He came over that night and even before she'd closed the door, he was covering her mouth with his, pulling her to him and letting her know how ready he was for her. She didn't resist, she wanted him just as badly.

They tore at each other's clothes, leaving a trail behind them as they moved to the bedroom, kissing, murmuring, groaning. The smell of him, the feel of his hard flesh and urgent tongue was driving her crazy. They were naked even before they reached the bed. He pushed her down, roughly, parted her legs and knelt between them . . .

CHAPTER ELEVEN

Marina can only feel thankful she's at home alone. She wouldn't want anyone to see the expression on her face – she doesn't even want to see it herself.

In other circumstances, it might have been the explicit sex scene she'd just read between 'Christy' and 'Johann Johannsen' that had shocked her so deeply. In these it's how hard she's suddenly found it to stop herself seeing 'Johan' as Maxim and 'Christy' as her old friend and nemesis, Shana Morales.

Whether this actual scene, or something like it, had ever taken place between Maxim and Shana, Marina has no idea, but she does know that they'd slept together early on in their relationship, and that Shana had fallen very deeply, very quickly.

I think he could be the one, she remembers Shana telling her. *Oh God, I shouldn't have said that. I've probably jinxed it now.*

Marina had been too heartbroken over Patrick's betrayal to take in much else of what Shana had been saying at the time, too wrapped up in herself and how everything around her was changing.

Had Maxim fallen for Shana in those early days?

No. He couldn't have. Things would have turned out very differently if he had.

Nevertheless, their affair had started out like this. A powerful attraction, an urgency to satisfy it, a need for more, and yet more.

There are pages of it, pages and pages.

Marina hasn't allowed herself to read any further than the first fall onto the bed; it had felt, ludicrously she knew, as if she were tormenting herself with Maxim's desire for another woman. It hadn't seemed to matter that the names were different, or that it had happened so many years ago, the scene had threatened to come alive for her in a way she didn't want to handle.

So she'd skimmed past it, the words blurring as she scrolled down the screen, turning them into pointless paragraphs that needed to be severely edited or erased altogether. She'd picked the story up again towards the end, where they'd finally engaged in conversation – she thought they were in the sitting room by then, but what difference did it make? It was Johan's mention of his family's ski chalet in Aspen that had caught her attention and made her heart turn over.

Maxim's family had a ski chalet in Aspen.

Had Maxim ever taken Shana there during the time they were together?

No. It wasn't possible. Marina knew for certain that couldn't have happened, so why is she even asking herself the question, when there's nothing in the book to suggest that Aspen had even played a part.

At least not so far.

Closing the lid of her laptop, she reaches for the glass of red wine she'd poured an hour ago.

She needs to get a grip of herself, to stop confusing her own life with E.L. Stalwood's story – unless that's exactly what she's supposed to be doing. And if it is . . .

Quickly opening her laptop again, she goes through to her inbox and calls up the message she received from Rosie Shell earlier in the day.

Some things are never forgotten, or forgiven.

At the time she'd assumed it was Rosie's bitter response to the poaching of one of her star authors – Rosie always had been a sore loser – but now Marina can't help wondering if the message, she might even call it a warning, was about more than Thomas Jackson. Rosie could be a vengeful and spiteful woman – is she using E.L. Stalwood as a pseudonym to rake up old ghosts? To cause Marina the deepest humiliation? To reframe events in a way that has the potential to destroy Marina's world should it turn out that Rosie knows something, and is using this book as some sort of slow-reveal.

Naturally, Marina has already googled E.L. Stalwood, but so far she's found nothing to connect the name to Rosie. Hardly surprising. If Rosie really is embarking on a long-awaited and carefully crafted method of revenge for how she'd been fired, and for what had happened to her old friend Shana, she'll have hidden her real identity well.

Or is Shana Morales E.L. Stalwood? In many ways, that seems more likely, but why now, after all these years? They hadn't been in touch since the day Shana was led from the court. What could have changed to make her believe that this is the right time to strike back?

There is a chance, of course, and Marina knows she'd be a fool to ignore it, that she is still so haunted by all that happened that her subconscious has started to plant reminders in places and people and words that have no connection to what went before.

Could she really be doing that to herself?

She has no immediate answers; she only knows in this moment that she is finding it hard to clear her mind of the almost pornographic encounter she's just read between 'Johan' and 'Christy'. Of course it's ludicrous to feel upset, jealous, after all these years, but the description – depiction – is so detailed and erotic that it feels disturbingly, hideously, as though it might have happened last week.

She takes a breath, and tries to push past the fiction to who they'd all really been back then. They'd worked in publishing, had only ever been connected to TV through their authors. Yes, there had been a power struggle between her and Shana when Shana had tried to move her aside in order to promote Amelia.

Had Maxim ever been involved in that?

Not as far as Marina knew, but there was probably a lot she didn't know and maybe Shana has chosen this time and this way to tell her.

Shana was never to be trusted, and that won't have changed.

She'd used Amelia once . . .

Amelia, the pretty, smart, quietly spoken young girl who Marina herself had employed as an assistant; who'd had no family connection to Shana, or none that Marina had known of.

Amelia, who'd destroyed her marriage to Patrick.

Shana and Rosie.

They'd both, in their ways, been good at mind games, so are they conspiring to try them out again?

Marina suspects they consider it clever, cunning, amusing, the way they've changed names and settings for *That Girl*, filtering the truth through a web of allusion and distorted reality. Told like this, only Marina would recognize the real story.

Maxim and Patrick would too.

Why is she suddenly thinking that one of them could be behind this? That is just plain crazy. Neither of them would want to relive those times, any more than she does. Much less would they want to hurt her with a book submission intended to screw with her mind.

What about Noel? Is he being used as an agent, or is he a part of it?

And then there's Georgia, who she ran into earlier coming out of the executive offices over at Pall Mall. She has no idea what Georgia had been doing there, who she'd been seeing, and there had been no time to ask because Marina was already late for a meeting.

Since the acquisition of Thomas Jackson, everyone has been saying that Georgia is destined to become the next publishing director. She deserves a promotion, Marina wouldn't argue with that, so has Georgia been discussing her future with Maxim, asking what her chances are of taking over Marina's position? But Maxim wouldn't stand for anyone going behind his wife's back like that.

Would he?

'Amy' had replaced 'Katie' on their TV show.

Is Georgia, in the dimension of reality, aiming to replace Marina?

Picking up her phone, Marina scrolls to Noel's personal mobile number and gets through straight away. 'I want you to tell E.L. Stalwood,' she says, 'that I'm not prepared to read any more until she reveals her identity.'

There's a pause before he says, 'She?'

'It's a woman. I'm sure of it.'

'OK. So is there a reason why this matters right now?'

Realizing she doesn't have a good answer for that, she

says, 'Please, pass the message on,' and ringing off, she's about to call Patrick when she decides against it. If she mentions the book again he might want to read it and, apart from everything else, she really doesn't want him imagining Maxim having rampant sex with Shana the way she just has.

No, what she needs right now is to start accepting that some deep, dark part of her psyche is at play, allowing a few adjacent-leaning coincidences to trick her into seeing the past in places it doesn't exist.

Weird and even a little psychotic, but she can always go back to her therapist if she feels it becoming a problem.

Hearing someone entering the house, she goes to check who it is and finds Ed kicking off his shoes in the hall.

'Hey!' he says when he sees her. 'I didn't know if anyone was in. Good day?'

'Yes, fine,' she assures him. 'You?'

'Yeah, pretty good. I'm just going to get changed for a run. Can I treat you to a pie and a pint later?'

She smiles. 'I'm meeting Maxim at the brasserie. You can join us if you like. What's this?'

Glancing over his shoulder, he sees her picking up a parcel he'd brought in and put on the console table.

'Oh, I found it on the doorstep,' he replies. 'It's addressed to you. From Amazon, by the look of it.'

Seeing that it is, she tries to remember what she ordered. Undoubtedly something for the girls.

As Ed runs off up the stairs she takes the parcel to the kitchen and forgets it for a moment as she reads a text from Maxim.

Running late. Should be there by 8. Saw Rosie Shell earlier. You're definitely not her favourite person. ☺

I never was.

No, I guess not, but you're certainly mine (don't tell the girls, they think it's them). Got to go. Love you.

Smiling to herself even as she tries to quell all the dizzying thoughts in her head, she puts the phone aside and reaches for the parcel.

It is easy enough to open, perforated cardboard and a blue, tie-top pouch, but as she pulls the contents free, she feels herself freeze with horror.

It is a doll, small and plump with ruby-red lips and rosy cheeks, and the name *Amelia* embroidered across the front of its Babygro.

Three days pass before she receives an email from Noel saying: *No response to your demand for E.L. Stalwood's identity reveal, but she's keen to know what you thought of the latest sex scene.*

Marina turns hot and nauseous with anger and unease.

Replying immediately, she says, *Poorly written and not believable.*

Do you want me to relay that?

Does she? In truth she has no clear idea of what to do next. The shock of the 'Amelia' doll is ebbing, but the reality of it and what it could mean is still very much there in her head. Should she mention it? Show it to someone even? No. She isn't going to play the game. Let the sender never be sure if she ever received it.

So she simply says, *Your decision. My request still stands, we want to know more about her.*

OK. I'm getting the impression there's more going on here than you're telling me. However, the attached came through an hour ago. Up to you if you read it, but I should let you know that if you're not interested, I've been instructed to contact Rosie Shell. Nx

CHAPTER TWELVE

That Girl by E.L. Stalwood

Katie was in a taxi on her way to Johan Johannsen's London offices. He didn't know she was coming; she'd been afraid he'd refuse to see her if she tried to make an appointment.

She could have rung, of course, or sent an email, but she wasn't going to allow him to hide behind a phone or a computer. She was going to force him to look her in the eyes when he told her she was wasting her time trying to persuade him to change his mind about the programme; about her.

Her phone bleeped with a message. She glanced down and saw it was from Rob, but she didn't bother to open it. She hadn't spoken to him in over a month. She had nothing to say to him, and nor was she interested in the reports of his heavy drinking, much less in the fact that his relationship with Amy apparently wasn't going well. God only knew what was happening about the pregnancy. It never got mentioned so, like Christy, Katie was not inclined to believe in it.

What was real, however, was the loss of her position on the programme and the way Christy, presumably with Johannsen's blessing, was planning to deepen her humiliation by turning her into some sort of floating presenter who didn't even get to be in every show, while Amy took the lead.

'Why are you agreeing to it?' she'd shouted at Christy when

she'd first heard about it. Funny how that had roused her temper when so far almost nothing else had. In fact, ever since Rob had left, it had been as though she'd died inside and only the shell of her had continued to function. Until this shocking blow had suddenly brought her back to life; had made her want to start fighting. 'Doesn't our friendship mean anything to you?' she'd snarled at Christy.

'It means everything,' Christy assured her, 'and I swear I'm doing my best to make this as easy, as painless, as possible.'

'Then fire her.'

Christy balked. 'I thought you didn't want that. You said you wanted her to stay around so you'd know what she was up to. So she had to look at you every day and know what she did.'

It was true, Katie had said that, and she'd meant it at the time, but where the heck was that stupid, misguided sort of pride ever going to get her? 'I've changed my mind,' she told Christy. 'I want her gone and you can make it happen.'

'Oh, Katie,' Christy groaned sympathetically. 'We're all ready to shoot the pilot. She's been rehearsing, and she's good. I'm sorry, I know it's not what you want to hear, but she has a natural talent for presenting and Johan's on board for it. Anyway, it's only a test run. We don't know yet how well the new format is going to work.'

'But we do know that I'm not even featuring in the pilot and all I'll get later, if a new series is commissioned, are the scraps you decide to throw my way. How do you think I feel about that, Christy? Do you even care?'

'Of course I do, and believe me, if there is a new series, I'll make sure that your slot is everything you'd want it to be.'

Katie hadn't argued any further, but she didn't trust Christy to keep her promise, and maybe it was the fact that their friendship was starting to fail, that their loyalty to one another wasn't what it used to be, that was making everything so much harder to deal with. They'd always had each other's backs, would do anything for one another, but ever since Johan Johannsen had come along, everything had changed.

The taxi dropped her outside the company headquarters and, because the receptionists and security guards recognized her, no one tried to stop her from taking a lift to the fifteenth floor.

Johannsen's secretary wasn't at her desk, the whole suite appeared deserted, so Katie walked straight on through to the penthouse office with its expensive furnishings and views down over Green Park.

As she looked around, she spotted a box of Christmas decorations in a corner ready to bring a tasteful blaze of festivity to this part of Johannsen's world. It made him seem more human, she thought; or maybe more callous, she couldn't quite decide. She wondered if he and Christy were planning to spend the holidays together. She wasn't sure how often Christy had seen him by now – Christy had more or less stopped confiding in her – but she was in no doubt that Christy nurtured high hopes where this relationship was concerned.

Katie wished she could feel happy for Christy, that she could drink wine with her and laugh and plan the way they used to, but imagining Christy with Johannsen and the future they'd probably have together, actually made her feel sick with misery and loneliness. She should resign from her job. God knew she'd thought about it often enough, but if she did what would she have left?

Her mother, God help her.

Sarah Right wasn't someone to be alone with in good times, certainly never during a crisis.

Hearing voices outside she turned, and started as she caught a glimpse of herself in a mirror. Her eyes were too bright, her cheeks flushed with random blotches of colour, her hair glinting like small shoots of fire in the overhead lights. She looked as wild and desperate as she felt inside.

The door opened and the moment she saw him she found herself tongue-tied, intimidated. His height, good looks and pervasive air of self-assurance reminded her of his power over her world. She felt foolish for being there.

'Katie,' he said, and his friendly manner threw her. She'd expected him to be surprised, or impatient with her for barging in uninvited, but he appeared almost pleased to see her. 'I'm sorry, do we have a meeting scheduled?' he asked, shrugging off his overcoat and slipping it onto a hanger.

She started to explain, 'I-I . . .'

'No problem. Have you been offered some refreshment?'

She ignored the question and tried to focus her thoughts, to remind herself of why she was there.

'Please, sit down,' he said and directed her to the sofas. As he took the one opposite her, she found herself understanding why Christy was so attracted to him. It wasn't just his physical appearance, although that was arresting enough, it was the way he had with him – attentive, respectful; apparently ready to listen even to someone who'd turned up uninvited.

She wondered what he was really thinking or seeing as he regarded her – a manic-looking woman full of anxieties and rejected-wife paranoia?

'Christy's told me about your proposals for change,' she began, sounding – hopefully – more confident than she felt.

He nodded for her to continue.

'I agree,' she said, 'that we would benefit from a fresher look, but before we get onto it I'd like to remind you of how successful we've been up to now. And I believe that my experience in the business could be put to good use going forward. Maybe not as a presenter, but as series producer.'

He seemed momentarily surprised, and no wonder, for he knew as well as she did that she'd just suggested taking over Christy's job. So what was he making of it? That she was treacherous, self-centred, never to be trusted?

Or maybe he considered her as determined and cutthroat as he was underneath it all.

'I've drawn up a list of my proposals,' she ran on, reaching into her bag. 'I can email everything over, but before we get into it, I'd like you to consider using someone else to front the show.'

'You mean someone other than Amy Summers?'

She flushed as she nodded. He obviously knew why she didn't want Amy, but she wasn't going to embarrass herself by spelling it out.

His tone was mild as he said, 'Have you discussed any of this with Christy?'

She had to admit that she hadn't.

He didn't react, simply encouraged her to carry on, all the time seeming to assess her, watching her far more closely than she felt comfortable with. His eyes were so blue and penetrating, so *knowing*, that she found it hard to meet them, even to keep herself on track.

She was still mid-flow when he suddenly said, 'If I'm understanding you correctly, you're advocating a more intellectual or factual-based format, whereas I'm sure you must know that the aim is to attract a broader cross-section of the viewing public.'

Refusing to be put off, in fact oddly energized by what seemed like criticism, she said, 'OK, I accept that you're looking for something . . . more commercial, shall we say, but I believe there's room for both the light-hearted and the serious, provided it's handled correctly. And of course it would be handled correctly, and professionally.'

He regarded her thoughtfully, curiously, before saying, 'I don't want to argue about this, but what you're—'

'So what do you want?' she suddenly blurted. 'To throw me out like I don't matter? To cancel my life because it no longer suits your agenda? The trouble with people like you is that you're all about the bottom line, profit, advertisers, greed . . . Reality, substantiality, worthwhile content means nothing to you.'

To her surprise he didn't appear particularly offended by her outburst, simply allowed a moment to pass before he said, 'You're making a lot of assumptions about me—'

'As you have about me and my ideas,' she cut in fiercely. 'Why don't you at least let me give them a try?'

He was already shaking his head.

'Then fuck you!' she cried, and shooting to her feet she grabbed her bag ready to leave.

'Katie, this isn't personal . . .'

'Well it certainly feels that way to me,' she seethed and, accepting she was getting nowhere, apart from further away from what she wanted, she started to leave.

'Katie,' he said again as she reached the door.

She turned back, still clinging to a last shred of hope in spite of everything.

To her annoyance he didn't actually say anything, merely looked at her as if still trying to work her out. In the end she said, 'The next time you look in the mirror, I want you to ask yourself: are you really always right, or are you just in a position that makes it that way.'

An hour later, she was alone in her dressing room, feeling about as wretched as it was possible to feel having just screwed up any modicum of a chance she might have had to hang onto her job. She barely even looked up when Christy let herself in, though she was tempted to tell her to go away. She didn't want to discuss the excruciating encounter with Johannsen, not least of all because of the way she'd tried to steal Christy's job.

Did Christy know that yet? Had she already spoken to Johannsen, and so knew the whole hideously embarrassing truth?

'Are you OK?' Christy asked, looking worried as she closed the door.

'I'm fine,' Katie replied crisply.

'You don't look it. Has something happened?'

Katie shot her an incredulous look and Christy held up her hands. 'Sorry, you're right, that was a stupid question.' She moved to a chair and asked if it was OK to sit down.

She'd never asked before, and the fact that she had hurt Katie deeply, for it seemed to say all she never wanted to be true about their deteriorating friendship.

She waved a hand for Christy to continue. No matter what Christy did or didn't know, or what her conscience was doing, she'd still rather have Christy here right now than be alone. Although she guessed that might depend on what Christy had to say.

'I thought you might like to know,' Christy began, 'that I've come up with what I hope is a workable compromise – one that will keep you in position. It's going to be a big ask, and I'll have to run it by Johan, but I thought I should sound you out first.'

So she hadn't already spoken to Johannsen, and Katie couldn't suppress the sudden bloom of hope. She was ready to grab onto anything that might feel like a lifeline, a thread of possibility that would keep her in a job and even a friendship with Christy. 'I'm listening,' she said.

Christy smiled, obviously pleased to receive the go-ahead. 'Why don't we explore the idea of you and Amy presenting the show together?' she said.

Katie reeled. She stared at Christy, unable to believe what she'd just heard. Christy had to know how abhorrent the idea would be to her, that nothing in the world would persuade her to go along with it. So was this Christy's way of making sure she had no choice but to walk away? Was that actually what Christy wanted? Were they, on some level, not only drifting, but actually starting to resent and despise one another?

Without thinking it through, only wanting to call Christy's bluff, she said, 'I guess it could work. I mean, I'm not going to like it much, but if . . . I'll think about it, but I don't see any reason yet not to give it a go, provided Johannsen is on board, of course.' After the way she'd just spoken to him, she doubted very much that he would be; however, for the moment she was only interested in Christy's reaction to the curve ball she'd just thrown.

Christy hid her surprise well and gushed, 'That's fantastic. I'm so pleased. I mean, I know it won't be easy at first, but I'll make sure to keep the girl under control, and I just know Johan will go for it. I'll make sure he does.'

Katie's insides were twisting and turning with all sorts of difficult emotions. She needed to end this now, to be alone to consider what she really wanted, if there was any way she could extricate herself from this new ignominy and get Amy Summers out of her life for good.

To get Christy back on side even.

They were a team, always had been. How had they been brought to this?

Changing the subject and her tone she said, 'Can I ask . . .? Am I allowed to ask, if it's serious between you and Johan?'

Christy's eyes sparkled and there was no doubt how much she hoped that it was, but instead of answering she sat forward and took Katie's hand. 'I know things are crazy for you right now, and he probably seems some sort of monster to you, but once all this is sorted out, you'll see him in a completely different light, I promise.'

Katie lowered her eyes. She had no idea what to say to that.

With a gentle sigh Christy said, 'I hear Rob's been arrested for drunk-driving again . . .'

Katie got up. 'Why don't you talk to Amy about him?' she snapped. 'He's nothing to do with me,' and, leaving Christy staring after her in despair, she slammed out of the room.

CHAPTER THIRTEEN

Marina is sitting up in bed, her laptop casting the only light in the room as she scrolls back to where 'Katie' confronted 'Johan Johanssen' over her position within the company.

As she reads the paragraphs again, she's aware of a harsh apprehension knotting her insides, for something like it had happened once.

The scene had taken place in Maxim's office, around the time of Forster Inc's takeover of Hawksley Maine. Marina had heard, through the grapevine, that there were plans for a big shake-up of the fiction division, and apparently Shana was onside for everything. Afraid that Shana couldn't be trusted to look out for anyone but herself, not even the authors, Marina had made it her business to try to save herself and those she feared were most at risk.

She'd made an appointment to see Maxim at the Forster offices in Pall Mall. (She hadn't barged in, the way 'Katie' had in the book; however she had, thanks to the state of her marriage, quite probably been wild-eyed and emotionally unstable.)

She remembered holding it together quite well at the start of the meeting, as she'd explained that she was a totally committed member of the team who had a very good track record of bringing on new authors. She'd gone on to say that she was dedicated to keeping the top sellers high in the charts and from being poached by other publishers. She'd conceded that the list might need culling, but a summary excision of those who'd generated profits below a certain amount in the past year, or of talented team members, was just plain short-sighted and would be to the company's detriment in the end.

That was more or less how it had gone. She can no longer remember the exact details, or even much of what Maxim had said in response, but she hasn't forgotten how politely he'd heard her out. Unfortunately, panic – and his silence as he'd considered her case – had made her lose her temper and say things she no longer wants to recall. She'd come away feeling wretched and deeply ashamed. Even so, she hadn't regretted trying to save herself or the authors who'd faced the threat and ignominy of being dropped.

(The book made it sound as though it was all about 'Katie', but the reality had been far more complex and even altruistic than that, for so much more had mattered to her, Marina, than was being transcribed. Of course, what was being transcribed was nonsense, because she'd never worked in TV, and had certainly never been a presenter with self-serving ambitions.)

Looking back to what she knows about the real story – set in publishing, not television – she can't be sure whether she confided in Shana after the meeting with Maxim. It's the only way Shana could know about it, unless she'd learned most of it from Maxim himself. They'd still been together then, so there's a good chance he'd told her. It's so hard to be clear after so many years.

What she knows for certain is that there's a deeply sinister intention behind this book. It's aimed straight at her, and she can think of no one other than Shana and/or Rosie who'd feel they had something to be gained from reawakening the past. So what do they have to gain? What do they know? What have they discovered to make the sending of dolls and the carefully crafted retelling of an old story seem like a good idea?

The mere thought that there might be something turns her cold to her core.

Could it be connected to the 'little something' mentioned in the prologue? Was all the horrific suspicion, fear and horror going to start up again?

'Hey you, what are you doing?' Maxim asks sleepily as he rolls over to reach for her.

She closes down her laptop and puts it aside before snuggling into him. 'Just reading,' she says. 'Sorry if I woke you.'

'What time is it?'

'Late and we both need to be up early.'

'We do? Isn't it Saturday tomorrow?'

'It is, but the girls want to be on the lake by midday. With a picnic and you driving the boat.'

'Again?'

'Always you – and don't forget they've got friends with them this weekend so we'll have a full house.'

He turns onto his back and pulls her with him as he says, 'I think I forgot to mention that I've invited Georgia and her boyfriend – can't remember his name – to come over on Saturday night.'

Marina's heart locks onto an unsteady beat. 'You invited Georgia?' she says mildly. 'How on earth did that come about?'

He stifles a yawn. 'I got chatting with her the other day when I was waiting for you, and she mentioned she's going to be visiting her godparents, or grandparents, in the Cotswolds at the weekend. So I said she should come on over. It's OK, isn't it?'

Is it? It doesn't feel as though it is, but what else can she say apart from, 'Of course.'

An hour later she's still awake, staring into the darkness as Maxim sleeps soundlessly beside her. Although thrown by Georgia's invitation, her focus is back on the book and – she's certain about this now – its clear attempt to head off a lawsuit by changing names and backdrops and keeping essential details vague.

She isn't sure yet how she's going to put a stop to it, but she'll come up with something, because for everyone's sakes, her own, Maxim's and the girls', this grotesque resurrection of a nightmare absolutely has to be shut down.

It's Saturday evening, and there are so many friends and neighbours milling around the terrace of the old rectory that some have spilled onto the lawn, while others are inside, grouped around the kitchen island, catching up on each other's news. Maxim and Noel are in charge of keeping the wine flowing, while the girls and their own weekend invitees are passing around the canapés they've spent the afternoon making themselves.

Though neither Maxim nor Marina had intended to have such a large gathering, it wasn't unusual for their parties to grow in number as the time drew closer, and they were always happy for that. They enjoyed having people round, especially friends they knew well. The more the merrier, Maxim always said, which was undoubtedly how he'd ended up inviting Georgia to join them, simply because it was the sort of thing Maxim did.

You're going to be in the Cotswolds? Of course you're welcome. It'll be lovely to see you.

Georgia turns several heads when she arrives looking stunning in a white sundress and high wedge platforms – a look that should be tarty, in Marina's opinion, but somehow didn't come over that way. Her legs are bare, tanned and long, her chestnut hair a glossy tumble of beach waves, and her smile as sultry and captivating as her large tawny eyes. Apparently the boyfriend has gone down with a summer cold, so Georgia hopes they don't mind that she's come alone.

'Of course not,' Marina assures her as Maxim approaches with a fizzing glass of champagne.

'Lovely that you made it,' he tells her, passing the drink to her. 'Cheers,' he adds, and Marina watches Georgia's eyes fix onto his. Adoringly? Gratefully? It's hard to tell.

'Cheers,' Georgia echoes. 'Thanks for inviting me. I've been looking forward to it.' And still only addressing him, 'You have a beautiful home here.'

'Thank you,' Marina replies, putting herself back in the conversation. 'I believe you're in the area visiting your grandparents. Where do they live?'

'Godparents,' Georgia corrects, turning to her. 'About half an hour away, towards Cirencester.'

'You should have brought them,' Maxim tells her.

Georgia's eyes light with a playful sparkle. 'My godfather's a little eccentric,' she confesses, 'so probably best he's not here. I see the twins are,' she runs on, looking across to where they're helping Ed to reattach some fairy lights to surrounding bushes. 'They're so grown-up now and utterly gorgeous. Like their mother,' she adds with a teasing smile in Marina's direction.

'Exactly like her,' Maxim agrees. 'Now, who shall we introduce you to?'

As he steers her off through the crowd, Marina stands watching for a moment, not much liking what she's seeing, his hand on Georgia's slender back, her lovely face turned up to his. Whether the physical contact means anything to him isn't possible to know, but Georgia certainly seems to be enjoying it.

Over the next hour or so, as Marina mingles, makes small talk and drinks more wine, she's conscious of continually checking where Georgia is and who she's talking to. Thankfully, it isn't always Maxim, although he's occasionally in the same group, and apparently Georgia is something of a comedian for she seems to have a knack for making him laugh.

Who knew she was such a social animal? Such an accomplished storyteller.

The jarring note causes Marina's heart to skip a beat – storyteller? Why had that word come to her mind, apart from obvious reasons – almost everyone in her world is a storyteller – so why is she suddenly unsettled by it? She can't answer that because Noel is calling out to her and an elderly couple from Bourton want to thank her for the advance copies she sent them of a book by their favourite author.

A while later she spots Georgia chatting with the twins, apparently absorbed in whatever they're telling her. Marina is so proud of the way her girls can handle themselves in social situations. They're always lively and gracious, can appear interested in whatever anyone's telling them, even if they aren't. And if they're questioned they're very good at giving answers – no teenage awkwardness or monosyllabic withdrawals for them, at least not yet.

Georgia throws back her head and laughs at something Livvy has apparently said and Livvy is so pleased that her ears turn pink. It's something that happens when her emotions are heightened, much to Sophie's enjoyment as she doesn't suffer the same way.

Is Georgia interested in them because they're Maxim's, or simply because she likes young people?

Marina moves on to chat with an author she'd first published over a decade ago, Lavender Hayes. Lavender is a large, luscious older woman with a wild nest of ash-blonde hair and a penchant for younger men. She's already had a long, lusty flirt with Ed and Maxim, and no doubt several others are in her sights, but for now she's keen to gush her thanks to Marina for her amazing insight into her stories.

'They'd never be any good without you,' she declares, clearly blissfully happy to share the credit. 'I don't mind telling anyone that. It's up here,' she insists, pointing to her head, 'I have it here in my brain, but it takes you and your amazing expertise to coax it onto the page.'

'You are way too modest,' Marina laughs, meaning it, for this particular author actually requires very little editing. 'You make my life easy, and you know I always love your books.' This is also true, for Lavender has a gift for dark and hilarious romance.

She's just noticed Georgia heading into the house and is now glancing around for Maxim.

'Let's do lunch,' Lavender declares. 'I'm in Sardinia for the next month, but when I get back. And you must come too,' she informs Noel as he joins them.

'To Sardinia?' he responds. 'Count me in.'

'You know you're always welcome,' Lavender beams. 'You might give me some inspiration for the next one.'

Knowing she's actually quite harmless, he grins. 'Anything for one of my favourite clients. Have you seen your latest royalty statement yet? If not, you're going to like it.'

'Oh, marvellous. Let's have some more champagne on that. Maxim! Darling. Over here with the bottle.'

Relieved to see him, Marina watches him top up their glasses and slips an arm around Sophie as she comes to join them. 'You look tired, sweetheart,' she murmurs into Sophie's cool blonde hair.

Stifling a yawn, Sophie says, 'That's because you use us as slaves.'

Maxim immediately scoffs. 'Didn't I agree to pay you twenty quid each for this evening?'

'Yeah, but we haven't seen it yet and, anyway, we need to renegotiate. Fifty would be fairer. Don't you think, Mum?'

'Don't answer that,' Maxim advises, 'on the grounds that you're my wife and you should be on my side.'

'Always,' Marina assures him dryly.

'Mum!' Sophie protests. To her father she says, 'Livvy reckons it should be a hundred, so I'm letting you off lightly.'

'Twenty it is,' he tells her. 'And I'll take it thanks, for all the taxiing around.'

Sophie rolls her eyes but, as Marina laughs, she does too. They are a lot alike, a little shy, thoughtful and naturally good-natured, whereas Livvy, with her full-on confidence and decidedly extrovert qualities, is all Maxim.

It's a while before Marina realizes that Georgia hasn't rejoined the party, unless she's inside chatting to someone.

Although there's no particular reason to go and find out when Maxim is caught up in lively debate with the local MP whose politics he doesn't share, Marina makes her way to the kitchen anyway.

No sign of Georgia, and she isn't in the sitting room or library either. The door to the downstairs cloakroom is open and no one is in the dining room.

Wondering if she might be unwell, or even trapped in one of the upstairs bathrooms, Marina decides to go in search. As she climbs to the first landing, she's aware of the party chatter receding and it feels bizarrely as though she's entering another sort of realm. One in which outside belongs to a normal world, and in here something else altogether is going on.

Blaming the fabulist novel she's currently reading for her overactive imagination, she's about to check the first bathroom when she notices Georgia coming out of the room Maxim uses as a study and quietly closing the door behind her.

It is so unexpected, so suspicious even, that it's a moment before Marina is able to say, 'Georgia?'

Georgia spins round, aghast. 'I'm so sorry,' she gasps. 'Oh my God! You made me jump.'

'What are you doing?' Marina asks curiously.

Georgia grimaces and turns it into a smile. 'I'm so embarrassed. I know I shouldn't . . . I mean, this is such a beautiful house and I really wanted to see it, so I thought I'd take myself on a tour. I'm sorry. I know I should have asked, but you have so many guests, I didn't want to drag you away, and obviously I wasn't going to ask Maxim.'

Why 'obviously'? Marina has no idea. She's still too thrown by finding her senior editor seeming to sneak out of a room that technically is off-limits.

Had she been in there because Maxim told her to meet him there and hadn't been able to get away?

For God's sake, Marina, get a grip.

'Shall we go down?' she says, sounding cooler than she'd intended, but why not, surely the situation calls for a less friendly tone?

'Of course. Again, I'm really sorry.'

As Georgia goes ahead down the stairs, she half glances over her shoulder as she says, 'I don't know if it helps, but you have exquisite taste when it comes to interior design. Décor. I should say décor. You're obviously not a designer. Unless you are, in another life.' She attempts a laugh.

'I only have the one,' Marina responds mildly, while wondering why the girl is so nervous. There's surely no need to be, unless she's lying about why she was in Maxim's office, and what reason would she have to do that unless she had an arrangement to steal some moments with him?

Later, after everyone has gone home and the girls are in front of a movie, Marina leaves Maxim on the terrace with Ed and Noel to go and have a good look around his study. She has no idea what she's expecting to find and, as far as she can tell at first glance, nothing is out of place. She raises the lid of his laptop and hits the space bar to bring it to life; after a beat his calendar comes up showing entries for the next month. She scans them but there are none she doesn't already know about, or that seem in any way anomalous.

Hating herself for it, she checks his email and private messaging links; there's nothing she wouldn't expect to find, no secret posts or links to connect him to anything suspect or in any way curious.

She turns away and looks around the room again just

in case there's something she might have missed. Of course she knows it's absurd to think a doll could be lurking somewhere, or a printed chapter of *That Girl*, but she can't deny she's looking for something like it.

She leaves the door open as she goes back downstairs, wondering if it's just plain crazy to suspect Georgia of being involved with Rosie or Shana when she's of a different time, another era. As she considers it, trying to link them up in her mind, she's thinking of how a reader – herself in this case – is often not aware of who is related to whom, much less of what might be developing behind the scenes. The twists and turns, red herrings, literary sleights of hand and timing of revelations are all entirely in the gift of the writer.

CHAPTER FOURTEEN

It is Tuesday morning before Marina is able to focus on *That Girl* again.

She's decided to work from home; it'll be easier to make calls with no one else around – although she had some difficulty persuading Maxim that he didn't need to take a WFH day too.

'We could go out for lunch, just the two of us,' he'd insisted. 'I don't mind paying.'

She'd laughed at that as he'd known she would but, as appealing as the prospect was, she really needed him out of the way for this. Thankfully, Ed had thundered down the stairs at that point and – whatever he was late for – Maxim was persuaded to drive him there.

Minutes after the door closed behind them Marina was googling Shana Morales, something she should have done long before now.

Unsurprisingly, just about everything that comes up is connected to the trial at the end of 2009. She doesn't need to read any of that, she'd been there, so knows only too well what happened. She continues to scroll.

Eventually she finds a brief *Daily Mail* article dated nine years ago stating that convicted murderer and ex-publisher, Shana Morales, had been transferred to a facility north of Bristol.

HMP Eastwood Park, a women's closed category prison.

Though it's no surprise to read this, Marina finds her head spinning at the thought of 'Christy Grant' in prison. It's disturbing how often she's seeing Shana as 'Christy', and the other way around. The same goes for Patrick and 'Rob', Amelia and 'Amy' and, worst of all, with Maxim and 'Johan'. There's also 'Katie', of course, but curiously she doesn't often see herself in the alter-ego that has been created for her, only in the events that are fusing fact with fiction.

Has Rosie been visiting Shana in prison all these years, or have they stayed in touch by phone and mail? This is presuming they are working together, and Marina can't see how else any of this is happening. Which of them came up with the sick idea of planting a doll outside Marina's Holland Park home, and to send another through Amazon? A doll with Amelia's name on its shirt, for God's sake! Rosie must have organized it, and only she would have access to email, so she has to be sending the chapters.

What is Georgia's part in it?

Does she actually have one?

Maybe she really had just been giving herself a tour of the house.

Going onto the prison website, Marina sets about requesting a visit. Though Shana might be the last person in the world she ever wants to see again, she needs to confront her, face to face, with the cruelty and pointlessness of what she's doing. Cruel to Amelia's family; pointless because she has to know the book will never be published.

Unless Shana and Rosie intend to develop the story in the way Marina fears the most.

Of course they are; there would be no other reason to do it.

After finding a link that allows her to make the visitor

request, she sits back in her chair needing to take a pause, to think, to decide whether or not to show the book to Maxim. The last thing she wants is to allow the spectre of the past to start haunting him the way it is her, and she sure as heck doesn't want to remind him of his apparently highly sexual relationship with Shana. However, her greatest reluctance is really all tied up with his father and how the all-powerful Paul Forster is likely to react if everything gets hauled into the public eye again.

She doesn't want to risk that. Maxim had taken her side the last time, had acted hastily and convincingly, but it had cost him and his reputation so dear that it was a miracle their relationship had survived. They had made it through, but the big difference now is that they have two children. If Shana and Rosie have found something to throw doubt on the outcome of the trial, or on how certain evidence came to light, then Paul Forster will waste no time in acting and it's likely Maxim would support him.

So, the most sensible course at this stage is to do whatever she can to shut things down before they get to a point where Maxim will need to know.

Her mobile rings and, without checking who it is, she clicks on.

'Marina, it's Georgia. Is this a good time?'

Marina blinks. Georgia/Amelia/*Amy*: their faces morph into one, then mercifully separate again. 'Yes, it's fine,' she hears herself say. 'What can I do for you?'

A few hours later, Marina is seated at a terrace table outside the Holland Park Café, a pot of berry tea and a slice of quiche untouched in front of her. She'd come here because she'd needed to get out of the house, to take in some different air and try to get over the shock of being told in a return email from the prison that Shana Morales had been released on licence over a year ago.

In spite of the warmth of the day, she shivers and looks around at the walkers, joggers, dogs, children and other café customers. She isn't expecting to see Shana, and yet she can't help looking for her, or feeling that someone is watching her.

How on earth does a convicted killer leave prison before serving even half their sentence, and without there being a record of it? Obviously there's some sort of documentation somewhere, the prison would have it, as would the parole board and the probation service, but for some reason the news hasn't been made public.

She has no idea if it's permissible to contact any of the relevant authorities to try to get more information. Since she isn't a family member, or even a close friend, it's probably safe to assume that no one would be forthcoming. Moreover, someone would be sure to recognize her name, in spite of her being married now, and that would beg all sorts of questions she really doesn't want to answer.

Anyway, the fact that there's nothing to be found on any of the social media sites, or news outlets, presumably means that Shana has, for some reason, been allowed to leave prison quietly and is now either doing an exceptional job of staying under the radar, or she's started again with a new name.

E.L. Stalwood.

In spite of knowing that a search for this name will lead nowhere, given how many times she's already tried, she decides to return home and try again anyway. This time she adds Shana Morales and even 'Christy Grant' to the search, but there are still no results of any use.

There is no point in ringing Rosie, she'd never get anywhere with her, the end of Noel's recent email more or less confirms that.

If you're not interested, I've been instructed to contact Rosie Shell.

A ruse, a threat, a smokescreen?

It's impossible to know, but one thing is certain, she isn't going to give Rosie the satisfaction of asking if she knows where Shana might be.

She could always try contacting the lawyer Shana used during the trial. He must know where she is, but if Shana doesn't want to be found, there's no way he'll give any details to Marina Forster.

What about Shana's half-Greek, half-Spanish mother, who used to live near Chester? Marina has no idea where exactly, and since she's never met the woman, and has no idea of her first name, she can't think how to begin with that. Besides, it's quite probable Mrs Morales is no longer alive, and – even if she is – why would she want to speak to Marina, much less tell her where to find her daughter?

'Hey, Marina,' Ed says, startling her as he comes into the kitchen through the back door and kicks off his Converse. 'Good day?'

'Yes, fine,' she replies, quickly switching focus while watching him dump his holdall on the far end of the table and pad off to the fridge. 'How about you?'

'Yeah, cool. Starving actually. I left at such a pace earlier that I forgot to take my phone. Couldn't pay for anything and my gym pass is in an app, so I need to call Maxim and let him know I'm going to be late meeting him.'

'Here, use mine,' she says, unlocking her mobile and passing it to him. 'I didn't realize you guys were going to the gym this evening.'

'That was the plan. Feel like joining us?'

Though she often did, usually for a swim, or a Pilates class, she says, 'I'll take a rain check and carry on working for a while. There's a slice of quiche in the salad drawer if you fancy it.'

'Hey, honey, right back at you,' Ed says into the phone as he connects to Maxim. 'I'm good, how are you?'

Realizing Maxim had presumed it was her calling, Marina laughs as she goes into the laundry room to take a pile of sheets from the dryer, only half listening as Ed says, 'Really? I'm gutted. I haven't been able to think about anything else all day. Yeah, sorry you couldn't get hold of me . . . So, what's come up? Oh, right, I kind of forget what an important dude you are . . . Sure, I'll tell her. Catch you later. Good luck behind the black door.' As he rings off, he says to Marina, 'He wants me to remind you of how important he is.'

Marina has to laugh. 'I'm guessing he's not meeting you at the gym?'

'No, apparently he's got a hot date at Downing Street, to discuss the present Incumbent's desire to produce an autobiography.'

Used to Maxim being called upon last minute for most things political (the non-fiction department relied heavily on him in the early stages of bidding for top politicians), Marina goes to put the kettle on.

'Wow! She's hot,' Ed exclaims, unwrapping the slice of quiche and devouring half with one bite.

Marina's insides flip as she realizes he's staring at her laptop, the screen filled by an old photo of Shana.

'Who is she?' he wants to know.

Thinking quickly, Marina says, 'An author we're considering publishing. That shot was taken fifteen or more years ago, so perhaps a little mature for you?'

He grins and tears off a square of paper towel to dab his mouth. 'She writing her memoirs?' he asks. 'Looking like that, I bet she has some stories to tell.'

Inwardly balking at how right he was, she says, 'Did Maxim give you any idea what time he might be home?'

He shakes his head, and nods to her phone as it rings.

Seeing who it is, she clicks on. 'Hi, Livvy, everything OK?'

'Yeah, Mum, all cool, but we've had this brilliant idea that concerns Ed and we can't get hold of him. Any idea where he is?'

'He's right here. Shall I pass you over?'

Livvy's exuberance drops a notch. 'Oh. Does that mean you're at home?'

'I am.'

'So Ed is too?'

'He is, but about to go to the gym.'

Livvy repeats this to someone at her end, presumably Sophie, and says, 'Why isn't he answering his phone?'

'He forgot to take it today. Here, I'll put him on.'

As he takes the phone, Marina closes down her laptop and goes to make some tea.

'Fuck no!' Ed suddenly cries. 'No, Livvy. Sorry, it's just not going to happen. Yeah, I get what you're saying, I really do . . . No way. You'll have to find someone else. Sorry. Apart from anything else, your parents would kill me.'

'We would?' Marina enquires, unable to imagine what this could be about.

'Don't tell her,' she hears Livvy shout.

'I've got to go,' he says, 'but the answer's definitely no.'

As he rings off, Marina regards him curiously.

Throwing out his hands, he says, 'They want me to be a live model for their art class.'

Marina can't help laughing, in spite of how inappropriate and outrageous it is, or maybe because of it. 'And you turned them down?' she teases. 'I didn't think you were the shy type.'

'Yeah, very funny. Shit, can you imagine being naked in front of a roomful of thirteen-year-old females?' He shudders violently. 'Hell, I could probably get arrested . . .'

'Don't worry, the school wouldn't allow it. It's obviously one of their crazy ideas to try and show off to their friends. I'm embarrassed by them. Would you like me to have a word?'

With a reluctant grin he shrugs it off. 'It's cool. Bit of an overreaction on my part. Anyway, I'm going to head upstairs and get myself together. I'll shower and change at the gym, meeting up with some mates from uni after so count me out for dinner.'

Left alone, Marina carries her tea and laptop up to the sitting room and curls up on one of the sofas. Now she has the evening to herself she really ought to catch up on some of the reading she's recently neglected.

However, it's hard to stop thinking about Shana and the fact that she is out there somewhere, almost certainly hiding behind a false identity, while writing her detestable – possibly libellous – book and sending creepy dolls. It has to be the build-up to some sort of payback for what she perceives Marina and Maxim did to her.

CHAPTER FIFTEEN

It might have happened over fourteen years ago, but Marina remembers very well the call she received from Maxim soon after the disastrous meeting in his office. It hadn't been to fire her, as she'd expected when she'd heard his voice, but, to her complete surprise, he'd wanted to invite her to lunch.

Of course she'd gone, full of nerves and confusion, planning everything she was going to say in every possible scenario, discarding it, rephrasing it, and promptly forgetting it the closer she got to the oyster bar in South Kensington.

He was waiting when she arrived, seeming both too important for such a casual venue, and yet perfectly at ease. He stood out amongst the other diners, of course; someone with as much presence and as good-looking as he was, he couldn't help it. Her heart tripped with all sorts of concerns and annoying insecurities as she shook his hand and sat down opposite him.

'Relax,' he murmured softly, 'it's going to be all right.'

Startled, and suddenly less anxious, she treated him to a playful scowl and consulted the menu.

After placing their order, he wasted no time getting to the point. 'I'm going to give you six months to do things your way before putting everything under review again,' he told her, holding her eyes with the mesmerizing intensity of his own.

She was so taken aback that she was only able to stare at him, until suddenly she broke into a laugh that made him laugh too and, as though to mark the moment, he called for two glasses of wine. At lunchtime! But who cared, she was wildly happy to celebrate this amazing and totally unexpected encouragement. And was she really going to say no to the boss? Who actually didn't feel quite so much like a boss at the moment, more like a . . . She wasn't sure how to describe his new status, except, of course, he was still the boss.

Naturally, Shana was furious when she found out. As publishing director she should have been the first to know about any change of plans, especially those coming from the top. Marina didn't even try to argue with that, for Shana was right, Maxim should have spoken to her first. Marina had no suggestion to offer as to why he hadn't, but what she did know was that Shana was actually far more upset about the lunch than she was about the change of direction.

Though pleased for herself and her unexpected 'stay-of-execution', Marina soon became increasingly upset by the distress it was clearly causing Shana. The last thing she wanted was Shana to think she might be gloating, or was in any way uncaring of her feelings, when she of all people knew how insecure Shana could be deep down. So, in an effort to ease the tension building between them, and maybe even to try to start repairing their friendship, Marina decided to splash out on a special Christmas gift for Shana. Although they were heading in different directions for the holidays, they always used to celebrate, just the two of them, during the lead-up to the big day, and to Marina's surprise and relief, when she suggested they get together, it seemed Shana was keen to keep the tradition going.

They met at Shana's flat and Marina was immediately touched when she arrived to see the effort Shana had gone to, filling her sitting room with candles and Christmas cheer, and having champagne ready to pour.

At first they talked around the safer, more generic aspects of their jobs, and even managed a few laughs at various things that had happened in the office over the past few days. Both were careful not to tread on anything personal, not wanting to risk this delicate détente, at least not yet, and it made Marina's heart ache to think of how much their friendship really meant to them both. Neither wanted to lose the other, and she was so glad she'd suggested this evening that she decided not to wait to hand over the gift she'd brought along.

It would help, she was certain of it.

Shana was clearly surprised, and seemed almost wary as she began to unwrap the exquisitely ribboned package, while Marina looked on smiling and hopeful. It was something very special, and she wasn't at all surprised when Shana's beautiful dark eyes suddenly lit with delight and even awe, the instant she realized what it was.

'Oh my God, Marina,' she exclaimed, lifting the heavy bronze figurine from its box. She was a collector of art deco sculptures and this one, of a reclined woman reading, was an exceptional piece.

'It's stamped,' Marina told her, her voice catching slightly on the pride she felt at having found it. 'Three of seven.'

For one heart-stopping moment, Shana seemed about to cry. 'I don't know what to say,' she murmured, swallowing hard. 'It must have cost you a fortune.'

It had, but all Marina cared about was how special the moment felt, how much the piece seemed to mean to Shana.

They sat for a while, admiring the slender female body and open bronze book that appeared enchantingly animated by the glinting candlelight. The thick, gold-veined marble of the base was weighing heavily in Shana's hand, and Marina reached out to take it, enjoying the pleasing heft.

'I love it,' Shana smiled, her eyes showing the truth of her words, 'and I love you for getting it.'

Marina returned the smile. As complicated and competitive as their relationship had become, this surely was a way back to how it had been before Amelia, before Patrick, before Maxim even.

Going to place the figurine in pride of place on her mantelshelf, Shana stood back to admire it all over again. 'I'm not sure anyone's ever given me anything so beautiful before,' she said softly, and seemed unable to look away from it. 'And now I'm embarrassed that I don't have anything for you.' She turned around and gazed helplessly, guiltily at Marina.

'This is what matters to me,' Marina told her. 'Us two, being together like this, the way we should be.'

Shana smiled as she nodded. 'It matters to me too. I've missed you.'

'I've missed you too. It doesn't seem right not to know what's happening in your world, how you're feeling about things, how much stronger we always seem when we're together.'

'I know, and I'm sorry. I've allowed myself to become too wrapped up in things that . . .' She looked dismayed and shook her head, as if not sure how to articulate everything she was feeling. 'No matter what happens at work, in our personal lives, or in the future,' she said, 'you'll always mean the world to me. I hope you know that.'

Swallowing the lump in her throat, Marina said, 'I do, and it's the same for me. We shouldn't have lost sight of one another the way we did, not when we're each other's rocks.' Her eyes sparkled and Shana laughed.

'We are certainly that,' Shana agreed, and refilled their glasses. 'So, tell me how you really are, and what's happening between you and Patrick these days.'

Marina's eyes fell to her glass as her heart contracted. 'I'm not sure how to answer that,' she said quietly, 'I know he's still crazy about Amelia, it's all he can talk about . . . Not that we talk often – not at all if I can help it. I've no idea what's going on with her, but I don't think she's interested in him any more and it's driving him crazy. I'm sure you've heard about how he's messing up in the marketing department, missing deadlines, drawing up bizarre plans, upsetting agents and authors. Half the time he's drunk or hungover . . .' She stopped, picturing it all, and feeling wretched for him, and for herself. How had they come to this? Was there really never any going back? Certainly none that she could see right now, not when he seemed more of a stranger than she'd ever imagined he could.

She looked up and made herself smile. 'Don't let's talk about things that are going to bring us down,' she said. 'If you're willing to tell me, I'd love to hear how things are going with you and Maxim.'

Shana immediately seemed cautious, but Marina threw out her hands as if to say, you have nothing to worry about where I'm concerned. A moment later, Shana's eyes started to shine, a sure sign that she felt ready to start trusting again. 'To be honest, I can hardly stop thinking about him,' she confided, unable to contain her smile. 'OK, I know his status counts for a lot – does that make me shallow? Sorry if it does, but even if he weren't who he is . . . Well, you've seen him, you've spent time with him, so you know how . . . *attractive* he is. And charming and a little bit ruthless – you can imagine what a turn-on that is for me.' She laughed and sighed. 'I just wish I could stop worrying that I'm going to do something to screw it up, the way I usually do.'

'You won't,' Marina assured her. 'This is different, I can tell.'

Shana's expression was soft and grateful as she said, 'Thank you for that. For me it is. I just wish I could be more . . . certain about him. I mean, it's early days for either of us to be talking about any sort of commitment, but our relationship is very . . . *physical*. Maybe that's all it is to him.'

'Physical sounds good to me,' Marina laughed. 'Isn't that where it all begins? OK, not always, but that sort of attraction, the whole chemistry and urgency of it, can make for a pretty powerful start. Are you seeing him over Christmas?'

Shana pulled a face. 'No, I have to spend it with my mother and he's flying to the States to be with his family.'

Marina didn't mention how she'd be filling the time and Shana didn't ask.

By 27 December Marina was back at her desk, trying to distract herself from the three days of torment she'd just spent in Devon. Being at the office was so much easier than milling around the hotel that her narcissistic mother owned and ran, or at home alone in the flat that she'd once shared with Patrick.

She'd cried enough tears over the past few months to

last her a lifetime; wallowing in her misery at one of the most emotionally difficult times of year wasn't going to get her anywhere. Whereas, throwing herself into the second chance Maxim Forster had given her hopefully would.

She was so engrossed in the creation of a new spreadsheet that she started when her mobile suddenly rang. It wasn't a number she recognized – in fact it was a New York prefix. Remembering her American colleagues didn't have as much time off for the holidays as they did in England, she clicked on.

The last person she expected to hear from was Maxim. He hadn't even crossed her mind; she wasn't even sure she knew he had her number, but apparently he did, and he was calling to find out how her Christmas had been.

Really?

Although awful, lonely and wretched would have been the honest answer, she summoned her dignity and said, 'Fine,' or something along those lines.

Unprompted he told her he'd just returned to Manhattan after spending a few days on Long Island with his family, and he was intending to fly back to London the following day.

'My brother and sister-in-law are going to be spending a couple of weeks in Europe,' he continued, 'and I was hoping you might think about joining us all for dinner on New Year's Eve. If you don't already have something planned.'

She was so stunned that she literally had no idea what to say. Had he really just invited her to spend New Year's Eve with him? And his brother and sister-in-law? Or was she losing her mind?

'You don't have to give me an answer now,' he said. 'I'll be back tomorrow. We can speak then.'

As she rang off, her mind was full of Shana, who she knew had already bought something new to wear in anticipation of spending New Year's Eve with him. How the heck was she going to take it if Marina decided to accept the invitation? How could Marina begin to explain it if she did when she and Maxim hardly knew one another? They'd never even met outside the office, apart from that one short lunch at the oyster bar.

Shana would never understand; how could she when Marina didn't either? She had to be misconstruing this in some way. She'd never sensed he was interested in her, apart from allowing her to move forward with her ideas. He'd been kind then, and yes, attentive, but nothing more than that. And this probably wasn't even a date. Except what else could it be on New Year's Eve?

It just wasn't possible that he'd be attracted to her – *her* – when he had Shana.

Actually, it hardly mattered what he thought of her when she was still far too distraught over the break-up of her marriage even to think about becoming involved with another man. And besides, she wasn't going to put her friendship with Shana back into jeopardy when it was still far from fully healed. So, as much out of loyalty to Shana as to protect herself from any further heartache, she decided she must turn him down, no matter how intrigued she might be by the invitation.

She'd gone.

When he called the next day and she told him it wouldn't be possible for her to join him, he'd taken almost no time at all to talk her into it. This was perhaps her first experience of Maxim getting his way while never seeming to exert any sort of power or pressure.

So, yes, in spite of knowing what her acceptance would do to Shana, she'd accepted his invitation. Not without trepidation or guilt, or fear of what it was going to mean going forward, but, she had to admit, with a much lighter heart than she'd imagined possible during such a terrible time in her life.

It wasn't that she hadn't felt shamingly disloyal throughout the evening, because she had, and yet somehow she'd seemed to sparkle. He was the most wonderful company, as were his brother and sister-in-law, and it wasn't until late into the evening that she realized she'd hardly thought about Patrick and Amelia at all.

At midnight, on the twelfth stroke, he kissed her, deeply and yet softly, seeming to commit his entire self to the moment. When he drew back to look at her, he seemed both amused and ready to kiss her again. She held his eyes and, as the music and laughter swirled around them, poppers popped and streamers streamed, there was a quiet intensity between them that left her in no doubt that he really was attracted to her. And to her surprise she realized she felt the same. Though her heart was shattered, and her life in danger of falling apart, this man was somehow lighting up parts of her that might not have felt fully alive before. Simply being with him, and returning his gaze this way as fireworks soared and lit up the night, was filling her with the kind of promise she longed to have the courage to embrace.

It was around two in the morning when he finally saw her into a taxi and said he'd call the next day. To her amazement he did, and they spent so long on the phone finding out all sorts of hilarious and irrelevant things about one another, that in the end he said it was crazy, he should just come over so they could stop wasting the battery on their phones.

He came, they cooked together, drank some wine and continued to chat about everything and anything. When he decided, around eleven, that it was time for him to go, he said, 'If I kiss you now I won't be able to leave, and I really don't want to rush this.'

She tried to answer, even to make light of it somehow, but found she couldn't. She was too thrown by the words and their meaning, too bewildered by how she felt too. Such a depth of connection and so soon after a first date, a first kiss, had never happened to her before – and maybe the only reason it was happening now was because she was on the rebound.

It was his fear that she might be. 'It would be the most natural thing for you to use our relationship to help yourself overcome your heartache,' he said, 'so I want you to have space and time to think, to give us a chance to get to know one another better before we make any further commitment.'

She didn't argue, as much as she wanted to, for she knew he was right. It was too soon, and already maybe too powerful for her to know how to handle it yet. So he'd left their second date without even as much as a kiss, but the teasing look in his eyes had made her heart sing.

By the next morning, Shana knew all about the New Year's Eve date and she was clearly incandescent. (The gossips hadn't been able to apprise her of the fact that he'd visited Marina's apartment the following day, so that, at least, had escaped exposure on social media.) There had been no mild-mannered or sensitive 'Christy' on the scene then. It had been pure hot-tempered, vengeful Shana who'd called Marina everything vile she could think of, from treacherous to conniving, to downright disgusting and disloyal to a point that could never be forgiven.

Marina didn't try to defend herself; how could she when she'd known from the start how deeply it would wound Shana, humiliate her even, to find out that her so-called best friend had seen the year in with the man she had invested so much hope in. The betrayal, of course, made a mockery of the gift Marina had given her to try to repair their friendship, and there had been no point trying to tell herself that – if the roles were reversed – Shana wouldn't have thought twice about hurting her. It was true, Shana wouldn't have had the least compunction about going behind anyone's back, including Marina's, however, there was no doubt Marina was the guilty party here. She had caused Shana the greatest injury of all, and for that she must be made to pay.

Within days Shana had moved Amelia to a workstation where Marina would see the girl's happy and lovely face every time she looked up. Shana's constant reminder of what deceit and betrayal looked like. At the same time, Shana did whatever she could to undermine Marina, to make her look incompetent, foolish, neglectful. It had been a nightmarish time, made all the more difficult by Patrick's disciplinary hearing – the start of the process of his eventual dismissal – and his constant urging for her to speak to Maxim on his behalf. She never did, she was in no position to; even if she were, she knew she'd be unable to change Maxim's mind.

It had all been so crazy, so mixed-up and disorientating, the only sane moments were those she spent with Maxim, but even then her mind was in such a vortex of fiercely conflicting emotions that it wasn't easy to relax. Amelia, Patrick, Shana; they started to feel like a bunch of angry nemeses she couldn't escape.

With a sigh, she puts a hand to her head and tries to shut it all down as she comes back to the present, to their beautiful home in Holland Park and the reality of where they are now in their lives. Though it was always wonderful to relive the early days with Maxim, the memories will always be tainted by the fact that neither she nor Shana, nor Patrick, had covered themselves in glory back then, or indeed later. Actually, later it got so much worse that she recoils from revisiting the horror of it now.

However, she is certain that E.L. Stalwood fully intends to confront her with it in future chapters. In fact, she's already dreading finding out what sort of spin Shana is going to put on it all – and it's definitely Shana behind the pseudonym, she is in no doubt whatsoever about that now.

CHAPTER SIXTEEN

That Girl by E.L. Stalwood

'Thanks for coming over this evening,' Johan said, passing Christy a glass of chilled white wine that came from the vineyards his family owned in Burgundy. 'I'm sorry it was such short notice, but I'm only just back from Paris.'

'It's not a problem,' she assured him, and managed to smile past the tearing ache in her heart as she feigned innocence, ignorance of the real reason she was there.

He was about to end it between them. Of course he was, and she could have spared herself the hurt and humiliation of it all by not coming tonight. She only had because she simply couldn't give up so easily, and nor could she extinguish the small, pathetic flicker of hope that he might change his mind.

For the next few minutes he talked about work and a colleague in Paris who'd apparently had a heart attack in the middle of a client meeting.

Christy listened and responded in all the right places and in all the right ways. She drank her wine and allowed him to refresh her glass. She watched his hands, strong and lean, the small hairs on the backs of his fingers. She recalled the feel of his muscular legs pressed against her own, the width of his shoulders enveloping her. She studied his face, the faint shadow of a beard across his jawline, the contours of his mouth, the length of his nose, the mesmerizing blueness of his eyes. She almost couldn't bear for this to go on any longer, was afraid that if it did she might end up doing or saying something she'd deeply regret.

It was a moment before she connected with what he was saying.

'. . . so I think you know that when I came to London to negotiate the takeover of the company that it wasn't my intention to be around for long. A month, maybe two. As it turns out, I'm going to be running things myself until the time is right for someone else to take the helm.'

She attempted to look pleased – wasn't that the appropriate response to having him around on a more permanent basis? – but her smile couldn't last when she knew exactly what he was leading up to. He was right on the point now of telling her that he'd only allowed himself to screw her because his stay in London was supposed to be temporary. He probably won't use those words, but it was what he'd mean.

'. . . and as we're both adults, and we knew what we were getting into when I first arrived, that it was . . . Well, I'm not sure what it was, apart from very enjoyable, of course. But now things have changed and I'm afraid I have to bring our . . . arrangement to an end.'

Arrangement?

Somehow, God only knew how, she regarded him with mock-humorous eyes, as if to say, *you really don't need to be making a big deal out of this.*

Seeming to pick up on this easy release, he smiled as he said, 'OK, no need to labour it? For my part, I want to say that it was good while it lasted – great, actually – you're an extremely beautiful, and exceptional woman—'

Cutting across him she said, 'I know you're seeing Katie, so please don't feel you have to flatter me or explain yourself any further. Obviously, your feelings are quite strong for her, and I don't blame you. She is, to quote you, an extremely beautiful and exceptional woman. She is also – I'm saying this now for your sake more than hers – still vulnerable after the break-up of her marriage. It's not so long since it happened, and with the way things have been with Amy, the betrayal, the dreadful feelings it's left her with . . . Well, I'm sure she's not using you to try to get back at Rob, at least not consciously, but I do know how much he still means to her.'

Though he frowned he said, 'I understand it's going to take time for her to get over everything she's been through, and I'll give her as much as she needs.'

But you won't give me anything.

The truth of that was excruciating for Christy. 'Then she's a lucky woman,' she said with a shaky smile, 'because I think you're a very special man and, as sorry as I feel that we won't be seeing one another on a personal level again, I really hope it works out for you and Katie.' Thank God he had no way of knowing that in her heart, in her very soul, she was wishing Katie straight to hell.

'That's gracious of you,' he said. 'She's fortunate to have such a good friend.'

Christy knew it was time to get up and leave, to wrench herself away from this exceptional man and the luxurious apartment that she'd hoped one day to share with him, the life that should have been hers, but she was afraid if she moved she might fall apart.

He took out his phone, as clear a signal as any that this meeting was over. 'There are some calls I need to make,' he told her.

'Of course. Yes, I must go. It was good to see you.'

'You too.'

As they reached the door she said, 'I'm not sure now is the

right time for this, but tell me, are you aware that Amy Summers is pregnant by Katie's husband?'

His expression was unreadable as he waited for her to explain why she'd brought this up.

'Obviously, it's extremely hard for Katie,' she rushed on, 'with her and Amy being in such close proximity each day, so I'm wondering if we should give her some time off to try to come to terms with everything.'

In a chill tone he said, 'I believe Katie herself should make that decision, but are you sure the pregnancy is real? From what I hear, there is some doubt.'

'Oh, there was, at first,' she assured him, wondering if Katie herself had told him about it, 'but we know now that it's very real. It's not what Katie needs, obviously, not what any of us does, actually; however, we'll find a way to deal with it. Sorry, I probably shouldn't have brought it up.'

'No, you probably shouldn't,' he agreed.

By the time Christy arrived home, she was no longer able to hold it together. She was completely and utterly devastated, simply couldn't bear knowing that she'd never really meant anything to him. She felt so used and discarded – and ashamed of herself for having been such a fool to fall so hard so fast.

She had no idea how she was going to get through the days and weeks to come, how she'd hide the pain each time she saw him, how she'd cope with everyone else knowing and pitying her, or maybe even laughing. Worst of all would be seeing him with Katie.

She'd give almost anything to avoid that, but she was no longer in a position to fire Katie, and now that they knew Amy really was pregnant, there was a good chance Katie would take over the show again.

*

Just over a week later Katie came into Christy's office and closed the door behind her. She looked pale, a little tired, and yet oddly radiant – surely to God she wasn't pregnant too!

'It's done,' Katie said quietly. 'I thought I should let you know.'

Christy frowned, not sure what they were talking about, while at the same time a wild hope was flaring – had Katie developed a conscience and ended her relationship with Johan?

'Amy is no longer pregnant,' Katie explained. 'I took her to the clinic myself, yesterday.'

Christy's eyes widened in shock. '*You* took her? How—'

'She came to me and asked what she should do, so I told her.'

Christy blinked. Was she understanding this correctly? 'You told her to have a termination?' she said, needing to be clear.

Katie nodded. 'I think she'd already made up her mind, she just wanted someone to say it was the right thing to do.'

'And she came to you?'

Katie shrugged.

Christy sat back in her chair, needing a moment to take it all in. 'Does Rob know?' she finally asked.

Katie frowned, as if the question hadn't actually occurred to her. 'I've no idea,' she replied.

Still trying to get ahead of this, Christy said, 'What about Amy? Is she OK? Where is she?'

Katie checked her watch. 'She'll be in later. Actually, it's probably best not to ask her about it, unless she tells you herself, of course. Given that you're her aunt, I thought she'd have come to you in the first place. I guess she chose me because she was pretty certain I'd give her the answer she wanted.'

Suspecting that was true, Christy couldn't help wondering

what Johan would think if he knew about it, for didn't this prove that Katie still wanted to be with Rob? Why else would she have involved herself in killing his child, if not to destroy the very thing that still held him to Amy?

CHAPTER SEVENTEEN

Marina can hardly believe what she's just read. The insinuation that she encouraged Amelia to have a termination in order to try to get back together with Patrick is so outrageous, and shocking, that she has to read it again to make sure she's understood it correctly.

She has.

In fact, the real truth is that she'd *never* actually known for certain if 'Amy's' – *Amelia's* – pregnancy had been real, so this *invention* of her involvement in an abortion is beyond offensive: it's utterly libellous. Or it would be if real names had been used.

Her eyes close as her head starts to spin. She's in a meeting that seems to be going on for ever, too many people droning on about budgets and forecasts and bottom lines for schedules that haven't even been fully approved. She's finding it almost impossible to concentrate, to stop herself thinking of what Maxim would say if he read this latest chapter. Would he believe it?

She glances out to the main office where Georgia is chatting with a handful of editors. Nothing unusual there, they often discuss the books they are working on. Occasionally Marina joins in simply for the pleasure of listening to their ideas.

She watches Georgia breaking into a smile as she gets

up to greet someone wandering over from the lift. With a jolt she realizes it's Maxim. He's driving her home this evening, but has turned up early and doesn't appear to be in any hurry to find her. He's clearly pleased to see Georgia and stands talking with her, apart from the others, making her smile as he smiles too.

There's nothing wrong with that; Maxim makes people smile all the time. He could be teasing her about her secret, self-guided tour of their Cotswold home, or maybe he's forgotten about it already. Marina hadn't made a big deal of it, had simply said she'd found it a little odd and Maxim, distracted by something he was doing with the girls at the time, had agreed.

What had it really been about? Could it have been as innocent as Georgia had claimed? She hasn't seemed particularly uncomfortable around Marina since, although Marina returned from lunch yesterday to find Georgia sitting at her desk.

'A quiet place to read,' Georgia explained, and there's nothing wrong with that, except Marina can't recall her doing it before.

At last the meeting breaks up and Marina returns to her office to find Maxim sitting with his feet up on her desk, chatting to the twins on FaceTime.

'Half-day?' she comments dryly as she begins packing up to leave.

He's still in Dad-mode, sharing his extensive knowledge of digital media in an effort to help his daughters with their homework. It's loud and argumentative because he keeps using words they don't understand until eventually he turns the phone around and tells them to say hi to Mum.

'Hey, Mum,' they chorus. Livvy adds, 'I've messaged you a list of things I need for the weekend.'

'Me too,' Sophie says. 'I've run out of cream for my eczema so don't forget that.'

'I haven't. It's all in hand,' Marina assures them.

'Where are they going?' Maxim asks.

'Oh, Dad, we already told you,' Livvy groans. 'We're camping in the New Forest with Tilly David and her family. Anyway, got to go now. Thanks for the help, Dad, love you both.'

Maxim's blue eyes are alight with mischief as the call ends. 'A whole weekend without them,' he declares, not actually rubbing his hands together, though he might just as well be. 'What will we do with ourselves?'

Laughing, Marina says, 'I'm sure we'll think of something. Now, are we ready to go?'

'Ah, that's why I'm here. To give you the car keys. Richard Dayes called. He's got a spare ticket for England v. Pakistan at Lord's this evening.'

'Richard Dayes?'

'Goldman Sachs? Anyway, I shouldn't be late home, but if we go on for dinner I'll let you know.'

As he presses a kiss to her mouth, she wonders if she believes that he's going to the cricket. She has no reason not to – it isn't unusual for him to take off to a match at the end of the day. Sometimes even during the day. 'Before you go,' she says, already knowing she shouldn't get into this, but doing it anyway, 'there's something I'd like to ask you.'

He turns around, all interest.

Don't do this, she tells herself as she says, 'I know this is a strange question, coming out of the blue, but did you ever hear that Amelia was pregnant?'

His eyebrows shoot up in surprise. 'You mean – *that* Amelia?'

She nods. In their world there was only one.

He's clearly thrown, but nevertheless casting around in his mind. 'No, I don't recall ever hearing that,' he says. 'Why are you asking? Why are you even thinking about her?'

She shrugs, dismissively. 'Something came up earlier that reminded me of her. It happens from time to time. Well, of course it does . . . Actually, I should take this call. It's one I've been waiting for.' She clicks on her mobile and blows him a kiss as she says into the phone, 'Hi, Ethan, how's the weather in New York?'

'We'll speak later,' Maxim says quietly and, dropping the car keys on her desk he heads out to the main office, not stopping to speak to Georgia, who doesn't even look up as he passes.

An hour later Marina is following Patrick into his sitting room, thrown by how she'd thought of him as 'Rob' when he'd opened the door. It's a strange transposal of character that's happening more and more; she's even found herself calling Maxim 'Johan' in her mind, and the moments of confusion are both annoying and unsettling. It means Shana is getting to her, and she'd almost rather die than let that happen.

'Is this going to become a habit?' Patrick asks cheerfully. 'If it is, I might start wondering if you have an ulterior motive.'

'Very funny,' she retorts, and looks around the room as she drops her bag on a chair, 'but thanks for seeing me.'

'Always a pleasure. I've got a bottle of Cabernet open if you'd like a glass.'

'Just one, I'm driving.' She realizes that the flat smells

different to the last time she was there, less flowery, more . . . him. 'Is Anthea still on the scene?' she asks.

'She left last week. It was all very amicable and a great relief. I expect we'll remain friends for a couple of months, but I can't see it going any longer than that. Unlike us, still friends after all these years. Isn't that something?'

She has to agree it is, considering all they'd been through, but she doesn't respond, simply sinks into one of the sofas.

'OK, so what can I help you with?' he asks, bringing her a glass of wine.

She takes it and raises it to salute him. Now she's here she isn't entirely sure how to go about things, except there really is only one way. 'I'm sorry if this opens up old wounds for you,' she says, 'but . . . Was Amelia really pregnant when you told me she was?'

His eyes darken with confusion. 'Wow! I didn't see that coming,' he mutters, looking as uncomfortable as she'd expected him to. 'Why on earth are you asking?'

'I guess . . . I've always wondered. You told me yourself that she was, but if it was true, what happened to the baby?'

He seems suddenly older as he turns to stare at the window, as if scenes from their past might still be playing out there somewhere. 'As far as I know,' he says, 'she miscarried around the time we broke up, although that was a pretty drawn-out affair.' His eyes return to hers. 'As you no doubt remember.'

'What do you mean, as far as you know?' she counters. 'Didn't you believe in the pregnancy?'

'I did at the time.'

'Do you now?'

He shrugs. 'Does it matter?'

Realizing that in many ways it probably doesn't, at least not for him, she shakes her head.

'So what's going on?' he presses. 'Why are you bringing this up now?'

She takes a sip of wine and debates with herself on how far she should go. If she tells him about the book he'll want to read it and, given the latest chapter, she doesn't want him, or anyone, to suspect, if only for a moment, that she helped to arrange an abortion for Amelia. (Noel, of course, has read the submission, but as he hadn't been a part of their lives back then, he probably hasn't yet made any connections.)

In the end, she says, 'Did you know that Shana's been released from prison?'

His glass stops mid-air as surprise catches him off guard. 'No, I didn't,' he replies carefully. 'When?'

'About a year ago, apparently. She's on licence.'

'So she served, how long?'

'Almost thirteen years. Have you heard from her?'

He balks as if she might be mad. 'No,' he replies, drawing out the word, 'but I'm starting to think that you might have.'

She shakes her head.

'Then how do you know she's out?'

'I contacted the last prison I knew her to be in and they told me.'

He's clearly at a loss. 'Why on earth would you do that? You surely don't want to be in touch with her.'

'No, not at all, but I guess . . . I was curious, and now, knowing she's no longer there . . . It's brought a lot back that I really never wanted to think about again.'

'Well, I guess no one can blame you for that.'

They sit quietly for a moment, each trying not to be overwhelmed by their memories. She wonders if he remembers things differently to the way she does – of course he does, no two people ever recall events the exact same way, especially after so many years.

'Did you want the baby?' she asks quietly.

He inhales deeply and puts his glass aside. For a while she thinks he isn't going to answer, and is beginning to regret asking, when he finally says, 'To be honest, I can't remember much of what I wanted back then, but I can tell you that it took me far too long to realize how badly I'd screwed up my life. She was . . . I don't know . . . It was as if she had some sort of hold over me. I was completely blown away by her and could never get enough . . .' He breaks off, seeming to realize that – even now – Marina wouldn't want to hear about his obsession. 'I guess I was relieved when there was no longer a child to make things even more complicated,' he says. 'As you might recall, I'd been reported to HR for being drunk on the job by then so I was about to be fired. People said she was behind the complaint . . . I don't know if that was true . . . Yes, she wanted out of our relationship, but would she have lied like that, kicked me when I was already down? Who knows? She never struck me as that sort of person.' He takes a breath and lets his eyes drift as his mind remains locked in the shame of it all. 'I still had a long way to go before I hit the bottom,' he says bleakly, 'and sometimes I wonder if I'd ever have made it back on my feet if it weren't for Maxim. The man who fired me, but who picked me up again when it looked like I was going under for good. I didn't deserve the help he gave me, but I'm sure glad I took it.'

After a moment she says, 'I am too. Everyone deserves

a second chance, and we know how strongly Maxim believes in that.'

His eyes meet hers and hold them for a while. 'Have you tried to find out where she is?' he asks.

She makes a small move of discomfort at having Shana brought back into the conversation. It was as though the ghost of her had suddenly slipped into the room. She doesn't want to admit that she has made enquiries, but she can hardly deny it when it wouldn't seem normal given that she'd gone as far as to find out if she was still in prison. 'I did a quick search,' she says, 'but I don't think she's using her own name.'

He takes that in. 'I guess I'd do the same if I were her,' he responds. 'New identity, fresh start and all that.'

She wants to say, *Writing something like* That Girl *is hardly a fresh start given it's raking it all up again,* but she doesn't. 'It feels . . . *strange,*' she says, 'knowing she's out there somewhere.' It's a ludicrous understatement, for there are moments when it makes her feel sick with fear.

'Do you think she'll try to get in touch with you at some point?'

A shiver goes through her as she thinks of the dolls. She could tell him about them, but given their significance, how Amelia's body had been found in a meeting room with her head caved in, she decides not to. 'Who knows what she's planning to do,' she replies. *Apart from write a book about the very worst time of our lives in a way that could cause people to wonder if justice had really been served.*

If the right person had gone to prison.

If Maxim had done something so utterly reprehensible that he never should have survived it.

'What would you do if she contacted you?' she asks, her voice slightly hoarse.

He gives a short laugh. 'Maybe it would depend on what was in it for me.'

Realizing from her expression that his jest hasn't been well received, he arches an eyebrow. 'She won't. She couldn't stand me, remember?'

Marina looks down at her glass, almost empty now. 'She hated us all in the end,' she reminds him.

A few minutes later, as he walks her to her car, he says, 'I know you're afraid she's going to turn up again, and I don't blame you after what she tried to do to you . . . So, would you like me to have a go at finding her? I mean, just so that we know where she is and what she's up to these days.'

She doesn't have to think about it. 'Yes, please,' she says, 'but if you do find her, don't get in touch. Tell me first, OK?'

'Anything you say,' he promises and, giving her a brotherly kiss on the cheek, he opens the car door for her to get in.

CHAPTER EIGHTEEN

That Girl by E.L. Stalwood

'Will you come away with me for a weekend?' Johan asked, his head propped on one hand as he gazed down at Christy lying stretched out on the bed beside him.

They're at his Knightsbridge apartment, their clothes strewn around the furniture and floor, their bodies still slick with the afterglow of love-making. His was taut and powerful, hers willowy and smooth and still tingling from his touch.

She knew she shouldn't have come running the instant he called, but she'd been unable to help herself. In all her years, she'd never met anyone who felt so right for her; even looking at him seemed to complete her. And why shouldn't she be with him when it was all she ever thought about? Did it really matter that he'd only got in touch because Katie had decided to try again with Rob?

They'd make it work this time; she was certain of it.

'Where do you have in mind?' she asked, reaching up to graze the backs of her fingers over his chin.

'Rome?' he suggested. 'I have a business dinner to attend and if you can get away too . . .?'

'I'm sure I can,' she murmured, watching her long, manicured fingers trace the masculine contours of his lips. Then, without having any clear idea of why, she said, 'Are you sure you wouldn't rather be taking Katie?'

His eyes closed and, as he rolled away from her, she wanted to bite back the words. What was wrong with her? Why was she trying to sabotage herself like this?

'How are things going with her husband?' he asked, his tone neutral, his eyes still closed.

She hesitated as she wondered how much to tell him. Being fired from his job had hit Rob hard and Katie, typically, felt partly responsible, given she was the one who'd complained to HR about him always being drunk about the place. She'd denied it, of course, but Christy knew she was behind it. She wanted him out of the way now that things were going so well with Johan; no more chances of embarrassing encounters or reminders of the kind of man she'd been involved with before. Then, bizarrely, she'd found it hard to live with herself after getting her way and felt some inexplicable compulsion to try to make amends by going back to him.

Nevertheless, no more fame as a sports presenter for Rob Nicholls, no more public adulation or endless free tickets to all the big matches. No money coming in, either. 'Not well,' she admitted in answer to Johan's question. 'I'm afraid he's still obsessed with Amy.'

'I thought that was over?'

'It's supposed to be, but he doesn't seem able to accept it. I think he took the abortion hard.' She wouldn't mention anything about Katie's involvement in that. The sooner they got off the subject, the better.

He threw back the sheet and walked across the room to fetch the glasses of champagne they'd abandoned soon after she'd arrived.

As she watched him she was aware of her heart beating too fast. She wanted him so much, too much.

Please don't let this turn into a one-night stand.

But no, he's invited her to Rome – unless she's ruined that already.

Coming back to the bed, he handed her a glass and said, 'We've given Katie a chance with her ideas, but I'm afraid they really aren't the right fit for what we're trying to achieve. And if there's friction in the office between her and Amy . . .' He let the sentence hang, and Christy understood that he expected her to take the necessary steps.

She sipped her drink and watched him slip back into bed. The crisis, thank God, seemed to be over. She must be more careful about what she said in future, think before she as much as mentioned poor Katie, whose life really wasn't going well. Christy was sorry about that, she truly was, but she'd had enough struggles in her time to know that they all passed in the end.

One day Katie would find the man who was right for her, but it wouldn't be Rob. Or Johan. 'Let's talk some more about Rome,' she said, 'and what we'll do there. I mean, besides the dinner and . . . a little more of this?' She dipped her finger into the champagne and reached beneath the sheet.

CHAPTER NINETEEN

It hadn't happened, any of it. 'Christy' and 'Johan' might have got back together in this so-called *book*, but Maxim had never returned to Shana following their break-up (apart from in Shana's dreams, apparently). He'd never taken her to Rome, and nor had he ever lived in Knightsbridge, although where he'd lived hardly seemed important.

In fact, Marina can't be entirely certain about the real sequence of events back then. What had or hadn't been said, or thought, or acted on had become like most memories, blurred or tangled by the passing of time. However, she's certain that she and Maxim continued to see one another after their first New Year's Eve date without interruption, so no matter how Shana tries to spin it now through 'Christy', it will only ever be herself she's deceiving.

Marina glances across to where Maxim has fallen asleep in front of the news, feet propped up on a padded stool, head resting on one hand and a frown deepening the line between his eyes. She loves him so much that it feels an actual physical part of her, as real and vital as every breath, every beat of her heart. When she considers the sliding doors of what could have happened all those years ago and what actually did, she knows how blessed she is to be his wife. He'd stood by her throughout, had never doubted her the way others had, and he'd done things few men would have been brave enough, or perhaps foolish enough, to do for someone they loved. He'd even married her and had children with her. It was true the twins hadn't been planned, but he'd been thrilled when they came along, and not once, over the years, had he ever voiced any regret for all he'd given up to be with her. Not Shana; he surely never wasted a moment regretting anything about her . . .

Feeling suddenly sickened by the image of him and Shana in bed together, brought about by these latest scenes featuring 'Christy' and 'Johan', she shuts down her laptop as if it might somehow swat Shana like a fly. She'd stopped reading before the real intimacy could come alive in her head, but it seems to be there anyway, just as Shana had presumably intended.

What fun she must be having with this, how powerful she must feel, thinking she is pulling all the strings, and knowing that trust, real trust, probably still doesn't come easily to Marina. It will all be a psychological game for her, her well-honed weapon of choice. She probably even has a fairly good idea of how Marina is reacting, because she'll know it'll be hard for Marina to protect herself from any level of doubt when she's been betrayed the way she has. Not by Patrick. No, he isn't the one who's caused the really lasting damage to Marina, it is Shana herself. It was because of her that Marina had come close to suffering a complete breakdown around the time the twins were born. She'd spent the first two years of their lives undergoing intense therapy, and she still, today, experiences painful, irrational, bouts of insecurity. They are behind the suspicions she sometimes has about Maxim and he really doesn't deserve it. He's a good man, a wonderful father, a brilliant businessman, who could have gone much further in his career a long time ago were it not for her. He's never complained about that, but he must surely wonder what, where and who he might be now were it not for her. Almost certainly he'd have returned to the States after straightening out Hawksley Maine, and would no doubt be heading up his father's business empire now.

As it stands, his younger brother, Mark, had taken over when Paul Forster retired, and the old man finally forgave Maxim for allowing himself to be dragged into the scandal of a junior employee's murder.

The mere whisper of another scandal involving his eldest son and the woman he'd married, much less the resurrection of the old one, and Paul Forster would be sure to act – and maybe this time Maxim would support him.

She glances down at her laptop, knowing she won't open it again tonight. She has no intention of going any further into the labyrinth of mind-manipulation and fantasy that Shana is spinning. She needs to start seeing this book for what it really is – a disjointed, structureless, mostly insubstantial set of scenarios that in a normal world she'd already have rejected.

Surely Noel doesn't still think it has merit . . .

A wave of frustration sweeps through her. And so begins the mistrust of a man she's long considered a good and true friend, for whom Maxim has as much respect and affection as she does. Is she really suspecting him of working with Shana on this, feeding it through with no criticism or comment, no input whatsoever?

Why would he do that? What on earth would be in it for him to help someone who'd been imprisoned for murder to retell, reinvent even, the events that had brought her down?

It could be a great story. Wasn't that what all agents – and publishers – wanted?

Leaving Maxim sleeping, she goes upstairs to the study and closes the door behind her.

Noel answers his mobile on the second ring. 'Hey, Marina, I wasn't expecting to hear from you tonight. Is everything OK?'

'Yes, no . . . Actually, it's this book.'

'Ah yeah, I'm guessing you think the latest sex is too graphic and I have to admit I agree. Some of it even made *me* blush, can you imagine that? But it can always be toned down in the edit?'

'To be honest,' she says, trying not to be annoyed, 'I stopped reading when it all started up. Does anything relevant happen after?'

'Well, they go to the Holy City, stay at the Hassler – do you know it? Fabulous, madly expensive. Anyway, there are some paras, quite well done IMHO; she builds Christy's feelings for Johan to a point where you just know she's going to get hurt again and you can't help feeling for her. I mean, we've all screwed ourselves over at one time or another, and she's flat out terrified of doing it again.'

Marina can feel her insides churning. 'So, does she get hurt again?' she asks tersely.

'It hasn't got that far yet, I'm just guessing.'

'So, in other words, it's a pointless chapter?'

'Well, I guess that depends on what comes next, but I grant you the sex seems gratuitous. I'll lay money the writer is getting off on it and that's why it's so detailed. You know that happens.'

Trying not to bite out the words, she says, 'But the whole thing – it's not exactly tying together, is it?'

'Mm, maybe not yet, but I'm sure it's going to happen and if it's worth it we'll help her get it sorted.'

Over my dead body. 'So you actually think it's worth pursuing?' she presses.

'I do at the moment. But you don't?'

No, she really doesn't; however, she knows she can't stop now, and not only because of the threat to take it to Rosie Shell who might or might not already know about it anyway. 'Have you had any discussions with the author yet?' she asks.

'Nothing, apart from on email.'

'But you're starting to agree with me that it's a woman?'

'Yes and no, but does it matter who's writing it as long as it's good?'

'I don't agree that it is. Tell me, do you actually care yet about where the story is going?'

He doesn't take long to answer. 'I'd certainly like to know more. I've asked for the rest to be sent in one go, but no response to that yet. However, I'm sure Stalwood would appreciate some feedback from you if you're up for it.'

She says, shortly, 'If I have time, I'll email you some thoughts in the morning.'

Moments after she rings off, Maxim comes into the study, stretching noisily and exposing his midriff. 'There you are,' he says, stifling a yawn and gasping and laughing as she puts a cold hand on his bare skin. 'Did I interrupt something?'

'No, I was just chatting with Noel. You're tired.'

'I am and I have to be up at the crack of dawn. Would you rather I slept in a guest room so I don't wake you when I leave?'

Remembering he had an early flight to the States she says, 'No, I never sleep well when you do that. Have you packed yet?'

'Just about to.'

'OK, I can either help, or fix you something to eat.'

He eyes her suspiciously. 'How did you know I was hungry?'

Matching his expression she says, 'Because neither of us has had any supper?'

He grins. 'True, how did that happen? Anyway, an omelette would be great, with mushrooms if we have them.'

'I think we do.'

Twenty minutes later, they're at the kitchen table with a six-egg savoury omelette and a bottle of Merlot between them. As they eat, they check their iPads to make sure she has his complete schedule for the next two weeks, which will see him in New York, Los Angeles, Florida, Boston, and finally Long Island to spend a few days with his father. It's several years now since Marina last saw the old man. Maxim generally goes alone and, once a year, usually February half-term, he takes the girls to Aspen for skiing. It suits both her and her father-in-law to have as little to do with one another as possible, and it's much easier on Maxim not to have to try to protect her from his over-bearing father's rancour.

'Oh, and will you look at this,' Maxim declares as if he hadn't noticed the diary entry before, 'I get back in time for your birthday.'

She feigns surprise and delight, while knowing he'd almost certainly planned it that way.

'We should go somewhere,' he decides, 'just the two of us.'

She hates the way his words send her straight to the chapter she's just read. 'You mean for dinner?' she asks. 'How about—?'

'No, for a weekend. Somewhere we haven't been before.'

'Christy's' story is still resonating like an unstoppable bell. 'Vienna?' she suggests, maybe a little too loudly. Actually, it isn't new to them; in fact it's a city they both adore, and Vestibul is one of their favourite restaurants in the world.

'Great idea,' he agrees, still looking at his calendar. 'But how about we go to Rome instead?'

Her heart flips as she stares at him. Had he really just said that, or is her own mind playing tricks on her?

'Not Rome?' he says, catching her expression.

'Why Rome?' she asks.

He gives a shrug. 'Because I've got a meeting there, and if memory serves me correctly, we've never been together.'

She feels herself starting to buzz, as if some sort of alarm is going off inside her and the next words come tumbling out before she can stop them. 'Did you ever go there with Shana?'

He frowns and stares at her, clearly confused.

She watches him put his glass down and sit back in his chair. For a long moment he simply looks at her, until finally he throws her completely as he says, 'Actually I was in Rome with Shana once.'

She freezes as the shock of it hits her. *The chapter was true? They really had gone to Rome?*

'It was a long time ago, obviously,' he continues, 'but since you ask . . . Why are you asking?'

'Continue,' she urges.

He's clearly baffled, trying to read what's going on with her and failing. 'OK, I'm finding it a bit strange that we're having this conversation, but it was at a time when I was due to go to Rome anyway, on business, and you were trying to repair things with Patrick, so I asked Shana if she'd like to come with me.'

She can hardly believe this. There's a whole chapter of his life with Shana that she'd not known about until now. But that isn't the worst of it. She could feel herself burning inside as she says, 'I never went back to Patrick after you and I got together.'

He seems perplexed by that. 'But you did. I remember how much I wished you hadn't.'

She hardly knows what to say. She has no memory of trying to repair her first marriage, and she surely wouldn't have forgotten something like that. Would she?

Frowning and laughing he says, 'You really don't remember it?'

She shakes her head. 'I thought . . . Once we were together, that was how it stayed.'

'Well, it did, more or less, apart from the brief period when I think you took pity on Patrick.'

She tries to cast her mind back to those distant times, to snare all the details and dramas and emotions they were embroiled in, to pin her memories to dates and other events, but it's all so dense, so caught up in the confusions and horror of what had ultimately happened that it's like trying to find her way through a thickening fog. Occasionally some things come clear, are so sharp that she has no doubt about them, but then others succumb to shadow and doubt and a version of truth that might not be truth at all. It's how memory works, she knows that, it's as unreliable as it's necessary, but to let her down over something like this . . .

He says, gently, 'There are things in our pasts that we all forget, or block out—'

'But us breaking up for a while?' she cuts in sharply. 'Me going back to Patrick?'

He shrugs. 'Even the big stuff can get lost over time.'

'Even the big stuff?' she echoes incredulously.

Except it hadn't turned out to be that big in the grand scheme of things, had it, because she hadn't *stayed* with Patrick. And what does any of it matter now? She and Maxim are together, they've come through all those terrible times, put them behind them and moved on.

And yet, here those terrible times are again, bobbing up like some voracious monster from the deep in the shape of an emailed book. 'I don't understand,' she says, 'why I'm only finding out now about you and Shana.'

Appearing at a loss, he says, 'Because you asked? And I thought you knew. Besides, there was really nothing to tell.'

'Apart from a trip to Rome?'

'And a few dinners. Marina, what's going on? Why are you getting so worked up about this?'

Ignoring the question she says, 'Exactly how serious was it between you and Shana?'

He seems incredulous. 'Obviously not at all, or you and I wouldn't be sitting here now.'

'But she wanted it to be?'

'Well, I think we know the answer to that, considering what she tried to do to you.'

Even the allusion causes her to wince. *What she tried to do to you.* Regretting even mentioning Shana's name now she says, 'Why don't we meet in Vienna after you've been to Rome?'

'OK. Let's do that. I'll have my PA set it up. Now, if it's safe to change the subject . . .'

*

The following morning Marina emails Noel.

E.L. Stalwood needs to make it clear what he/she is trying to achieve with the story.

Does she actually want an answer to that?

Didn't she already know what it was?

If she's right . . . No, she can't be, because if she is, she doesn't even want to think about what it might do to her life. Not least as a publisher – although that hardly matters when weighed against her far more vital roles of wife and mother.

CHAPTER TWENTY

That Girl by E.L. Stalwood

Christy was finding it hard to move a single muscle. Each time she tried, it was as if so many cracks were opening inside her to let in even more grief and despair that she was in danger of completely falling apart.

Katie and Johan were back together and she, Christy, had been thrown aside again.

How could she have allowed this to happen, never mind for a second time? How was she ever going to get over the wrenching pain and humiliation, or the inescapable longing for a man she loved so deeply and yet she can't have?

'I know you understand,' he'd said when he'd told her once again that it was over – this time it had been on the phone, he hadn't even bothered to see her face to face. He might as well have added, *thanks for filling the gap,* or: *it was fun, wasn't it? Great that you were available to come to Rome.*

She didn't understand, and couldn't imagine she ever would. He had completely and utterly broken her heart, shattered it into so many pieces that it would never be possible for her to put it back together again.

And Katie? How did *Katie* feel about what she was doing to Christy? Did she think about it at all? Did she know Johan had been sleeping with Christy while she was nursing Rob's wounds after he was fired, trying to save him from all the damage he'd caused himself? Even if she did, she'd no doubt forgive him. He was Johan Johannsen, after all.

While Christy spent hour upon hour trying to hold herself together, she was, at the same time, concocting every conceivable revenge she could think of to pay Katie and Johan back for what they'd done to her. At times she worked herself into a state of uncontrollable and abject fury, but it was a state that all too often collapsed into a terrible, desperate bout of hopelessness and yearning.

'She'll end up going back to Rob,' she warned Johan during one of the many calls she couldn't stop herself from making. 'She's as obsessed with him as he is with Amy.' *As obsessed as I am with you.* The truth of that made her feel as wretched as the loneliness he'd left her with.

'Christy, I have to ring off now,' he told her, 'but please come to my office next Friday morning when I'm back from Milan. We need to talk.'

Since then, Christy had been unable to sleep or eat. She hadn't even been to work – she couldn't face seeing Katie, couldn't face anyone. She was terrified he was going to fire her and knew she should resign before he had the chance, but so far she'd been unable to make herself pick up the phone or send an email.

On Friday morning, more anxious than she'd ever been in her life, she went to his office. She was wearing the blue silk wrap-around dress that she'd bought while they were in Rome. He'd chosen it, and had taken so much pleasure in removing it later.

Her heart was in her mouth, her legs not quite steady as his PA, Jacinda, showed her through to the inner sanctum. It was all she could do to stop herself sobbing when he looked up from his desk and gave her a welcoming smile. He seemed genuinely pleased to see her, much as he would be an old friend, or respected colleague.

How could she feel the way she did about him, while he seemed to feel something else altogether?

Somehow she returned the smile, and even managed to be a little jokey with Jacinda as the older woman filled two cups with coffee and spilled some in a saucer.

'This is the trouble with Johan,' Jacinda chirped, 'he just can't get the staff.'

Christy rolled her eyes and Johan laughed as he came to the sofas, gesturing for Christy to make herself comfortable on the one opposite his.

She did so and allowed the skirt of her dress to fall open for a moment before closing it over her knees. She was embarrassed, wished she hadn't done that, even though he didn't seem to have noticed.

'I'm sorry to hear you've been unwell this week,' he said, picking up his coffee as Jacinda left. 'I hope you're better now.'

She nodded and sipped her own coffee. 'I'm fine, thanks. Some sort of stomach bug. How was Milan?'

He grimaced and tilted a hand from side to side. 'Partly good, partly frustrating, but it was worth going.' He put his cup down again and sat back to cross one leg over the other, to stretch one arm along the top of the sofa. She found it almost impossible to look at him.

'I'm glad you made it today,' he said, 'because I'd like to discuss you taking over as executive producer for the whole of the features department. It's a position I'm hopeful you'll accept.'

Shock, relief, then bile rose to stick in her throat; it was a moment before she could say, more honestly than he'd managed, 'You're making me this offer because you want to move Katie into my job?'

He didn't even attempt to deny it. What he said was, 'She's learned a great deal from you during the time you've worked together, and I'm sure you'll agree that this is a natural progression for her. Of course, you'll still be in charge, you just won't be as hands-on with the day-to-day decision-making as you've been used to. Your role will be more . . . overarching.'

Everything in her was resisting, wanting to throw it back in his face, to walk out now and never return, but where would that leave her? Precisely nowhere, unless she considered 'out of a job' as somewhere. It would also mean she'd never see him again, and she wasn't yet ready for that. 'So what exactly will my new role entail?' she asked, attempting to show interest, while wondering how he was viewing this weakness. She'd given in too easily, should have stood up to him, threatened to sue, even, and yet here she was, trying to be onside. 'I understand the title,' she conceded, 'but if you could talk me through what you'll be expecting from me.'

The irony in his smile turned her heart inside out. 'I know you're far more familiar with the actual running of things than I am,' he replied, 'so I won't embarrass myself by trying to answer that. What I will say is that there is quite a substantial salary increase that goes with it, and a bigger office for you on the floor above the one you're on now. You'll be responsible for a substantial amount of the company's output.'

She could feel how pinched her face was as she tried to look grateful, reasonable even. 'And if I decide to cancel the programme I'm leaving?' she enquired mildly.

His eyes were steady, hard, as he said, 'You would need a good reason to do that.'

She didn't press it. There was no point when she knew he'd never let her cancel anything without his approval, especially Katie's programme.

'Once you're settled,' he continued, 'I'd appreciate it if you could find something else for Amy Summers.'

She managed to hold his eyes, trying not to see him as a lover, but as someone she didn't know. 'Why would I do that?' she asked. She knew, of course, but she was going to make him spell it out.

'Katie is keen to make a few changes,' he replied, with no apparent compunction. Why should he have any when he was in charge? 'Not overnight,' he continued, 'obviously these things take time, but she'd like to start by cutting back the number of times Amy fronts the show in a week. I believe she's looking into adding a few guest presenters.'

Christy could feel the tightness in her jaw as she put her coffee cup aside. 'So Amy and I are to lose our jobs to make room for—'

'Let's not go any further with that,' he interrupted coolly. 'I simply want you to be assured of my continued support when you take over your new role, and to know that—'

'—you don't want to fuck me any more so you're buying me off with a promotion that you know I don't want.'

He rose to his feet and walked around his desk. 'I think this meeting is over,' he said in a tone that allowed no challenge.

She stood, and for one terrible moment she almost tore open her dress. She wanted to remind him of what he was giving up, of how irresistible they had found one another, of how *meagre* blonde and fair-skinned Katie was by comparison.

He went to open the door. 'Thanks for coming today. The changes we've discussed will take effect in the next few weeks, and if there's anything you'd like to discuss further, just let me know.'

That night, a little drunk and deeply distraught, Christy picked up the bronze Katie had given her and turned it over in her hand.

Though it was one of the most beautiful objects she owned, she hated it now, even more powerfully than she'd once loved it. It was a brutal, mocking symbol of Katie's falseness, and she didn't want it in her home, or her life, a moment longer.

Taking it to her car, she drove to Katie's flat with it resting on the seat beside her. She had no clear idea of what she was going to say or do when she got there. She was simply following an urge to confront Katie tonight; to let her know that – whatever the future held – they would never be friends again.

It was past nine o'clock when she turned into Katie's street. There were two parking spaces outside the ground-floor apartment. Katie's car was in one, Johan's was in the other.

Christy knew she should have prepared herself for this; nevertheless, the shock and hurt of seeing their cars together was the worst kind. She couldn't bear it. She just couldn't.

The lights were on inside; she could see Katie through the open blinds, curled onto a sofa, a laptop open in front of her. There was no sign of Johan, but he was obviously in there somewhere.

Christy picked up the bronze, stepped out of the car and, without a care for who might see her, or who might end up hurt, she hurled it through the window. The satisfying sound of glass smashing and Katie's shriek stayed with her as she got back into her car and drove away.

CHAPTER TWENTY-ONE

Marina would never forget the night the bronze figurine had come crashing through her window, glass shattering like shrapnel, flying everywhere, even into her skin and hair. She'd leapt up, crying out in terror as the missile smashed into the coffee table and Maxim rushed in from the kitchen.

'What the hell?' he exclaimed, going to her. 'What happened, for God's sake?'

She took a breath, attempting to pull herself together as she stared at the sculpture she'd given Shana in a gesture of friendship – a gesture of falseness now, she had to accept. It was a small but heavy bronze, so appropriate to their world.

Clearly understanding without having to be told, Maxim said, 'Do you want me to call the police?'

She shook her head and her mouth trembled in a bleak sort of irony as she said, 'I suppose it's one way of returning a gift.'

Taking out his phone he quickly dialled. 'Pack a bag,' he instructed. 'You can't stay here with the window like that. We'll go to mine.'

As he arranged for a temporary repair, she stared around at the mess, thousands of jagged shards scattered all over the half-finished manuscript she'd been reading while Maxim cooked. It felt oddly as though something inside her had shattered. She picked up the sculpture and ran a finger over the smoothness of the exquisitely carved female curves and sharp edges of the book. If it had hit her, it could have killed her.

Looking back on the incident now, with Shana's account of it in front of her, Marina can feel the same quickness of fear that had hit her that night, but also the weight of Shana's pain. She'd understood the anger and despair that had driven her to do something so crazy: hadn't she felt the same during the early days of her break-up with Patrick?

She remembers trying to call Shana that night, but there was no answer. She'd even considered going over to see her, but Maxim had refused to let her go alone. If Shana was in that sort of mood, there was no knowing what else she might do, and seeing him would probably only inflame things further, so they hadn't gone.

In the end Marina took the sculpture to the office early the next morning and put it on Shana's desk before anyone else arrived.

Shana never mentioned it when she came in, so Marina didn't either.

The following week, Shana moved up to the fourth floor and invited everyone for drinks in her new executive suite to celebrate her promotion. Feeling sure she wouldn't be welcome, Marina waited until everyone had left the office before packing up to go home. Although by then she was officially the publishing director, she hadn't felt comfortable about moving into Shana's office.

'Are you coming to the drinks?' she heard someone ask.

She turned to find Amelia standing close to the lift, looking slightly nervous but as lovely as ever. Marina wondered what her relationship with Patrick was these days, if they saw one another at all, and how responsible

– guilty – she felt about all the heartache she'd caused, about the mess his life was in.

'I'll walk up with you if you like,' Amelia offered. Was she concerned about her position now that Marina was taking over? No one had told her yet that she was being moved aside, but it would happen, and after that Marina would devise another way to move her along until she was finally out of the door.

Such a shame it couldn't happen right away. Given the choice, she'd happily never see the girl again.

She turned away. 'I have other plans this evening,' she said shortly, 'but before you go, have you been in touch with Corey Millar yet about the video promotion for *Watch the Eyes*?' Millar was one of their leading thriller writers, who'd recently delivered a truly chilling horror story set in a remote house inhabited by a deranged woman and hundreds of dolls. The art department had dressed a deserted old cottage in Berkshire to shoot a trailer for the book's publicity.

'We're doing it tomorrow,' Amelia assured her. 'Corey's going to be there and Will Robbins is on camera. It'll be seriously spooky, but I guess that's the idea.'

Marina shouldered her bag and said, 'I'll see you tomorrow.'

As she walked to the lifts, she felt Amelia's eyes on her back, a direct, penetrative stare that could almost be physical. She wondered what the girl was thinking, feeling even, but doubted she'd ever know the answer to that.

She was already at home with a glass of wine poured and the news on TV when Maxim rang to find out where she was.

Confused, she said, 'Am I supposed to be at yours?'

'No, you should be here at Shana's drinks.'

'You mean you're there?'

'Of course. How do you think it would look if I didn't show?'

Not entirely sure about that she said, 'Well, I can't imagine Shana wants me there so I hope it all goes smoothly and everyone has a great time. Are you giving a speech?'

'Just a short one. I have some Stateside calls to make after, so I'll go straight home and see you tomorrow?'

'OK. Sorry if I've let you down?'

There was a smile in his voice as he said, 'You haven't.'

Now, with Shana's latest chapter open in front of her, Marina has no problem guessing where the story will go next. Shana is going to claim that she and Maxim – 'Johan' and 'Christy' – had spent the night of the drinks party together, and she, Marina, all these years later, will feel enraged and doubtful and worried that it was true.

She really has to stop letting it get to her like this. She's handing all her power to Shana by reacting at all, never mind by reading the book, and yet how can she not? The recreation of another intimate scene with Maxim notwithstanding, Shana is very close now to recounting what happened to Amelia, and it's this, more than anything, that Marina is dreading.

Putting her laptop aside, she goes to stand at the half-open sash window of the sitting room and gazes out at the street beyond their small front garden where cars are parked against the kerb and lampposts are just starting to come on. She watches a young couple stroll hand in hand away from the park, and follows the progress of a Range Rover as it comes to a stop outside a neighbour's house. The man who gets out is in his sixties, grey-haired and dapper; a professor of physics whose wife is the creator of a range of beauty products. Marina and Maxim don't know them well, but they've joined them for drinks a couple of times before operas in Holland Park, and walked home with them after.

She's about to call out as the professor drops a book from the pile he's carrying, but he notices it himself and stoops to pick it up. As though sensing she's there, he glances up and waves.

She waves back and is grateful she isn't close enough for him to see the shock on her face.

She hadn't noticed it at first, but it's there all right, illuminated by a streetlight, and perched on the gatepost outside her house, legs akimbo, arms outstretched, eyes staring right at her.

A terrible doll.

She pushes the window closed and turns away, hands pressed to her cheeks as a torrent of blood rushes to her head. Had Shana put it there? Or had she got someone else to do it? Rosie? Georgia? Noel? Not Noel, he was in Cardiff today. *Ed?* For God's sake, what is wrong with her? Ed is in Scotland, mountain-biking.

Is someone still out there watching the house, watching her, waiting to see what she will do? Where are they hiding? In a car, an apartment opposite?

She sinks to the floor and wraps her arms around her head. She suddenly feels like a prisoner in her own home. She can't go out there. She won't. In her mind's eye, it is still staring up at her, face impassive and yet grotesquely threatening. It's appalling, horrifying, menacing, a memory come to life straight from the night of Amelia's brutal murder . . .

CHAPTER TWENTY-TWO

The following morning the doll has gone. Marina searches all around, up and down the street, throughout their small front garden, in the bins even, but it might never have been there. She could almost have dreamt it, or conjured it from her imagination, but she knows she didn't. Someone put it there for her to see, and at some point during the night they came to take it away again.

What are they hoping to gain from this?

She expects to receive a message on her phone, or an email, maybe a note through the door, but nothing arrives, and no further chapters turn up over the following days. Her insistence that Noel should tell his author to let them know what she's trying to achieve with the story continues to be ignored.

Though it's small comfort not to be faced with any more unbridled sex between 'Christy' and 'Johan', Marina still isn't finding it easy to sleep at night. She's even short with Maxim when he rings, causing him at one point to tell her to sort out what's stressing her and stop taking it out on him and the girls. This obviously means that one or both of the twins have been in touch with him to complain about her irritability every time they try to talk to her.

Even her colleagues are starting to ask if she's all right. Of course she is, she tells them, while wishing she could just get up and walk out of a meeting that is being dominated by an egotistical author – or agent – or even one of her own team.

The longer E.L. Stalwood's silence goes on, the more ominous it's becoming.

It doesn't seem to help that whatever Shana writes it can't change what was investigated, recorded and reported at the time. She, Marina, has all the cuttings, printouts, photographs and court documents in a box in the attic. Maxim doesn't know it's there, nor do the girls. She should get rid of it, has no idea why she's kept it when she has no intention of reading any of it again.

She doesn't have to when so much of it is imprinted on her mind. The first article she recalls reading ran more or less as follows, and even now she can feel the chilling horror of it coursing through:

Amelia Spence, aged nineteen, editorial assistant at the London publishing house Hawksley Maine, was murdered at the company's South Kensington premises last night. Police were called after her body was discovered in a fourth-floor meeting room and the building has now been closed to anyone not involved in the forensic search.

It's believed that the weapon used to strike a fatal blow to the head was a small, bronze statuette which was found next to the body. It has been taken away for analysis.

A company spokesperson issued a statement soon after the event saying that the CEO, Maxim Forster, has been in touch with Amelia's family to express his shock and deepest condolences and he's given his reassurance that everyone will be working closely and tirelessly with the police to find out who committed this terrible crime.

No arrests have been made so far, but staff members are being interviewed, as are Amelia's close friends and family. We're informed by someone who wishes to remain anonymous that Amelia was an extremely popular rising star in the publishing world, but apparently there had been some difficulties lately between her and other staff members.

Marina hadn't been named at that point, no one had, but she'd been amongst the first the police had interviewed that very night. They'd come to her home around ten o'clock and had questioned her for what had felt like hours, wanting every last detail of her relationship with 'the deceased'. That was how they'd described Amelia; also as 'the victim' and 'former colleague'.

It had been almost impossible for Marina to take it all in.

She struggled to recall all the details now, it was so long ago, but of course they'd asked how well she'd known Amelia; if Amelia had any particular friends or enemies; how and when had she, Marina, found out about her husband Patrick's affair with Amelia?

It had shocked Marina deeply when she'd realized how much they knew already.

'Did you ever threaten to kill Amelia?' one of them had asked. His name was Detective Chief Inspector Colston; he was bald, sharp-eyed, and almost as wide as he was tall.

'No!' she'd cried emphatically. Although she'd had no memory of speaking those words aloud, she couldn't deny she'd thought about doing it often enough. Maybe she'd yelled it once in a state of a grief and despair and someone had heard.

And that someone had told the police?

'I've never laid a finger on her,' she insisted, implored. 'It's true there were difficulties between us because of what happened with Patrick, my husband, but I'd never do something like this.'

'You wanted her to leave the company?' the female detective stated, making it a question. She was Detective Sergeant Jenifer Sands, tall, rangy, dark-eyed and ginger-haired.

'Yes, I did, but not like this.' How could they even think it, for God's sake? This was crazy!

'Where were you between seven and eight this evening?' Colston asked.

She reeled with shock. 'I was here, at home, reading a manuscript. It's there, on the table, you can see . . .' She pointed and they glanced at it.

'Did you return to the office for anything?' Colston wanted to know.

She swallowed hard, trying to keep herself calm. 'No, I was here the whole time.'

'Can anyone verify that?'

A rush of unease tripped her voice. 'N-no,' she managed, 'I don't think so.'

Sands didn't look convinced. 'Are those the clothes you were wearing today?' she asked.

Marina glanced down at her T-shirt and leggings. She'd changed when she'd come in, the way she always did.

She was asked to remove the items and to retrieve those she'd been wearing earlier so they could be taken away for analysis.

'Please, I swear! I never hurt her,' she cried as she handed over the plastic sack containing her black Gucci trouser suit and a pale green silk shirt. 'It's true I hated her for breaking up my marriage, but we've moved on . . . I-I . . . things have changed.'

'In what way?' Sands enquired.

'She . . . I . . . I'm with someone else now.'

They hadn't asked *who* that night, but they did when they'd called her to the station the next day.

That was when she'd told them about Maxim and had watched them exchange long, expressive glances; Sands had even noted something down, but what it was, or what they'd deduced from her admission, she had no idea. She was in such a state of agitation by then that she was unable to gauge anything.

It wasn't until she saw Maxim later in the day, at his flat – her own was still being searched – that she finally got a clearer picture of what was thought to have happened to Amelia. Apparently, she'd been working alone in a meeting room, packing up the dozens of dolls that had been used in a video shoot the day before. Will, the cameraman, had popped upstairs from his edit suite because she wasn't answering her phone, and what he'd found was a sight he'd probably never forget.

Amelia with a fatal injury to her head, her blood and brain matter dripping from dolls' hair and eyelashes, and pooling on the floor.

Marina's hands were over her face as she listened; she couldn't look at Maxim, didn't want to see how shaken he was, or how close he might be to suspecting her of doing this terrible thing.

'Marina,' he said gently, 'if you know anything, anything at all, you need to tell me now.'

Her head came up, eyes flashing with disbelief and horror. 'You think I could do something like this?' she shot back at him.

He seemed stricken. 'Of course not. I know you never would, but the police have to investigate everyone, and you were at your flat alone . . .'

'Yes! I was there the whole time. I didn't go back to the office.'

'OK. I believe you and I'm sure the police do too, they're just being thorough. Now tell me about Patrick. Did you talk to him at all yesterday?'

'No, but he didn't do it.'

'How can you be certain of that?'

She couldn't, but nor was she willing to believe it. 'How would he get into the building?' she demanded. 'He no longer has access.'

Maxim shook his head.

Brokenly she said, 'I need an alibi, don't I?'

'At the moment it might be useful, but it's still early days, and right now I believe Will, the cameraman, is being held for further questioning.'

She tensed with shock. 'Because he found her? How could they think—?'

'I'm sure as far as they're concerned, everyone is a suspect.'

Everyone is a suspect. Her thoughts buzzed around her head like wasps trying to burst free.

She looked at him. 'Does that include you?' she asked hoarsely.

He shrugged. 'I guess so, or it did. I have an alibi for around that time.'

'Where were you?' For one heart-stopping moment she

thought he was going to say he'd been with Shana. That they were going to alibi each other.

'I was at the gym.'

She stood up, paced about the room, then turned to him. 'Has Shana been questioned?' she demanded.

'I have no idea.'

'Do they know the sculpture belonged to her? It was mentioned on the news. We need to tell them . . .'

'At this stage, I think we let them find everything out for themselves.'

She didn't argue. She was in no position to, when she had no idea how to.

Two days later she received a call from DCI Colston. 'I'd like to ask you about the bronze figure Shana Morales threw through the window of your flat,' he said, coming straight to the point.

Marina's heart stood still. She could see the sculpture, feel it in her hand, even, and now . . . 'What about it?' she asked, her voice barely more than a whisper.

'Perhaps you can tell me what happened to it after that night.'

'I- I returned it to Shana the next day. I left it on her desk.'

'Did anyone see you put it there?'

'I-I don't know.'

'She claims she never saw it again after that night.'

Marina's head spun. Shana was denying seeing it again! 'But I gave it back!' she cried. 'I put it on her desk.'

'Can you think of a reason why Shana Morales would want to harm Amelia Spence?'

Marina searched her mind in a panic, trying to come up with an answer, but she didn't have one.

The detective said, 'We've spoken to your husband, Patrick Cain . . . You are still married?'

Marina's heart jolted as she said yes.

'He confirms that his relationship with Amelia ended badly a short while ago. Is there anything else you can tell us about that?'

What was she supposed to say? She didn't, and yet she did. 'I knew it wasn't working out for them,' she replied, 'but Patrick and I didn't discuss it. I don't think he'd have hurt her, though, and it's definitely not in him to do something like this.'

The detective said dryly, 'A lot of people don't have it in them to kill another human being, until suddenly they do.'

Now, as Marina stands in her Holland Park home, the detective's words spin out of the past as clearly as if they'd only just been spoken.

A lot of people don't have it in them to kill another human being, until suddenly they do.

She'd never have considered herself capable of murder until the urge had all but overtaken her when she'd found out about Patrick and Amelia. But she wasn't alone in feeling that way; most did when they were hurting as much as she was then. It didn't mean they acted on it.

She'd thought for a while that Patrick might have become so drunkenly crazed that he'd decided to punish Amelia in the worst way imaginable for rejecting him.

He hadn't.

He'd been at a football match that night, in a hospitality box, with three friends who all vouched for him.

The only other suspect who'd been unable to come up

with an alibi was Shana, but she had no motive, no reason at all to want to harm Amelia.

It was four days after the killing that CCTV footage came to light showing Marina's car parked fifty yards from the entrance to Hawksley Maine, between seven ten and seven twenty-five on the evening in question. It had been recorded by a rotating camera on the front of a bank adjacent to the company's front door.

The fact that her phone showed she'd been at home during that time meant nothing; she could simply have left it there. Although there were no images of her entering or leaving the building, or witnesses to claim they'd seen her, there were digitized security doors at the back, unmonitored by CCTV at that time, and she had access to the codes.

The police were discreet about her arrest, at least at first. They asked her to come to the station and, within minutes of entering the building, she was being read her rights. Someone told her her car had been impounded, and she was allowed to make a call before being locked into a cell. She'd known no appropriate lawyers then, so in a state of terror she'd rung Maxim.

His voice was calm and firm as he said, 'I'll speak to someone right away and we'll get you out of there.'

She sat waiting and waiting, racked with fear, flying into a panic at the slightest sound, and somehow bringing herself back again. She was terrified Maxim would abandon her. They'd only known one another a matter of months; he didn't owe her anything and he really didn't need this in his life.

Eventually, a lawyer came. His name was Nathaniel Dayson and he was, it turned out, one of London's leading defence solicitors.

Maxim was with him, but was instructed to wait outside.

In an interview room scuffed and worn by time, Dayson listened carefully as Marina repeated everything she'd told the police. The lawyer's presence – his whole demeanour – felt more intimidating than comforting, but she continued to speak while he made notes. He asked questions and gave simple, straightforward advice about how they were going to proceed with the upcoming interrogation.

Suddenly someone knocked on the door and asked Dayson to step outside.

Marina waited again, hands clutched under her chin, heart thudding out of control. She wondered if Maxim was still nearby, if she could go to find out, but then the door opened again and Dayson came back. His expression was so taut and grave that her heart went into freefall.

'They've found blood in your car that's a match to Amelia's,' he told her.

She was charged with murder that very day, and from there she was remanded in custody. She thought, hoped, it would be for just a few days – maybe a week – until, between them, Maxim and Dayson could manage to sort things out.

The next five months turned into the most traumatic of her life. It wasn't only trying to live with the sickening horror of what she'd been accused of, that she was actually going to stand trial for, it was the burning fear of the women around her. There were so many, and the things they'd done, did to each other . . . It was another world, an inescapable dimension of hell, full of people with bad teeth and bloodied piercings. The beatings she received for no reason, the threats and jeering were an almost daily occurrence. The dread of never getting out of such a diabolical place, of this being the rest of her life, was all-consuming.

She couldn't sleep, and when she did she often woke screaming, in the throes of a panic attack. She was made to suffer for disturbing her cellmate in ways no one should ever be made to suffer. The sadistic cruelty and derision seemed unending.

Though not everyone was part of the gang that had decided to make a sport of posh-girl baiting, those who were there for non-violent offences, or were close to release, knew the self-preserving wisdom of turning a blind eye. She had no friends, no security from the officers, no one to turn to at all.

Apart from Maxim. He visited as often as he could, which on a good week could be two or three times. The lawyers came too, Dayson and the barrister he'd appointed.

One day her mother turned up; Marina was so surprised and relieved to see her that for the first ten minutes she couldn't stop sobbing. Sarah Rush watched her impassively, the way she had so often over the years. They'd never had an easy relationship; Marina had learned as a child that it wasn't possible to reach someone like her mother, for she had no natural warmth or understanding, and virtually no sense of empathy. It was a mystery to Marina how a dear sweet soul like her father, who'd died when Marina was ten, had stayed married to the woman.

Sarah's gravest concern, when they were finally able to speak without Marina dissolving into tears again, was for how her daughter's unfortunate situation might impact on her when people found out.

'Of course, if you tell me you didn't do it, I believe you,' she insisted, 'but if you're found guilty, I've no idea what'll happen to me.'

The visit hadn't lasted long after that.

Maxim's father, Paul Forster, was even worse. As far as he was concerned, his son must have lost his mind even to think about standing by this 'editor person'. The police didn't bring charges without evidence and everyone knew she had means and motive. She was clearly a sociopath and it was time for Maxim to return to the States. There were any number of Forster executives who could take over in London, someone who would cleanse the company of everything connected to this egregious scandal.

Maxim paid no heed, not even when his father threatened to fire him and cut him off. In the end, Paul Forster did neither. Instead he retreated to his mansion on Long Island, believing that once the trial was over and Marina had been sentenced, Maxim would come to his senses and get on with his life.

CHAPTER TWENTY-THREE

Marina can't believe she hasn't seen this before. How on earth could she have missed it when it's been right there staring her in the face all along. In fact, it's so obvious to her now that she can no longer see E.L. Stalwood's name.

It's an anagram of Stella Wood, an author Shana published early on in her career, even before Marina had joined the company. It was the success of that book that had catapulted Shana through the editorial rankings to become publishing director at such a young age.

Later, after everything, probably around ten years ago, Stella Wood had submitted a second book, this time to Marina, and Marina had turned it down. Stella hadn't taken the rejection well; she'd tried to hold Marina to a promise Shana had apparently made at a time she was in a position to give one. Marina had remained resolute: she wasn't going to publish a book that she didn't believe in.

You'll pay for this, she recalled Stella telling her. *You'll pay for everything.*

Though Marina had felt unnerved by the threat at the time, knowing that Stella had once been close to Shana, who was by then a few years into her sentence, to her relief she'd never heard from Stella again and had more or less forgotten all about her.

But here she is, submitting another book clearly designed

to carry out her promise of revenge. Unless Shana is hiding behind a convolution of Stella's name.

Or it could be both of them.

The very idea of being up against both women causes Marina's insides to churn with an even deeper and more chilling dread than she's known before. Separately they'd be fearsome adversaries; together they could prove a formidable, unstoppable force.

It's late on Friday afternoon now and she has to leave soon to pick up the girls, but having solved the anagram, she needs to carry out an online search for Stella Wood. She isn't surprised to discover that the book Shana published fell out of print a long time ago, and with there being no electronic version, it isn't possible to get hold of a copy right away. However, Marina is recalling with an awful intensifying of foreboding what that book had been about.

The following morning, she and the girls are at home in the Cotswolds. Though it's never as much fun without Maxim, they love it here anyway, and Marina had rarely felt the need to get away from London more.

Now, with sunlight and countryside smells drifting through the open window, all three of them are still in their nighties, sprawled out on Maxim and Marina's bed, laughing at crazy TikTok videos and weird Insta photos. In spite of how badly she'd slept and how distracted she's feeling, Marina loves being with the twins like this, all limbs and sweet morning breath and no pressure to be anywhere else. Maybe she could even detach from the darkness at the back of her mind, at least for some of the time. The only cloud she's prepared to let through is how much she's missing Maxim.

'I miss you too,' he'd told her when they'd spoken last night, 'and believe me, I'd far rather be there with you guys than where I am right now.'

'Which is?'

'At Louis Armstrong Airport waiting for a flight to JFK.'

'And how was New Orleans?'

'As humid and crazy as ever. I used to love the place, but these days twenty-four hours is enough. Dan sends his love, by the way.'

Dan was Daniel Gibbons, one of Forster Inc's senior executives and oldest son of Louisiana's state senator, Grant Gibbons.

'I hope you remembered to send him mine,' she said. She'd only met Dan a handful of times, but he'd always be a favourite with her for the way he'd defied his boss, Paul Forster, and come to her and Maxim's wedding. Maxim's younger brother, Mark, had made it too, to stand as best man, and Mark's wife would have flown over with him too if she hadn't been heavily pregnant at the time.

Maxim's only sadness on the day was that his mother had no longer been alive to share in it. He was certain she'd have loved Marina as much as he did.

'So, it turns out,' Maxim was saying from the airport lounge, 'that Dan and Tina are planning a vacation in Southern Italy for the whole of October, and they've invited us and the girls to join them for however long we choose.'

How wonderful to think about a time that might be free of the menace of this damned book. 'If we go during half-term that would be wonderful,' she'd said. 'The girls would love it. It might help them get over the loss of Ed, having all those ripped young Italians to focus their attention on.'

With an amused groan he'd said, 'Remind me when Ed's leaving us?'

'Middle of July. He's meeting up with his parents in New York for a few days then they're driving to their Long Island home for the summer.' Right next door to the Forsters' lavish shorefront estate. It was how Joel and Maxim had become friends, during long, hot, sporty vacations as children. 'I expect you already know that,' she added.

'I kind of do,' he replied wryly.

Did he wish he could spend the summer on Long Island with his family and old friends too? It had been a long time since he'd been able to, and she knew his father would welcome him with open arms, even send a plane to fly him over if he had to; but there was no way Maxim would go without her and the girls. And if they did all go, he'd only end up in a fight with his father for making Marina feel, all over again, that his son was only half the man he could be because he'd married her.

'My flight's going to be called any minute,' he said, 'and I want to know about you. You're sounding better than the last time we spoke.'

Realizing that at least some of her tension had begun to unravel during the drive from London, she said, 'You know what it's like coming here. We both find it much easier to relax after a difficult week than if we stay at home. I just wish you were with us. The girls do too.'

He laughed. 'They miss their driver, cook and banker more like. Are Ed and Noel joining you?'

'Ed's still in Scotland, but Noel's aiming to get here late morning tomorrow. Apparently Helena James is coming with him.'

'Oh? Interesting. Does this mean they're officially an item now?'

'That could be overstating it. You know Noel, a bit of a commitment-phobe, but he doesn't bring anyone here unless he's keen.'

'Great, because we like her.'

'We do,' she confirmed, 'and apparently they have tickets for Glastonbury next weekend so we can all go together. Now, what's on your agenda in New York?'

'Nothing exciting. I'll stay with Mark, as usual, and we'll drive upstate on Tuesday night to check in with the old guy. Apparently he's not been too great lately, so we'll be able to find out more about that. OK, that's me,' he said as a flight announcement drowned him out. 'I'll call again tomorrow and maybe you'll tell me what the issue was this week that got you so worked up.'

'Maybe,' she said, fighting down a surge of apprehension. 'I love you.'

'I love you too. Tell the girls I'm going to post a song to TikTok all about it.'

She laughed – and laughed again when she told them and they yelped in protest.

'He will! He'll do it!' Livvy cried in high-pitched alarm.

'He is *totally* embarrassing,' Sophie declared hotly. 'I'm going to message him right now and tell him we'll leave home if he does.'

She did and Maxim messaged back saying, *All the more reason to do it.*

They'd found that hilarious because they were nothing if not contrary.

Now, having finally showered and dressed, they are on the front lawn helping Marina to weed the beds when Noel and Helena arrive. Marina watches with a smile as the twins bound up to greet them as if they're family – in Noel's case he practically is. Helena, as the hugely popular author of a teenage romance series that the girls can't get enough of, both in book and TV form, is duly greeted like a rock star.

'Helena, I'm so glad you came,' Marina smiles, going to hug the elegant and colourfully dressed author.

With an infectious note of irony, Helena says, 'You know how exclusive he is about you, so I'm feeling very honoured. And you girls, I have to wonder just how lovely you're intending to get?'

'No limits,' Livvy assures her, 'but it can be a pain having someone who looks just like you.'

'Tell me about it,' Sophie retorts. 'Can we help you carry anything in?'

'How delightful, thank you.'

Hauling a heavy bag out of Noel's car, Sophie, always the considerate one, heads for the door. 'This way, I'll give you the grand tour.'

'Have you got any more books coming out soon?' Livvy wants to know, skipping after them. 'We're totally in love with Captain Cavendish . . .'

Marina doesn't hear the rest as they disappear along the hall towards the stairs.

Turning to Noel, who's laughing and rolling his eyes, she hugs him as she says, 'I'm glad you brought her. She's always a breath of fresh air.'

'You all are,' he insists, 'and I'm going to love being the only bloke – unless Ed's joining us?'

'He might if he gets back in time, but it won't be until tomorrow. Here, let me take something,' and, helping him to unload the rest of the gear from the boot, she leads the way inside. Now isn't the time to talk about E.L. Stalwood when he's only just turned up, but she's decided they must try to find an opportunity to discuss it at some point over the weekend.

Half an hour later they are strolling down through the fields and along the river bank towards Lower Slaughter, the girls skipping around Helena, wanting to know how often she goes to the film sets, if she ever gets involved in the casting. They have lots of suggestions in case she does.

Marina and Noel walk on ahead, discussing one of his clients who's suffering from an untimely bout of writer's block and another who's deeply unsatisfied with her marketing plan (neither author with Janus). Marina does her best to be supportive while trying to choose the right moment to broach what's uppermost in her mind.

'Oh my, will you just look at this place,' Helena enthuses as they enter the centuries-old Cotswold stone village where the River Eye slows and narrows into a shallow, pebbly stream as it meanders and babbles through the centre of the idyll.

It's impossible not to be entranced by the place, especially on such a beautiful sunny day, with abundant rose of Sharons tumbling and tangling over huge stone pots, hydrangeas and lupins bursting with colour, and honeysuckle climbing the limestone walls. Almost no traffic comes through to disturb the peace, and there is nothing for tourists to do apart from admire their surroundings and maybe treat themselves to an ice cream from the only shop.

As they reach the small bridge that crosses to the pub, Marina glances along the road to check for traffic and hesitates as she notices a woman sitting on a bench outside the churchyard. There's something familiar about her . . .

Her heart gives a horrible jolt as the woman glances her way then stands and walks in through the side gate of the Manor Hotel.

Marina starts to run.

'Mum! What the . . .?' Sophie shouts after her.

People turn as she races across the road into the hotel's gravelled topiary garden. No one is there. She runs on, past a fountain and out onto the lawn in front of the house. She looks frantically around, but there's no sign of the woman so she dashes up the steps into the entrance lobby.

She stops on the threshold, breathless, a hand clasped to her chest as a receptionist regards her curiously from his desk.

'Can I help you?' he asks.

She stares at him, not sure what to say. 'Do you – do you have someone staying here,' she begins. 'Her name's . . .' Would Shana have used her own name? 'Stalwood,' she says. 'A Mrs or Miss Stalwood?'

'I'm sorry,' he replies, 'we can't give out the names of our guests . . .'

'Can you call her, tell her I'm here?' He looks about to refuse, so she says, 'Please. She's an old friend. I saw her come in and it's been so many years. You'd be doing me the most enormous favour. Her too. She'll want to know I'm here.'

Eyeing her carefully, he begins tapping into his computer. After consulting the residents' list, he says, 'I'm afraid we don't have anyone by that name.'

'Morales?' she states hopefully. 'It was her maiden name. She might have gone back to it.'

He checks again and shakes his head. 'Maybe you were mistaken. If you haven't seen her for a long time . . .'

Marina turns to survey the front lawn, where a dozen or more diners are seated at tables with parasols.

'Marina? What's going on?'

Noel is coming towards her, his face creased with concern.

'Are you OK?' he asks. 'What happened?'

She attempts to swallow and, glancing back at the receptionist, she thanks him, descending the steps as Noel reaches them. After satisfying herself that none of the diners is Shana, she links his arm and starts back to the topiary garden. 'We need to talk,' she tells him. Her heart is still thudding, and she continues to look around as they leave the hotel grounds, certain Shana is close by and very probably watching. 'I've just seen someone,' she says. 'I'm certain it was her . . .'

'Who are we talking about?'

She braces herself. 'Her real name is Shana Morales and I think . . .' She glances at him, 'You've heard of her, haven't you?'

He doesn't deny it as he waves out to the others who are still by the bridge waiting and wondering. 'You're right,' he says, 'I have heard of her, I've just been waiting for you to bring it up.'

CHAPTER TWENTY-FOUR

Later in the day, after Helena and the girls have left in Noel's car to make a tour of Stow-on-the-Wold, Marina carries two glasses and a bottle of rosé wine onto the terrace and sets them down on the table.

As Noel pours, she's picturing the woman who walked into the side gate of the Manor Hotel, seeing her clearly in her mind and still feeling certain it was Shana. Moreover, the way the woman had glanced up before walking away suggested she'd wanted to be seen, although there had been no further glimpses of her while they were having lunch in the pub garden. Nevertheless, Marina had sensed her watching them, probably from one of the Manor's upstairs windows.

If she was right, then Shana had been able to see the girls. The mere thought of that cracked her anxiety wide open, making it virtually impossible to still.

'OK,' Noel says, putting the bottle down, 'I'm going to cut right to it. I've heard the gossip over the years, you know what this industry is like, so recently, after a few chapters of this submission, I went to Google to find out more. I now know that fourteen years ago Shana Morales tried to frame you for the murder of Amelia Spence.'

Marina's throat turns dry. It is still hard, even after all this time, to hear those words and know the appalling truth of them. 'There are those,' she says quietly, 'who still say I did it and got away with it. Rosie Shell being one of them.'

His distaste of Rosie shows as he says, 'But there was a trial and Shana was found guilty.'

Marina nods. This was indeed true. She takes a sip of wine and returns the glass to the table. 'Before we go any further,' she says, watching a butterfly skitter past, 'let me tell you first about E.L. Stalwood.'

He tilts his head, curious to know.

'I can't think why I didn't see it before,' she admits, 'but I'm certain it's an anagram of Stella Wood, and not even a very good one.'

He frowns as he shifts the letters in his mind. 'I'm not familiar with the name,' he tells her.

She shakes her head. 'I'm not surprised. She's an author Shana published way back when, before I even knew her. I believe she and Shana were quite close for a while, but I didn't meet her until much later, a few years after the trial, when I turned down her second book.'

His tone is ironic as he says, 'So you weren't her favourite person a long time ago, and now you think she's behind this book? Or that Shana's using an anagram of her name?'

'Possibly, probably both,' she replies.

Clearly puzzled, he gestures for her to elaborate.

Knowing she has to, she presses out the words she hasn't even wanted to say to herself. 'Stella Wood's first book was about the life sentence she received, and partly served, for a murder she claims she didn't commit.' She waits for the resonance to establish with Noel, the shifting sands of guilt and innocence, the recognition of what they're reading now, of how the stories are fusing. When she's sure he's there, she continues. 'After her release, Stella was approached by several publishers for her story, but it was Shana, young, ambitious and very persuasive, who struck up a bond with her. This was when our department wasn't exclusively fiction; Stella's book fell into the category of true-life crime. It was a huge success. As you can imagine, everyone wanted to read about the beautiful – and Stella was very lovely – young woman who, according to her, had been wrongly imprisoned for a terrible crime. She was a TV executive before everything changed for her.' She watches Noel again and attempts a smile as he registers this new symmetry with *That Girl*.

He says, 'So this book is something like an analogy, albeit a tortured one?'

'Definitely tortured,' she agrees.

'And who was Stella Wood supposed to have murdered?'

Marina picks up her glass, swirls the wine around and drinks it down before she says, 'Her niece.'

His eyes open wide and a moment passes before he says, 'So was Amelia Spence Shana's . . .?'

Marina shakes her head. 'They weren't related. It's just presented that way in the book, presumably to . . . tie in with Stella's story? To mess with me. Probably both.'

'Jesus Christ,' he mutters. 'This is a bit fucked up.'

Marina could hardly disagree.

When she doesn't continue he says, 'So, given what happened today, can I assume that Shana Morales is no longer in prison?'

'She was released on licence a year ago.' Marina picks up her glass and puts it down next to the bottle.

Refilling it, he says, 'Have you tried to find out where she is? Of course you have.'

'So far I haven't got anywhere.'

'But now you've cracked the anagram, you're thinking she could be with Stella Wood?'

'It's possible. However, I can't find Stella either.'

He gives that a moment before saying, 'Did they ever find out who actually killed Stella's niece? I mean, if it wasn't her.'

'She always maintained it was her sister, the girl's mother. Just as Shana tried to claim that it was me who killed Amelia.'

'Holy shit,' he murmurs, and stares thoughtfully, worriedly out at the garden. In the end he says, 'She's having a second go at putting the blame on you, isn't she? That's what this book is about?'

As Marina nods, she feels the horror of it all rising up again: the hatred and bitterness, the horrendous accusations against her and Maxim, the prison, the terror of never getting out, of losing everything and everyone . . .

Steadying her breath, she forces down the onslaught and says, 'You're right, it seems pretty certain that she intends to throw everything back into doubt and create a new nightmare for me by telling the story again. The change of names and backdrop, and carefully calculated use of lies, are a way of protecting herself from the possibility of a libel suit, I guess until she's ready to reveal . . .' Her voice lowers and falters, 'Whatever she's planning to reveal.' Hearing the words, feeling them giving life to the fear that there might actually be more, makes her reach for the wine again.

Noel sounds concerned – alarmed even – as he says, 'From what I've read about the case, you were charged with the murder right after it happened, correct?'

She's starting to feel queasy now.

'So how come she ended up going down for it?'

She takes a breath, not wanting to go through any of it ever again, but she needs him to hear the story from her, certainly not from Shana through her fake characters, or from anyone else who might be harbouring a grudge, such as Stella Wood. 'Remember, I was in prison at the time she was arrested,' Marina says, 'so I wasn't really aware of what was going on outside, but I had a great legal team, thanks to Maxim. They knew the police had found Shana's DNA in my car, but obviously there was no way of establishing when, or how, it had got there. Then, about five months after my arrest, with the trial looming, the police received an anonymous call asking how thoroughly they'd searched Shana's flat. It turned out they hadn't searched it at all, so they did, and that was when they found Amelia's phone.'

The intention is simply to leave a little something where she won't immediately find it.

Recalling those words from the prologue of *That Girl* makes her breathless.

She watches Noel, certain he must be connecting with that line as well, but even if he is, what he says is, 'Let me get this straight. She stole your car . . . How would she even know how to do that?'

Marina shrugs. 'It's a good question, easily answered. We used to keep copies of each other's keys, front doors, cars; anything that mattered really. I returned hers when things started to go wrong between us. I had no idea she'd made duplicates of mine before giving them back, she never mentioned it, and I never thought to ask, but we weren't exactly on good terms at the time so we wouldn't have spoken about it. I don't know if she had any particular reason for keeping them, but it's the kind of thing she'd do, just in case. You need to understand,' she continues with feeling, 'that Shana is nothing like the character she's drawn for herself in Christy. They might look similar: Shana was certainly beautiful and successful – obviously she wasn't a TV producer, she was a publisher – and she had all kinds of qualities as well as insecurities. But fundamentally, as a person, she was unpredictable, egotistical, vain, spiteful if anyone crossed her, and when her relationship with Maxim, who you must realize by now she's calling Johan in the book . . . when that relationship didn't work out, she became obsessed with him, and vengeful to the point of . . .' She's lost for a moment, unable to find the right words to sum up such a complex and ultimately unknowable character. 'The worst of it began,' she continues, 'when she hurled a bronze sculpture through my window, yes, that really happened, and now, fourteen years later,' she throws out her hands, 'here we are.'

Noel is regarding her intensely, taking his time to assimilate what she's telling him with what he's read so far, and Marina can't blame him for seeming to doubt her version of Christy (was he really?). It was hard to make a sudden change of perspective, opinion, even loyalty. She knows that because it happens often when reading a novel. The reader starts out committing to one character, then suddenly has everything pulled out from under them with an unexpected plot twist, or the revelation of an erstwhile hidden personality flaw.

In the end, apparently deciding to leave the more esoteric points of storytelling to one side, Noel reverts to the reported events as they'd unfolded. 'OK. So she took your car . . .?'

Going back there, Marina says, 'She took it and parked

it where it could be seen by CCTV, but not in an obvious spot inside the company's premises. From there she presumably let herself in through the back door and went up to the fourth floor, where Amelia was working in a meeting room. It's possible she was on her way to my office to leave the bronze on my desk, but then she saw Amelia and . . .' She hates imagining this next bit, is always repelled and distressed by it. She pushes some stray strands of hair from her face, and presses on. 'I've no idea if they spoke, if Amelia even knew she was there. I guess no one knows that apart from Shana. In court she denied everything, so she wasn't questioned about any exchange they might have had. All we know for certain is that after the attack she dropped the bronze next to Amelia's body, because it was found there, and she must have been wearing gloves because apparently there were no prints on it. Then she left the building and returned my car to its place outside my flat before driving her own home. Of course she denied all that too.'

Noel is shaking his head incredulously and Marina isn't surprised. There is so much about her story that challenges belief. Even she has a difficult time with it herself, in spite of how long she's known it.

He says, 'Let me get this straight – she managed to take your car from outside your apartment and bring it back less than an hour later without anyone seeing her do it?' Before she can answer he adds, 'I guess, by the same token, no one could say they saw you go out and come back?'

'They couldn't,' she confirms. 'And no one saw her going into the building or leaving. They didn't see me either, but of course they couldn't have because I never went back there that night.'

Throwing out his hands, he says, 'But what the hell was her reason for doing it? An innocent girl, for Christ's sake!'

Understanding his need to make sense of it (everyone had tried at the time, so why wouldn't he now), she feels more nausea rising as she says, 'You will have read this in your research, but I – we – have always believed that what drove her was the need to get me out of Maxim's life. You've seen how the book is building up to that? "Christy" is crazy about "Johan" – obsessed, even. Her claim – and her lawyers built her defence on it – was always that I had a motive for killing Amelia, because of her affair with Patrick, my first husband. And I had no alibi for that night. The fact that I was in a relationship with Maxim by then held little weight, they argued, because it was still early days and it was known, apparently, that I was still bitter about the break-up of my marriage. Actually, I probably was, but definitely not to the extent that I'd do something like that. However, I admit I was working towards getting Amelia moved from fiction – and if I could, I'd have got her fired.'

Noel sinks back in his chair, apparently needing more time for evaluation, at least one that works for him. And because Marina knows him so well, she understands how important it is for him to be certain he is understanding everything correctly.

Finally he says, 'You have to excuse me for this, but I'm going to ask it anyway . . . Why the hell didn't Shana just kill you if she wanted back into Maxim's life?'

It isn't as if Marina hasn't been asked the question before, she has by the police and was again in court, but it still manages to make her feel as though she was lying the entire time.

Being asked it by Noel gives her a horrible, wrenching feeling inside, one that's almost insupportable; however, she knows she has to accept it the same way she always has, without protest or anger, only steady rationale. 'I'm sure she wanted to,' she replies, 'but it would have been much harder for her to get out of that. So she apparently decided that Amelia was the answer, and that if Maxim saw me as a murderer, he'd never want any more to do with me.'

Noel's eyes seem to glaze as he deals with the unconscionable horror of it all, and Marina feels his confusion, for even now, after all this time, it's still close to impossible for her to accept what happened at that unthinkable time of her life.

'Amelia's family must have been devastated,' he finally says quietly.

Marina is surprised and touched by that; to put Amelia's family at the front of his mind, after all he'd just heard, showed what a decent man he was. It had always seemed that everyone was focussed on her and Shana, Maxim too, following the double shock of her release and Shana's arrest. She herself had thought about Amelia's parents often over the years, the tall, rangy woman and her stricken husband who'd been in court every day, listening to how their precious only child had become collateral damage in Shana's desperate need to win back the man she insanely believed should be hers. 'Maxim tried reaching out to them after the trial,' she says. 'He was determined they understood that the company was prepared to give them all the support they needed, but they wanted no more to do with us. I guess you can't blame them.'

Noel shakes his head, seeming to accept that, while also apparently lost for words. Since Marina doesn't feel the need to speak again for the moment, she lets the silence run. She wants to bring herself back to her surroundings, to tune into the sound of a tractor in a nearby field and the bleating of sheep carrying across the meadows. This is where she belongs now, in her beautiful home in the middle of the English countryside, so far away from the hell she might have known that the fear of it, the memory of it, can only be a dream.

In the end Noel says, 'What does Maxim say about the book?'

She continues staring out at the fields. Answering this question isn't going to be easy, far from it in fact, but she's been expecting it and, since there is no avoiding it, she says, 'I can't tell him.'

Noel's shock is almost palpable.

'We went through so much at the time,' she continues, 'it was horrendous and . . . You've read about it, you know what they accused him of, what he also had to go through.' She locks her eyes to his and wills him to understand what she's about to say. 'I've never told anyone this, and I've definitely never said it to Maxim, but I'm afraid that if we hadn't found out I was pregnant when I was in prison, he'd have done what his father wanted and walked away.'

Noel's jaw slackens as his eyes dilate with shock. 'Oh, come on,' he protests.

'You weren't there,' she reminds him. 'It was awful; his father is extremely powerful and our relationship was still so new . . .'

'But this is Maxim we're talking about. He adores you . . .'

'I know that's how it seems, but if this were to blow up again and become as toxic as it was the last time, he won't want the girls around it. He'll take them to the States, or at least send them, and frankly I wouldn't try to prevent it, because *I* don't want them harmed by it either.'

Noel is staring at her in disbelief and confusion. This is all very hard for him to grasp in such a short time and with so much at stake, but she can see that he's trying. In the end he says, 'I still think you should tell him. If anyone can deal with this—'

'Noel, please. I don't want him to know unless he has to. I need to put a stop to it, and I need you to promise that you'll keep it to yourself, or at least between us.'

He is clearly struggling with what makes sense to him and yet apparently doesn't for her.

'This is my marriage,' she reminds him. 'Please let me handle it my way. Can you do that?'

Though he continues to look troubled, and as if he might still argue, he finally says, 'OK, if it's what you want, but one thing's for certain, we can't leave things as they are. We need to find her and, as you say, try to shut her down before it goes any further.'

Relieved by the 'we', she says, 'I couldn't agree more, but—'

'If she's who you saw at the Manor Hotel today . . . Is it possible you could have been mistaken?' he asks. 'She's obviously over a decade older than the last time you saw her, and prison is sure to have aged her even more than the years.'

'Of course, but I'm pretty certain it was her. Actually, I'm not in any doubt.'

He nods, seeming to acknowledge the powerful nature of her instinct. 'But why would she be there?' he asks. 'I don't get it. If she wants to see you, she obviously knows how to find you.'

'I don't think she does want to see me; not yet, anyway. She's stalking me . . . Actually,' she shoots him a look, hoping he's ready for more, but even if he isn't she needs to press on. 'There have been some dolls,' she tells him. 'I'm sure you read about them when you did your research, how Amelia was surrounded by them when it happened?'

His eyes narrow as he nods slowly.

'I've found a couple outside the house in London, and one was sent to me via Amazon with the name Amelia sewn onto the front of it.'

He balks and grimaces at the creepiness of it, and raises a hand as if to stop her. 'Where are these *dolls* now?' he asks.

'I threw them away. Maybe it was the wrong thing to do, but I couldn't bear to have them anywhere near me.'

His eyes remain on hers, thoughtful and determined. 'She can't be that hard to find,' he declares, 'not now we know who Stalwood is.'

Unravelling with relief at his words, to have it confirmed that he really is on her side and willing to help, she says, 'So far I haven't got anywhere, but my ex, Patrick, said he'd look into it. I haven't heard from him so I'm guessing he hasn't come up with anything yet.'

Astonished, Noel says, 'You've talked to him but not Maxim? Why would you do that? I didn't even know you guys were still in touch.'

'We aren't very often, but I thought he might have heard from her. Actually, I was afraid at first that he might have been involved somehow . . .'

'And you aren't now?'

She covers her face with her hands, as if to contain the craziness of her own thoughts and suspicions. 'Half the time I don't know what to think, or who to trust, and now she's stopped sending chapters. What's that about, if it isn't to mess with my head?'

Noel picks up Marina's phone and hands it to her. 'Call your ex,' he says. 'Ask if he's found out where she is, or if he has any leads. And tell him I'm on board for finding Shana, just in case he's interested. I'll get more wine while you make the call.'

As he goes inside, keeping the door open so he can hear what's being said, she connects to Patrick's number. 'Hi, is this a good time?' she asks when he answers.

'Not really, I'm at a conference in Oslo, but is everything OK?'

'I just wanted to know if you've made any progress in trying to find Shana.'

'Actually, I haven't had much time, but so far I've drawn the same blanks you have. I'm thinking we should speak to someone in the probation service. They're bound to know what name she's using these days.'

'I've tried them, but they won't give out that sort of information.'

'Then we need to find someone on the inside of the service. I don't know anyone myself, but one of your crime writers is sure to have a contact or two who could be useful. Or why not try the lawyers you used back then? I'd say try her lawyers, but I doubt you'd get anything out of them.'

Bracing herself, she says, 'I've confided in Noel Hadigan, the agent she's using to filter the book through to me—'

'Christ! Why did you do that?' he cries. 'How do you know he's not involved in some way? I mean, obviously he's involved if he's the agent . . .'

'He's also a good friend and I trust him.'

He sounds angry, impatient, as he says, 'I'm not sure that was wise, but listen, I'm sorry, I have to go. Let me know if you get anywhere and I'll call when I'm back.'

As she rings off, Noel returns with a fresh bottle of rosé and a bowl of marinated olives. 'He thinks we should talk to a crime writer who might have an "in" with the probation service,' she says.

He nods as he sits. 'Not a bad suggestion. Richard Olaf is a client of mine. He did a book a couple of years ago, published by Orion, all about a probation officer. I'll talk to him. You'll have someone on your list too, bound to have, but leave this one to me while you carry on trying to find out more about Stella Wood.'

'It's possible she's changed her name too, given her history.'

'Great.' He bites into an olive. 'OK, so I think our next move, today, is to email "E.L. Stalwood" to find out when any more chapters might be coming our way. Agreed?'

Marina's heart lurches as she nods. The fact that this is ongoing – that she has no idea yet how to stop it – is creating so much havoc for her that it's surely only a matter of time before she loses any chance of controlling it.

'The question is, do I let her know we've worked out who she is?' he prompts.

After considering it, picturing Shana's face as she realizes she can no longer hide behind E.L. Stalwood, the laughter, the glee even, or maybe she's not yet ready for full exposure, she shakes her head. 'I think we need to continue playing it her way for now. It's our only chance of finding out where she's actually intending to go with the book, and I guess we have to do that.'

He frowns thoughtfully as he nods. 'So I'll tell her you're eager to read more . . .? No, I think I should say something along the lines of being surprised not to have heard from her in a while, keen to know how the writing is going, can I offer any help, that sort of thing. I'll keep you out of it.'

Happy to agree to that, Marina looks up at the sound of a car coming to a stop in front of the house.

'Must be Helena back with the girls,' he says and starts to get up. 'She'll probably be needing one of these.' He gestures to his glass and pops into the kitchen for a fresh one that he has filled by the time Helena comes through to join them.

'Where are the twins?' Marina asks, when there is no sight or sound of them.

'At the gates talking to a woman we found there,' she replies, sinking into a chair with a satisfied sigh.

Marina's heart turns over as she and Noel exchange glances.

'We'll be right back,' Noel says as Marina takes off towards the house.

He catches up with her on the drive.

As they reach the gates, the girls are coming through carrying a punnet of strawberries each and their usual breezy attitudes. 'She was so sweet, this woman,' Sophie tells them, 'she gave us these and they look delish.'

'This is a bit weird though,' Livvy added. 'No idea why she gave us this.'

When she sees what it is, Marina feels the world slip its axis.

The doll's hair is dark and plaited, just like Marina's, its expression is horrifically gurning, and embroidered across its denim chest are the letters HMP. *Her Majesty's Prison.*

Noel says, 'Where's the woman now?'

Livvy turns around. 'I don't know. She just walked away.' Clearly confused she adds, 'What's the big deal?'

'What did she look like?' Marina asks as Noel runs off down the lane.

Livvy shrugs and turns to Sophie.

'Kind of tall, grey hair, maybe foreign,' Sophie says uncertainly.

'She didn't have an accent,' Livvy objects, 'so I don't know why you said that.'

'She just looked kind of . . .' Sophie shrugs.

'Why? Who is she?' Livvy asks Marina.

Marina shakes her head, thinking fast. It doesn't fit the description of the woman she saw earlier, whose hair had been long and dark, but that was an easy feature to disguise. 'Apparently someone's been stealing one of the local farmer's strawberries and giving them away,' she says randomly. 'I don't think we should eat them. If she's got mental health issues, there's no knowing what she might have done to them.'

Livvy and Sophie both look aghast as they stare down at their punnets.

'What about the doll?' Livvy asks, holding it aloft as if it might bite.

'We should probably get rid of that too,' Marina replies, and looks up as Noel reappears at the gates.

He is shaking his head. 'Village is deserted,' he tells her.

'Were you going to make a citizen's arrest?' Sophie asks excitedly.

He frowns, until catching Marina's eye he says, 'Something like that.'

'Let's go in,' Marina urges, gesturing for them to start up the drive.

As soon as the twins are out of earshot she says quietly to Noel, 'Would you mind closing the gates? I know we don't usually, but maybe tonight we should.'

CHAPTER TWENTY-FIVE

It's late on Tuesday afternoon and Marina is in her office with the door closed, only vaguely aware of the raised voices outside as she rereads an email that arrived a few minutes ago.

She looks up, startled, as someone knocks and comes in. It's Toby, Georgia's number two in general fiction, a slight, wiry lad with a mop of curly red hair, pale green eyes and an engaging smile. He's excellent at his job, and a great favourite with many authors as well as with the rest of the team.

'Do you want the good news or bad?' he asks, leaning against the door frame and folding his arms.

Deciding the email in front of her is enough bad for today, she says, 'Start with the good.'

'OK, great! So, according to our reckoning, we have three paperbacks in the Sunday Times' top ten next week – numbers nine, six and two – and, wait for it, a hardback at number one.'

She manages to break into a smile. This really is good news. 'Ellison Graves has gone straight in?' she guesses.

He nods, beaming all over his face. 'As he's one of Georgia's, and with her being off this week, I wasn't sure if you wanted to call and let him know. Happy to do it if you prefer.'

Normally Marina never shies away from delivering good news to an author, especially Ellison Graves who, though a regular at the number one slot, is always so genuinely thrilled to hear he's made it again. No expectations or sense of entitlement with him. Today, however, she decides to let Toby have the pleasure of making Ellison's day.

'Cool, happy to do it,' he replies. 'The paperback best-sellers are being contacted by their editors, as usual.' He grimaces. 'Now for the bad news. I'm afraid Della Parrish has announced that she won't be renewing her contract with us if we continue to publish Fiona Simmons.'

Marina's eyes close in exasperation. 'Who has she announced this to?' she asks.

'Me, and I presume her agent, although I haven't heard from him yet.'

'Remind me who it is.'

'Bart Jefferson at Farradays.'

'I'll speak to him, but before I do, can you pull up her sales for the past three years? Let's see how well she's actually doing.' She doesn't add that she'd be quite happy to see the back of the self-aggrandizing, pushy, truly irritating historical novelist, as she doesn't encourage negative-speak about authors, even this one.

'On it,' he salutes, and starts to leave.

Stopping him, she says, 'Remind me where Georgia is this week? I seem to have forgotten she was going on holiday.'

'Oh, it was kind of a last-minute thing that came up on Friday, and as we don't have anything big about to land, I said I'd cover.'

Not pointing out that Georgia should have checked with her first, she says, 'Do you know where she's gone?'

He shrugs. 'All I can tell you is that "Boo" called and told her to get herself on a flight . . .' His enthusiasm tails off as he realizes this isn't going down too well.

'Boo?' she queries tightly.

'I know – gaggy, isn't it? – but it's what she calls her boyfriend.'

Marina is poker-faced as she nods and asks him to close the door as he leaves. Then, returning to the anonymous email still open on her screen, she reads it again.

In case you haven't worked out where Georgia is this week, I'm sure you will once you receive this.

Her heart lurches painfully. Georgia wouldn't have needed Marina's clearance for time off if it was Maxim who'd asked her to join him.

She turns from her computer and back again. The thought – the fear – that Georgia could be with Maxim is overwhelming her, and this email is so distressing and aggressively provocative . . .

Reaching for her phone, she's about to call Noel when she realizes she'd prefer him not to know that she has trust issues where Maxim's concerned. With all that's going on, it will just complicate things further.

She sits back in her chair, trying to make herself think straight.

If Shana is behind the email, how on earth would she know about Georgia's movements? Or that she, Marina, has doubts about Maxim? The former gives even more weight to the fear that Georgia might be working with Shana, possibly with Rosie Shell and/or Stella Wood as a go-between. The second is something Shana has no way of knowing, for Marina has never admitted her insecurities to anyone; although Shana would have little trouble working it out for herself. It's virtually impossible for someone with Marina's past to feel fully secure about anything.

Is there anyone else who could have sent the email? Georgia herself is a possibility, of course, or maybe it was Stella Wood. And why haven't she and Noel received any more chapters yet?

'I can't answer that,' Noel says when she rings him. 'I've no idea what's going on. I take it you haven't heard anything since the episode at the gates?'

Shuddering at the image of the hideous doll that Noel had taken charge of, in case it was needed at some point in the future, she says, 'Nothing, but I can't get it out of my mind that the woman, whoever she was, talked to the girls. It could easily have been Shana, but I've been wondering about Stella Wood. The two women don't – or didn't – look dissimilar, and they're around the same age.'

'I've been wondering about Stella too,' he admits, 'but like you I can't find anything about her online after 2016 when she apparently moved to Glasgow. She'll be on the same sort of life-licence as Shana, though. She has to be; it's how it works when someone is released after being convicted of murder. On which note, my author who wrote about a probation officer is making some calls. He'll get back to me as soon as he has news. Meantime, I've been thinking we might need some professional help with this. Someone who knows how to trace those who don't want to be found.'

'You mean a private detective?'

'Exactly. They'll have ways and means of following trails or cracking email addresses that we don't have the first idea about.'

Wondering if she could ask them to track the email in

front of her, or find out where Georgia was, Marina says, 'I think it's a good idea. Do you know anyone?'

'Not personally, but once again we can turn to our authors for a recommendation.'

What a terrific resource they are, especially crime writers. 'Will you do it?' she asks. 'I don't want any of my authors, or editors, to know that I'm in need of that sort of service.' She doesn't add that she might have reason to feel mistrustful of her team now, but it's there in her mind and tying her up in knots with the frustration of not knowing what to do about it.

'Sure I'll do it,' he replies. 'Tell me again when Stella Wood was released and how old she was at the time.'

'In 2005, and she was thirty-eight. That would make her mid-fifties now.'

'And we know Shana is fifty-eight. Your sighting in Lower Slaughter tells us that she's still tall, dark-haired and slim. Stella, who was once a brunette version of Kathleen Turner, could have done anything to her appearance by now and we would have no way of knowing. I'm still wondering if we should be telling the police about the dolls. It's intimidation, harassment . . .'

Dread surges through Marina. *No more police. Please. I can't go through anything like that ever again.* 'Let's take the PI's advice on that,' she says, stalling.

'OK. Before I ring off, you were going to give some thought to who might have known you were spending the weekend in Gloucestershire. I know we don't want to suspect anyone on your team is giving Shana information, but let's at least try to rule it out.'

Only wishing she could, she says, 'I have thought about it, and I don't recall discussing it with anyone here, but we go most weekends so it would have been an easy presumption to make.'

'I wonder if they knew Maxim wouldn't be around?'

She stares at the email and feels a wrenching sadness as she pictures him with Georgia, somewhere in the States, Georgia's beautiful chestnut hair spilling over a pillow, or tumbling down her naked back as she moves towards him.

She lowers her head to fight down the pain of it as she hears Noel saying, 'So I'll get back to you as soon as I have news about a PI. Meantime, you know where I am if any more mysterious dolls turn up.'

CHAPTER TWENTY-SIX

Marina can't stop herself constantly checking the street outside.

Everything appears normal, a few passing cars, neighbours coming and going, no strangers lurking; no dolls.

'Are you expecting someone?' Ed asks when she goes to the window for the umpteenth time since she came in. He'd returned from his mountain bike adventure a few hours ago after disappointing the girls by not making it to Gloucestershire on Sunday. However, he's definitely joining them for Glastonbury next weekend. He's even messaged them to confirm it, which Marina knows will have delighted them.

In answer to his question she says, 'No, no one. I'm just . . . sometimes it helps to get up and down when I've got a lot on my mind.'

'Anything I can help with?'

She looks at him, wanting to ask if Maxim has really been with him on all the occasions she'd thought they were together, but of course she can't. 'Thanks. There's a . . . a troublesome author I need to sort out and I'm trying to decide on the best way to handle it.'

'Well, I'm here if you change your mind.'

Leaving him to watch a game on TV, she goes to her

study to read through *That Girl* again in case there's something she's missed that matters.

She gets no further than the end of the prologue, stops and reads it again. Someone entering 'Christy's' apartment and leaving a 'little something' in a bedroom drawer. Something that is going to blow up Christy's world.

Of course she has no reason to trust anything Shana has written, when so much of it is a wild distortion of truth, but she'll never be able to get away from the fact that it was the discovery of Amelia's phone in Shana's flat that had turned everything around for her and led to Shana's arrest.

This is clearly Shana claiming – again – that it was planted. She'd shouted it from the rooftops at the time, and her lawyers had made much of the sudden search of her flat. It had surprised everyone. No one, not even the police, had been able to explain why the anonymous call had come when it had, so long after the event. Nevertheless, the phone was there, and with no evidence of a break-in, the only explanation could be that she'd put it there.

Shana had always insisted that Maxim was behind the scheme to frame her – and she hadn't been alone in her suspicions, for there had been a constant barrage of press speculation about it too. Naturally, nothing had ever been proved – how could it be when it wasn't true – but no journalist of the time was interested in allowing the truth to stand in the way of a good story.

For the intruder there will only be anonymity.

Realizing she's becoming more agitated than ever, Marina shuts her laptop down and takes herself off to bed.

It is the middle of the night when she's woken by the phone on her nightstand. Her first thought is for the girls, then Maxim, then *Shana*.

Reaching for her mobile she sees a US number, and fears for one wild moment that it might be Georgia.

What is the matter with her? Is she losing her mind?

'Hello?' she says, struggling to sit up.

'Honey, it's me,' Maxim says. 'Did I wake you?'

'It's OK, is everything all right? What time is it?'

'Just after midnight your time, seven with me. I'm at Mark's, but we're heading out to Long Island in a few minutes. Dad's had a fall and been taken to hospital. Kathleen, the housekeeper, is worried it might have been a stroke, so we don't want to leave it till tomorrow in case it's serious.'

'Oh God, I'm so sorry,' she replies, meaning it – she might not like the old man herself, but he's Maxim's father and she knows this news will have affected him deeply.

'Mark's talking to Godfrey, Dad's physician, on the other line,' he tells her. 'He's already on his way there. It could be we're getting excited over nothing. I should know more by morning.'

'OK. Should I tell the girls?'

He goes off the line for a moment, talking to someone, presumably Mark, or Cher, Mark's wife, since the other voice is clearly female. Coming back he says, 'Maybe hold off on telling the girls until we have more news. I should go now, sorry to have woken you.'

'Don't be, I'm glad you did. Call as soon as you can. Love you.'

'Love you too.'

After ringing off, Marina sinks back into the pillows and stares, wide-eyed, into the semi-darkness. She knows it's beyond crazy to think he'd create such an elaborate and atrocious lie to prepare her for not making it back at the weekend, but she hadn't been able to stop it from entering her mind. She was even wondering if he'd been talking to Georgia when he'd gone off the line.

Swinging her legs over the side of the bed, she sits for a moment trying to still her thoughts. She is her own worst enemy and Shana's easiest victim – presuming it was Shana who sent the email about Georgia, but of course it was.

She's tempted to read it again, but manages to stop herself. She could search for nuances she might not have noticed before, or even try to trace the sender – not that she has the first idea how to begin – but it isn't going to make the suspicion disappear. The only way she can do that is to find out who Georgia's boyfriend actually is. But how foolish is she going to make herself look if she starts asking members of the team if they've ever met this 'Boo' and do they know his real name?

She can't imagine Maxim enjoying being called 'Boo', but maybe he has a pet name for Georgia. What does she know of their private world that probably doesn't even exist except inside her head?

Realizing she isn't going to get any sleep for a while, she goes downstairs to fetch her laptop and brings it back to bed. She opens up a manuscript she's promised to read by the end of play on Friday. Thankfully it's by one of her favourite literary authors, who has the knack of drawing a reader right into the heart of a story and closing the door behind them.

It works well until she gets to an Orwellian-ish line that reads, *You can hide from the truth, but remember, it's always watching and one day it will reveal itself whether you're ready for it or not.*

She can almost hear Shana saying it and laughing, as if

she had somehow guided Marina to this very book and the ominous prediction of these words.

She closes down the manuscript, knowing she won't be able to go any further with it now, and goes down to the kitchen to make some coffee.

CHAPTER TWENTY-SEVEN

Maxim rings just after noon the next day. By then he's already texted to let Marina know that his father is being kept in for observation and will probably be allowed home sometime in the next forty-eight hours.

Going to catch some sleep now, his last message had said, *speak later.*

She's in the back of a taxi on her way to lunch with an agent when he finally gets hold of her.

'So it seems he dodged a bullet,' he says with a sigh. 'They've fitted a pacemaker and for the time being he's stable. It gave him a fright, that's for sure. Lucky Kathleen was there.'

Lucky indeed. 'So will you fly back on Friday, as planned?'

'No, I'm going to stay on a while. It's what the old guy wants, his loved ones around him for a few days, so that's what we're going to do. I know that kind of screws up Glasto, but I'm hoping you and the girls will make me feel better about that by going anyway.'

Her mouth is dry, her heart hurts as she says, 'Yes, we can do that. Ed's going to be there with a couple of mates, so the girls will be happy and I'll have Noel and Helena for company. I'll miss you though.'

'I'm sorry. I was really looking forward to it, but you understand why I have to stay, don't you?'

'Of course.'

She heard someone speaking at his end and, before she can stop herself, she says, 'Who's with you?'

'Kathleen. She's made breakfast for us all, so I should go. I'll catch up with you again later. Oh, and don't worry about saying anything to the girls. Just tell them I've been delayed and I'll explain everything when I'm back.'

After ringing off, Marina sits numbly holding her phone, wishing she knew how to silence the damnable inner voice that seems to have a life and agenda all its own. In her heart she knows he wouldn't lie about his father's health like this, so why can't she make herself believe it? She's even doubting what Toby told her earlier, that Georgia is in Florida, because for all she knows, Georgia was lying to him.

Looking down as her mobile pings with an email, she sees it's from Noel and opens it.

Meeting with a PI later. Meantime my author's probation service contact claims to have no information about Shana Morales using a false identity. However, he offered up a Dorset address for her. We could check it out after Glasto at the weekend, as we'll kind of be down that way.

Marina looks away from the email, but has little time to digest it, as her taxi pulls up outside the restaurant. After paying, she climbs out and is about to read the message again, standing in the street, when her lunch date arrives and sweeps her into his favourite eatery.

It isn't until she's on her way back to the office that she realizes she's had another email from Noel. It simply says, *See below.*

Scrolling down she reads,

Dear Noel, I'm sorry for not being in touch sooner, but very glad to hear that you are keen to read on.

I'm wondering if you or Marina Forster have guessed where the story is going yet. With your literary expertise it's possible that you have, but for the average reader I think it's important to keep up the mystery, don't you? I hope I'm succeeding with that. Perhaps you'll let me know.

Meantime, more for your appraisal.

E.L.S.

CHAPTER TWENTY-EIGHT

That Girl by E.L. Stalwood

Dear reader, I am sure by now that you have guessed Christy is me, or, put another way, I am Christy. It's quite hard writing about yourself in the first person, I find, so I'm going to continue in the third person if you don't mind.

Congratulations on working it out, by the way – E.L. Stalwood is Christy Grant. I knew you would eventually, and I feel quite excited about it.

And now to continue my story . . .

It had come as a complete surprise to Christy when two detectives had turned up at her flat one evening, months after Katie was remanded into custody, asking if they could come inside and talk to her.

Of course she had said yes: she was curious, and wanted to be helpful. Also, she had nothing to hide, so she pressed the buzzer to let them in. Actually, if truth be told, she was a little anxious, but that was only to be expected; she'd been on edge ever since the terrible time of young Amy's murder. Everyone had. The shock of what happened to the poor girl was still reverberating through the company's corridors and offices, through all their lives, rumbling away like an earthquake that couldn't quite give up. People couldn't stop talking about it, obsessing over it even. Many were in counselling; a few had actually resigned their jobs. Johan had announced a few weeks earlier that the entire company would be relocating as soon as suitable alternative premises could be found. Few would feel more relieved about that than Christy.

She had been haunted, tormented by what happened to her poor niece, and would never go near that meeting room now. And she certainly couldn't think about the killing without feeling subsumed by the sheer ugliness and enormity of it.

As she waited for the detectives to climb to the fourth floor, she found herself irrationally wondering if Johan might be with them. She could think of no good reason why he would be, but he was always on her mind, no matter the situation. She simply couldn't stop herself hoping that, one day, when all this was finally behind them, he'd come to his senses and realize that they were meant to be.

She had seen little of him since those horribly dark days when everyone was questioned, over and over, so many times that there were moments when Christy had felt close to delirious. The fact that she had no alibi for that night had been terrifying, especially when she learned that Katie had claimed she'd left the bronze, the actual murder weapon, on her desk the morning after she, Christy, had thrown it through Katie's window.

It was a lie – a wicked, shameful lie. Christy had never seen the bronze again after that night, and how could anyone think she would want to harm her own niece?

She had no idea what the interrogations were like for Johan, it wasn't something he was likely to discuss with her, and besides, she'd hardly seen him since it happened. He'd appointed others to run the day-to-day business while he, apparently, spent most of his time with lawyers. It was a complete mystery to Christy why he'd chosen to stand by Katie when he couldn't be in any doubt about what she had done. He must surely have recognized the malignant streak in Katie's character by now. She kept it well hidden, it was true – Christy had only seen it once or twice herself over the years they'd known one another – but it came out when Katie was stressed, or felt under threat, or when she believed someone had wronged her. It must have taken her over when she'd bludgeoned poor Amy to death. No matter that she had Johan now and no longer wanted Patrick, Amy had needed to be punished.

'Miss Grant,' DCI James Colston announced as he arrived on the landing. Christy remembered him and his balding head only too well; had hoped never to see him again after Katie's arrest – other than in court, of course. The red-headed woman with him was DS Jenifer Sands.

Before she could invite them in, Colston held up a piece of paper. 'We have a warrant to search your flat,' he informed her.

Christy's heart leapt into her throat. 'What for?' she cried. 'Why? I don't understand.'

Sands said, 'We've received information that makes it necessary, so if you don't mind . . .'

To Christy's horror, other officers started swarming up the stairs and into the flat. She tried to protest but could only watch, speechless with confusion, as they began to toss around cushions, open cupboards, turn out drawers. She kept telling herself that she had nothing to fear. They wouldn't find anything, because there was nothing here. *She had done nothing wrong.*

After a while, someone shouted from the bedroom, and Colston went through, followed by Sands, leaving Christy wide-eyed with dread. 'What is it?' she'd demanded when the detectives returned to the sitting room. 'What's happened?'

'Is this yours?' Colston asked, holding up a mobile phone in a gloved hand.

She looked at it, blinked uncertainly. She had one like it, but hers was there, on the coffee table. 'I-I don't—'

'Do you have a charger?' Sands interrupted.

'Yes, course.' With a terrible trepidation building inside, she fetched one from her study.

Colston took it, plugged in the mobile and watched it come to life. He glanced at Sands before turning back to Christy. 'This appears to belong to Amy Summers,' he told her. 'We spent a lot of time looking for it after her murder. Would you mind telling us how it got here?'

Christy was panicking, shaking her head and backing away. 'I have no idea,' she cried desperately. 'I've never seen it before. I swear. Where . . . where was it?'

'In your bedroom,' Sands replied. 'I always said we should have searched your flat. An oversight on our part, but we have it now.'

'No! No!' Christy shouted, putting up her hands to ward them off, though neither had moved. 'I don't know how it got there, I swear. Someone must have put it . . . Did you? Oh my God, have you just—?'

'Who else has keys to your flat?' Colston interrupted.

She could hardly think straight. 'Katie had them. She gave them back, but . . . She must have made copies. It's the only—'

'Katie Beech is in custody,' Sands reminded her coolly. 'Are you really trying to say she brought it here?'

'No! She must have . . . She could have told someone where to find it and they . . . Oh God! I can't believe this is happening.' Her mind was in so much chaos it was hard to pull any sense from it. Suddenly she cried, 'Johan Johannsen! He knows where I keep my spare keys . . . Katie must have hidden the phone after she . . . After . . . And he . . . he brought it here.'

Colston and Sands regarded her incredulously.

'Or he paid someone to do it,' she ran on frantically. 'I don't know. All I can tell you is that I have no idea how it got here.

For God's sake, if I had taken it at the time, don't you think I'd have got rid of it by now?'

Colston turned to Sands and nodded.

Sands stepped forward. 'Christy Grant, I am arresting you on suspicion of the murder of Amy Summers—'

'No!' Christy yelled, snatching her hands away. 'I'm telling you, someone planted it there. For God's sake, don't you find it odd that you can walk right in here after all this time and . . . Stop! I had nothing to do with . . .'

'. . . but anything you do say . . .'

'Please listen to me,' she sobbed. 'They've plotted this together, Johan and Katie. They're trying to blame me for what *she* did. Ask yourselves, why would I hold onto the phone if I did it? It doesn't make any sense.'

Neither detective appeared to be listening, nor was anyone else as they began filing out of the door.

'Where are you taking me?' she demanded as she was led after them. 'I need a lawyer. You can't do this . . .'

'You'll be able to call someone when we get to the station,' Colston informed her. 'Meantime, I would remind you that you're under caution.'

Christy was charged two days later and remanded in custody. There was no sign of Katie when she got to the prison, but she was certain it was the same one. It was only later that she learned Katie had been released before she'd been brought in.

She waited, hoped and prayed that her lawyers would be able to prove she'd been set up, or at the very least that the presence of Amy's phone in her flat was not proof of guilt.

It didn't happen. She had to face a trial.

Each day she sat in the dock, straight-backed and dignified, and abjectly terrified of how this was going to end. She had entered a plea of not guilty. Of course she had. She would never admit to something she didn't do, especially when her very freedom was at stake, not even for a reduced sentence.

The only time she saw Katie during that horrendous travesty of a trial was when Katie took the witness stand and lied many times under oath. Lie after lie after lie, all mixed up in truths that lent a credibility to her story that at times made even Christy unsure of what was and wasn't real.

Christy knew she couldn't match the performance. Katie, with her smart lawyers and convincing demeanour, was winning over the jury with each hour that passed, while Christy could see that she herself was garnering very little sympathy. Everyone seemed to believe that she'd tried to frame Katie for Amy's murder, and that her motive had been to try to break up Katie's relationship with Johan so she could have him for herself.

It was insane. Why on earth would anyone believe that?

Apparently they did.

Katie was in court when the verdict was announced. Christy couldn't see her, but she knew she was in the public gallery, watching and listening. She had no idea how Katie was feeling. How did anyone feel when they knew they were sending someone to prison for a murder they hadn't committed? A murder they'd committed themselves.

Christy had learned by now that Katie was pregnant, so she understood at last, with a horrible, wrenching despair, why Johan had chosen to stand by her. He couldn't have the mother of his child serving a life sentence, and he certainly couldn't allow the child to be born in a prison.

So Katie had successfully trapped him into a situation he couldn't escape and had, at the same time, secured her freedom and Christy's imprisonment.

As she was led away, Christy knew with a certainty that had no room for doubt, that one, or both of them, had arranged for the phone to be planted in her flat. What she didn't know – yet – was how she was going to prove it.

CHAPTER TWENTY-NINE

Marina can't go to Glastonbury.

Livvy called on Friday morning to complain that her time of the month was so bad there was no way she could go to class, never mind a festival.

Marina promptly rearranged her day and drove to the school to pick her up, while Noel, Ed and Helena collected Sophie in the early evening to take her and a lucky friend to Somerset. There was no point in everyone missing out.

Over the weekend, Marina commits herself to being a caring mother, allowing Livvy all her favourite foods and treats, wiping away the tears each time she sobs over all she's missing out on. She even gives her quite a generous budget to do some internet shopping to try to cheer her up, while all the time she herself is in a state of desperate agitation.

She doesn't know yet what Noel might have made of Shana's latest chapter, or the way she'd addressed Marina directly at the beginning as 'dear reader'. There had been no opportunity to discuss it, but she'd heard his tone when they'd spoken on the phone. He'd sounded worried, cautious, as though something in him had shifted since reading those pages. It seemed they'd managed to wield the very power Marina had dreaded. Anyone who read it would be questioning her and Maxim's innocence by now. God knows, she would too, if she didn't know better.

She keeps reminding herself that there's no way Shana can prove something that hasn't happened. It simply isn't possible. Shana killed 'Amy' – *Amelia*. Everyone knows that. The jury found her guilty, unanimously, but Marina's greatest fear now is that Shana might have found someone to lie and say they'd been paid to plant the phone in 'Christy's' – *Shana's* – flat.

Surely if that were the case, Shana would already have gone to the police.

Maybe she will when she's finished having her fun with this literary attempt at destroying Marina's sanity and, much as Marina might be struggling against it, she knows she's in danger of feeling unstable again, the way she did all those years ago.

She remembers with both a blurred and frightening clarity how the trauma of Shana's trial and sentencing had ended up sending her into an early labour. And because she was still so stressed after the births, and Maxim was so worried, he'd insisted she couldn't think about returning to work until she was fully recovered.

She will never forgive Shana for stealing the first years of her twins' lives from her. Those all-important precious firsts, when she should have been focussing only on them, seeing and storing their first smiles, first teeth, steps, giggles, tantrums, and the beautiful bonding with their father. But she'd been unable to escape the nightmare of what had happened to Amelia, to her and to everyone else in Shana's orbit.

The girls were three by the time she returned to the office to take over from Rosie Shell, who'd been acting publishing director for the time Marina was away. Though there had been no mistaking Rosie's hostility right from the start, it was less clear what everyone else thought about her being the boss's wife now. She knew that many, throughout the industry, were still wondering how the mobile phone had got into Shana's apartment, and had they, Marina and Maxim, somehow arranged for it to be planted there?

Now, she can only feel thankful that she hasn't told him about the book yet, for the last thing she'd want him to start wondering is if she really had got pregnant on purpose to trap him. Into marriage, of course, not into getting her out of prison, for she couldn't possibly have known when she conceived what was about to unfold. She knew that plenty of others thought she'd planned it, his father being one of them.

She doesn't know how the old man is doing now; she hasn't heard from Maxim since Friday when she'd told him that she and Livvy weren't able to go to Glastonbury. He'd been sympathetic, of course, and had spoken to Livvy to reassure her that he'd do his best to get tickets again next year. Since then he hasn't called again, has only messaged to say: *I think everyone we've ever known has heard about Dad's 'episode' and now they all want to come visit. There's a bunch of old friends from California staying for the next couple of days who I haven't seen for years, so you can imagine all the catching up that's going on. Dad's loving all the attention, of course. It's pretty full on and every time I go to call you, I realize it's too late with you. Thinking of you and Livvy; Sophie obvs having a fantastic time going by her videos and messages. Love you all, Mx*

He hasn't said yet when he's planning to come back, and she can't help wondering if a part of him wishes he could stay where he is at the heart of everything he's so familiar with – and that she doesn't know at all. It's obviously hard for him not to be able to introduce his girls into that world, to show them off with all the wonderful fatherly pride he has in them. She imagines – if he really is there and all he's said is true – that he's talking about them non-stop, showing around photographs and delighting in the praise. Or maybe he isn't mentioning them at all, has found a way to compartmentalize his two worlds so that he's only a son, a brother and an uncle while he's in his father's home. He almost certainly wouldn't want to talk about her, the wife who'd only escaped being tried for murder because she was pregnant and he'd found the best lawyers that money could buy.

Do they, his friends over there, believe in her innocence, or is there still gossip and speculation amongst them too?

As the tide of it all keeps coming back at her, she isn't always able to hide it from Livvy.

'Mum, are you OK?' Livvy had asked only a few minutes ago. 'It's like your head is somewhere else and you seem a bit . . . I don't know . . . Not right.'

'I'm fine,' Marina assures her, 'just a few issues I have to deal with tomorrow at work.'

'Want to talk about it?'

Marina smiles into her dear, beautiful young face, with its small smattering of teenage spots and freckles. 'Thanks, but it's all quite complicated, and really I ought to be putting it out of my mind for now. Are you ready to go back to school?'

'I guess so, but it's going to be seriously gagging having to put up with Sophes banging on and on about what a brilliant time she's had. It was bad enough getting all her messages and videos. It's like she was trying to rub my face in it.'

'No, she was trying to make you feel a part of it the

best she could, and I heard you singing along with them. You didn't seem too fed up then.'

Livvy shrugs. 'No, but it's not the same as being there, is it? I just better not get one of these TOMs next year or I'll shoot myself. Do you think Dad really will be able to get more tickets?'

'I'm sure he'll do his best, and you know how good he is at making things happen.'

Livvy breaks into a smile. 'He's the best, isn't he, and I suppose it's been pretty cool having you all to myself this weekend. You're a really good listener.'

With an arched eyebrow, Marina says, 'Just as well when you've got so much to say, but I loved having some special time for us too. You know Sophie will probably want it next?'

Livvy assesses that. 'It's OK. I'll just go somewhere with Dad, but if she says anything about me I want you to tell me. Promise?'

'No deal. Unless you want me to tell her everything you've said about her this weekend.'

Livvy laughs. 'She's cool really – most of the time, anyway.'

'And so are you. Now you should go upstairs and fetch your things while I get the car out.'

Much later, after dropping Livvy at school and spending some time admiring Sophie's new non-permanent tattoos, Marina returns home feeling absurdly lonely without them. Or was she afraid it was the last time she might see them?

No, she isn't thinking that at all. It hasn't even properly entered her head and nor is it going to.

After messaging Ed to find out when she might expect him back, she pours herself a glass of wine and decides to settle with her laptop to prepare for the coming week.

It's a good idea, but one she simply can't carry through. There is so much going round and round in her mind, from Shana's latest chapter and how convincing it had sounded; to Noel's distance since it had arrived; to Maxim not ringing and is he really at his father's house, or somewhere with Georgia?

Her eyes close in despair. Why can't she stop picturing them together? It's as though she's determined to sabotage her own life before anyone can beat her to it. Anyone being Shana, who surely knows by now how afraid she is.

Maxim isn't with Georgia.

Georgia is in Florida and due back tomorrow.

Maxim is with his father and will fly home surely by the middle of the week.

Staring at her phone as it rings, she takes a moment to register that it's Patrick.

'Hi, can you talk?' he asks when she answers.

'Yes, are you back from Oslo?'

'Since Wednesday. Sorry I didn't call sooner, a lot going on, but here I am. Have you made any progress on finding Shana?'

'Not yet, but Noel's going to talk to a private investigator.' *Is he still intending to do that?* 'I think I saw her last weekend, just before I rang you.'

'Are you serious? Where?'

'In Lower Slaughter.'

'Isn't that near where you and Maxim have a house?'

'It is.' Without giving herself time to think about it, she says, 'There's a book. She's writing it, using other names . . . I'm going to send it to you.'

There's a beat of surprise before he says, 'Yes, do that. You know, I had a feeling something more was going on. I guess it's about what happened. What's she saying in it?'

'More or less what you'd expect. You need to read it.'

'I will, but before you go, I've been thinking about this agent. Noel, is that his name? You said on the phone that you trust him, but who is he exactly? And *why* do you trust him?'

She glances up at the sound of Ed coming in. 'He wasn't here when it happened,' she replies. 'He moved to London from Sydney about eight years ago, and in that time he's become a good friend. To Maxim as well as to me. If you met him, I think you'd trust him too.'

'All right, but for what it's worth, I reckon you should be there when he speaks to a PI.'

'Actually, I'd rather keep myself out of it for now, but I'll bear your advice in mind.'

After ringing off she attaches *That Girl* to an email, sends it to him, and is about to call Noel when she realizes she isn't sure what to say, given how his manner towards her has changed. That he, of all people, could be doubting her, is telling her more clearly than anything just how powerful Shana's book is going to be *if* it's ever published.

And one way or another, Rosie Shell will make sure that it is.

CHAPTER THIRTY

'Are you kidding?' Noel cries when Marina finally catches up with him two days later. 'Of course I don't believe her. I grant you she tells a good story, and others might be taken in by it, but why the heck would I when I know you?'

She wants to say, *Maybe because it's taken you until now to call me back*, but she says, 'You seemed a little . . . distant when we spoke at the weekend.' *And I wasn't sure if you'd deliberately avoided me when you returned Sophie to school, because you'd already gone by the time Livvy and I turned up.* 'I thought maybe she'd got to you.'

He gives an incredulous laugh. 'I can promise you she hasn't, and I'm sorry if I seemed a bit off. I just had a few things on my mind. Family stuff, back in Aus. Anyway, like I said, she's convincing, so I can understand why you're worried.'

Marina's insides churn. *Worried?*

'But we're going to do our best to cut this off before it goes any further.'

'Have you received any more?'

'Actually, something came in about an hour ago, but I haven't had time to look at it yet. I'll send it on to you now, but before you go, I've had a chat with the PI my author recommended. Her name's Brenna Isaacs and she sounds pretty switched on.'

Pushing aside Patrick's advice to meet the PI herself, she says, 'What have you told her?'

'Everything she needs to know. She doesn't reckon it'll be too much of a problem tracing either of them – Shana Morales or Stella Wood. She's promised to get back to me by the end of the week. Her rates are pretty high, but we want the best. I'll send the details over.'

Seeing his email arrive in her inbox, she tenses as another drops in right after it. It's from the same anonymous address that had asked her last week if she'd worked out where Georgia was.

Could Noel have sent them both? It seems ludicrous to think it's anything more than a coincidence that they've turned up at the same time.

'Are you still there?' he asks.

'Yes, I . . . Your email's here. When are you planning to read this latest offering?'

'I have to run to a meeting now, but I'll definitely get round to it by the end of the day. What about you?'

Knowing she won't be able to wait, she says, 'Let's speak later, or tomorrow, once we know what it says.'

After ringing off, she calls the classics division to tell them to start the meeting without her, and with a horrible apprehension burning all the way through her, she opens the anonymous email first.

Georgia not back yet? Or Maxim?

Her heart thuds as if it's been struck a physical blow.

Neither of them is back.

Maxim had called last night to let her know he was intending to be home by the weekend.

Georgia, according to Toby, is still in Florida having a

fabulous time with 'Boo' and is due to fly back on Sunday ready for work next Monday.

Reaching for her mobile, Marina opens her rarely used Instagram account and searches for Georgia's. She's surely posting shots of herself and the boyfriend, the way everyone does these days, showing off what an amazing time they're having and enhancing the images to make themselves look utterly gorgeous, tanned and deliriously happy.

There are no posts.

In fact, Georgia hasn't posted anything on social media since the launch party she and Marina had both been at a few weeks ago, when Marina had noticed her and Maxim talking quietly together.

Was that when they'd decided on this holiday together?

Unsure whether she wants to scream or cry, Marina drops the phone and tries to breathe. They're together, she's sure of it, maybe on Long Island, where Maxim could be introducing her to his family, and his father is making her feel as welcome as he's always made Marina feel unwanted.

She gets up, walks to the door and turns back again. She has no idea what to do. She's desperate to speak to Maxim, to hear him assure her it's nonsense, that he has no idea where Georgia is and nor does he care. But even if he did say that, would she believe him? She has no way of knowing what's really going on at his father's home, who's actually there or even if the so-called 'episode' is real. The only way of finding out is to ring her sister-in-law, Cher, but how can she do that without making herself seem paranoid and foolish – and what on earth is she going to do if Cher tells her she hasn't seen Maxim in a while?

Maybe should she fly over there.

Nothing in the world could induce her to humiliate herself in front of Paul Forster.

Staring at her mobile as it buzzes, it takes her a moment to register the message. *We need some answers here, any idea how long you're going to be?*

Realizing she has to get to the meeting, she quickly exits her email account, packs up her laptop and the files she needs and starts downstairs. Her mind is still reeling, trapped between the past and the present and with no idea of what the future might hold.

She doesn't have time to read Shana's latest chapter now. It will have to wait until later.

CHAPTER THIRTY-ONE

That Girl by E.L. Stalwood

Christy waited.

For days, weeks, months stretching into years, she waited like a captured bird in an ugly cage to hear from Katie. She sent visiting orders but they were never taken up; she tried to call but was never answered – of course Katie and Johan had changed their numbers. The frustration and impotence was overwhelming. The burning need to speak to them – to beg them to do the right thing – was in danger of driving her from her mind.

Why, she wanted to know, was Johan staying married to someone he knew was a killer? What sort of man allowed his children to be brought up by a woman he had to help escape a murder charge? Once they were in the world and he was able to take full custody, why hadn't he taken them to the States and left Katie to her fate?

If he were a decent man, and in her heart Christy still wanted to believe that he was, he wouldn't leave her to rot in prison when he knew she was innocent. He wouldn't even have to admit that he'd arranged for the mobile phone to find its way into her bedroom. He could say it was all Katie, that she'd arranged it somehow – and for all Christy knew, she had.

Over time she came to realize that the only way she'd survive the unspeakable injustice, never mind the physical hell she was in, was by taking better control of herself. She started to make friends, signed up for yoga and meditation sessions; for spiritual counselling and holistic healing. She turned herself into a model prisoner, someone who helped others to read and write, to learn English and how to communicate less aggressively with one another. She kept her head below the parapet, but not so low that the officers didn't notice her and so would, hopefully, when the time came, support her early release.

In spite of her resolve and the progress she made with her self-improvement, it was still a constant struggle to stop herself wondering if Katie ever spared a thought for her. How many times in a day, week or month did she have to wrestle with her conscience, knowing what she'd done not only to her, Christy, but also to Amy? Was it really possible for her to live her life as though none of it happened, as if there was no blood on her hands?

It was through letters from old and loyal colleagues that Christy found out when Katie returned to work after a prolonged maternity leave. She was told how Katie fired or relocated those who'd been running things during her absence; how she set up a new division and, as the CEO's wife, was apparently answerable to no one.

She was living the life that should have been Christy's.

Years rolled by and, through a regular supply of trade magazines, Christy was able to keep up with Katie's success. She read about all the star acquisitions, the industry awards, the expansion of her new division and the international recognition. She also learned about the homes Katie and Johan bought in London, and in Gloucestershire. She even knew that their children were at a boarding school in Surrey.

It was twelve long years into her sentence, just before her first parole hearing, when she received a letter, out of the blue. It had, she quickly realized, the potential to change everything for her.

She read it once, twice and a third time, taking it in and becoming increasingly unsteadied by the bloom of hope forming inside her. It was like receiving a message from destiny, a divine reassurance from all the gods in heaven that she hadn't been forgotten, after all. Someone out there knew she'd been wronged and was prepared to help.

Here, at last, was the way she could finally make sure justice was served.

CHAPTER THIRTY-TWO

Marina hardly knows what to fear most about this latest chapter, Shana's continued insistence that the mobile phone had been planted; the fact that she'd been gathering information about Marina for years and knew where to find the girls; or that she'd been given a way to make sure 'justice was served'.

Who had contacted her two years ago to give her such hope of clearing her name? A lawyer? A friend of Amelia's? *Patrick?* Could it have been Maxim?

Her mind spins with the shock of his name even entering her head. Surely to God he'd never do something so treacherous as to conspire with Shana to try to end his marriage. Things aren't that bad between them.

They aren't bad at all – unless he is involved with Georgia . . .

She has to clear her mind of this paranoia, to stop giving in to it and remember that everything she's just read is pure Shana-invention.

Taking it line by line, she goes through it again until she reaches the part about a letter arriving 'out of the blue'. It can't have been from Rosie if they'd stayed in touch all along, which presumably they had. Much more likely was that it had come from Stella Wood.

Definitely not from Maxim.

Or Patrick.

She feels sick with herself for even thinking it.

'I've got to admit,' Noel says when they get together at Marina's home later to discuss the latest submission, 'that if I didn't know better, she might be winning me over by now about that phone . . . No! Don't look like that, it isn't happening, but do you really think she had it there in her flat all that time?'

Marina's movements feel stiff as she puts a plate of cold meats and cheeses on the table. 'Maybe not at first,' she replies, 'but when her flat wasn't searched and everything was looking so grim for me, she had no reason to carry on hiding it wherever she'd put it while the investigation was ongoing. Maxim always said he thought she was planning to get rid of it once and for all after the trial was over, when no one was even thinking about it any more.'

Noel grimaces as he thinks. 'I guess I could buy into that,' he responds, 'but you have to admit, purely objectively, that it's not as convincing as the tale she's telling—'

'Because she's had a long time to work out the most believable way to tell it,' she reminds him sharply. 'She has no idea if anyone really broke into her apartment and left the phone there, but suggesting it in a prologue the way she has makes it seem completely credible. Anyway, don't forget she was found guilty in a court of law, so a jury was clearly convinced by the case the prosecution presented.'

Conceding the point, and apparently finding no need to carry on as devil's advocate, he says, 'OK, so it's a question now of deciding what elements of it all really matter.'

'It all matters,' she retorts, feeling both drained and agitated, even oddly distanced from where she is and what they're saying.

'When's Maxim back?' he asks.

'Saturday morning, first thing.'

'OK, good. I still think you should tell him about this, but I understand it has to be your decision. Now, who the heck is this someone who writes to Shana out of the blue and is "prepared to help". My money's on Stella Wood.'

Marina agrees.

'Actually, I have some news about her, but first, as far as we know she wasn't around at the time of Amelia's killing, and if they weren't in touch until twelve years into Shana's sentence, we have to ask ourselves what could Stella bring to Shana's party after so long? Or, put another way, what would be in it for Stella to suddenly pop up from nowhere to help Shana, and how the heck is she going to do it?'

'Presuming the letter was from Stella,' Marina replies, 'all we really know about her is that she was convicted of a similar crime to Shana's – but in her case it really was a niece.'

'So maybe Stella got a delayed surge of empathy towards the person who helped publish her side of the story and decided to get in touch and help put a different spin on things.'

'But what could she possibly know – or do – that could change the outcome of Shana's trial?'

Noel shakes his head, clearly having no answer for that. 'It's my guess that Stella Wood provided accommodation for Shana following her release and that's quite possibly where Shana still is. Which brings me nicely on to our PI, Brenna Isaacs, who was in touch earlier to say that if she has the right Stella Wood, then she got married in Scotland back in 2006, at which point she dropped the "St", and changed her name to Ella Neavis. This would be why we amateurs lost track of her in our search. Brenna's still working on where Ella Neavis is now.'

Impressed by the speed of the result, even if it doesn't get them anywhere yet, Marina says, 'Has Brenna Isaacs had any success locating Shana?'

'If she had, I'm sure she'd have mentioned it. However, if I'm going to ask her to get involved any further, she'll need to know about you.'

Marina nods slowly, realizing she'd been foolish to think she could avoid it.

'In fact, it'll make her job a lot easier if we can give her the full picture,' he coaxes. 'And bear this in mind, she wouldn't have such a successful business if she couldn't be trusted.'

'It's not a question of trust,' Marina replies, 'it's . . .' She shakes her head, unsure for a moment what it *is* a question of. 'Once you tell her what it's really about,' she says, 'she'll obviously look into the whole thing and then maybe she'll be someone else who starts suspecting me. Or Maxim. Or both of us.'

He frowns. 'I didn't,' he reminds her, 'and frankly, I think what she'll be most interested to know is how we – you – are planning to stop Shana from publishing the book when we do find her.'

It's a good question, and one Marina doesn't have a proper answer for yet. She only knows that not knowing where Shana is, and being stalked and baited by dolls along with twisted, accusatory narratives, is something that has got to be made to go away.

'OK,' she says, 'give Brenna everything, including the book, and arrange for us to meet,' and reaching for her mobile as it rings, she feels her heart flip when she sees who it is. Showing Noel the screen she clicks on. 'Hi, Patrick,' she says, 'is everything OK?'

'I'm not sure,' he replies. 'I've read the chapters you sent, but I'll come on to that. I'm ringing because I've had an email . . . I'm guessing it's from Shana, but the sender's address is just a bunch of letters and numbers . . .'

'What does it say?' Marina urges, certain it was going to be the same address as the emails about Georgia.

'You know, I'm not sure I want to read it out loud,' he tells her. 'Why don't I send it to you? Are you alone?'

'Noel's here.'

'OK, I hope you're right to trust him. Call me back when you've got it, or come over if you like. I'm in all evening.'

As she rings off, Marina looks at Noel, not even trying to hide the anxiety building inside her. 'Did you hear any of that?' she asks.

He nods.

Should she tell him about the anonymous emails she's also received?

Not yet; they need to stay focussed on finding out where Shana is, not on what else Shana is doing to try to screw up Marina's marriage.

When Patrick's email arrives, she opens it, and as she reads the words she turns icy cold. It is no wonder Patrick hadn't wanted to say them out loud.

You were lucky to have a rock-solid alibi at the time of Amelia's murder or you could have ended up being found guilty of a crime you didn't commit. Yes, they'd have come after you, be sure of that. Maybe you already are. You know your ex-wife is the killer. Don't you think it's time to persuade her to admit to what she did? If you don't, you'll be complicit in the cover-up.

CHAPTER THIRTY-THREE

'Are you sure?' Toby asks, with a quick glance at the editorial team behind him. 'You're going to tell Della Parrish's agent to take her to another publisher if she insists we drop Fiona Simmons from our list?'

Marina glances up from her computer. Her expression is harsh, her eyes glazed by her troubles. 'I think we've all had enough of Della's self-importance,' she replies, 'not to mention her one-sided rivalry with Fiona. She needs putting in her place and the best way to do that is to call her bluff.'

Toby looks impressed. 'And if she decides to go?'

She raises an eyebrow. 'The way I'm seeing it is that either way we win. Sure her numbers are good, but not good enough to start making hysterical demands about who we do and don't publish.'

He grins. 'You know, this is what I love about you, Marina, you never let yourself be pushed around. Shall I get her agent on the line?'

'I have other calls to make first, so I'll get round to him by the end of the day. With any luck, a spell of silence will convey the message without any shots being fired.' As he starts to leave, she changes tone, making it sound like a passing thought as she consults a file in front of her. 'We're still expecting Georgia back on Monday, I take it? Or has she decided to stay where she is for another week?'

With an *ouch* sort of look, he says, 'As far as I know she's back on Monday. Apparently she has some news, and do you know what I think it is? I reckon "Boo" has popped the question. Or maybe she's preggers.' He claps his hands and gives a little shimmy of delight as he returns to his desk.

Marina's mouth has turned dry; she can barely move.

Echoes from the past when Patrick told her that Amelia was pregnant are so loud and jarring that she's finding it hard to hear anything else, or to force herself past the coincidence.

Except 'Boo', whoever he is, absolutely cannot be Maxim. She isn't going to allow herself to believe it, not even for a minute. Maxim had emailed only this morning saying,

Can't wait to see you all. Will you and the girls go to Glos on Friday evening? If so I'll get a car to bring me from the airport on Sat morning. Provided no delays, I should be with you before midday. Is Ed joining us?

There was nothing in that – *nothing at all* – to suggest he was with Georgia, or that he had any horrible surprises planned for the weekend; but nor is there anything to say he isn't – and doesn't.

No! This . . . *madness* isn't real. It's only Toby guessing at Georgia's news. He doesn't know what it actually is. He's just leapt to a conclusion that apparently makes sense to him.

She looks out to the main office where he's at his desk, speaking to someone on the phone. His back is turned so she can't gauge what kind of call it is: secretive, serious, personal, professional.

She turns away, opens up her emails, and is about to send one to Noel when one arrives from him.

Meeting with Brenna Isaacs at my office, Monday 6 p.m.

OK with you? If so, will send what we have of the book and speak to her before you arrive. N

After giving him the go-ahead, she forces herself to put everything out of her mind so she can focus on her day's commitments. There is much to do: various business strategies to formulate; marketing spends to sign off; publishing dates to review; a foreign rights meeting to organize; an author presentation to attend; Della Parrish's agent to call . . .

She also needs to get back to Patrick about the email he received last night, so she messages to ask if she can come over later, around seven.

'So,' Patrick says, after pouring her a drink and setting a bowl of nuts on the coffee table between them, 'I want to know if it's true. Would you and Maxim have come after me if I hadn't had an alibi?'

Marina's hand freezes mid-air. She stops eating and stares at him.

'Why are you looking at me like that?' he protests. 'It's a perfectly reasonable question. Isn't it?'

'That sounds very like you believe Shana's story,' she cries furiously. She slams down her glass and starts to stand up.

'Hang on, hang on,' he laughs, reaching out to stop her. 'That's not what I said, but you've got to admit that it wasn't until the lawyers dug right into the case that the police found evidence to nail her. So we have to ask ourselves how all those forensic experts missed it the first time around.'

She blinks. 'Because they weren't looking for it,' she reminds him, tightly, 'at least not in Shana's flat.'

He regards her carefully, pulling his lips between his teeth as he waits for her to connect with what he's actually saying.

As she does, her eyes widen with shock. 'You actually do believe it was planted?' she murmurs.

His eyes remain on hers. It's answer enough.

'Don't you see,' he says, sitting forward, 'Shana framed you well and good that night, and she was getting away with it until someone – a lawyer, I guess – makes a call to suggest something might have been overlooked, i.e. Amelia's phone in Shana's flat. Curious that, isn't it? A tip-off after so long, and at the point when things really weren't looking good for you.'

She really doesn't want to utter the next words, but forces herself anyway. 'Maxim would never do something like that,' she protests. She'd never wanted to believe it, had always accepted it when he'd told her it was nonsense.

'To save you, he might. *Might* being the operative word, because obviously I don't know that he did. And your reaction to my suggestion has me more or less convinced that if it did happen – and it's a big *if* – you didn't know anything about it. Which is fine. It was obviously better for you that you didn't. I just can't help wondering where yours truly might be now if they – Maxim's lawyers, I mean – had decided to come after me.'

She gets up, walks across the room and back again. 'Let me get this straight,' she says, 'you *do* think Shana did it, it's just that no one could prove it, so it was arranged for Amelia's phone to be "found" in her flat.'

'Succinctly put and accurate, that is what I think.'

She stares at him in disbelief and bleak dismay. 'You realize, don't you,' she says, 'that what you're saying is Maxim quite probably thought I was guilty so, just in case, he avoided a trial by getting someone to frame Shana?'

Patrick pulls a face. 'What matters is that you got the right result, isn't it?'

Yes, they had, but like this? 'Where the hell would he have got the phone?' she challenges.

He throws out his hands. 'Perhaps it was always there, at Shana's place, and no one planted it at all,' he counters.

'But who, apart from Shana, could have known it was there? And even if she did have it, tell me this, why didn't she get rid of it right away?'

Picking up his wine he says, 'You're asking me questions I have no way of answering, but you were in court, you heard the prosecution case. It had its flaws, I grant you, but in my view the scenario they painted of her retrieving the phone from its hiding place when she thought the danger of her flat being searched was over had some merit. You must agree?'

Yes, of course she did, hadn't she been saying the very same thing to Noel earlier?

There is no other explanation, there simply can't be, unless Shana's suspicions are correct and it was planted there.

It isn't until she's at home later, staring into the darkness with everything spinning around in chaos, that Marina realizes Patrick hadn't actually answered her question. He hadn't said that he thought Maxim believed in her innocence. She knows that shouldn't bother her, that it's probably just something Patrick assumed went without saying, but it's in her head now and she can't get past it.

CHAPTER THIRTY-FOUR

When Maxim arrives at their Cotswolds home just after midday on Saturday, he looks tired, Marina thinks as he hugs her hello, but pleased to see them all. The girls are certainly thrilled to see him, especially when he sets about lavishing them all with gifts from his travels. He doesn't mention his time on Long Island, apart from to say Grandpa is much better and that everyone is looking forward to seeing Ed soon, especially his parents who are already at their summer home. At that, Marina notices the girls exchanging glances and wonders what they're up to, but the moment passes as they remind her that they'd planned to go into Stow to pick up the necessaries for a barbecue later.

Ed fires everything up when the time comes – Maxim had gone upstairs for a lie-down around four, and when Marina went to check on him at six, he was so deeply asleep that she decided not to wake him. Instead, she stood looking at him for a while, loving him so much that it was making the fear racing around in her mind even harder to bear. But she's not going to bring anything up this weekend. The last thing she wants is to spoil his homecoming.

On Sunday morning, as they're strolling down to the pub, Marina gets to find out what the look between Livvy and Sophie had been about, although it comes in quite a roundabout way. Holding her mother back from the others, Sophie slows their walk as she says, quietly, 'Livvy and I have been talking about this quite a lot, and we're wondering . . .' She glances up at Marina, seeming unsure of herself for a moment, so Marina squeezes her arm.

'What are you wondering?' she prompts.

'Well, the thing is, you never talk about what happened to make Grandpa Forster the way he is with you. And we've been thinking . . . I know this might sound weird, but do you reckon there's something we – me and Livvy – could do to, you know, get him to change his mind? Because we're sure, if he really knew you, he'd love you as much as we do. As much as Dad does.'

Marina continues to walk in step, watching Maxim's back as he rambles on ahead with Livvy and Ed, wondering how he might answer this if Sophie were to put it to him. 'Have you ever asked Dad about it?' she counters, waving for the others to go on and not hold the gate.

'Kind of.'

'And what did he say?'

'He just says it's complicated and he's sure something will sort itself out.'

Disappointed, though not surprised that Maxim hasn't ever mentioned this, Marina says, 'Well, it is quite complicated, and it probably isn't a conversation for today, but you're wonderful for wanting to help in some way.'

'We're right though, aren't we?' Sophie says earnestly. 'The reason we hardly ever go to Long Island is because Grandpa has got something against you?'

With a sigh, Marina says, 'You know that Grandpa has his own way of looking at things and he doesn't like it too much if someone disagrees with him.'

Though Sophie leaves it there for the moment, she brings it up again in a slightly different way a few minutes later as they stroll through the village. 'How would you feel,' she says in a tone that makes it clear she's expecting to be told no, 'if Livvy and I went to New York with Ed when he goes?' Before Marina can answer, she rushes on, 'We've already asked him and he says he's sure his parents will be OK with driving us to Long Island too. Honestly, it's got nothing to do with us being mad about him, but of course we are, it's just that we haven't been to the States for ages and it's so lovely at Grandpa's place, and we could learn to sail . . . Think about that. Dad's always saying he's going to teach us, but according to Ed, Uncle Mark is a really good instructor and he and Aunt Cher are going to be there all summer, and there are loads of people around our age . . .'

'Sophie, take a breath,' Marina says gently. 'It's all right. If you want to go to the States and Dad says it's OK, then we'll make it happen.'

Sophie stops and clasps her hands to her face in disbelief. 'Are you serious? Oh, Mum, you are just the best,' and, throwing her arms around her mother, she almost topples them into the river. 'Livs. *Livvy*,' she shouts, but before she can speed off to her sister, Marina holds her back. 'Remember to clear it with Dad first,' she says. 'I don't think he'll have a problem with it, but you need to be sure.'

'Yeah, definitely we'll speak to him first,' and breaking into a heart-grabbing smile, she throws her arms around her mother again. 'He'll say yes, now that you have. I just know it.'

She turns out to be right, Maxim does say yes, and though Marina is going to hate parting with them for the summer, she could hardly have felt more relieved. To her mind it confirms he really has been there this past ten days – he could hardly let the girls go if he hadn't been, it would be bound to come out – and Georgia couldn't have been with him, for much the same reason.

She feels foolish and furious with herself for allowing that stupid email from Shana to have got the better of her the way it did.

For the next hour or more, they sit beneath a parasol in the pub garden, tucking into Sunday roasts and drinking Italian wine, while the girls complain about their boring fizzy elderflower, and chat excitedly about all the things they're going to do on Long Island. Ed is full of who he's going to introduce them to, while Maxim listens and laughs, clearly entertained, but not making any suggestions himself. Marina suspects it's because he doesn't want to make her feel left out, and loves him for it.

When the meal is finally over, he stretches out his long legs and lets his head fall back as he reaches for her hand.

'Oh God, not in public,' Livvy protests.

He laughs and raises Marina's fingers to his lips.

Marina turns to him, about to whisper something, when she catches a glimpse of a woman strolling through the dappled shade along the pavement outside the pub.

Maxim looks round. 'What is it?' he asks.

Marina shakes her head. 'Nothing, I just—'

'Oh no, not again!' Sophie cries in mock horror. 'Hold her down, Dad, before she goes zooming off after some stranger like she did two weekends ago.'

'You should have seen her,' Livvy joins in. 'She sprinted like a mad woman into the Manor Hotel gardens, abandoning us all like we weren't even her children, and Noel had to go and get her back.'

Maxim regards her curiously.

Marina laughs. 'They're exaggerating, as usual,' she scolds. 'I didn't run—'

'You did,' Livvy insists. 'You went into that hotel like someone had shot you from a gun. Didn't she?' She's asking Ed for confirmation.

'I wasn't there,' he reminds her.

'Oh no. I forgot. Well, she did, and it wouldn't have been so bad if it hadn't turned out to be the wrong person. I mean, talk about embarrassing.'

'I didn't catch up with them, so I don't know if it was the wrong person,' Marina points out.

'So who did you think it was?' Maxim asks, his eyes remaining on hers.

Trying to keep it light, she says, 'No one, just someone I . . . used to work with. A long time ago.'

He continues to regard her in a way that tells her he's more curious about this mysterious sprint after an old colleague than she wants him to be. She smiles at him with raised eyebrows, and fortunately he lets the subject drop as friends from a nearby village turn up at that moment and are persuaded to join them for coffee.

As everyone falls into various conversations, Marina does her best to be discreet as she tries to spot the woman again. Between the sun and shade, it's impossible to say if it had been Shana – what is Shana even like these days? As Noel had pointed out, prison must have taken its toll, so the tall, dark-haired woman she'd hared after into the Manor Hotel, and who'd seemed to move with a careless elegance through the trees a few minutes ago, could have been anyone.

Except every instinct she possesses is telling her that she hasn't got it wrong.

'So,' Maxim says, when they're in their room later, packing before returning the girls to school, 'who did you really think it was?'

Managing not to miss a beat as she continues to strip the bed, Marina says, 'I told you, an old colleague. She worked for the company before your time, so you wouldn't know her.'

'But I do know when you're not being straight with me, so, I'll ask you again. Who did you think it was?'

She stops, takes a moment to turn around and lets out a long breath as she says, 'OK, I admit she reminded me of Shana and I apparently overreacted.'

Clearly thrown, he says, 'But how the heck could Shana be in Lower Slaughter when she's in prison?'

She meets his eyes. She has to do this now, there's no avoiding it. 'Apparently she's been released,' she says, 'and I don't know where she is.'

He frowns in bemusement. 'Why on earth would you *want* to know?'

She shakes her head. 'I guess it unnerves me to think of her out there, that we could run into her at any time . . .'

'Put it out of your head,' he instructs. 'I'm not even convinced she's been released, it seems far too soon to me, but even if she has, she's not going to come anywhere near us.'

'How can you be so sure of that?'

'Because everyone knows what she tried to do to you and she won't want to risk being sent back to prison, which is what would happen if she started harassing us. She'll—' He breaks off, muttering under his breath as his mobile rings. He snatches it up, and seeing who it is he says, 'I have to take it.'

She watches the door close behind him but hears him say, 'No, it's not a bad time. Yes, fine, back in one piece. Now tell me what's going on with you.'

She picks up the sheets and begins to fold them. Her head is swimming in all sorts of nonsense again, asking why he hadn't said who was calling, or why he has to speak to them now, in another room. He'd sounded tender and humorous; it was the kind of tone he used with the girls, and her, when in a particularly affectionate mood.

There is no opportunity for her to ask him about it, or – thank God – to talk about Shana again, with Ed and the twins in the car on the drive back, and by the time they're finally home he's already engrossed in all the catching up he needs to do in the coming week.

She can't be sure whether she's sorry or relieved that he seems to have forgotten their conversation about Shana, although she is beyond thankful that she hadn't been forced to tell him about the woman who'd given the girls strawberries at the gates two weeks ago, along with the ghastly doll in prison gear. If he knew about that, if for a single moment he thought anyone had been anywhere near his children with possible malintent, there would be absolute hell to pay. Even worse would be if he found out that Marina hadn't told him about it right away.

So what is she going to do? How is she going to explain what's been happening for the past few weeks and why she's kept it back from him when it's going to mean admitting she had – *has* – suspicions about him?

CHAPTER THIRTY-FIVE

Isn't Georgia's news wonderful?

Marina is staring at the anonymous email with a sickening dread. She has no idea what Georgia's news is, because Georgia hasn't come in today. She's ill, apparently, but will be working from home, catching up on all the reading she has to do, should anyone need to contact her.

To make matters worse, she hasn't called Marina to explain this, which would have been the right thing to do. She spoke to Toby and asked him to pass the message on.

And now this bloody email has arrived with all its mockery and menace.

It is midday, Marina is due to leave any minute for a lunch with the sales team, but first she makes a quick call to Patrick.

'Have you been able to find out yet who that email was from?' she asks, knowing he'd understand she means the one that told him to consider himself lucky that no one (she and Maxim, or maybe just Maxim and his lawyers) hadn't come after him for Amelia's murder.

With a sigh, he says, 'To be honest, I don't know how to go about it, without asking someone in our IT department, and I'm not keen to go that route.'

She has the same problem. 'It can only have come from her,' she states. 'Have you tried replying?'

'Do you want me to?'

She thinks about it, not sure what good it would do, if it would even get through without being blocked or bounced back. 'Give it a try,' she decides, 'and ask her . . . Ask her where she is, and can you meet up to talk?'

There's a pause before drawing out the word in a long thread of doubt, he says, 'Okaaaay. And if she agrees to see me?'

'We'll go together.' Is that the right answer? She has no time to be certain. 'Sorry, I have to ring off now,' she says, 'but I'll speak to you later.'

She's on her way out of the door when Maxim rings, sounding his usual breezy self as he says, 'Seems everything's gone crazy during my absence. It's making me feel kind of indispensable, but it's also screwing up my plans to spend every evening this week with my wife. I'll send over my schedule and please try not to hate me when you see that I have to be in Paris for the next two nights and Milan on Wednesday. I'm on my way home now to pack a bag.'

Though she's used to him hopping over to various European cities at short notice, she comes very close to objecting this time. She doesn't want him to go away again so soon. She needs him here, to know where he is and who he's with. Of course his schedule would tell her that, but can it really be trusted? 'If I were able to get away, I'd come with you,' she says, hoping it's what he wants to hear, 'but I've got a pretty full week myself. In fact, I have to rush now, but call me when you get to Paris?'

'Of course. I'm going to try not to miss you, but that's something I'm not particularly good at.'

With a smile she says, 'Same here. Love you and don't

forget to message the girls when you can. You know how they always want to know where we are.'

With a laugh he says, 'If we weren't in touch for days on end, they probably wouldn't notice, but don't worry. I'll be sure to text or FaceTime.'

The next few hours both race and drag for Marina, depending on how well she's able to focus on the demands at hand. The most difficult moments are those when she's exchanging emails with Georgia. They start off on a friendly note, Marina saying she hopes Georgia had a lovely holiday and will feel better soon, and Georgia replying that she had a fabulous time, thanks, and is really gutted about not being able to come in today. *Hope all's good with you.* From there they only deal with work issues, and Marina doesn't ask what Georgia's news is. She can wait to find that out – and she isn't going to allow herself to wonder either if Maxim is actually with her and not in Paris.

If the schedule he'd sent her is false, his PA would have to know about it and, even in her near-paranoid state, Marina can't believe in that level of collusion and deception.

She leaves the office just after five thirty, and by ten past six she's pulling up in a taxi outside Noel's office, while talking to Patrick on the phone.

'Nothing yet,' he tells her, 'but I haven't had a "return to sender", so I guess that means it's gone through.'

'Is there a way to find out if she's read it?'

'No idea. You know I'm not techie enough for that. The book though . . . We haven't actually discussed that yet, so what the fuck?'

Great question. 'I'm sorry,' she says, 'we'll have to talk about it another time. I need to go into a meeting now, but let me know if you hear anything.'

A few minutes later she's entering one of Noel's plush meeting rooms on the second floor of a concierge-managed block in Chelsea, where Brenna Isaacs, the private investigator, is waiting. She's a stout, serious-faced woman, probably in her forties, with neatly cut auburn hair and piercing grey eyes. When she smiles it's a transformation that makes Marina blink; she hadn't expected it to be quite so lovely.

'It's a pleasure to meet you, Mrs Forster,' Brenna Isaacs says. 'May I call you Marina?'

'Of course.'

'And you must call me Brenna.' Her gesture for Marina to join the conference table next to Noel shows that she's used to being in charge of a situation, and Marina decides she appreciates that.

As Noel passes around drinks, Brenna studies her laptop. 'OK,' she says, looking up and regarding Marina with unabashedly assessing eyes, 'I've gone over everything Noel sent me and I want to thank you for trusting me with it. I can quite understand why you're concerned, because as I see it she's gearing up to fight the case again, possibly in the court of public opinion, unless she's able to conjure up evidence, or a witness, to prove her claim that the mobile phone was planted. If she can, then we could be looking at the quashing of her conviction, even a retrial.'

Marina inwardly reels. Even the word is anathema to her, never mind the reality.

'However,' Brenna continues, 'if she does have proof, it begs the question why hasn't she already produced it?' Without waiting for an answer, she says, 'Am I right in thinking that – as far as you're concerned – there is no such evidence or witness?'

Marina shakes her head. 'I can't see how it's possible, unless she's going to pay someone to lie.'

'Or, unless someone has come to her in more recent times to admit they put the phone in her flat?'

Marina's heart turns over.

'I'm sure you must have considered the fact that your husband or his lawyers might have had something to do with it?'

Marina opens her mouth to answer but no words come out.

Seeming unconcerned by that, Brenna says, 'My next observation is that this book is probably a bluff. In other words, she's no more certain now than she ever was about the phone being planted, but she's hoping this method of intimidation will force you into acts of self-incrimination that could end up proving her case for her. What's your answer to that?'

Swallowing hard, Marina clenches her hands as she says, 'She's certainly capable of playing that sort of game. She'll even be enjoying it, I'm sure.'

Brenna regards her fixedly, as though evaluating how unnerved she really is by this unusual mode of attack, or maybe she's thinking something else entirely, it isn't possible to tell. 'OK,' Brenna suddenly states, 'our first goal is to find her and I'm glad to say I've made some progress since Noel and I last spoke.'

Marina's insides seem to fall away from her as the PI draws an iPad from her large leather bag.

'You were right,' she says, 'to connect E.L. Stalwood with Stella Wood, who's been known as Ella Neavis since her marriage to Tom Neavis, a Glasgow-based artist, in 2016. His death was registered in 2018 and, soon after that, in the same year, Ella returned to the south of England. I haven't been able to establish when she first made contact with Shana Morales, but the address in Dorset that Shana Morales gave to the probation service at the time of her release is the same as the last known address for Ella. The property is in Ella's father's name, Graham Stockton. The man himself is in a nursing home near Dorchester and the house – Sodeham Mill – is not, at first glance, showing any signs of occupancy.'

Marina's heart is beating fast as she tries to take it all in. 'You've been there?' she asks, surprised.

'I went yesterday – I was down that way visiting a friend, so we went for a drive. It took us some time to find the place, it really is at the back end of beyond; no actual road leading to it, just an overgrown track and the windows of the cottage – mill – are shuttered closed. There are a few outbuildings, all derelict.' She hands over her iPad to show the shots she'd taken of what had clearly once been a picture-book greystone cottage, but is now overrun by weeds and brambles at the front. At the back, a small table and chairs have been placed beneath low hanging branches, and a pathway of flat stones leads down to the stream.

'Is this in use?' Noel asks, pointing at the stable door of the cottage. 'It looks quite new.'

'It's certainly a recent addition, or replacement,' Brenna replies, 'and it's probably safe to say that it's being used by whoever is going in and out these days.' She leans over to flick the photographs on, and stops at the shot of a green recycling box. It contains an assortment of bottles – wine, milk, water, juice – and piled next to it are some newspapers, with a close-up of the date on the top one.

Marina glances at Noel as he announces with some feeling, 'That's just over a week ago.'

Brenna nods. 'My best guess is that this place is being visited to satisfy the probation service that licence conditions are being met, by both women. It's interesting that they committed very similar crimes, albeit some years apart, and both are claiming their innocence. Ella seems to have given up on it now, at least I haven't been able to find anything recent about her, but clearly we know that's not true of Shana. Anyway, it's possible they're going about other lives in a different location, maybe with other names. As far as I can tell, E.L. Stalwood is only being used for the submission of this book, but I'm still looking into it.

'The recycling tells us that someone has been there quite recently, but without twenty-four-hour surveillance there's no way of knowing who it is, or how often they come and go. However, I did locate a local shop about a mile and a half from the cottage where milk is sold by the bottle – an unusual thing these days – and when I asked if anyone ever came in from Sodeham Mill, I was told that "old Graham's daughter" stops by once in a while.'

'Meaning Stella? Ella?' Marina prompts.

The investigator grimaces. 'It's possible, but apparently there are two daughters, and the young man I spoke to didn't know either of their names. However, I'm working on the assumption it's Ella, and I believe it's highly likely she'll lead us to Shana once we find out where she actually lives.'

'Why do you think that's proving so difficult?' Noel asks. 'I mean, Stella – Ella – doesn't have anything to hide, does she? Isn't her name on the electoral roll, or something?'

'It could be, if she's changed it from Ella Neavis; and actually she does have something to hide.'

Noel frowns; Marina says, 'Shana?'

Brenna nods. 'For whatever reason, it seems Shana is flying below the radar and Ella is helping her, so as a next step I recommend stationing a couple of our surveillance people at the mill to find out who's visiting. We can then put a tail on that person to track where they go. I'll give you rates for that, if you're interested in pursuing it.'

'Yes, yes, I am,' Marina assures her.

'In which case I'll activate it immediately.' Brenna quickly taps something into her laptop before fixing her eyes on Marina again. 'I'm not going to ask you to comment any further on the actual detail of the claims in this book, but I'd like to know what course of action you intend to take when we catch up with Shana Morales. And we will, you can be certain of that.'

Unnerved by the directness of the question, Marina turns to Noel. *Was this woman afraid she might be planning to do away with Shana?*

Noel says, 'I hope it doesn't sound rude, but once we know where she is, we can probably take it from there.'

Brenna's high-wattage smile makes a return. 'That's fine,' she says. 'I'll be in touch as soon as there's more to report. Would you like me to copy you both in?'

Marina says, 'Yes, I think so, but before you go, do you have someone trying to trace the E.L. Stalwood emails?'

'I do indeed, and will report on that as soon as there's some news. I'm afraid these things can take longer than we might like. We used to call it a needle in a haystack. Today we call it an @ on Twitter, although it's not generally quite so polite.'

Surprising Marina, Noel says, 'Marina's ex-husband, Patrick, has received a message from a different address, but we're pretty sure it's Shana. Shall we forward it to you?'

'Yes please.'

He turns to Marina.

'I'll do it right away,' she says, and picks up her phone to do so, feeling thankful that she doesn't have to mention anything at this stage about the emails she's received from the same address. They can deal with the Georgia business when they know for certain who's behind the messages.

After Brenna has left, Marina sits quietly, staring at the seat she's vacated, turning it all over in her mind, trying to straighten it out, while Noel quietly watches her. 'She asked a good question,' she says, looking at him, 'what am I going to do when we find her?'

He raises an eyebrow as he says, 'I know what I'd like to do, but why don't we cross that bridge when we come to it? More importantly right now – brace yourself – I've received another chapter which I haven't yet shown to Brenna.'

Marina's insides jar as she stares at him.

'It's different to the rest,' he says. 'It's more . . . I guess you could say, direct.'

'In what way?'

'You need to read it.'

She waits, watching his fingers on the laptop keyboard as he calls up the email. 'Can I stay here while I read it?' she asks. 'Or do you have to be somewhere?'

'I can be late,' he replies and, pressing send, he leaves her to read the latest submission while he goes to refresh their drinks.

CHAPTER THIRTY-SIX

That Girl by E.L. Stalwood

Something Katie never allowed herself to think about during the long, lonely years Christy spent paying for a crime she didn't commit, is what she would do if Christy ever found a way to prove her innocence. It's true enough to say that it gave her nightmares from time to time, not to mention witching-hour terrors, but during the day she was always quick to banish her fears to the place she kept poor Amy; the bottomless black hole that serves as her soul.

Then the day arrived when she found out Christy was no longer in prison and she knew, in that deep, dark moral vacuum of hers, that she was facing the beginning of the end. One way or another, Christy was going to clear her name and – when she did – Katie would be exposed for the brutal killer that she actually was – that she *is*.

Katie worried and fretted and tore herself apart, trying to come up with ways of getting to Christy before Christy can get to her. But even if she managed it, what then? The truth can't be changed, or erased, or ignored any longer, and they both know that Christy has right on her side.

However, Katie has decided not to give up without a fight. She even believes in a deluded part of herself that she can win, which is a little sad when she already knows deep down that she has lost Johan. He might still be living with her, going through all the motions, but he's in love with another woman. He's even planning to move his children out of their school, to take them out of the country, away from their mother's shame. He wants them to have the life that he, and they, would already be living if it weren't for Katie.

It might be comforting for Katie to know that actually he won't be allowed to fulfil his plans, because the part he played in Christy's wrongful conviction will soon come to light. So, his hope of starting afresh with a new wife and the baby they are expecting in a few months will never come to pass.

Those poor teenagers, with all their security and privilege, their hopes and expectations of the future, they've done nothing to deserve the parents they have. But let's be clear about this, and fair, Christy never did anything to deserve what happened to her either.

CHAPTER THIRTY-SEVEN

Marina's face is ashen.

A baby?

Is that Georgia's news?

Is that why she didn't show up at the office again today? Morning sickness?

She wants to speak, to say it's all lies, that Shana is evil through and through, manipulative and calculating to Machiavellian levels, but she can't push the words through the tightness in her throat.

Noel says, gently, 'I'm sorry you had to read that. I guess using the present tense as much as she has makes it seem more . . . current, more *here*. But the main thing is it still doesn't prove anything.'

It doesn't, but Marina isn't sure it even needs to.

She continues to stare at her iPad, no longer reading, only trying to make her mind function past the shock.

'She's doing this to fuck with you,' Noel persists. 'Pull back from it—'

Interrupting she says, 'There's something you need to see,' and, calling up the anonymous emails she'd received about Georgia, she hands her iPad over for him to read.

It takes him only moments, and almost the same amount of time passes before he finally lifts his eyes back to hers. He looks shocked, sorry, confused. 'Why haven't you said anything about this before?' he asks. 'Did Shana send them? It has to be her.'

She nods. 'They're from the same address as the email Patrick received, so I'm sure it is her.'

'Obviously, it's not true,' he states, 'I mean about Maxim and—'

'I think it's highly possible Georgia is pregnant,' she interrupts, her voice strangely steady, though flat. 'I've wondered for some time if she and Shana have been collaborating in some way. It's hard to think otherwise when confronted with this.'

His eyes remain on hers, bleak and regretful, as he says, 'You're going to have to talk to Maxim now, you do realize that?'

She knows he's right, there really is no avoiding it any more, but it makes her feel so wretched inside, so afraid of what it's going to lead to. Her voice is hardly more than a whisper as she says, 'He's in Paris tonight. Or I assume he is. He's not due back until Thursday and this isn't a conversation we can have over the phone.'

'No, it isn't,' he agrees. He waits and, when she doesn't speak again, he says, 'Can I make a couple of suggestions?'

She moves her eyes to his, desperate for something, anything that might guide her through this nightmare.

'First, I think Brenna needs to know about these emails. Second, it might be a good idea to let Maxim read the book before you talk.'

She agrees to both, and drops her head into her hands as Noel cancels his plans for the evening and goes to pour them both another drink. There's still a lot of talking to be done, outcomes to assess and actions to be decided, and she's never felt more thankful for his friendship in her life.

In truth, he's the only real friend she's had since the good times with Shana, so many years ago. She has been too afraid to trust anyone since, apart from Maxim, and she only has to look at how that's turning out to realize that her instincts about people, even those she loves, are not to be depended on.

CHAPTER THIRTY-EIGHT

Georgia is pregnant.

This is the news she's been dying to break and now, here she is, in the middle of the office, radiant and joyful as she sucks up the congratulations being showered all over her. She is so beautiful that Marina can barely look at her, although it isn't her beauty that is making it hard, it's imagining her with Maxim, their shared happiness and intimacy, hearing what they might have agreed about her . . . The speculation and dread are half killing her.

Of course she'd tried to join in with the well-wishers (how foolish that must have made her look in Georgia's eyes), but it seems she'd come across as sincere, for no one had looked at her askance when she'd hugged Georgia, not even Georgia herself.

Does Maxim know she's making her announcement today?

Is he the father?

Is this some cruel, despicable game they're playing to make her doubt herself, to run her around in so many circles that she can no longer see what's real and what isn't? Is the plan to force her back to the therapist, who'll have no choice but to restrain her for her own – and everyone else's – good?

And yet, in spite of everything, she finds it almost impossible to make herself accept the idea of Maxim and Georgia, just as she'd once found it all but impossible to believe the idea of Patrick and Amelia.

Christy and Johan.

Rob and Amy.

The madness of history repeating itself, the appalling synchronicity of the worst of memories, playing out in the present, is doing horrible things to her mind. How on earth could Shana make it happen? She couldn't, is the answer, not without Georgia's help – and here is Georgia, pregnant . . . Except, is she really? No one had ever really known the truth about Amelia . . .

She continues to listen as everyone chatters and laughs; there is no mention of the father, at least not by name, it's only Georgia saying, 'We're so thrilled.' Or, 'We don't mind if it's a boy or a girl.' Or, 'Yes, we're going to be moving in together; not sure when, but soon,' that seems to acknowledge there is such a person.

Marina closes her office door, needing to pull herself together before something inside her gives way completely and she does something everyone will regret, her most of all.

She hasn't spoken to Maxim since reading the latest chapter last night. Apparently he was out for dinner when she rang, but he'd emailed later to say he'd been in touch with the girls, who hadn't got back to him yet. He'd finished with, *Going to be in meetings all day tomorrow so I'll try you and them again in the evening.*

Bisous.

His use of the affectionate French sign-off had made her want to weep as she thought of all the wonderful summers they'd spent in Provence over the years, their attempts to speak the language making the girls hoot with laughter – or cringe, depending on what was said, and who was there.

Somehow she gets through the rest of the day, constantly aware of Georgia at her desk, tanned and flushed and apparently sharing the wonderful news with her authors each time one rings. Marina can't remember ever feeling so isolated or trapped. It's as though she's caught between two worlds, the past and the present, and she has no idea how to make herself move forward into what might come next.

Finally Georgia is ready to leave for the day, and comes to put her head round Marina's door.

'Thanks for allowing me some slack today,' she says, grimacing and twinkling in a way that Marina can imagine appealing to Maxim. 'I promise I'll be properly back on it tomorrow. God knows, I need to be. There's so much catching up to do.'

Summoning a smile, Marina says, 'It's good to have you back. It seems you had a wonderful break.'

Georgia's eyes come to hers and Marina's heart turns over. There it is – the look. The triumph, the tiniest of tiny smiles.

She says nothing, simply feels the blood drain from her face.

As if nothing unusual has happened, Georgia gives her a wave and sets off across the office.

Marina stays where she is, watching her new nemesis as she waits for the lift while tapping a message into her phone. She is reminded of the time Amelia stood outside a lift, suggesting that they might go to Shana's promotion party together. Marina had rebuffed her, had told her to make sure she was on top of the video shoot planned for the next day. The shoot that had included hundreds of dolls.

Marina can hardly bear her own thoughts, her tearing fear and fury, her need to stop this without knowing how to. After Georgia has gone, she considers going to search her desk and computer; maybe she would have done if other people hadn't still been around.

She needs to speak to Maxim, but she rings Noel instead.

'Holy fuck,' he swears, when she tells him Georgia's news. 'I really didn't think . . . Did she actually say it's his?'

'She didn't have to. If you'd seen the way she looked at me . . .'

'Remind me when he's back.'

'Thursday. I'm not sure if he's actually in Paris . . .'

'There's one way to find out. Stay where you are, I'm going to try his number. The ringtone will tell us whether or not he's in this country.'

As Marina waits, she struggles hard not to cry. It is all getting too much for her. She has no idea what she's going to do if he's still in the country. It will confirm everything and she just doesn't feel ready for it. She never will be.

'Right,' Noel declares, coming back on the line, 'he's definitely abroad, which I guess is good news.'

Almost sobbing with relief, she puts a hand to her head as she says, 'Did you speak to him?'

'No, I just waited for the ringtone.'

'He'll know you've called.'

'I'll deal with that if he rings back. Now, tell me, have you looked at Brenna Isaacs's email yet?'

Thrown, Marina goes to her inbox. 'I didn't know there was one. When did it arrive?'

'About fifteen minutes ago. I thought it was why you were calling. Give it a read and get back to me when you're done.'

Marina finds and opens it. Her heart is thudding so hard it's like a lead weight trying to burst out of her chest. How much more can she take?

Hi Marina,

We've had quite a productive day at our end with some results I hadn't expected so soon.

I drove to the nursing home near Dorchester this morning to try and speak to Graham Stockton (owner of Sodeham Mill, and father of Stella Wood). Happily, in spite of being incapacitated physically, he does not have dementia and was willing to chat.

The daughter who visits him and the mill is indeed Stella, aka Ella. Apparently she lives with her husband, Oscar Wiley, near a place called Birdlip, about 6 miles from Cheltenham – I have an address. Stockton hasn't ever met Wiley, but he's sure that his other son-in-law, Tom Frobisher, has. (He gave me Frobisher's number, also Ella's, but I'm holding off contacting anyone until I've spoken to you.) Tom Frobisher's wife – aka Ella's sister – is apparently no longer with us. She died back in 2017, but her husband, Tom, 'a good man' says Stockton, has stayed in touch. Stockton talked some about his granddaughter, who I assumed to be the girl Ella (Stella) was convicted of murdering. He spoke as if she was still with us, not as if it had happened over twenty-five years ago, but maybe in his mind time no longer has the same meaning.

I've already sent someone to check out the address in Birdlip. (Photos attached.) It's a good five miles west of the main village, and seems to be a rundown farm with a number of outbuildings. Though it appears to be an isolated place, it has reasonably easy access to the A417 and M5.

No sightings yet of anyone coming or going from any of the properties, but none of the mailboxes lock so my operative was able to look inside and found an EDF bill addressed to Oscar Wiley. No other letters.

Please call me at your convenience so we can discuss our next steps.

Brenna

Marina quickly opens the photographs. Just as Brenna had said, they show a cluster of old farm buildings, mostly constructed in stone, with two open-sided barns, a mobile home and an assortment of rusting machinery cluttering up the grassy yard. The main house is at the heart of it all, three storeys high, weathered and missing roof tiles, but it could be occupied. It's hard to tell through the scaffolding that masks most of its frontage.

She sits back in her chair, not sure what to make of it. Is this where Shana is staying, with Ella Wiley and her husband? It's about half an hour's drive from Lower Slaughter, so not exactly local to her and Maxim's Cotswold home, but not that far either.

She's about to read Brenna's email again when another message turns up from the detective addressed to both her and Noel.

I've just had a voicemail from Tom Frobisher. (He got my number from Graham Stockton who rang to tell him about my visit.) He lives in London and is happy to tell us anything we'd like to know about Ella Wiley and what she did to his wife and daughter. (He's assumed

that's why I'm in touch. I can put him right when I call back if you like, just let me know.)
I could see him alone if you prefer.
Brenna

Marina's mobile rings.

'What do you say?' Noel asks. 'Should we go to see this guy?'

Marina is thinking about what Stella – Ella – might have done to Tom Frobisher's wife, who was clearly the mother of the niece Stella had been found guilty of murdering.

'Yes,' she says, 'I'll ask Brenna to set it up.'

CHAPTER THIRTY-NINE

It turns out Tom Frobisher is so keen to see them that by eight o'clock that evening Marina, Noel and Brenna are being served drinks in his Hammersmith riverfront cottage. It smells of lemony polish and old furniture, and is far larger inside than it appears from the waterside walkway.

The man himself has to be well into his sixties. His hair is thin and grey, and his cobalt blue eyes at once gentle and wary. Marina detects an air of sadness about him, hardly surprising when he's lost both his daughter and his wife. It doesn't appear from the photographs dotted about the room that he's married again.

Once they're all seated, he turns his attention to Marina and speaks softly as he says, 'As soon as Ms Isaacs here told me you were coming, I had a fairly good idea of what this was going to be about.'

Thrown, Marina says, 'You know me?'

'I know of you,' he replies, 'and I have done for many years. To explain, I used to be a publisher myself, mostly tech stuff, magazines and books. I had a small company based in Kent until I sold it, back in 2016, but while I was still working I used to subscribe to all the industry magazines. That's how I know something of your story. Of course, the business with Shana Morales was in the mainstream media as well. My wife Jayne and I only took an interest because of Ms Morales. As you no doubt know, although I think it was before your time, she published Stella's book about our daughter's murder.'

Marina's heart contracts. Though his tone is matter-of-fact, she can tell how much it pains him to say the words.

'Have you ever met Stella?' he asks.

Noting how he doesn't refer to her as Ella, Marina says, 'Not in person. We had a short correspondence by email nine or ten years ago when I passed on her second book.'

He nods vaguely, as if hardly listening. 'There's much I could tell you about her,' he says, 'but I've no idea if she kept in touch with Shana after the book came out, and I think that's what you want to know.' He reaches out a shaky hand and picks up his drink. 'I never read it,' he continues, 'but I know she used it to try and blame Jayne, my wife, all over again for what had happened to our daughter, Zoe. She even managed to get the investigation reopened for a while . . . It was much like the first one because it was still a case of her word against Jayne's. There was nowhere else to go with it, so they shut it down again.'

As he falls silent, Marina can feel her insides knotting. It is so similar to what happened between her and Shana, her word against Shana's. Had she, Marina, left the bronze on Shana's desk, or hadn't she? Had Shana taken Marina's car on the night of the killing, or had Marina driven it back to the office and home again without being noticed?

Frobisher's eyes are unfocussed as he continues to speak. 'Jayne wasn't in the house when Zoe was strangled and drowned in the bath. Stella was with her, but the way Stella tells it is that she was the one who came in to find Jayne in the bathroom trying to revive Zoe after losing her mind.'

He rubs his eyes and looks so weary all of a sudden that Marina feels compelled to say, 'If you don't want to go on—'

'The first time around,' he continues over her, 'the police believed Jayne, and Stella was sent to prison. She served thirteen years before she was released on licence. After the book and all the heartache she caused us with it, she moved to Scotland . . . I wish she'd stayed there. If she had, Jayne might still be with us.'

Startled by that, Marina allows several moments to pass as he composes himself. Then she says, gently, 'What happened when she came back?'

He nods, as though he'd expected the question. 'She moved in with her father for a while. I know you've already met Graham,' he says to Brenna. 'He's a good man, kind to a fault, and couldn't see in Stella what the rest of us saw. To be honest, I don't know what he really believes happened to Zoe, I only know that he's never been able to blame either of his girls. I suppose he just shuts it out, doesn't allow himself to think about it, but I do know that losing his granddaughter broke his heart.'

He seems lost in the tragedy, no longer aware of his visitors or the chattering voices of people passing outside. Eventually he looks up and his rheumy eyes move to each of them in turn. 'She killed Jayne,' he says. 'She killed my wife, her own sister.'

Marina's heart jolts as she looks at Noel and Brenna, who are clearly equally as thrown.

'It didn't happen quickly,' Frobisher continues. 'She took her time over it, and did it in a very clever way, some might say. She kept sending Jayne messages – texts, emails, letters – asking her what sort of mother killed her own daughter and let her sister pay for it? They just kept coming, phone calls too. I contacted the police, and a lawyer, I even tried speaking to her, but she wouldn't stop. It was like she was obsessed. She wasn't going to let it go until Jayne confessed, she said. In the end it drove Jayne mad. She couldn't stand any more, so she took her own life.'

Marina stares at him in shock as she realizes this could very well be what Shana is trying to do to her.

'Of course,' he continues sadly, 'in Stella's eyes that proved Jayne could no longer live with the guilt of sending her sister to prison. She didn't even mention Zoe. It was all about her.'

It's almost ten o'clock by the time Marina arrives home, tired, and still troubled by the interview with Frobisher, and the clash of similarities between the two cases. Somehow she manages to sit chatting with Ed for a while about his plans to take the girls to New York at the end of the month. She wants to say they can't go, that she needs them to be at home with her for the summer, but she has no reason to block the trip now. They would never forgive her, and maybe this was all part of Maxim's plan to get them away from her.

Maxim.

Has he rung, or messaged?

She hasn't checked her phone since leaving Tom Frobisher's and she doesn't have the energy to start panicking about him and Georgia now, although she can barely think of anything else. It's becoming all tangled up in Frobisher's story about Stella, whirling and snaking around her head until she has no idea how to separate them.

'Looks like we now know where Shana got her idea

about the book from,' Noel had commented during the taxi ride from Hammersmith. As Brenna lived two streets from Frobisher, she'd said goodbye on the waterfront with a promise to be in touch first thing in the morning.

'You think she's trying to drive me to suicide?' Marina responded disbelievingly, and yet, because she knew Shana, she did believe it.

'She could only do that if you were guilty.'

Marina turned to look at him, alarmed and puzzled. 'Does that mean you think Jayne Frobisher killed her daughter?' she countered.

He shook his head. 'That's not what I said. We don't really know anything about the Frobishers, or what happened to their daughter, but if Shana is copycatting Stella's actions with this book and the coercive emails, we need to let her know that she isn't going to succeed.'

'No, she sure as hell isn't,' Marina agreed, and she'd felt certain of it when she'd said it. Now, as she gets ready for bed, and everything begins to overwhelm her again – Georgia's baby, Maxim's extended stay in the States, his sudden trip to Paris, her dread of speaking to him, Stella's awful revenge on her sister, *That Girl*, the mobile phone and the encroaching horror of being accused of Amelia's murder again – she knows she is getting dangerously close to the edge.

CHAPTER FORTY

That Girl by E.L. Stalwood

Christy's release felt like a spring day in the middle of winter; a long-awaited cure for terrible pain; a gift of endless fresh air after year upon year of smothering injustice.

There was much to be done, so many wrongs to be righted, and she could hardly wait to get started.

Her very good friends – the Woolleys – were waiting to whisk her from the prison to the safety and welcome of their home, to settle her into a new and wholly unrestricted routine. They were eager to help her in any way they could, even to clear her name if it proved possible, for they believed wholeheartedly in her innocence.

It was probably only a few days after Christy's first glorious steps back into freedom that her friends revealed some information they'd been keeping from her until now.

And what a shocking and completely game-changing piece of information it was.

As soon as she realized what it could mean for her, for them all, Christy found herself overcome by the pent-up emotions she'd carried through the worst years of her life. Not for the first time since her friends got back in touch, just before her parole hearing, she felt as though the gods were finally smiling down on her in the shape of these two very special people.

Through them fate, that marvellous and capricious manipulator of life's events, had been working away in the background all this time, putting everything into place ready for her return.

Although the Woolleys were clearly committed to helping her, they insisted that the means of achieving her aims must be undertaken with great care and patience, as no one wanted to risk any missteps when so much was at stake. Christy wholeheartedly agreed. Everything had seemed to happen so fast at the time of her arrest, had spun so irrevocably out of her control almost before she'd known what was happening. She wasn't going to let that happen again.

As the days and months passed, she realized that one thing hadn't changed since she'd left prison: she still thought about Katie all the time. It was like a curse that she couldn't throw off, and yet it was also a powerful driving force.

She had little difficulty imagining what was going on in Katie's head. A guilty person will always fall prey to fear and paranoia, especially when they find out that their past is about to catch up with them.

Katie would most assuredly be terrified by now. As for Johan, Christy was less certain of his state of mind, although she was inclined to think he might not know anything yet or he'd surely have tracked her down weeks ago. Katie, in her deluded and pathetic way, could be trying to protect him, for she, more than anyone, knew that he had a lot to be afraid of – and his ways of dealing with people were decisive and effective, as Christy knew to her cost.

Though Christy wasn't, by nature, a vindictive person, she had no problem making an exception in Katie and Johan's case, for they deserved everything that was coming to them. It had been a slow process so far – at least slower than Christy would have liked – but they had now reached the point where Katie had learned about the child Johan was expecting with another woman. It was so redolent of what happened all those years ago with Rob and Amy that even Christy felt shocked by Karma's mischievous ways.

As far as she was aware Johan hadn't yet admitted to his treacherous affair, but he will soon, because he'll have to and the conversation will begin the way so many of these conversations do. 'Darling, we need to talk,' or something along those lines. And maybe Katie will hit back with the appalling secret she's been hiding for even longer than they've been married.

She's never been certain that her children are his.

That's correct, dear reader, Katie has never been certain about the paternity of the babies she gave birth to a few short weeks after leaving prison.

They could as easily be Rob's, conceived during the dark and turbulent days when Katie tried to repair her marriage. Poor Rob was in a very bad place at the time, so perhaps it wasn't any wonder that Katie, who was in prison when she found out she was pregnant, decided the child could only be Johan's? He was the one whose family was worth billions, he had the power to help her escape a murder charge, so of course choosing him was the right thing to do.

Almost fourteen years later, and there sat Katie atop the mountain of privilege and falsehoods she'd concocted, still trying to tell herself that she was unreachable, invincible, when she knew deep down that it was turning volcanic. Her marriage couldn't survive, nor could Johan's new relationship, nor any of his plans for after he'd dumped Katie. Once the truth came out about the mobile phone and how he got it into Christy's flat, it would all be over.

Justice would finally be served.

And how on earth could Katie be a mother from a prison cell?

CHAPTER FORTY-ONE

Marina is sitting with her face in her hands, tears of helplessness leaking through her fingers as she struggles to contain herself. This awful, vile chapter is just about destroying her. She hardly knows what to do next, is paralysed with dread, can only sit waiting for Noel to ring her back. *Don't show anything to Maxim yet*, he'd said in his covering message. *I'll call in next ten minutes.*

As if she would show it to Maxim. She'd rather die than let this poison anywhere near him.

Did Noel's caution mean he was worried she might not be certain about the twins?

What could she say to persuade him they were Maxim's when she suddenly feels uncertain herself? Until a few weeks ago, she'd had no memory of trying again with Patrick, but apparently she did, and now *this*. But she knew she'd never have taken a conscious decision to claim she was pregnant by Maxim if she'd ever been unsure.

Of course she hadn't; it had never happened. This was more trickery and malicious guesswork on Shana's part, designed to undermine confidence as well as memory.

The only truth is Georgia's pregnancy.

Not the worst truth of all, but God knows it's bad enough.

Her phone rings and, seeing it's Noel, she snatches it up.

'Where are you?' he asks.

'Still at home, thank God. I wouldn't want anyone to see me like this. I can hardly believe . . . The things she said. Noel, you have to know it's not true about the twins, I swear it isn't, but if Maxim sees it—'

'Listen to me,' he breaks in urgently, 'it doesn't sound as though you've seen the latest email from Brenna. Shana's at the farm near Birdlip, or she was last night. I'm coming to collect you, so clear your calendar. Brenna will meet us there.'

Throughout the journey, Marina's insides are continuously knotting and unravelling in overwhelming onslaughts of nerves made worse by her attempts to rehearse what she is going to say and do when – if – she comes face to face with Shana. She has no clear idea yet of how to approach the situation, except she knows she can't allow Shana to control the narrative any longer. She needs to turn it all around, to take the initiative so that she is no longer behaving like a victim, reacting to everything Shana throws at her as if she's some sort of punchbag that has no means of hitting back. She must find a way to fight this, to discredit Shana and her sick, monstrous efforts to destroy everything and everyone that makes up Marina's world.

Part of her – no, all of her – wishes she could get Shana out of their lives once and for all. To make sure she never speaks to anyone about anything ever again.

There is so much to deal with, to feel afraid of, that it's close to impossible to decide what to prioritize: the book, her marriage . . .

She waits until Noel is taking yet another phone call and opens up her instant messaging app. She sees that Patrick is online, but needs to be certain it's him before going ahead.

Patrick: *Of course it's me, who else would it be?*

A girlfriend, the cleaner, a colleague – how would she know?

She types: *I need to ask you something. Back when our marriage fell apart, was there ever a time we decided to give it another go? I'm talking about after I got together with Maxim. Probably in January some time.*

He takes an unforgivably long time to respond, during which she feels herself dying a thousand deaths. *You won't have forgotten that I was drinking heavily then, so if you're referring to the time you thought you ought to try and save me, I suppose you could say we had a go at making it work.*

Her heart contracts so harshly that she actually winces. *When was it exactly?*

I can't give you dates, if that's what you're after. It didn't last long before you gave up on me. Not that I blame you, just stating a fact.

Bracing herself, she makes herself tap in the next question. *Did we sleep together during that time?*

You mean in the same bed, or sex?

Sex.

Honest answer? No idea. What's going on, why are you asking about this now?

Having no intention of answering, she sits for a moment, still not remembering anything, but desperately trying to. It's like trying to navigate roads she's never travelled, with no map or compass, only vague recognitions of old signposts that end up leading her nowhere.

She looks down as he messages again. *Where are you?*

Without thinking: *On the way to see Shana.*

Are you serious? Where is she? Hope you're not going alone.

Noel's with me.

The agent? Christ, Marina, why do you trust him so much?

She looks away from the phone, irritated by the question and by Patrick. Why does he have to call this into question now? She really doesn't need it when she's trying so hard to stay on top of it all.

Tell me where she is and I'll get there asap.

No! It won't help to have you around and the private investigator will also be there.

You mean the PI he found?

And who I've now met. Please stop doing this. I'll let you know how things go.

She clicks off and shuts down the notifications, so she won't know if he replies. It won't stop him from ringing, of course, or emailing, but she'll just ignore those attempts too.

'Are you OK?' Noel asks, glancing over at her.

'I guess so,' she replies. What other kind of answer could she give?

Looking out at the passing landscape, she sees that they've left the M4 now and are on the road to Cirencester. How is it possible to dread something so much without being able to turn around and run from it?

'No calls from Brenna yet,' Noel states. 'Do you want to check if she's emailed?'

Marina opens her phone, scrolls down, sees there's a message and reads it out loud. '"I'm close to the location, parked outside a small complex of luxury barn conversions. The farm isn't visible from this spot. I don't want anyone to see me until you get here, but Jason – my operative – is hiding out in one of the farm's derelict outbuildings and has just sent this through."'

Marina opens the attachment and feels she might choke.

'What is it?' Noel asks worriedly.

'A photograph of Shana,' she replies, her voice as strangled and taut as her nerves. 'She's there. Oh my God, she really is there.'

'Is it the woman you saw in Lower Slaughter?'

'Yes. Yes, it's her.'

CHAPTER FORTY-TWO

Fairbyrne Farm is situated at the top of a mountainous grassy ridge overlooking mile upon mile of rambling Cotswold countryside. Cows and sheep graze the undulating fields, small dots in the vast, patchworked landscape, while birds of prey soar and swoop overhead, masters of all they survey.

The decrepit five-bar gates leading into the farm are propped open amongst brambles and hollyhocks, providing no obstacle to Noel driving through in his 4x4. Brenna is in the backseat now, while Jason, the operative, is apparently still somewhere on the farm complex, out of sight. Marina looks around, sick with apprehension for what could lie ahead.

Everything is as still and ramshackle as it appeared in the photographs; a perched and sprawling enclave of partially collapsed outbuildings with smashed windows and weeds growing out of gaping roofs. The yard is a dumping ground for abandoned tools and building materials, while the old barns with their rusting frames and corrugated-iron shelters provide scant protection for the remains of what looks to be a combine harvester and various old stone troughs for animals no longer there.

As Noel bumps the car along a track gouged out by tractor tyres, Marina's heartbeat is jolting and slowing with the motion.

They are approaching the main house now, three storeys high, flat-fronted with tall chimneys and windows covered in plastic sheeting. The scaffolding is a steel skeleton seeming to hold everything together. The entire place might have appeared deserted, were it not for a muddied Land Rover next to the house with its tailgate open, and a cat leaping onto a window-sill to curl up in the sun.

'Jason has seen three people coming and going this morning,' Brenna tells them, 'so they're either around the back, or they're . . .' She stops as the front door opens and a woman in baggy denim dungarees and a red checked shirt comes out to stand and watch them. She is tall, rangy, short-haired, with narrowed eyes, and is brazen in her stance. She is a faded but still instantly recognizable version of the vibrant beauty she used to be. She must have been wearing a wig the day Marina spotted her in Lower Slaughter, for there is no evidence of her long hair now.

Though Marina has known for some time that this meeting had to happen, she sorely wishes she could tell Noel to turn around and drive them away. Anything rather than have it play out on Shana's terms instead of her own. However, she gets out of the car, her entire body wired with dread and anger, her mettle ready to take charge.

'Marina,' Shana drawls as if the last time they'd seen one another might have been weeks rather than years ago, and even on friendly terms. 'What kept you? I expected you long before now.'

The words and the tone tip Marina's nerves even closer to the edge. Her eyes move to a slightly shorter, heavier-set woman in similar dungarees and a white T-shirt as she exits the house to take up position beside Shana.

'Do you recognize Ella?' Shana asks, not taking her eyes

from Marina. 'She used to be Stella, but you already know that, don't you?'

In spite of the years that have passed and the weight the woman has gained, Marina can see that Stella – Ella – is indeed the author whose second book she turned down.

Shana's eyes spark with mischief as Noel comes to stand with Marina. 'Ah, you must be my agent,' she declares with a chuckle. 'We haven't formally met, but I know who you are. Thank you,' she presses her palms together, 'for reading my book.' To Marina she says, 'I guess I should thank you for reading it too. I expect it's brought back a few memories?'

Marina feels the heat of anger on her face and blood pulsing in her veins. She sounds sharp, defensive, as she says, 'Why are you doing this, Shana?'

Shana turns her surprise towards Ella, who raises a sardonic eyebrow. It is as if neither can quite believe the question.

Instead of answering, Shana says, 'Shall we go inside? There are so many bugs flying around out here.'

Marina doesn't move.

'Don't worry,' Shana says, 'you're perfectly safe and, anyway, given our history, I think I'm the one with most to fear around here but, look, I'm fine.' She throws out her hands as if to prove it. 'I'm more than happy to invite you into my home, in spite of everything. Your friends too.' She seems amused by herself and looks past Marina to Brenna, who is still standing next to the car. 'I'm guessing you're the private investigator,' she says, 'so it's probably you I should congratulate for finding me. Although, I don't suppose it was one of your more taxing assignments, I never intended to make it difficult.'

Marina bristles, hating the way they're being treated as playthings to be tossed and kicked around until Shana becomes bored and decides to . . . what?

What is going to happen here today?

She lowers her head to speak quietly to Noel, but he gestures for her to turn back. Shana and Ella are disappearing into the house.

'Do we follow?' Brenna asks, coming to join them.

Impatiently Marina says, 'We haven't come all this way to leave in less than five minutes with nothing resolved.'

Brenna glances at Noel. 'The invitation was for all of us, so,' she gestures for him to lead the way.

The house is dark after the brightness of the sun and smells of old wood, marijuana and fresh paint. They progress along a narrow hall, floorboards creaking beneath their feet, the distant sound of hammering coming from somewhere upstairs, or outside.

'In here,' Shana calls out, as Noel steps into a lozenge of sunlight streaming from an open door to the right.

Marina and Brenna follow him into a large, high-ceilinged room with newly whitewashed walls and two tall, arch-topped windows that overlook the panoramic view beyond.

'As you can see,' Shana says, waving them towards a cluster of armchairs shrouded in dust sheets, 'we're decorating – renovating actually – so I hope you don't mind the lack of usual comforts.'

The last thing Marina wants is to sit, but is afraid she'll look cowardly or foolish if she refuses.

Shana chatters on in an airy, friendly way as she and Ella pull up a couple of spindle-backed chairs to sit facing them. 'We're staying in the mobile home until the place is ready,' she explains, 'but now and again we pop down to

Dorset so Ella can check on her father and I can satisfy the conditions of my parole. I'm sure you've seen Sodeham Mill by now – quaint little place, isn't it? I stayed there, with Ella and her husband, for several weeks after I was released, until we relocated here. Oh, don't worry, my probation officer knows all about this farm. He's visited a couple of times, in fact. He sees it as a wonderful opportunity for me to be involved in a project. It'll be a big job, of course, and it'll take some time, but I think it'll be worth it when it's restored to its former glory.'

Ella says, 'It's been in my husband's family for over two hundred years, but they fell on hard times a few decades ago and it was left to rot, until Oscar – my husband – learned a while back that he'd inherited it. The black sheep of the family and now it's all his. Hah! Isn't that remarkable. Funny how things turn out. Of course, we knew right away we wanted to do something marvellous with it, but as Shana says, it's going to take a lot to make it workable as a farm, if that's the way we decide to go. We've been thinking about turning the outbuildings into holiday lets, or maybe we could rent the whole place out as an artist's, or writer's retreat.'

'I'm in favour of writers,' Shana adds, apparently enjoying her little witticism.

Marina is staring at them in disbelief. This is surreal. Do they seriously think she, or anyone else, is interested in what they're trying to achieve here? Of course they don't, they're just playing with her again, and she will have no more of it. 'You know very well that I'm never going to publish your book, Shana,' she says, 'and I'm quite sure no one else will either, given its false – libellous – allegations. So what is this really about?'

Shana's eyes widen with surprise. 'Well, of course you know the answer to that, but before we get into it, I'm curious to know how long it took for you to realize the story was all about you? And me, of course, but mostly you.'

Marina's eyes are glacial as she stares back at her.

Shana smiles. 'I thought the TV setting – courtesy of Ella, naturally – was quite a nice touch. A parallel that isn't quite aligned with publishing, but close, and characters that don't look much like any of us, or have our names, but the essence of it all is there, I believe, almost from the start. Incidentally, did you enjoy the way I turned Patrick into a bit of a lowlife? I know I did, and frankly it's no more than he deserved.' She laughs and Marina notices that one of her back teeth is missing. No dental care in prison? Or something more sinister?

'You and I both know,' Shana continues, 'that Rosie Shell will happily publish if you refuse to – we'll need to fill it out more, of course, get right down to every last detail, but that shouldn't be too much of a problem. And as for the "allegations" being "libellous" – well, you surely must be aware that you'd only be confirming the supposed identity of the characters within if you decide to start a lawsuit.'

Much as Marina hates it, she knows she can't argue with that; she really would bring about her and Maxim's downfall if she as much as attempts to block the book once it gets into Rosie Shell's hands. If it isn't there already.

Aware that everyone's eyes are on her, including Noel's and Brenna's, Marina says, 'I take it you've already discussed the book with Rosie so shall we—'

'Oh no, no, that's not true,' Shana interrupts. 'I've thought about it, I admit, and we discussed it at some length, didn't we?' she refers to Ella. 'But we've decided to keep her as our trump card, should we need one. How is dear Rosie, by the way? Do you see much of her now? She stopped writing to me a few years ago, which was a bit of a disappointment, but she got married, didn't she, and I guess life moved on.'

Having no idea if any of that was true, apart from Rosie's marriage, Marina says, 'Whatever you're planning for this book, you know very well that you can't prove anything about the mobile phone, and if you try—'

Shana's hand shoots up. 'I think you're about to threaten me,' she cautions, 'and I'd rather you didn't, especially when you know full well that your husband, or someone on his legal team, organized everything so I'd be found culpable for a murder *you* know I did not commit. And as for not being able to prove anything . . . well, I'm afraid that's where you're wrong. However, we shall come on to that. For now, as you're here, let's get down to what *you* did to me and—'

'I did nothing to you,' Marina snaps back furiously. 'And I had nothing to do with what happened to Amelia either. *You* killed her to try and get me out of the way so you could have Maxim to yourself.'

'But you're the one who had the bronze,' Shana cries as if Marina must surely remember that. 'The murder weapon,' she explains to Ella.

'I gave it back to you,' Marina seethes. 'The next morning, I left it on your desk—'

'Says you, but no one saw you put it there and I *know* I never saw it again after I threw it through your window.'

Marina feels close to murderous. 'You're lying and you know it.'

Shana smirks. 'You can tell yourself whatever you like, Marina, God knows you've been doing it long enough, but it'll never alter who you really are or what you did to me and that innocent girl.'

Marina's eyes flash; her jaw is tight as she bites out her reply. 'It was more or less over between her and Patrick by the time she died, and I was already with Maxim. So you can't seriously believe I'd *kill* her as some sort of revenge.'

'Frankly, I was never entirely sure what you might be capable of, given the vicious little streak you have running through you, but then we found out in the most appalling way just how far you'd go. Poor Amelia. Anyway, *why* you did it is of little interest to me. All that matters is that I get my life and my reputation back. Oh, and that you and Maxim are made to face the consequences of your actions; that you pay for what you've put me through. I think that's fair, don't you?' She's addressing the others now as if they're some sort of jury.

Ella says, 'Completely fair. They've got away with everything for too long already. It's just a shame about the children, is what I say. It'll be hard on them when they find out their father isn't actually—'

'They're *his*,' Marina shouts over her. 'If you saw them—'

'Oh, but we have,' Shana interrupts. 'So sweet and pretty . . .'

Marina's tone is deadly. 'If you ever go near my girls . . .'

'Too late,' Shana laughs. 'Did they enjoy the strawberries?'

'Stop this!' Noel cuts in forcefully. 'It's not getting us anywhere.' To Shana he says, 'You know you can't force Marina to publish, and if you had any proof of your innocence you'd have used it by now. So, I'll put the question to you again, what is really going on here?'

Shana looks impressed, as if she hadn't realized he could speak and now discovers he's rather good at it. 'I'm actually quite sure I *can* force her to publish,' she begins, then pauses and turns to Marina, appearing puzzled and curious. 'What does Maxim think of the book?' she asks. 'Has he enjoyed his little trip down memory lane?'

Marina stares at her with hatred.

Shana breaks into a smile. 'You haven't shown him yet, have you? Of course you haven't, I'd have heard from his lawyers by now if you had, even though there isn't a single mention of either of your names. So why are you keeping it from him, I wonder? I guess you were always afraid it might come out about the children. Well, here it is for everyone to see, little rabbits out of a hat – or, more accurately, dirty secrets out of the past.'

Marina's fury is at exploding point, her face is flooding with colour. 'Believe me, changing a few names isn't going to save you if you try to claim my children aren't Maxim's. You have absolutely no proof of it.'

'Are you sure about that?'

'If you did, you'd never have kept it to yourself, so let's stop this . . .' She breaks off as a tall, broad-shouldered man with ruddy cheeks and greasy grey hair strides into the room with a rifle in one hand and the arm of a slight young man in the other. Marina can smell the alcohol on the older man from ten feet away.

'Jason!' Brenna exclaims.

'So that's your name,' the drunk responds in a clipped, plummy voice. 'I meant to ask, very remiss of me.' To Ella he says, 'I found him lurking about the old wood shed, so thought I'd bring him in.'

Ella says to Brenna. 'He belongs to you?'

'He does,' Brenna confirms. 'Would you mind putting the gun down, sir?'

'Yes, best do that,' Ella tells him. 'Not something we want in the vicinity should things start to get heated. This is my husband, Oscar,' she announces as if no one had guessed. 'The one who inherited the farm.'

Oscar salutes with the rifle and says, 'What do you want me to do with him?'

'Take him back outside,' Ella replies. 'And give him some water if he wants it. It can be thirsty work, spying on people.'

As soon as they've gone, Marina turns back to Shana. 'I know what's really going on here. You're trying to use my children, your book, those ridiculous dolls, your outrageous accusations and everything else you can think of to do the same to me as Stella did to her sister. Well, it isn't going to work.'

Seeming startled, Shana and Ella exchange glances. 'Do you know what she's talking about?' Shana asks.

Ella shrugs. 'Beyond me.'

'You are going to hound and torment me until I have some sort of breakdown,' Marina says through gritted teeth, 'or until I end up confessing to something I didn't do.'

'Gosh! That sounds to me as though she still believes her own lies,' Shana remarks incredulously to Ella.

'She wants to hold onto those girls and her marriage,' Ella explains as if Shana might not know that.

'Ah, yes, the marriage,' Shana smiles, turning to Marina. 'How's that working out for you?'

Marina fervently wishes the gun was still there, able to be snatched and used to wipe the ugly smirk off Shana's face.

Noel steps in again. 'Shana, you've got to know that

Marina's never going to confess to a crime *you* committed.'

'How do you know that?' she snaps at him. 'Just because she tells you she's innocent, doesn't mean that she is. And, I'm afraid she's far from it.' Her eyes narrow as she fixes them on Marina, although she continues speaking to Noel. 'Of course, no one actually saw her kill Amelia, they'd have come forward if they had, but we do know that the bronze was in her possession until it was found at the murder scene. And we also know that the mobile phone found in my flat was planted there. If that hadn't happened, she would have faced the trial that was inflicted on me, and she'd have gone to prison for what *she* did.'

Marina is about to speak, but Noel says, 'How are you going to prove the phone was planted? You said we'd come on to it, so let's get there. We're dying to hear.'

Shana simply smiles at him.

'She can't tell you because it didn't happen,' Marina cries, sounding more convinced than she felt. 'I don't know why you kept it,' she says to Shana, 'and I don't really care, but—'

'Stop, stop, we can argue this as long as you like,' Shana says over her, 'but you know very well that the police only searched my flat when they did – many weeks after your arrest – because they'd received an anonymous tip-off. I can't be sure of actual dates, but I'm pretty certain you'd have known you were pregnant by then, so how very convenient for you that there was now some evidence linking me to the murder. Amazing what money and influence can do, isn't it? Maxim pays someone to bring the phone—'

'This is all nonsense and you know it.'

'What I know is that the person he paid is standing ready to confess to his crime and who he was acting for.'

Marina reels. She has no idea if this is true, but can see that it has all been leading up to this. Someone, the intruder, has come forward, has approached Shana . . . Except why wait? Why bother with this book?

'I fully believe you should go to prison for Amelia's murder,' Shana is saying in reasonable tones. 'The girl and her family deserve at least that, I'm sure you'd agree. However, it doesn't actually have to go that far. You see, there's a way forward that could avoid you having to experience what I did for twelve years. I think that will make you happy. Yes, I'm sure it will, although considering the state of your marriage and what you're going to have to do to stop me going to the police, "happy" might not be quite the right word.'

Marina's mouth is dry; she has a horrible sense of what might be coming next and can only wonder why she hasn't seen it before.

'You, Marina,' Shana says, 'as the publishing director of Hawksley Maine, are going to offer me a three-million-pound advance for my book – though you, Noel, will *not* take the commission because Ella is now my agent. She will negotiate the contract, including the payment schedule and, once it's all agreed, the book will become yours, Marina, to edit however you see fit before publishing. I promise I won't have a single objection to any changes you wish to make. You can even say what you like about the bronze and the mobile phone.'

Marina's breath is short; her mind is spinning with all that this is going to mean and on so many levels. Taking just the publishing aspect, Shana would know as well as she did that the board would have to approve that sort of advance – unless Maxim acted independently. He probably would if it meant avoiding any further investigation into the mobile phone.

But how can she be sure there really is someone ready to confess to planting it? And even if there is, who is going to believe him? This could all be a high-stakes bluff, carefully crafted by Shana and the Wileys . . .

She gets abruptly to her feet. 'We're done here,' she tells Noel and Brenna, and starts to the door.

Before leaving she turns back to Shana and says, 'If you think you're going to blackmail us into anything, you are out of your mind.'

Shana only laughs.

CHAPTER FORTY-THREE

Marina is pacing the rear garden of her and Maxim's Cotswolds home. Noel had driven her here before returning to London; he has an important dinner this evening that he can't miss. He'd offered to try to get out of it, but she'd told him not to worry about her, she'd be fine on her own. It would give her some time to think, and she'll use the old Volvo to drive back to London when she's ready.

She hadn't opened up the house when he left, had simply gone to the kitchen poured herself a large glass of water and brought it outside.

Clouds are gathering overhead as she comes to a stop at the centre of the lawn, drink in one hand, her phone in the other, as she continues going over everything that had been said at Fairbyrne Farm. It's clear that blackmail has always been at the heart of Shana's intentions, she just hadn't seen it in this form until today.

She keeps picturing the two ex-convicts, less than twenty miles away from where she is now, congratulating one another on how well this next stage of their plan has gone.

Stage one: write the book. Stage two: reel Marina in. Stage three: collect the advance. Of course it won't stop there. It could go on and on, royalties, reprints, foreign rights deals, even a sequel, but only if the book is published – and for that to happen, Marina will have to go along with their plan and rewrite it in such a way that no one, least of all her and Maxim, can be recognized.

The very thought of allowing herself to be manipulated that way makes her sick with rage. She can't do it, she knows that, and no doubt they know it too. They're probably finding it hilarious imagining her attempting to unpick the web Shana has spun, and no less entertaining would have been listening to her today insisting that she hadn't killed Amelia, and that no evidence had been planted. Her denials had sounded weightless even to her, while Shana's supercilious stance, her flagrant claiming of the moral high ground, galling and despicable though it was, had come across as convincing and irrefutable.

But you're the one who had the bronze, she had declared, as if everyone knew it, so why was Marina still trying to say otherwise.

I left it on your desk . . .

. . . but no one saw you put it there . . .

How could she, Shana, have known Amelia would be in the office at that time, and alone? She couldn't, but Marina could have because she was the girl's boss, so would quite possibly be aware of her movements. Why would Shana wish the girl any harm – other than for the reason Marina's legal team had presented? It never had sounded entirely credible to Marina, and yet a jury had found Shana guilty anyway. It was the mobile phone that had swayed them, of course.

Going back to the kitchen, she sets her glass aside and begins dousing her face in cold water. She needs to decide how to move forward from here, what to do to derail this monstrous blackmail plan and all that's going to come with it.

Reaching for a towel, she presses it to her face and goes to stare out at the rain that has begun drifting across the landscape. Her thoughts, her solutions, are becoming crazier by the minute as she imagines luring Shana here and stabbing her to death. (She can always claim self-defence.) Or she could return to Fairbyrne Farm, grab the rifle and kill them all. If it weren't for Noel and Brenna, the police might decide it was the act of a random maniac.

Turning around, she sinks into a chair at the table and buries her head in her hands. She'd never do it, of course, and not only because she'd never get away with it, but for all sorts of other reasons that begin with her girls, move on to her conscience and end with Maxim.

No, there's only one way forward that she can see. She'll have to tell Maxim everything and let him decide what needs to be done, because only he knows the truth about the evidence, and only he is in a position to deal with the blackmail.

The business with him and Georgia will have to wait.

Reaching for her phone, she connects to his number and feels her heart twist painfully as he answers on the second ring. Are they coming to the end of the time when he takes her calls so readily?

'Hey you,' he says, 'I was just about to call. How're things?'

Having no idea how to answer that, she says, 'It's been a long day, and there's—'

'Hang on,' he interrupts, 'I'm guessing this is room service. I'll just let them in.'

As she waits, she can hear him directing someone to 'put it there, yes, that's great. Thanks.' She knows he'll give a generous tip, because he always does.

'Sorry,' he says, coming back on the line. 'As you know, I don't normally suffer with jetlag, but it seems to be getting to me this time, so I've decided to eat in the room rather than join the others at Jean-Jacques.'

'You sound tired,' she tells him.

'Mm, it's been hot here today and I've had back-to-back meetings with no break for lunch. Unheard-of in Paris.'

She almost smiles. 'I should let you eat,' she says. 'When do you expect to be back?'

'Thursday late morning, and I might go straight home.'

Should she tell him she's sending a book now that he needs to read before she sees him?

'Any chance you can finish early that day?' he asks. 'We need to talk.'

'Yes,' she replies, 'we do.'

It isn't until after she's rung off that his parting words properly reach her.

. . . the conversation would begin the way so many of these conversations do, 'we need to talk,' or something along those lines.

CHAPTER FORTY-FOUR

It's five in the morning when Marina starts the drive back to London. She's hardly slept. Knowing what Maxim wants to talk about, and that Shana had predicted it, is deepening the darkness and confusion inside her and making it more terrifying than ever. She still hasn't sent him the book – if it can even be described as that; maybe she'll do it later.

Before leaving she'd packed his and the girls' toothbrushes into her bag. Brenna Isaacs had provided her with details of a rapid DNA service, without asking any questions as to why she might want it. Or maybe Noel has shown her the latest chapters by now, so Brenna knows the paternity is in doubt. It hardly matters. All that does, for the moment, is finding out who the girls' real father is. She knows, of course, in her heart, but once Maxim sees what Shana has written he will almost certainly demand proof that they're his.

Is she worried that his plans for a future without her are going to come to nothing? The very last thing she wants is him to leave her, to go and start a new life in the States with Georgia – it's tearing her apart even to think of it – but she'd almost rather that than see herself, or him, go to prison. If it happens she will be to blame, for he'd only acted to save her and the unborn babies, while she, it will be said, acted out of malice and vengeance.

Once he knows what's going on, he'll surely agree that they must do whatever it takes to remove the power Shana is wielding over them and make sure it never happens again. He will know how to do that, please God. He'll find a way to make it all disappear before he leaves.

It is past eleven o'clock by the time she finally takes the lift to her office. She has the DNA results now (they are exactly as she'd expected), and she's been home to change out of the clothes she'd worn the day before. She feels shaky and light-headed, dazed by hunger and disoriented by everything that is happening as she walks through the open-plan area. She doesn't seem to have a handle on anything at all, it's slipping further and further away from her, leaving her stranded in a state of abject dread.

If anyone notices she isn't herself, they don't show it. They simply give her a friendly wave as she passes, and someone asks if she saw the bestseller lists yesterday and isn't it brilliant news? Janus is doing well in a really tough market, and they surely have to be on track to win publisher of the year. It wouldn't be the first time; they've made the top three regularly in the past ten years. She can only hope that her successor – who would have been Georgia in a normal world – turns out to be someone who knows how to nurture and reward all the talent Marina has brought together.

Her mind is so full of who it might be and where she, herself, might be by then, that it takes her a moment to register what is sitting on her desk, beside her computer. She stops at the door, staring at it, unable – unwilling – to believe her own eyes. She blinks several times, still certain she's imagining it, but it's there, as exquisitely beautiful as ever, the figurine she'd bought Shana all those years ago.

The murder weapon.

Her heart stumbles into thick, heavy thuds.

She moves awkwardly, shakily towards it, having no idea if anyone is watching her, not even thinking about it until she realizes Shana couldn't have put it there herself. And if Shana hadn't . . . She looks round, half expecting to see Georgia staring at her, but Georgia's desk is empty and no one else is looking her way.

'Does anyone know where Georgia is?' she calls out.

'At a meeting with Angela Greene,' Toby replies, referring to one of Georgia's authors. 'She should be back about midday.'

Marina nods. 'Did she . . .? Was she here earlier?'

'Briefly, to pick up the jacket proofs she needed.'

Marina looks at the bronze again. She has no idea what to do with it, what she's even supposed to do. She sits down in her chair and continues glancing at it as she opens up her computer.

It doesn't surprise her to find an email from the anonymous sender; it flat-out horrifies her when she reads the message.

Just in case you feel like doing the same to Georgia as you did to Amelia.

Her hands fly to her mouth. She bites down on her knuckles to stifle a cry. She can't stand this. It's too much. She has no idea what to do or think, who she can even turn to.

Noel, she must call Noel, but she can't move her hands from her face, can't even stay sitting in her chair. She slides to her knees, clasping her head and sobbing wretchedly. She can't do this any more. It's driving her crazy. She has no control. She is on the brink of losing everything, or maybe she already has and just hasn't caught up with it yet . . .

'Marina? Are you OK?'

It's Toby, peering down at her worriedly. 'Did something happen?' he asks gently.

She tries to speak, but only sobs. 'No – I . . .' She starts to get up, but there is no strength in her limbs, no will in her heart. She wants to stay here, curled up under her desk, safe from the world while someone takes that hideous bronze away.

An hour later she's at home. Toby had called a taxi to take her, had even tried to insist on coming, saying she shouldn't be alone, but she'd somehow persuaded him she'd be fine.

'I had some news,' she'd tried to explain. 'It was . . . I'm sorry, I can't . . .'

As sympathetic as he'd been, he'd seemed relieved in the end to let her go, and she didn't blame him. He'd never had to cope with her in such a mess before; she'd never been in that state, not at the office, at least not for many, many years. He'd tell Georgia when she came back, obviously, and though Marina had no idea what else they might say, Georgia would soon realize that the figurine had gone.

Was it Georgia who'd put it there? If not, then who else could it have been?

It's here now, on the kitchen table in front of her and Noel. He'd come as soon as she'd called, excusing himself from a meeting and no doubt making himself unpopular with whoever he'd abandoned.

'Is it the same one?' he asks.

Calmer now, but still pale-faced and edgy, she shakes her head. 'The one I gave Shana was three out of seven, this one is number six.'

'Meaning they were cast in the same mould?'

She nods. 'I don't know how she found this one. Maybe it wasn't difficult.'

'What matters is how she got it to your desk.' His eyes come to hers and his sorrow makes her heart turn over. 'Georgia,' he says flatly.

'I can't think of anyone else. Shana or the Wileys would never have got past security.'

'So we have to conclude that she knows them?'

Marina gets up from the table and goes to refill their coffee mugs.

'Is Maxim back yet?' he asks.

Her heart contracts painfully as she says, 'Tomorrow.'

'Have you sent him the chapters?'

'No. I've decided to deal with his . . . affair first.' She is so close to tears that one falls onto her cheek as she says, 'He's so good at hiding it. Just like Patrick was. Men can be . . .' She stops, not wanting to lump him in with what she'd been about to say. 'Or maybe I'm a fool for not seeing what's right in front of my face while the whole world talks about it?'

Regarding her soberly, he says, 'There's no gossip that I've heard.'

She shrugs. 'I don't expect anyone would say anything to you. They know we're friends.' Her eyes go to his as she realizes how true that is for her. 'I don't know how I'd be coping with this if it weren't for you,' she tells him frankly. She adds with a grimace, 'I'm not coping, of course, but you know what I mean.'

He looks at the figurine again. 'What are you going to do with it?' he asks.

Her voice is cracked, bitter as she says, 'Perhaps I should return it to Shana the same way she returned hers to me, by throwing it through a window.'

'She'd know she was getting to you if you did.'

She gives an unsteady laugh. 'She knows that anyway.' She looks at the bronze and shakes her head. 'If you're wondering will I use it on Georgia . . .'

'I'm not, so don't let's go there. I think you should keep it as proof of Shana's threats and intimidation. I know the emails are anonymous, but it can't be much longer before Brenna's techie finds out who's behind them.'

Marina nods. 'Actually, I should probably collect them all into one file to show to Maxim when he . . . when he gets . . .' As she starts to break down, Noel comes round the table to comfort her, but she pulls away. 'I'm OK, honestly,' she insists. 'I just need to get everything straight in my head so I can decide on the best way to deal with it.'

He glances at the time and grimaces as he says, 'I'm afraid I have to get back. Lunch with an Irish author who's flown over specially so I can't let him down. I'll keep my phone on in case you want to call.'

'Thanks,' she says, and goes to see him to the door.

After he's gone, she returns to the kitchen and stands staring so hard at the figurine that it seems to float and warp before her eyes. Small black dots begin to rain down on it as old memories surge . . . Then she's thinking about Noel and what a good friend he is – and how he's never once come right out and asked if she'd killed Amelia.

CHAPTER FORTY-FIVE

Marina emails her team the following morning to let them know she'll be working from home all day. She doesn't imagine anyone will be surprised by that, given her bizarre meltdown yesterday, and she isn't going allow herself to think about what they might be surmising or predicting.

Toby is the first to email back saying he hopes she's feeling OK and please let him know if there's anything she'd like him to do. He makes no reference to what happened the day before, and Georgia doesn't mention it either when she gets in touch. The reason for Georgia's call is to discuss the details of a six-book deal for one of her authors. Her tone is friendly, even quite warm when it comes to thanking Marina for greenlighting the contract.

At home in her study, Marina is finding it almost impossible to stay focussed. She keeps getting up from her desk to look out of the window, knowing Maxim won't be back yet, but having to find out what might be happening outside anyway. Although nothing is, apart from the usual intermittent flow of traffic and dog walkers, she keeps imagining dolls are hiding in trees, or behind cars, or in neighbours' windows. She thinks, for one terrifying moment, that she hears something smash downstairs but, when she goes down to the kitchen, the bronze figurine is right where she'd left it, in the middle of the table. And nothing is broken.

It's just after two when Maxim finally drives into the garage behind their garden. He'll be surprised to see the Volvo in her space – her car is in a resident's bay just down the street. She watches him come through the connecting door, a carry-on bag in one hand, laptop case in the other. He doesn't notice her at the upstairs window, but she can see already how tired he looks. His eyes are shadowed, and the furrow between them is deeper than ever. She imagines smoothing it, the way she often does when he's had a difficult day, holding his head in her lap and almost feeling his tension melting away.

Does Georgia do that for him?

Steeling herself, she goes downstairs to greet him.

By the time she reaches the kitchen he's already there, staring at the bronze on the table. He looks up as she comes in. 'What's this?' he asks, sounding puzzled and even annoyed. He'd recognized it, of course, how could he not, given the part it has played in their lives?

'I found it on my desk yesterday,' she tells him. 'It's not the exact one, but it's from the same mould.'

'So what's it doing here?'

'I brought it home because I didn't know what else to do with it. Shouldn't you be asking who left it for me?'

He flips his hand in a gesture for her to continue.

Not missing how cold he seems; in fact, hardly like himself at all, she makes herself say, 'I'm pretty sure it was Georgia.'

She'd expected him to look shocked, or disbelieving, but he simply scowls impatiently before turning to the fridge to take out a bottle of water.

'Doesn't that surprise you?' she asks, so tense herself she might snap.

He fills a glass, drinks and turns back to her. 'I guess so,' he replies. 'Do you know where she got it?'

Her voice is shaky, her heart fracturing, as she says, 'I know what's been going on, Maxim.'

His frown deepens. 'What?'

'I'm not sure when you were planning to tell me, but I think it was probably today, so I'm—'

'Stop!' he says sharply. 'I have no idea what you're telling yourself, or what's led up to this, but if you're accusing me . . . Are you accusing me of having an affair?' He regards her angrily and incredulously. 'Is that what you're saying?'

'You said you wanted to talk,' she reminds him, 'and I'm telling you that I already know what it's about.' She doesn't feel so certain now, about anything.

He presses his fingers to his eye sockets, as though to push away the build-up of tension. 'Sure I want to talk,' he says, 'but . . .' He shakes his head as if to clear it. 'Why the hell would Georgia leave this thing on your desk?' he demands, as if only just fully connecting with it.

'I think she got it from Shana . . .'

His eyes widen in shock. 'You think *Shana* gave it to Georgia? Have you gone crazy, or something?'

Why is he being so hostile, so caustic even? 'Shana's been writing a book,' she says. 'It's about what happened fourteen years ago, or her version of it and I've . . . She wants us to publish it.'

He gapes at her in disbelief, then quite suddenly he laughs, although it isn't a pleasant sound. 'She is clearly out of her mind,' he declares. 'Why the hell would we even look at it, never mind put it into print?' His eyes suddenly narrow. 'You've already looked at it,' he states.

She doesn't answer.

With a mutter of irritation he says, 'So where is it? How long have you had it?'

'A few weeks.'

'And you're only telling me about it now?'

'I-I didn't want you to be reminded of it all, or to feel afraid it was going to kick off again. It was so awful the first time around. The accusations, suspicions, the gossip, and now we have the girls . . . I kept hoping I'd find a way to stop her, but I don't think I can.'

'I want to see it,' he snaps.

She nods. 'I'll go up to the study and send it to your private email.'

A few minutes later, it's done. She doesn't go back down to make sure it has gone through, she knows it will have, and she wants to give him some time to read without her being there. Or maybe she just doesn't want to see or feel his reaction when he reads the part about the girls not being his.

She allows half an hour to pass before returning to the kitchen. The fact that there might not be an affair with Georgia is providing almost no comfort, given where they are and what the future could hold if they don't find a way to deal with Shana. She wants desperately to believe that he'll know what to do, because if he doesn't, they really are in trouble.

She half expects to find him still reading, but he's standing at the window staring out at the garden. She can sense his anger – fury – even before he turns around to fix her with a look that chills her right through.

'It's the twins, I know,' she cries. 'They're yours, I swear it—'

'Of course they are,' he growls. 'Do you seriously think my father didn't check it out within days of their birth?'

Her eyes widen with outrage. 'I didn't know that. And you let him?'

'It happened before I knew anything about it. He'd never have got off my case about staying in England if they turned out not to be mine. *I* never doubted it, whereas you . . .' He tilts his head. 'Maybe you did?'

'No!' she protests. 'But you know there are gaps in my memory, like me not recalling trying again with Patrick. Apparently you do remember it, and I was afraid you'd believe what she's written, so I decided to take your DNA and the girls' to a lab—'

'In order to reassure yourself.'

'No. To reassure you, in case you doubted me or . . . Maxim, why are we arguing about this? Isn't it enough that we know the truth? We can't let her come between us.'

'But apparently we can hide this . . .' he slams down the lid of his laptop, '*monstering* of the truth from me . . .'

'Like I said, I kept hoping you wouldn't have to know, that I'd find a way to end it before it exploded in our faces again.'

'So have you? Ended it?'

Bracing herself, she says, 'She's claiming to have found the person who put the mobile phone in her flat. He says you paid him.'

There's a moment's appalled silence before, in the deadliest of tones, he says, 'Please tell me you're not serious.'

She doesn't answer, he obviously knows she is.

'And what did you say to this . . . *bullshit*?'

'I told her we wouldn't be blackmailed and walked out of the room.'

His incredulity makes her want to take a step back. 'That sounds like you've seen her,' he says balefully.

Swallowing, she says, 'I went to the place where she's living.'

'Alone? Tell me you didn't go alone when you know—'

'Noel came with me, and the private detective who found her.'

He looks as though she's just hit him. Figuratively speaking, she supposes she has. 'So you've discussed this with Noel and some PI,' he says, 'and not with me? For fuck's sake, Marina . . .'

'She's been submitting the chapters through Noel and he's not stupid. It might have taken him longer than some to realize it was our story, but—'

'Did it ever cross your mind that he might be working with her?'

'Why is everyone saying that? You know him—'

'Everyone? Jesus! Who the hell else have you told?'

Realizing her mistake, she can only say, 'Patrick.'

She flinches as he thumps a fist on the table. 'You discussed this with your ex-husband, before coming to me? Why the hell would you do that? In what world did it make sense to you to go to him?'

'I thought she might have been in touch with him too . . . And I was afraid he might be working with her, in spite of everything you've done for him.'

'And is he?'

'I don't think so.'

'But you don't know? And you've got no idea about Noel either.'

'We can trust him, I swear. You know him as well as I do, but talk to him yourself if you like—'

'Oh, don't worry I will, and I'll also be talking to her probation officer – I take it she's still on licence?'

'Given her crime, she has to be.'

He takes a moment, clearly needing to collect himself and try to calm things down. She's grateful for it, but is still bracing for more. 'I don't understand why you've let it get to this point,' he growls. 'Surely to God you realized she was in breach of her parole simply for contacting you?'

'I don't know what the conditions are and, as you can see, she hasn't used her name. She hasn't used ours either, anywhere.'

'That still doesn't give her the freedom to rewrite the past.'

'Yes it does, unless we want to get into fighting her and having it all come out anyway.'

'All what come out? The fact that she killed an innocent girl to try and frame you?'

'I don't know who'll believe that once they've read the way she's telling it. It was touch and go the first time around, and now she has someone who's prepared to swear he planted the phone under instruction from you . . .'

'But you know that person can't exist, right?' He's looking at her oddly, as if expecting one answer while sensing he might get another.

'Of course,' she says. 'I mean . . .'

'Tell me you don't believe – that you've never believed – I was in some way involved in securing your freedom in the way Shana tried to claim back then, and is claiming again now?'

His expression is so chilling, so menacing even, that she can't be sure whether this is a genuine question or some sort of coercive control.

'OK, answer me this,' he says, 'where the hell do you think I'd have got the phone from?'

Her eyes return to his, haunted and heavy with guilt. 'I-I've never wanted to ask,' she replies. 'I kept hoping it was all a lie, but the fact that it turned up when it did . . .'

His tone is scathing as he says, 'I don't think I know you any more, and it seems you never knew me.'

'That's not true.'

'It patently is. *She* went to prison because she killed that girl. It was what she deserved – unless you're going to tell me something now that I might not want to hear.'

Her mouth falls open as she reels. 'You know I didn't do it,' she cries desperately. 'I could never have hurt her, no matter how much I hated her, and I didn't hate her any more . . . I had no reason to kill her. Jesus, Maxim, you can't believe I'd do something like that.'

'But apparently you can believe that I would frame an innocent woman for a murder . . .'

'No!'

'Yes! You've as good as admitted it. Think about all you've just said and tell me I'm not right. You think I fixed it for her to go to prison in your place.'

She can only stare at him. This is turning out to be so much worse than she'd feared. She's losing him; she can feel it, and she doesn't know how to bring him back. 'Not in my place,' she says, 'I should never have been charged . . . Maxim, please,' she implores as he starts to turn away. 'We need to discuss this rationally. Can't you see, attacking one another is exactly what she wants.'

'Oh yes, I can see that, but I'm afraid I can't discuss anything with you right now. Frankly, I don't even want to be in the same room as you.'

Stricken, she watches as he snatches up his keys.

'Where are you going?' she asks, feeling for one panicked moment that she's reliving the night Patrick snatched up his keys and left her with the words, *Amelia's pregnant*.

At the door he turns back, 'Tell me this, what the hell did I ever do to make you believe I'm the kind of man who'd stitch someone up like that? And, while you're at it, perhaps you can tell me what I ever did to make you think I was having an affair.'

He doesn't wait for an answer, simply yanks open the door and leaves.

CHAPTER FORTY-SIX

Knowing there is no point trying to go after him now, it would only get worse if she does, Marina takes several deep breaths to try to push down the panic that's building and reaches for her phone.

Noel answers on the third ring.

'Maxim's read it,' she tells him as soon as he answers. 'He stormed out a couple of minutes ago. The worst of it is that he thinks I believed her story about him planting evidence, and I have to admit a part of me . . . I mean, I can see how crazy it is now, but we never discussed it and I thought that was because—'

'Where is he now?'

'I'm not sure.'

'OK. Tell me about the twins? How did that go down?'

'Apparently his father had a DNA check at the time they were born.'

'Nice. Still, I guess it's worked in your favour. Did you bring anything up about Georgia?'

'He denies there's an affair. I suppose he would, but actually I think I believe him.'

'Did you show him the anonymous emails?'

'Not yet, but he saw the bronze figurine. He knows I think Shana might have given it to Georgia to put on my desk.'

'Well, if it turns out you're right about that, then I'd say young Georgia has some serious explaining to do.'

The following morning, Marina walks to the office. She wants to keep a clear head, no traffic mishaps or careless cyclists, as she tries to prepare herself for the difficulties that lie ahead. Maxim had slept in a guest room last night and had clearly left before six this morning because there had been no sign of him when she'd gone downstairs. He hadn't yet responded to the email she'd sent yesterday explaining about Stella Wood – Ella Wiley as she now is – and the part she'd played in Shana's life many years ago, and again now. She'd also sent copies of the anonymous emails concerning Georgia. There had been no acknowledgement of that either. However, an hour ago she'd received a message asking her to join him in one of the HR meeting rooms on the seventh floor at ten o'clock today.

It seems crazy to think he's going to fire her, his own wife and mother of his children, and yet she's afraid that's exactly what he intends to do. She tries to imagine what grounds he'll put forward and – whatever they might be – how the heck she'll respond. Her mind keeps skipping from one devastating scenario to another until she realizes she's getting everything way out of perspective. She needs to calm down, to remind herself of what the real issue is here: dealing with Shana.

She knows how pale and strained she must look as she steps out of the lift onto the seventh floor of the building, but there's no time to do anything about it. Maddie Raines is waiting – the same HR manager who'd been around at the time of Amelia's murder. She's still in the same job after all this time; older, of course, a lot greyer and certainly heavier, but her smile is as warm as it's ever been towards Marina.

'We're through here,' Maddie says, her voice gentle and musically Welsh. 'I've ordered some coffee; it should be here any second.' She pushes into one of the larger meeting rooms, often used for staff training exercises, and waits for Marina to follow. 'Maxim's already here,' she says. 'I'll just leave you for a minute and be right back.'

Marina's throat is dry, her heart is in chaos, as she comes to a stop with the width of the conference table between them and waits for him to look up from his laptop.

'Good morning,' she says tightly as he continues to consult his computer.

'We need to deal with Georgia first,' he informs her. 'She'll be joining us in a few minutes. Is there anything you'd like to say before she gets here?'

Thrown by the unexpectedness of the question, she takes a moment to say, 'I sent you the anonymous emails last—'

'Yes, and you think they're from Shana. I don't disagree, but someone's been passing her information and we need to find out who. As they concern Georgia, she's the obvious place to start. Did you bring the bronze?'

Reaching into her bag, she pulls it out and sets it down on the table between them.

He barely looks at it, merely begins typing into his laptop again.

'Maxim, we can't just—'

'You need to come and sit here,' he interrupts, pointing to the chair next to him.

She walks around the table and is about to speak again when the door opens and Maddie comes in, a worried-looking Georgia close behind her.

As they sit down, Marina watches Georgia's eyes alight on the bronze.

'Have you seen it before?' Maxim asks, coming straight to the point.

Without looking at him she gives a brief nod.

'Tell us about it.'

'I – uh . . . I was given it . . . I was asked to put it on Marina's desk as a surprise for her.' Her eyes flick to Marina and quickly away again.

'Who gave it to you?' Maxim asks.

'My . . . godfather's wife. Her name's Ella Wiley.'

Marina instantly flashes on the Cotswolds godparents, and the secret the "Woolleys" had shared with "Christy" just after she was released from prison. This must be it. Oscar Wiley's goddaughter is a senior editor working for Marina Forster – what a god-given opportunity for the Wileys to use Shana's desire for revenge to renovate their farm.

And for some unknown reason, Georgia has gone along with it.

'Do you know anything about the history of this bronze?' Maxim demands. 'Or one like it, anyway.'

Georgia shakes her head, but Marina feels certain she's lying.

'Has your godfather's wife ever asked you to pass on information about my or Marina's whereabouts?'

Georgie's colour rises. 'Once or twice,' she admits.

Marina is staring at her hard, understanding now why she'd been in Maxim's study the night of the party. She'd been checking his diary to make a note of his movements.

'And you agreed to pass on this information because . . .?' Maxim prompts.

Georgia's colour deepens as she shoots a look at Marina. 'I did it because they told me what you did to that girl and how you'd let an innocent woman go to prison for it. I read all about it and I could see . . .' She gulps and presses a trembling hand to her mouth.

'Continue,' Maxim barks coldly.

She takes a breath. 'They – they said, if I helped them, they could make sure justice was served and your job would come free at last. I didn't know if it was true, but I've waited and waited, Marina. You know I have. I deserve to be in your position, everyone says so, even you, but you never accept any promotions, never make space for anyone to take over, to spread their wings and rise to their full potential. You stifle us, or that's what you do to me. OK, I could go to another company, but I don't want to leave my authors. Why should I, when I've built up such a great list and I'm close to them all . . .' She stops, pressing a hand to her mouth again to stifle the sobs that are drowning her voice.

Maxim gives it a moment and says, 'When you came to talk to me about your ambitions to take over from Marina, I believe I advised you to be patient. Is that correct?'

Marina flinches. *To be patient?* Not, *you know that can't happen? Or, go elsewhere?*

'But apparently, instead of taking my advice,' he continues, 'you decided to move things along for yourself by becoming involved in this . . . I'm not sure what to call it, apart from a blackmail attempt, which you will know is illegal.'

Georgia cringes.

'Out of interest, did they pay for you to go to Florida while I was in the States myself?'

She swallows noisily and tries to toss her head as she nods.

'Did you send Marina emails from an unidentifiable address insinuating you and I were together?'

Her eyes fly open with shock. 'No!' she cries. 'If that happened, I swear it wasn't me. Oh God, this is awful. I'm sorry, I truly am. I wish to God I'd never got involved . . . I was stupid. I should have listened to Boo – Brody, my boyfriend – he said I shouldn't do it . . .'

Maxim rises to his feet and says to Maddie, 'Do whatever needs to be done, just make sure she's out of the building by the end of the day,' and before anyone can utter another word, he leaves the room.

CHAPTER FORTY-SEVEN

Marina is on the way down to her office when Patrick rings.

'How's everything going?' he asks.

'This isn't a good time . . .'

'Just tell me, did you see Shana?'

'Yes, but I can't speak now. I'll call you later.'

After ringing off, she stops at a water-cooler and fills a cardboard cup to the brim. She's still shaken by the last few minutes, Georgia's attack on her; Maxim so direct, ruthless and swift to action. He has a reputation for it, of course, but she rarely gets to see it herself. She'd almost felt sorry for Georgia, who she'd left sobbing in Maddie's arms. Marina hadn't allowed herself to engage, it would only have complicated things further, and she certainly wasn't going to try to change Maxim's mind.

She has no idea what to expect next from him. In this frame of mind, he is as unreadable as he is unapproachable, and much of his anger is obviously and understandably still directed at her. She feels the same, utterly furious and appalled with herself, as much for her lack of trust as her shameful suspicions. She should have gone to him right away with the book, allowed him to take control of the situation, even if it had meant thrusting him right back into the nightmare of the past.

As she walks through to her desk, she notices how quiet everyone is and wonders if the news has already reached them about Georgia. Certainly they'd be asking themselves why she'd been summoned to HR at such short notice. An announcement would have to be made, but she'd discuss it with Maddie first. Are they going to say Georgia resigned, thereby making it possible for her to get another job? Or should they make it clear she's been fired?

Once in her office she closes the door, a signal that she doesn't want to be disturbed, and goes to sit down at her computer. It's going to be virtually impossible to carry on as if nothing has happened, but for the moment she at least has to try.

She notices the anonymous email at the same instant as her phone chimes with a text.

She opens the email first, certain it's going to be about Georgia's dismissal, but she's wrong. It's from the same sender, but the message reads,

Have you worked out where they are yet?

She has no idea what that means, so she checks to see if she's missed an earlier email, but there's only this one.

Her phone gives a second chime so she picks it up, and is alarmed to see the same message.

Have you worked out where they are yet?

She looks out to the main office to see if any of the team is missing but, apart from Georgia, everyone is at their desks.

Another message arrives, a beat before her phone chimes again.

Better get to work on that contract. Figure non-negotiable.

She is so thrown and unnerved that it takes her a moment to realize there's also an email from Maxim.

Please send the address of where Shana can be found.

After forwarding both anonymous emails she picks up her mobile to call him. To her relief he answers right away.

'I've just sent you two more anonymous messages,' she tells him. 'I don't understand what the first one's about; the second speaks for itself.'

There's a brief moment as he read the emails. His voice is terse as he says, 'OK, let me have the address . . .'

'I will, but if you're planning to go there . . . I'm not sure that confronting her – them – is the right thing to do.'

'Then what would you suggest? That we give in to the blackmail?'

'No, of course not, but I thought – aren't there other ways of doing this? You said you were going to speak to her probation officer.'

'It's in hand, but I want to see her myself. So the address please, or I'll get it from Noel.'

'I'll send it now, but Maxim, can't we get her to meet us somewhere?' She has no clear idea of why she's saying this, it just instinctively feels wrong to turn up at the farm for the kind of showdown he's undoubtedly planning.

'Where would you suggest, given the nature of what needs to be discussed?' he counters. 'And please don't think I'm going to invite her into either of our homes, because that really isn't going to happen.'

Since it's the last thing she'd want either, she says, 'How about Noel's office? I'm sure he—'

'No, not there. I'm still having difficulty with why he didn't shut it down as soon as he realized what was happening?'

'How was he supposed to do that when we didn't even know it was her at first? And when we did—'

'When you did, you chose to believe her ludicrous story about planted evidence. I don't need any reminders of that, thank you. I'll be leaving in the next few minutes. If you want to come with me and give me the full details of what happened when you saw her, my car is parked under the building.'

CHAPTER FORTY-EIGHT

The traffic is unusually free-flowing as they drive out of London on the M4 heading for the Swindon turn-off over seventy miles away. If it continues this way, they should be at the farm by midday.

Maxim says little as they progress, mostly listens as Marina recounts everything that happened when she and Noel confronted Shana and Ella Wiley.

'I should have seen earlier that it was building up to a classic blackmail attempt,' she says, trying to keep her anger and sense of foolishness in check, 'but even so I can't see the threat of publishing the book going away, no matter what we do.'

'It'll be taken care of,' he tells her shortly, and clicks on to take an incoming call via the hands-free. It turns out to be company business, so she opens her phone to check if there are any more messages from the anonymous sender.

Nothing.

She reads the cryptic message again – *Have you worked out where they are yet?* – but is still unable to make sense of it, and as Maxim moves on to another call, she begins replying to other emails that need her attention. Anything to try to distract herself from what lies ahead.

A little over two hours later they are closing in on Cirencester when she receives a message from Brenna Isaacs.

The email account you requested information on has now been traced through various servers to a William Wiley – could be a brother of Oscar, or his middle name, maybe a son or brother.

Not sure how this can help them for the moment, but glad to have the connection to Shana, Marina reads the email to Maxim. 'Presumably it's an account set up for her,' she says, 'as she seems to have no internet or social media presence herself.'

'Forward me the investigator's email,' he says, 'and I'll send it on to the lawyers. With an impatient sigh, he indicates to overtake a lorry and speeds on around the ring-road to join the A417. 'Can you remember how to get to the place?' he asks as they draw closer to Birdlip.

'I think so. It's a small turning to the left just after a pub called the Highwayman. From there it's about three miles, mostly uphill. I've got it on satellite so I can check where we're going.'

Eventually, after the long and twisting climb through steep lanes and dense, rambling wilderness, they reach the gates to Fairbyrne Farm. Marina can feel herself recoiling. It's like revisiting a nightmare. She really doesn't want to be here. She flashes on Oscar Wiley's rifle. Had it been loaded? Would he use it if pushed? Why would he need to? They aren't here to cause trouble, only to try to avoid it.

Maxim brings the Mercedes to a stop just past the gates – there are too many potholes and random rocks to chance going any further. After he turns off the engine, they sit looking around. Everything is more or less the same as the last time she'd seen it: part derelict farm, part building site. There is no sign of the Land Rover, or any other vehicle apart from the broken-down tractors.

The stillness is eerie.

Her trepidation is mounting.

Maxim gets out of the car.

She does the same and walks alongside him towards the half-open front door. They are almost there when a shadow appears across the threshold and Shana follows with a display of mock surprise to see them.

'Here you are,' she declares warmly, much as she had the day before, as though they're the welcome guests she's been expecting. Her watchful, sloe eyes go to Maxim. 'I knew you'd come,' she says affectionately. 'You never could stay away from me for long, could you?' She gives a laugh that cuts right through Marina's nerves. 'You have told her, haven't you, Maxim, how often you came to visit me? She does know . . .'

Marina turns to him.

He stretches an arm out to stop her going any further. 'Don't fall for it,' he mutters.

Shana simply shrugs. 'Still keeping secrets, I see. Well, you've always been very good at them, haven't you?'

He remains silent, his eyes baleful and cold.

Shana smiles. 'You're very welcome to join me inside,' she says. 'Both of you, of course, unless, Marina, you'd rather wait out here.'

Maxim says, 'You need to know that your ludicrous attempt at blackmail is going to send you right back to prison.'

Her eyebrows arch in surprise. 'Oh no, no, no, you've got that wrong, Maxim. *She's* the one who's going to prison, finally, for what *she* did to Amelia – and *you* are going to go for planting evidence in my flat. I warned you it would come to this if you didn't get me out.'

'What is going on?' Marina hisses.

'Don't let her do this,' Maxim says through his teeth, his eyes still boring into Shana.

Shana continues to smile. 'Tell me,' she says, 'has she been worth all the trouble you went to in order to get her out of prison? I know you only did it because she was pregnant – you couldn't have the mother of your babies behind bars for murder, now could you? And now, here we are, and you're not even sure they're yours.'

As Marina draws breath, Maxim says, 'I know you've confessed to Amelia's murder. It's how you earned your parole, by admitting responsibility and expressing remorse.'

Shana's eyes narrow slightly. 'Someone's been doing their homework,' she comments dryly. 'But I'm sure you understand that I had to do something to get out of that hellhole. I should never have been there in the first place. So yes, I did confess and say I was sorry. It doesn't mean that I did it though. Does it, Marina? You know you never returned that bronze . . .'

Marina isn't listening; she's checking her phone and, quickly showing the screen to Maxim, she turns away to take the call.

'Mrs Forster?' the voice at the other end asks. 'It's Jemima Shilling here, Acting Head of School. I was wondering what time you're intending to bring the girls back today.'

Marina's heart turns cold. 'I-I don't understand,' she stammers. 'Aren't they there?' Her eyes fly to Maxim.

Sounding confused, Jemima Shilling says, 'You took them home last night—'

'No! I didn't. They should be there. Oh my God! Are you saying they're not?'

Maxim snatches the phone. 'It's the girls' father here,' he barks. 'Where are my daughters?'

'I-I'm sorry, sir,' comes the reply, 'your wife collected them yesterday—'

'She's already told you that she did not, so someone has apparently taken the girls without our permission. I want you to call the police right now and get them to the school. As soon as you hear anything, ring this number.'

Clicking off, he rounds on Shana. 'Where are they?' he seethes. 'Tell me right now or so help me God—'

'I have no idea,' she shouts over him. 'I'm not interested in your children, only in clearing my name. So get *her* to confess and I'm sure they'll be back with you before you can say *I planted the evidence*.'

'You are out of your mind,' Marina yells at her. 'They're innocent children . . . Jesus Christ! That's what the message was about, wasn't it, asking me if I knew where they were? Maxim! She has them.'

'I don't know anything,' Shana insists, and takes a step back as he comes towards her. 'It'll be Ella and Oscar. They're desperate for the money *she* promised . . .'

Maxim is already pushing past her into the house.

'They're not here,' Shana calls after him.

'Check the other buildings,' he shouts to Marina.

She's already on her way, shouting the girls' names at the top of her voice while frantically trying their mobile phones.

No replies from anywhere.

She turns back to the house, so afraid now that she stumbles and almost falls.

'Satisfied?' Shana sneers. She's still at the front door, watching and gloating. 'I told you they weren't here.'

'So where are they? For God's sake, you surely don't want to add kidnapping to your crimes . . .'

'I've never committed any crimes,' Shana shoots back at her, 'and whatever this is, I'm telling you it has nothing to do with me.'

Maxim comes out and grabs Shana's arm so hard her feet almost leave the ground. 'Get on the phone to your *friends* and tell them to bring my daughters back, right now, and don't bullshit me again that you don't know where they are . . .'

It suddenly comes to Marina. 'Maxim, I think I know where they are.'

He turns to her.

'Come on.' She's already starting for the car.

Before letting Shana go, he speaks right into her face, 'The prologue you wrote, the person who entered your flat, *it never happened*, and if you have someone prepared to swear it did, he's as big a liar as you are.' He pushes her roughly away and starts after Marina.

'Tell yourself whatever you like,' she shouts at his back, 'it still doesn't change the fact that your wife is a murderer and you helped her get away with it. And very soon the whole world is going to know all about it.'

CHAPTER FORTY-NINE

'It's a place called Sodeham Mill,' Marina is explaining as she and Maxim speed away from the farm. 'It belongs to Ella Wiley's father and it's where Shana went when she was first released. Oh God, Livvy, pick up, please, please,' but once again she goes straight to messages. She tries Sophie with the same result.

'Darling, it's Mum,' she says to the voicemail. 'Where are you? Please call me as soon as you get this.'

'So where is this mill?' Maxim demands, turning onto the dual carriageway and weaving through traffic in the only direction they can go from where they are.

'Dorset, so once we get to the motorway, head south. I'll get the address from Brenna Isaacs.'

As she does, he rings the police. It takes a matter of seconds for his call to be picked up but considerably longer for him to explain what's happened. As soon as he ends the call he rings the school, and swears as he has to leave a message for someone to ring him straight back.

Soon they're tearing down the M5, with Marina entering the mill's address into the satnav. 'It's really remote,' she warns. 'I've seen photos. Brenna's trying to find a mobile phone number for one of the Woolleys – Wileys.' For God's sake, she's sick of getting these names confused. It means Shana's hideously subliminal attempts at control are rooting inside her head.

Maxim clicks to take an incoming call and both he and Marina tense as a brusque male voice introduces himself as Detective Inspector Sutton of Dorset Police.

Maxim barely keeps the impatience from his voice as he's forced to explain everything again.

'So, let me understand this correctly,' the DI says, sounding far too untroubled for Marina's liking, 'you didn't take them out of school?'

'No! We did not!' she cries frustratedly.

'Do you have any idea who might have? A family member? A parent?'

'*We* are their parents,' Maxim shouts angrily.

'There's a woman called Ella Wiley,' Marina says, repeating what Maxim's already told him. 'We think she and her husband have taken them to the address we gave to the operator.'

'Sodeham Mill. Yes, I've got it. Are these people related to you or your daughters?'

'No, not at all. The girls have never met them—'

'So why would they go with them?'

'I've no idea,' Marina cries helplessly. 'I don't know how it happened, how they made contact, or got them out of class . . .'

'Do you have any reason to believe they'd harm the girls?'

'I don't know why they would,' she sobs. 'They're innocent children, but she . . . She's killed a child before. Her own niece, and she's helping someone we know . . .' Her voice, along with all attempts at explanation fail, and Maxim's hand claims hers so tightly that she knows he's as afraid as she is. 'Oscar Wiley has a gun,' she suddenly cries. 'They're crazy people . . . You should probably know that before you go there.'

'Yes, we should,' the detective agrees. He goes off the line for a moment and they can hear him talking, but not what he's saying. 'Can you send us some photos of your daughters?' he asks, coming back to them. 'Someone is going to text you an email address to use. Is either of them on medication, or do they have any special needs?'

'No, they're in good health,' Maxim tells him.

'And you've obviously tried calling their phones? Do they have mobile phones?'

'Yes. I'll send you the numbers.' Marina is so glad to have something to do that she almost loses perspective of what's happening. 'They're not answering,' she adds. 'It's going straight to voicemail.'

'OK. We're speaking on my direct line now so if they get in touch, or if you hear from the Wileys, ring me straight away. I'll contact the school to get a picture on what's happening there.'

'The acting head is Jemima Shilling,' Marina informs him. 'She'll have spoken to Surrey Police by now.'

'Thank you. Before you go, I should tell you that in the case of a possible child kidnapping we're obliged to notify the National Crime Agency.'

'Do whatever you have to,' Maxim tells him urgently.

Marina's phone rings and she almost drops it before clicking on. 'It's Livvy,' she cries in panic. 'Oh my God! Darling! Where are you?' She switches the call to speaker so Maxim can hear; presumably the detective too.

'Uuuh, at school?' Livvy replies, making it a question. 'We've just got back to the dorm to find like fifty missed calls from you. So what's going on? And you've got to tell us Dad's OK, or we're going to start like, *really* panicking?'

'I'm fine,' Maxim tells her. 'We thought . . . You're at *school*?'

'Are we supposed to be somewhere else?' Sophie asks.

'No,' Marina hastily assures her. 'It's just . . . We had a call. It was a . . . mistake. We were worried for a moment, but as long as you're OK.'

'Mistake?' Livvy repeats, incredulously. 'Like how?'

'They're always so busy,' Sophie reminds her sister. To her parents she says, 'Looking forward to the weekend. Our last one with you guys before we go to the States. Sad, but yay!'

Marina's head falls forward as a rush of dizziness overwhelms her.

Maxim says, 'We need to ring off now, but we'll be there to collect you by five tomorrow.'

As the call ends, DI Sutton's voice fills the car. 'Am I to take it the emergency is over?' he asks dryly.

Maxim says, tightly, 'It seems to be. I'm sorry if we . . . overreacted.'

'As long as you're satisfied your children are safe.'

Maxim glances at Marina. Her head is still in her hands as she tries to nod. 'I believe we are,' Maxim says, and after a curt thank you, he rings off, swerves onto a slip road, circles a roundabout and comes to skidding halt in a layby.

'What the *fuck*?' he roars, banging a hand on the steering wheel. 'What the *fuuuck*!' He turns to Marina. 'What the hell just happened?'

Equally as shaken, and still assimilating, she says, 'The call from Jemima Shilling . . . I can only think . . . It must have been a hoax.'

'No kidding.'

'It must have been Ella Wiley . . .'

'You don't say, but why, for Christ's sake? What is she getting out of this?'

'It's what she and Shana have been doing all along. You've read the book, all the insinuations, allusions, crazy retelling of what happened, it's all been a way of getting to us, of terrifying us – *me* . . . I'm sorry. I should have realized as soon as I got the call from Jemima Shilling that it couldn't be her, because any real contact with the girls would send Ella straight back to prison. So their plan is to keep on coming at me with chapters and emails, lies, accusations, false information about the children – anything they can think of until I do what they want.'

He starts the engine and spins the car around.

'Where are we going?' she asks, gripping the seatbelt.

'Back to the farm.'

Alarmed she cries, 'But why? The girls are safe and—'

'Do you have any evidence of the blackmail?' he barks, accelerating down the northerly slip road.

'What do you mean? I told you—'

'I mean hard evidence? Anything in writing?'

Knowing she doesn't, she says, 'Noel and Brenna Isaacs heard it all. Maxim, please don't let's go there again. Let's just talk to Shana's probation officer, or call the lawyers and ask them to—'

'The lawyers are already on it, and they've seen the book, if we can even call it that. They say, as it stands, there's nothing we can do to stop it being published, unless we want to apply for a court order. And if we do, it'll be as good as telling the world we're afraid of her.'

'And if we don't, it'll be giving her free rein to shout her accusations from the rooftops all over again, but this time with the girls listening and watching.' Marina can feel a blinding headache coming on. 'So she gets to carry on accusing me, harassing me and taking our money, until I have some sort of mental breakdown, or I do what Ella Wiley's sister did and kill myself.'

He reaches out to take her hand. 'I don't think we're in any danger of you doing something like that,' he says, making it an order, an impossibility, in the way only he can. 'She's not going to win this, Marina. We didn't let her before, and we sure as hell aren't going to now.'

Though reassured and relieved to feel his strength and support enfolding her, she still can't help willing him to change his mind about going back to the farm. She isn't sure she can take much more of Shana's accusations, especially when Shana sounds so certain of getting everything she wants out of this.

The first thing she notices as they drive into the farmyard is the Land Rover parked in front of the house with some sort of trailer attached to the back.

'The Wileys must be here,' she says, trying to get her head around it, around anything.

'Good,' Maxim replies with no apparent misgiving at all.

'But it's not good,' she snaps, turning to him. 'Didn't you hear what I told the police? He has a gun and he's a drunk—'

'Then stay in the car,' and, pushing open the driver's door, he gets out.

She watches him start towards the house, then quickly follows, unwilling to let him go alone. As she reaches him, Ella Wiley emerges from the house and smirks pridefully as she says, 'I guess you found your girls.'

'What is wrong with you?' Marina hisses in disgust. 'Why would you do something like that?'

Wiley waves a dismissive hand. 'You're an easy target, Marina, and I wonder if that's because your conscience is interfering with your judgement? Yes, I think that could be it.'

Before Marina can respond, Maxim says, 'Tell Shana to get out here.'

As though he hasn't spoken, Wiley says to Marina, 'I believe Oscar's goddaughter, Georgia, has lost her job, which would have been a great shame if you weren't about to rehire her. I think this time in a more senior role, don't you? Such as the one you currently occupy. Do you still have the bronze, by the way? A lovely piece, isn't it? I'm glad you didn't use it on Georgia, she's a sweet girl—'

'You're sick,' Marina spits at her.

Wiley laughs. 'And you'd know all about that. Now, we'd be very grateful for an advance on the sum we agreed—'

Maxim cuts across her. 'You're out of your mind if you think we're going to give you anything.'

Seeming astonished, she says, 'Oh, but you will, unless you want us to go to the police with what we know about the mobile phone. In my opinion, paying someone to plant it in Shana's apartment was a truly, *truly* despicable act—'

'Inventing stories doesn't make them true,' he interrupts, shutting her down. 'So go to the police, we have nothing to hide.'

'Really? Then why are you here?' When he doesn't answer, she smiles triumphantly. 'You think you can stop Shana, don't you?' she says. 'You think you can stop us all. The trouble is, you don't actually know how to do it, or did you bring the bronze, your wife's weapon of choice?'

Marina stiffens with repugnance.

Maxim says, 'Time for us to go,' and, taking Marina's hand, he starts to lead her back to the car.

'Just a minute, Marina.'

They turn back to find Shana standing in the doorway with Ella Wiley.

Apparently glad to have their attention, she says, 'Personally, I don't care about the money, that's for my friends. What I want is the truth from you. I know, *we all know*, that you did it, Marina.'

Marina cries, 'You've been telling yourself that for so long I think you actually believe it, but even if you do, it'll never change what really happened.'

'*You killed her*,' Shana seethes. 'You know it – and *he* knows it too.' She thrusts her face forwards as she snarls, 'I don't know what you tell each other, and I don't know how you sleep at night, but I do know that you're not getting away with it any longer.'

'So who is this person I'm supposed to have paid?' Maxim challenges. 'If he exists, why not produce him?'

'Oh, believe me, I will, unless my friends get their money.'

'But they're never going to get it.'

Shana's eyes blaze into Marina's again. 'I could kill you right now for what you did to me,' she hisses. 'You cheated me of everything – my job, my reputation, my freedom, my *entire fucking life* . . .' Without warning she lunges forward, hands outstretched.

Maxim cuts between them and catches Shana's wrists in an iron grip at the same instant as a sudden, deafening explosion tears through the air.

Everyone freezes, startled and afraid, not knowing where the blast has come from, or if it will happen again.

The echo of it fades and birds resettle in the trees.

Oscar Wiley comes striding towards them, a rifle sight pressed to one eye, its barrel pointing straight at Marina.

Maxim quickly shoves her behind him as Ella says, 'Put it down, Oscar.'

He isn't listening.

'I said, *put it down*.'

'Let him do it,' Shana says scathingly. 'It's what she deserves.'

Ella walks forwards and positions herself right in front of the gun.

Seizing his chance, Maxim grabs Marina and runs her to the car.

'It isn't over,' Shana yells after them.

'We'll be in touch,' Ella adds.

As Maxim reverses out of the gates, they hear another gunshot boom through the farmyard but they don't stop to find out if anything or anyone has been hit.

CHAPTER FIFTY

During the drive back to London, Maxim calls Nathaniel Dayson, head of the law firm who'd acted for Marina during her time in custody. Apparently he and his team are back on the case.

The man's voice is instantly recognizable and sends chills right through her, as it brings everything surging out of the past: the terror that she might never get out of prison; that she'd have to give birth there; that Maxim would take her children to the States so she'd never see them again.

'. . . and someone's going through the book again now,' Dayson is telling them. 'At the beginning she's claiming that "a little something" was left at her flat. No mention of a phone . . .'

'A small detail that can be changed at any time,' Maxim says impatiently. 'If she'd been specific upfront, Marina would have known right away what she was facing.'

'Nevertheless, we need to go through everything with the proverbial fine-tooth comb, and from as many angles as we can, because if we're able to make a case for libel it might deter any other publisher from going to print. So far it seems she's been extremely careful, especially where names and settings are concerned, although there is mention of twins.'

'What about the blackmail?' Maxim prompts. 'Surely we can get her back to prison for that.'

'I've spoken to her probation officer and he's not prepared to act unless we can bring him proof of a breach of her conditions. Same goes for Ella Wiley. Marina, has Shana Morales ever initiated direct contact with you?'

Knowing she hasn't, that even the stalking around Lower Slaughter could be construed as coincidence, or even non-existent, Marina says, 'Not in a way that would be helpful to us, but there were witnesses to the blackmail attempt.'

'Yes, I have their names, Noel Hadigan and Brenna Isaacs. I'll speak to them, of course, but we'd get a much better hearing if we had something in writing.'

Sounding as frustrated as he clearly feels, Maxim suddenly says, 'Why don't we just publish and be damned?'

Marina turns to him in disbelief.

'I wouldn't advise it,' Dayson responds coolly, 'not if you want to avoid a very public and potentially disastrous outcome—'

'What if it ends up prompting the police to reopen the case?' Marina cuts in, glaring at him.

Dayson says, 'That can't happen unless new evidence comes to light. Is it possible she could have any?'

'She can't find things, or people, that aren't there to be found,' Maxim says shortly. 'We know Marina didn't do it, and the proof Shana did was discovered in her flat. That's all there is to it.'

'Indeed,' Dayson agrees. 'Let's speak again tomorrow, or before if there's anything more you want to discuss.'

As the call ends, Marina sits numbly in her seat, feeling certain the lawyer has never really believed in her innocence in spite of, or maybe because of, the mobile phone.

She glances down as Maxim's hand closes around hers and turns to look at him.

'It'll all be over soon,' he says softly.

She attempts a smile, and turns to stare out of the window as a deepening, stifling sense of trepidation swells its awful portent all the way through her.

CHAPTER FIFTY-ONE

That Girl by E.L. Stalwood

Katie knows it's time to confess. She is paralysed by the inevitability of it, smothered by the horror of what it's going to mean for her, and for Johan, and their children.

She hasn't yet found the words, or the courage, to release herself from the darkness in her soul, but she will because she has to. The guilt is consuming her, stalking her day and night, and turning every waking hour into a living hell.

It is after seeing Christy, the woman whose life she stole and made her own, that she finally comes to accept that she can no longer live in her shameful state of denial. The truth of what she did, the knowledge of how it happened, is always going to be with her. The violence of it erupted between her and Christy the instant they met. It was like an electric force, invisible, powerful, incontestable. They both knew, and will always know, that Christy has suffered the worst imaginable injustice, that Katie and Johan are responsible for it and nothing will ever change that.

Let me remind you again, dear reader, because I believe it's important to spell it out once more at this stage: together Katie and Johan brought about the death of a blameless girl and the incarceration of an innocent woman.

Ask yourselves, what kind of people does that make them? The very worst kind, of course, and though it can be said that

Christy, who never had anyone to fight for her the way Katie did, who never set foot outside her flat the night Amy was murdered – though she has many flaws, and possibly isn't very likeable for some, never deserved what was done to her.

Katie is now living in hourly terror of how she's going to break the news to her children. It will be devastating for them, of course. It will shatter their privileged little world along with their belief, their trust in everyone and everything, for the rest of their lives.

Their father might manage to get away with his crime, his expensive lawyers will do their best to see that he does, and if they are successful his all-powerful father will absorb his son and grandchildren into the bosom and safety of the family.

Katie will not be welcome.

She will have no one to turn to.

It's possible that books will be written about her in the future and films made, but when the last page is read, or the credits roll, she will still be where she is, in a prison cell where she belongs.

Poor Katie.

Still, at least the guilt will no longer be eating away at her like a cancer. Or maybe it will, because paying for Amy's untimely death won't ever bring Amy back. She'll always be responsible for it, as she will for what she's done to her children, the incalculable damage she's inflicted on their tender young minds. And deep down, in her wretched, withered little soul, she'll always know that there can be no restitution for what she did to Christy. She'll never be able to make any of it right, no matter how hard she tries or how long she lives.

So, the truth will not set her free, I'm afraid, but it will, at last, allow others to move on with the lives that should always have been theirs.

CHAPTER FIFTY-TWO

Marina's face is ashen as she lowers the lid of her laptop.

She can feel Maxim watching her, assessing her response to this latest chapter and its continued menacing use of the present tense, giving the impression that times and stories are now merging. He's also read it, but she's unable to look at him. She's too afraid of what she might see in his eyes.

Noel is the first to speak. 'She's been careful with the names again,' he says. 'However, she's certainly piling on the pressure.'

Marina continues staring at nothing.

They are at home in Holland Park. Noel had come because Maxim had wanted to hear from him exactly what his involvement had been from the start. Noel had jumped straight in a cab and, while he was on his way, Shana's latest chapter had arrived.

'Have you seen Brenna's email?' Noel asks. 'Apparently Oscar Wiley has some serious gambling debts.'

'Where is the private detective?' Maxim asks. 'I think we should get her here.'

'She's on assignment somewhere in the north,' Noel replies. 'Back tomorrow.'

Marina blinks, finding herself faintly thrown to think of other people in need of Brenna's services.

Finally she forces herself to look at Maxim and, seeing

the strain in his eyes, she feels her own burn with tears. 'She really seems to think I'm going to confess,' she says hoarsely.

Maxim shakes his head. 'You can't let her . . .'

She turns to Noel. 'Sorry, but do you mind if Maxim and I speak alone for a few minutes?'

After he's gone, she goes to refill her and Maxim's glasses with wine and brings them back to the table. Neither of them drinks. She is too tense, too fearful, and he rarely does when stressed.

'I'm starting to feel afraid,' she admits, not looking at him, 'that I might have done it and somehow blanked it from my mind. Can that be possible? Some kind of mental blackout? I know I returned the bronze, but maybe . . . I didn't. I have no memory of trying again with Patrick and yet both you and he say it happened. So what if—'

'You *didn't do it*,' he says forcefully. 'For God's sake, look at me, Marina. Listen to what I'm saying. You did not do it.'

She stares at him. Is this his way of trying to convince her out of a truth, or does he really believe she's done nothing wrong?

And what about his own part in planting the phone?

Had that actually happened?

She doesn't know because after her release from custody she'd been afraid to ask. She hadn't wanted to know the answer and had understood that he didn't want to discuss it. The strain they were under was already too much; any more and she would have broken completely. So for years they've left it unspoken on all but the most posturing levels of denial.

Gentler, kinder now, Maxim says, 'I know you, Marina. You could never have done anything like that.'

Her breath catches on a sob.

'You've said yourself,' he continues, 'that you had no reason to harm Amelia. We'd all moved on by then, I guess apart from Shana.'

'But she really seems to believe I did it, and that someone planted the phone in her flat.'

'It's all designed to do exactly what it's doing now: to make you doubt yourself and me. Don't let her do it. We need to carry on believing in each other and focus on getting her out of our lives.'

'But how are we going to do that if she has someone to claim you paid him to plant the phone?'

'There is no one . . .'

'She's just going to go on and on with everything. Even Nathaniel Dayson doesn't seem confident about returning her to prison. The next thing we know, she'll be sending emails to the girls . . . Oh God,' she chokes, unable to bear even the thought of it. She glances at her phone as a text arrives.

Are you avoiding me?

'Who is it?' Maxim asks.

'Patrick,' she replies, showing him the message.

His eyes widen. 'Are you? Avoiding him?'

She shakes her head. 'Not really. I just haven't had much time to talk to him lately.'

'You say he's not involved with Shana, but is there a chance he's not being honest about that?'

Feeling her head spin again, she says, 'They always detested one another.'

'But things change. People's priorities and loyalties shift. For all we know he could be Shana's fake witness.'

'But he . . . What would be in it for him?'

'Money, of course.'

Another text arrives. *Is Maxim around?*

She messages back. *Yes, why?*

I wanted to be sure you're not on your own.

Her eyes return to Maxim.

Taking the phone he texts back, *What's that supposed to mean?*

Just looking out for you. I know you've been going through a difficult time. Any more news on Shana?

Before she can send a reply, Maxim passes the phone back and says, 'Ask him if we can go round there tomorrow. Or invite him here. We need to talk to him.'

A reply comes a few minutes later, *In Frankfurt until Monday, but happy to see you guys asap after that. Just give me a date and time.*

CHAPTER FIFTY-THREE

It's just after nine the following morning when Marina receives an email from Brenna Isaacs. She's at her desk, and knows Maxim is in the building somewhere heading up a meeting, but as soon as she realizes what Brenna has sent, she forwards it to him and rings to make sure he picks it up immediately.

'Why? What is it?' he demands.

'Go to the second attachment,' she instructs. 'Open it and listen, but make sure you're on your own. Do it now, please, and call me back.'

As soon as he's rung off, she plays the audio recording again, still shaking with the shock of what it contains.

Shana is speaking,

'You, Marina, as the publishing director of Hawksley Maine, are going to offer me a three-million-pound advance for my book – though you, Noel, will not *take the commission because Ella is now my agent. She will negotiate the contract, including the payment schedule and, once it's all agreed, the book will become yours, Marina, to edit however you see fit before publishing. I promise I won't have a single objection to any changes you wish to make. You can even say what you like about the bronze and the mobile phone.'*

Apparently Brenna had secretly recorded the entire

encounter at Fairbyrne Farm and now, here it is, in a zip file for Marina and Maxim to use however they please.

She snatches up her phone as Maxim rings. 'I've already sent it to Nathaniel Dayson,' he tells her. 'The probation officer will have to act once he hears it. Jesus Christ, I can hardly believe it . . .'

'Me neither. I didn't ask Brenna to record it. I guess it's something she just does. Do you think they'll take Shana in today?'

'I've no idea, I don't know how long these things take, but I've asked Dayson to keep us up to speed. Do you want to go down there?'

Incredulous, she says, 'To watch them arrest her?' She thinks about it. 'If we knew exactly when it was going to happen, maybe I would.'

'Well, I guess it's best we stay away, if that maniac's there with his gun. I should warn Dayson about that.'

'Yes, you should.' She presses her fingers to her mouth as relief rises in an explosive sob. 'Is it going to be enough to make her stop? Please say it is.'

'It should be. Christ, Marina, I hope you're paying that PI well, because she's sure as hell delivered.'

'I should call Noel,' she says. 'He put me on to her.'

'If he's supposed to be joining us this weekend, tell him to come on Saturday rather than Friday. There's something we need to discuss, and it can't wait any longer.'

Unable to silence the echo of Shana's words, *we need to talk*, she says, 'OK. Call me as soon as there's some news from Dayson.'

In the end, they are on their way to pick up the girls from school when Dayson finally rings to update them. 'I've just had word that Shana Morales and Ella Wiley are both back in custody,' he says. 'I'm glad you didn't decide to go down there. I'm told shots were fired and Oscar Wiley has been shipped off to Gloucester Royal. It was good we were able to warn the police that he was armed.'

Picturing the kind of chaos that must have broken out, Marina says, 'Was Shana hurt?'

'Apparently she didn't go willingly, there was a bit of a struggle – a chase, I believe – so there might be a few bruises, but by now she's either on her way to Eastwood Park, or she's already there. I'm told the police have confiscated various computers and mobile phones so I'm sure we'll hear more about that in the not too distant.'

'OK, thanks for letting us know,' Maxim says.

'Before you go,' Dayson says, 'Shana Morales had a message for Marina – she wants you to know that she's already sent the book to Rosie Shell.'

CHAPTER FIFTY-FOUR

'It makes no difference who has it now,' Maxim declares, bringing a bottle of Sauvignon and two glasses out to the terrace where Marina is watching the news on her phone. They'd arrived at the rectory a couple of hours ago, but this is the first opportunity they've had to talk now that dinner is over and the girls and Ed are inside watching a movie.

She looks up from the aerial footage of a deserted Fairbyrne Farm and holds the phone out so Maxim can hear the voice-over explanation of what happened at the remote location today when convicted killer, Shana Morales, had her parole revoked.

'It turns out,' the reporter was saying, 'that Morales was released on licence over a year ago, after serving more than twelve years of a life sentence. She was found guilty back in 2009 of murdering nineteen-year-old Amelia Spence, a publishing assistant, who worked at the same London-based firm. Morales has always proclaimed her innocence. We're still waiting to find out how she broke the terms of her release, but I'm told there were two other arrests today, including the owner of the farm, Oscar Wiley. Apparently he was shot in the leg when he turned his gun on one of the officers who'd come to arrest Morales.'

Marina shuts it down and puts her phone aside. 'How long

is it going to be before someone from the press contacts us?' she says, reaching for her glass.

'I'll give it twenty-four hours, if they can find us here. We need to work on a statement and run it past Dayson. Unless anyone mentions the blackmail, we won't either, but even if it gets out I don't see we have anything to worry about. Now we've got the recording, no one's ever going to believe anything Shana has to say, which is why it makes no difference who has the book. In its current form, incomplete and with no recognizable names, it's just a draft of a story that needs a lot of work. Once it's known that it was concocted as part of an extortion attempt, and if necessary we'll make sure it's known, no publisher in their right mind will touch it, including Rosie Shell.'

Marina nods as she absorbs the truth of his words. She's thinking of Shana and how furious she must be feeling now – murderous, even, were she able to get to Marina. And how much worse it was going to be when she realizes that her own careless words and failure to check if she was being recorded are responsible for destroying her crazed bid to bring Marina and Maxim down.

Is she still telling anyone who'll listen that she's innocent?

Of course she is.

'. . . so I'll call Ron Gibbs on Monday,' Maxim is saying, referring to Rosie Shell's boss, 'and recommend he has a word with Rosie before she gets too excited about her new submission. She'll back off as soon as she knows it's part of a criminal act.'

With a sigh, Marina says, 'I think, at some point this weekend, we should sit the girls down and tell them what happened. Finding out that their mother was once arrested for murder and remanded in custody, and still remains guilty in some people's view, and that their father was accused of securing her release by planting false evidence, might be better coming from us than from social media.'

She thinks about it for a moment and turns her eyes to his. 'It's going to be a hell of a lot for them to take in, never mind to deal with.'

'It's true, but given where we are today with Shana's arrest, and knowing them as I do, I reckon they'll be completely fascinated and turn us into some sort of romantic heroes who managed to outwit the bad guys.'

Marina suppresses a smile as she shudders and turns to gaze out at the fading blush of twilight. 'You know, I wouldn't put it past Shana to do some sort of media interview claiming her innocence,' she says. 'Anything to kick up the doubt and speculation again and to punish me for the crime she seems to have convinced herself she didn't commit.'

He starts to answer, but Marina says,

'She must be bitterly regretting her involvement with the Wileys by now, because, as she said herself, it was never about the money for her. I'm sure they talked her into it, and she went along with it because they gave her somewhere to live and promised to help her with "the book". For all we know, her false witness is Oscar Wiley.'

'I'm almost certain of that,' he replies, 'so it would never have worked; any lawyer with a degree of skill would be able to blow that man's credibility apart.'

Agreeing, Marina picks up her glass as she says, 'You know, I can't see Shana giving up trying to make me prove my innocence. She'll find a way . . .'

'That's not the way the law works, and you know it. And the same applies to media interviews as it does to her book: no one will want to get themselves mired in a very expensive libel suit that they just can't win. And that's exactly what will happen if anyone decides to give her airtime.'

Staring down at her drink she says, 'That at least is true, but I still don't think we've heard the last of her.'

'Maybe not, but there's a way to create a far greater distance between us and her than we have now.'

She frowns and regards him curiously.

'OK, big change of subject here,' he warns, 'but it's what I've been wanting to talk to you about.'

Bewildered and suddenly nervous, she waits for him to continue.

'I'd like us to move to the States,' he announces.

As her eyes widen with shock, he quickly adds, 'Please hear me out, because this is important. My brother, Mark, has been diagnosed with multiple myeloma, and the survival rate isn't good. Five years, maybe less.'

Feeling a great rush of concern she says, 'Is that a form of cancer?'

He nods. 'It affects the plasma cells and is going to involve a lot of treatment, so he won't be able to continue running the company. I've said, provided you agree, that I will take over as soon as we can make the move.'

She hardly knows what to say. She's still reeling from the news about Mark. Unable to move on from it yet, she says, 'How's Cher taken it?'

He swallows and starts to nod. 'Stoically, I'd say. They both have. I don't think they've told the kids yet, but I haven't spoken to Mark for a couple of days so they might have done by now.'

Thinking of her niece and nephew, both still in their teens, and how this was going to be for them, she covers her face with her hands. 'When did you find out?' she asks.

'Just before Mark and I drove out to Long Island last week. We haven't mentioned it to Dad yet, he's still dealing with his own health issues, but when we do break it to him I'd really like to be able to tell him that I'm making plans to return to New York. Sorry, I know that's pressure, it's just . . . how it is.'

She takes a breath, and then another. There's so much to process, so many reasons she doesn't want to go, but – given the circumstances – how can she possibly refuse?

'If you're concerned about what you'll do when we get there,' he says, 'you know Forsters has a lot of publishing interests. We could find you a position with any one of them, but Mark's recently acquired a smaller concern that he says has a lot of potential. It's Manhattan based, and already has a fiction division, but it could really benefit from someone with your experience and skills to put it on the map. OK, starting to sound like bribery. I'm just not sure of the right way to go about this.'

Having no idea if there even is a right way, she says, 'What about the girls? Please don't tell me you're intending to board them full time—'

'They'll come with us, of course,' he interrupts. 'There are some great schools in New York and I thought, if we lived on the Upper West Side, your favourite part of the city, we could get them into Brearley, or Trinity . . .' Clearly realizing he's going too far too fast, he says, 'It's all up for discussion, obviously. I'm not making decisions without you; these are just suggestions.'

Her mind suddenly spins in another direction, whether in search of objections or reassurance, she doesn't really know. 'What about your father? He won't want me . . .'

'He'll be fine. Once he knows what's happening with

Mark and that I'm going to be around . . . Listen, if he is insufferable, we don't have to see him, but I don't think he will be. He's mellowing in his old age. Don't tell him I said that, but is he is.'

She doesn't smile, she can't when she's feeling so bombarded by the proposed change that she's still struggling to grasp it.

'I won't go without you,' he tells her. 'I need you to know that—'

'You don't have a choice,' she interrupts. 'You have to go. I understand that. I'm just . . . I'm not sure what I am, apart from shocked and upset about Mark, obviously. Actually, I don't know what the buts are, only that I'm thinking about our homes here, and my job . . . I started Janus, built it up.'

'I know, which is why you'll get to choose who fills your shoes. It could have been Georgia, but she's not an option now. So maybe we can see it as your last poaching operation before leaving the UK, unless there's someone in-house I haven't thought about?'

How hopeful he is, and how utterly wretched she'll feel if she crushes him. 'No one who is ready,' she says. Is it going to sound petty to remind him of how much they love their house here, in the Cotswolds, and the one in London? Yes, at the moment it will, because it has to be all about Mark.

After drinking more wine she says, with some irony, 'The girls will be ecstatic, of course. A new life in New York City with their "romantic hero" parents, weekends and holidays on Long Island, skiing in Colorado, trips to California, Canada . . . All the great colleges they'll have to choose from later.' She isn't sure why, but tears are welling in her eyes and one falls onto her cheek.

He moves quickly around the table to sit beside her and takes her into his arms. 'I'm sorry,' he says, 'I probably should have waited . . .'

'No, you have nothing to be sorry for. You're doing the right thing – *we* will do the right thing, it's just that . . . Oh God, Oh God . . . What I'm trying to deal with right now is that you've had all this on your mind while we've been going through so much hideousness with Shana . . . I feel so awful, so . . .'

'Hey, come on, we don't get to choose the timing of these things, and maybe this one isn't so bad. A fresh start, away from her, away from the media scrutiny?'

Unable to argue with that, she says, 'When exactly are you thinking we should go?'

The sheepish look she knows well, and can never help loving, comes into his eyes. 'Well, I guess it would make sense to try and start the girls in a new school while they're over there.'

Shocked, she cries, 'That soon!'

'It doesn't have to be. I just thought if we went for a couple of weeks ourselves this summer, we could make use of the time, look for a place to live, introduce you to the current board of Mallosi – yes, it needs a new name – and spend some time with Mark and Cher . . .'

At last she finds herself able to smile. 'You really have been thinking about this, haven't you? And I reckon the next thing you're going to tell me is that you'll be commuting between London and New York for the next however many months as you hand over to your replacement here.'

'It's possible,' he concedes, 'and actually I do have to go to New York on Monday. There's a meeting I need to be at if I'm going to take over from Mark.'

She regards him with an arched brow. 'So you won't be here for the girls' sports day, summer play, or last hurrah before they leave – for good it seems – on Wednesday?'

He grimaces. 'I'll try to make it back, but I can't promise anything.'

'Then I'll let you break it to them yourself, but I don't think they'll mind too much if you tell them first that we're planning to move to New York.'

He laughs and presses a kiss to her mouth. 'We can keep talking,' he promises. 'I don't want you to feel you're being railroaded into—'

'Of course I'm being railroaded, but if you think I'm going to try and stop you, or let you go without me, well, it just won't happen.'

He gazes at her tenderly. 'And that,' he says, 'is one of the many reasons I love you so damned much.'

She sinks into his embrace, loving the feel of him wrapping around her, and the power of him that always seems to make sense of everything.

How incredibly lucky she is that he loves her so much. It has always secretly baffled her, but then why does anyone love anyone? It just happens, the way it did for her with him. It's not possible to reason with love, it isn't open to that sort of scrutiny and never will be. It just is, or isn't, with all the complications and unfathomable dimensions that fit in between.

And this is no time to be thinking about Shana. The time for that is already behind them.

CHAPTER FIFTY-FIVE

The rest of the weekend is one of chaos and excitement, with the girls googling their possible new schools, or messaging friends to share their amazing news, and even trying to find a great place to live on the Upper West Side. They are throwing themselves so wholeheartedly into plans for their new life that Marina begins to wonder just how long they'd been hoping it might happen one day. She doesn't ask, mainly because she hardly gets a chance, as they are so eager to share news of their latest discoveries, or to embrace 'the world's best parents'. (Confessions from the past have yet to be shared, but they can wait a while, let the celebrations come first.)

Noel and Helena arrive late on Saturday afternoon, bringing a friend of Ed's with them, and Maxim lights the barbecue while Marina opens champagne. By the end of the evening, four bottles down and more to go, Noel is talking about buying the rectory, 'to keep it in the family', and Helena has invited the girls to join her on the set for her latest movie adaptation somewhere in New England.

'This won't be our last weekend here, I'm sure,' Marina remarks to Noel as they sit watching a bizarre and hilarious game of moonlit badminton with three players on each side and frequent stops for 'refreshment'. The girls are tiddly, but it doesn't matter, tonight is special, they can all feel it, and why shouldn't they celebrate too?

'Let's hope not; I'm counting on you being regular visitors when I take over as lord of the manor.'

She smiles. 'Are you serious about buying it?' she asks. 'I'd absolutely love to think of you here.'

'Sure I'm serious, and we'll take the furniture too, if you're selling it.'

Her eyes widen. 'We?'

He grins. 'I haven't asked her, but I think she knows it's coming and she hasn't run for the hills yet.'

Marina laughs. 'She'll be lucky to have you, and yes, you'll be extremely lucky to have her too. And while we're on the subject of luck, it was shining on me, albeit in a weird way, when Shana chose you as her agent. I don't think anyone else would have stood with me, and carried on believing in me the way you did. So thanks for being the best friend I've ever had.'

He raises his glass and clinks it to hers. 'Likewise,' he says. 'You and Maxim mean a great deal to me and nothing will change that, no matter where you are in the world.'

'You'll stay with us whenever you're in New York?'

'You can count on it.'

As Maxim, laughing and breathless, comes to sit with them, he says, 'Please don't tell me you're talking about the unmentionable woman.'

Marina's heart flips as an image of Shana in her prison cell flashes in her mind. Such a brutal and depressing contrast to this beautiful garden.

'Not at all,' Noel assures him. 'She fired me as her agent, remember, so no longer interested in her.'

Marina smiles.

Maxim says, 'Marina thinks we haven't heard the last of her.'

'Let's hope I'm wrong,' Marina breaks in. 'I just want it all over with now. In fact, I've been thinking about cancelling seeing Patrick on Monday, but I guess he'll have seen the news, so he'll want to know exactly what's been happening.'

'I'm sorry I won't be with you,' Maxim says, 'but it could be a good opportunity for you to tell him about our plans. Oh, and don't forget to let him know that I was never in any doubt about the twins.'

CHAPTER FIFTY-SIX

'So you're off to New York?' Patrick comments wryly as he brings a bottle of chilled Pecorino to the table that he's already set for dinner. The apartment seems freshly cleaned, Marina notes, and is lightly fragranced, suggesting there might be a new woman on the scene. She hopes so for his sake; he sometimes seems a little lonely. 'You know,' he continues, filling her glass, 'I had a feeling it would happen one day, that you guys would up sticks for the States, and what better time than now, after all this . . . Whatever it was? I'll miss you, of course, I hope you know that.'

She smiles and says, 'Given how rarely we see one another, apart from recently, I think you'll survive, but we'll be back from time to time, so hopefully we can get together then.'

'You bet. Just let me know when you're coming so I can make sure I'm around.' He returns to the kitchen and a few moments later carries in a huge bowl of pasta topped with cheese, bacon, mushrooms and peppers. 'My signature dish,' he quips. 'Hope it's OK.'

'It smells delicious,' she says, meaning it, and watches as he ladles out two generous helpings and passes the first to her.

'So, when do you think you'll be off?' he asks, sitting down opposite her and shaking out a paper napkin.

She reaches for the Parmesan. 'Realistically speaking, it

might not happen until after Christmas, but Maxim's hoping to pull it off by the girls' half-term. There's not enough time to get them in for the new semester at either of the schools he's set his sights on in New York. He also has to get me sorted out with a green card, of course, but – as we know – money talks, and the Forsters are not short of that, and nothing if not well connected.'

Patrick chuckles and sprinkles a generous amount of cheese over his own meal. 'He's a good guy, your husband,' he comments. 'Of course, I should hate him, but he doesn't make it easy.'

She laughs and winds some spaghetti around her fork. They could go on like this for some time, but she's keen to get to the real reason for her visit, so she says, 'You've never actually told me what you thought of the book.'

He finishes a mouthful and reaches for his glass. 'Well, she didn't paint me in a glowing light, that's for sure,' he comments archly. 'More of an ass, actually. And "Rob"? Why choose that name for me?'

'I've no idea, but she didn't use names that could easily connect to any of us – apart from Amelia as "Amy", I guess.'

He sighs and shakes his head slowly. 'Everyone forgets about her, don't they?' he murmurs sadly. 'It's as if she was merely incidental to all our lives, when if it weren't for her . . .' He breaks off and glances at Marina.

She gives it a moment and says, 'It's OK, I know that you really cared for her. In fact, I was only thinking to myself the other night how we can't explain love, so maybe we shouldn't try.'

Seeming to appreciate her words, he nods slowly, still introspective. 'I hated what it did to you,' he says. 'I still loved you, but I couldn't give her up, and for a while I think she felt the same.' He's gazing into the distance now as if he can see her, a long way away, but somehow there. 'She had so much going for her. I know you thought so too, before . . . You were a perfect mentor for her until I stepped in and ruined everything, for us all.'

'You can't take all the blame. She had choices, she didn't have to get involved with you.'

'She never found it easy, you know. She was devoted to you . . .'

She puts up a hand to stop him. 'There's no point going over it all again,' she says. 'No matter what she felt about either of us, she betrayed me and broke your heart . . .'

'She devastated me. Shana doesn't bring that out much in the book. A little, yes, but obviously it wasn't the point of her story, and it wouldn't really matter to her how I felt about anything. It was all about her, and you, and "Johan".' He regards her curiously and says, 'It couldn't have been easy for you reading all that sex, knowing that really it was a recreation of scenes between Shana and Maxim.'

Feeling an uncomfortable heat, she says, 'I didn't read them. When I knew they were coming I put it aside.'

'Smart move. Does she know that?'

'I don't see how. I never told her.'

'Have you asked Maxim about them?'

'No. Why would I?'

He shrugs. 'I guess you wouldn't. I imagine she got off on writing them – in more ways than one.'

Unwilling to think about it, she says, 'The main purpose of those sections was to mess with my head, so I wouldn't put too much store in their veracity.'

His smile is small. 'Tell me,' he says, 'that final chapter . . .

The one where "Katie's" conscience is getting the better of her. Did it ever make you feel like confessing?'

Her heart gives a thud of shock. 'Why on earth would I?' she challenges, glaring at him and making ready to leave.

'Sorry, sorry. It came out wrong. Stupid of me. I just thought, the way she kept at it . . . What she wrote . . . I guess what I meant to ask is, how much did she actually get to you?'

Ignoring the question, she says, 'You know, I sometimes wonder about you, Patrick.'

'Honest to God, I didn't mean to offend you,' he insists. 'I need to think before I speak, always a failing . . . Obviously you weren't going to confess when we know you didn't do it.'

She regards him harshly. He doesn't sound as though he means that, so what the heck is going on with him?

'The big problem Shana had with that book,' he continues, 'with everything, actually, is that she's always believed Maxim arranged for the phone to be planted in her flat. She thought, if she could prove it, her conviction would be overturned. I don't actually blame her for thinking that. I'm sure I would have too, if I were her.'

Marina puts her glass down. 'But Maxim didn't plant the evidence,' she says, feeling the tightness in her face.

His eyes flicker to hers and away again. 'No, he didn't,' he agrees.

Her mind is moving so fast she can hardly keep up with her own thoughts. She sits back in her chair, seeing him almost as a stranger, as everything seems to shift and resettle at angles she hadn't seen before. 'Patrick, was it you?' she asks quietly. 'Did you kill her . . .?'

'Christ! No, no not me,' he quickly protests. 'I have a

rock-solid alibi for that night, you know that. No, they've always had the right person, no matter what she keeps trying to claim about that stupid bronze, and never leaving her flat. She did it – and then,' his eyes flick to hers, 'I did what had to be done to make sure you didn't go down for it.'

She is so stunned by his words that she can hardly begin to make sense of them.

'That's how it was looking,' he reminds her. 'You know that. They weren't interested in anyone else, until Maxim's lawyer insisted on a more thorough search of Shana's apartment.'

She's taking too long to process this, to catch up with what he's actually leading to.

'I made an anonymous call to the lawyer,' he says, 'suggesting it could be worthwhile going over the apartment again.'

She swallows dryly, imagining phone calls and anonymous break-ins, the planting of a phone, the arrest that followed. 'And you knew the evidence would be there,' she says, 'because you'd planted it?' She lets go a half-breath, as if it were all she has left.

'As I said, you were going down if someone didn't act.'

Appalled, transfixed, she says, 'So you . . . The phone . . .'

'Amelia didn't have it with her that day,' he says. 'She'd left it at home . . .'

'But how do you know that? You weren't living with her . . .'

'I went round there before going to the match. I still had a key, so I let myself in. When I saw the phone I thought, if I take it she'll have to see me to get it back.'

Though struck by his desperation, she's still too horrified by what he's actually telling her to properly assimilate.

'You remember how they were searching for her phone after,' he says, 'but they never could find it. I thought about getting rid of it, but then, when things started to go the way they did for you, I began to see how it might be useful.'

Appalled by the way his mind had worked, while quietly fascinated, she says, 'But how on earth did you get into Shana's flat?'

He shrugs. 'I knew where she kept the spare key. You told me yourself, a long time before it all happened. When we were all still friends.'

Marina stares at him for several moments, wondering if it's true that she'd once told him where the keys were. Is this something else she's forgotten? It could so easily be. How did anyone ever remember every single detail of their lives, especially when they'd happened during a time of emotional distress? It would be the same for Shana, surely. She'd seen what had made sense to her, and in many ways she hadn't been wrong. Her only mistake had been in making the intruder someone sent by Maxim. She'd clearly never considered Patrick.

Marina turns away and back again. She's so disturbed by all that this has thrown up that she can barely ground herself.

Patrick doesn't look repentant. He simply gestures with a glass as he says, 'The only reason I'm telling you now is because I want you to know that I did it for you.'

She's suddenly breathless, almost panicked, as she tries to seize the right way forward from this. 'You realize, don't you,' she says, 'of course you do, that I can never tell anyone because if I do you'll end up in prison . . .'

'As will you. And she, who did it, will be out.'

Marina sits with that, so stunned that she feels she might be losing her mind.

'I owed you,' he explains. 'After what I'd put you through, all the heartache, the betrayal . . . It wasn't right to let you pay for something I knew you didn't do. She tried to frame you, Marina, and she's never been able to get over the fact that she failed. And what drives her crazy to this day is that she knows the phone was planted, she just can't prove it.'

Marina says quietly, 'And because it was Maxim's lawyers who insisted on the search, in her mind they – he – had to be behind how it got to where the police found it.'

He nods.

She gets up from the table and begins to pace. She's so agitated she hardly knows what she's thinking. 'I don't know what to do,' she says, wretchedly, 'if I tell Maxim—'

'You don't need to do anything,' he interrupts gently. 'If you do, you'll be right back where you started, in custody, but taking me with you this time – and quite possibly leaving Maxim free to continue his life without you. Maybe to go back to Shana?'

'He would never—'

'She wanted everything you have now,' he says over her, 'and, let's face it, she would probably have it if things had gone her way . . .'

'No . . .'

'*Yes*. Remember when you tried again with me, it didn't take him long to go back to her then, did it?'

She's suddenly so close to smashing something that she has to clasp her hands to her head.

'OK, maybe I'm wrong about what he'd do,' he concedes, 'but if you go to the police with what I've just told you, it'll throw everything about your involvement back into question. They'll probably believe her about the bronze –

that you never gave it back – and her claim that she was at home all night . . . Marina, *think* what it'll do to your family. And for what? The sake of a truth that will serve no one apart from the one person who's right where she's supposed to be?'

'Says you?'

'Says me, and my conscience is clear.'

She stares at him hard without really seeing him. She's looking into the future, the horror of what it really would do to her family if she were to report what he's just told her. She knows she didn't kill Amelia, and Patrick's alibi has always proved that he didn't either.

That only leaves Shana.

'Sit down,' he says gently.

She isn't sure she can, and yet she does.

'Sometimes doing the wrong thing ends up getting the right results,' he says. 'That's just life. Maxim will know that as well as anyone, if you do ever decide to tell him.'

CHAPTER FIFTY-SEVEN

Maxim doesn't interrupt as Marina relates everything Patrick told her. She leaves nothing out, not even Patrick's assertion that Maxim would have returned to Shana if she, Marina, had gone to prison.

They're on their way back from the airport after seeing Ed and the girls off on their flight to New York – Maxim had arrived on the same plane only a few hours ago, so had gone straight from arrivals to departures. In a couple of weeks, he and Marina would fly over to spend some time looking at schools and apartments before driving the girls to Long Island for the rest of the summer. Marina isn't looking forward to seeing her father-in-law, in spite of Maxim's assurances that Paul Forster has promised to do his best to make her feel welcome.

Much more important right now is what Maxim is thinking of Patrick's role in her release from custody and Shana's conviction.

They're almost home and Maxim still hasn't spoken. When he does, her heart gives a thud of uneasy surprise.

'So now we both know for certain that you didn't kill Amelia and I didn't plant any evidence to get you released.'

After taking a moment, she says, quietly, 'So you did suspect me?'

Arching an eyebrow he counters with, 'No more than you suspected me.'

It's such a typical Maxim answer that it almost makes her smile.

'And for the record,' he adds, 'Patrick was wrong about Shana. I'd never have gone back to her – if the worst had come to the worst.'

She turns to look at him, and glances down as he reaches for her hand. 'Yes, she was set up,' he says softly, 'and she clearly knows it, but it wasn't by me, and it doesn't mean she's not guilty. So there's no reason to tell anyone else about this, least of all the police.'

She could remind him that she hasn't actually proved her innocence, but she decides not to. To continue the conversation, or the story Shana has tried to tell, would risk giving life to a book with no ending, and no editor, or reader – no one at all – wants that.

ACKNOWLEDGEMENTS

Well, here's something I never imagined being able to say: this book marks a huge milestone in my writing career: it is my 50th novel! I'm not sure whether this extraordinary truth leaves me more shocked, or thrilled, grateful (definitely grateful) or bewildered – probably all of the above.

How on earth has it happened?

The answer is: it only could thanks to exceptional publishing teams, and there have been a few across the years.

I had no idea the best was being saved for last, but it certainly seems that way today. It is truly exhilarating and inspirational to be a part of the team at HarperCollins, headed by Kimberley Young, my outstanding editor. I still don't know, Kim, how you have such an uncanny knack of knowing what I'm writing about when I seem to have lost the plot. Your belief in me and my stories is, without question, what makes all the difference to the book. It's an absolute truth that I couldn't do it without you.

It's a while since I signed the first of my contracts with HC, but throughout these last eight years I have been made to feel so welcome that it's as though I've known everyone forever. I can honestly say that everyone who's been a part of taking my books from me to you, the reader, has been an absolute pleasure to work with. And enormous fun!

Here are a few names, starting at the top: Charlie Redmayne, Kate Elton, Roger Cazalet, Kim Young, Elizabeth Dawson, Olivia French, Belinda Toor, Meg Le Huquet, Martha Ashby, Katie Lumsden, Sophie Burks, Amber Ivatt, Maud Davies, Fleur Clark, Rachel Quinn . . . There are so many more, including every member of the sales team who do such a magnificent job behind the scenes, and the immensely talented Claire Ward and her artistic creators who have produced some truly excellent and memorable book jackets.

Going back over the years to my earlier – and younger – days there are literally hundreds of editors, publicists, sales and marketing teams I'd like to thank for many exceptional contributions to the Susan Lewis oeuvre. I have some wonderful memories to cherish from those times, and it is a great relief to know that we all survived the bumpier rides.

Outstanding amongst the many faces of the past is my wonderful agent, Toby Eady. Sadly, Toby has passed now, but I know I'd never have got as far as I have if it weren't for his encouragement, wisdom, friendship and unfailing support.

Luigi Bonomi is my agent now and how fortunate I am to be able to say that. Thank you, thank you, Luigi, for your incredible insight and humour, your kindness, your patience, your brilliant advice and unerring eye. You are every bit as much a friend as you are an agent and I am so proud of that. I just love how much chat and laughter we share on a regular basis.

I cannot, of course, forget my family and friends whose love, forbearance and unfailing support have buoyed me through the more challenging times. My husband, James Garrett; my brother and sister-in-law, Gary and Jill Lewis;

my stepsons, Mike and Luke Garrett; my niece and nephew, Grace and Tom Lewis. My wonderful friends: Denise Hastie, Lesley Gittings, Fanny Blackburne, Ellie Gleave, Sonia Gourlay and all the very special people I am so blessed to have in my life.

Lastly, and without a doubt most importantly, my biggest and warmest thanks of all go to you, my amazing readers for your fantastic loyalty and inspiration. Many of you have been with me throughout the years, while others have dropped in for a while, left and come back again. I feel as though we are part of an enormous family with so much to share and even more to look forward to. I can't promise another 50, but I'll do my very best to get to 60 or even beyond.

Susan